The SMILE of the STRANGER

JOAN AIKEN

sourcebooks
casablanca

Published by Sourcebooks Casablanca, an imprint of Sourcebooks,
Inc.
P.O. Box 4410, Naperville, Illinois 60567-4410
(630) 961-3900
Fax: (630) 961-2168
www.sourcebooks.com

Originally published in 1978 in the United States by Doubleday &
Company, Inc. This edition issued based on the paperback edition
published in 1978 in New York by Warner Books.

Printed and bound in Canada.
MBP 10 9 8 7 6 5 4 3 2 1

Beware of blind Love, lest the dart from his bow
And the smile of the stranger should bring you to woe.
—Anon.

One

BEGUILED BY THE AMAZINGLY LOW PRICES MARKED ON a silk collar and pair of matching gloves that lay temptingly displayed in a milliner's window between two silversmiths' booths on the Ponte Vecchio, a tall foreign lady had entered the little shop haughtily glancing about her and demanded to buy the articles in question, pointing them out with her parasol and authoritatively announcing: *"Vorrei comprare questo paio di guanti e colletto!"*

The slatternly but astute-looking proprietress subjected her would-be customer to a swift, comprehensive scrutiny.

The Englishness of the purchaser had been beyond question as soon as she opened her mouth—no other nation could pronounce Italian so villainously. At first glance it might have seemed that she was a wealthy lady of fashion, for she appeared to be rigged out, if not in the first, at least in the second stare of the mode. Her walking dress of black-and-white-striped poplin was gathered around the shoulders into a fichu, which came to a knot low on the bosom; and it was worn over a pink quilted satin petticoat. Yellow Roman boots completed her toilette and she carried a silk reticule and an ivory-handled parasol; her elegantly tilted broad-brimmed hat had a silk scarf tied round its shallow crown, and revealed short ringlets, skillfully curled, of dark hair slightly streaked with gray. Her long pale face wore a supercilious expression, and her voice had the timbre of one accustomed to command. Yet closer inspection would have revealed that none of her articles of wear were in their first youth—indeed, they were of a style that had been worn since 1780—at least fourteen years; moreover, her silk gloves were darned, her parasol handle was cracked, and her petticoat was somewhat faded. But the light in the shop being decidedly obscure, the proprietress naturally took the Inglesa to be a lady of rank and fashion; she therefore had no hesitation in asserting that the cheap goods in the window were not for sale.

"Sold already to another person. They have been paid for and are but awaiting collection!" she kept repeating over and over.

The customer's Italian was not equal to grasping the meaning of these words, and she, for her part, continued to point to the gloves, and to declare, "*Preferisco questo!* I want this! *Those* ones. *Not* these"—pushing aside the various much more expensively priced items which the shopwoman persisted in fetching out from her store and displaying on the counter.

At last, quite out of patience, the shop owner fairly snatched the disputed gloves and scarf out of the window, and locked them up in a box, proclaiming, "Not-a for sale!"

"Then I consider it a perfectly outrageous piece of imposture that you should be exhibiting them in your window!" exclaimed the customer, relapsing into her mother tongue, "and I have a great mind to report you to the Prefecture!"

Either failing to understand this threat or, more probably, choosing to ignore it as quite impossible of execution, the shopkeeper shrugged up her expressive shoulders, protruded her lower lip, and rolled her black eyes heavenward in total scorn.

Feeling herself defeated, the English lady glanced sharply about her, hoping to pick up another bargain in default of the one she had failed to secure. A rack of shawls attracted her eye, and she moved over to it, having observed a ticket with a promisingly low price at the end of the rail. After some consideration, she selected a mulberry-colored shawl and held it up.

"*Mi piace questo!* I will have this."

But when she laid her money on the counter— having carefully extracted it from her purse, coin by coin—the proprietress burst into a flood of expostulation, and, as the customer showed no signs of comprehension, she wrote down the true price on a piece of paper and angrily thrust it forward.

"*What?* What can you mean? *E costa troppo!* That is three times the price stated on the ticket!" And the indignant lady pointed to it.

Exasperated, it seemed, beyond all bearing, the shop owner turned to a young girl in a gray cloak and straw bonnet who had just entered the place. To the newcomer she poured out a furious complaint and a demand for assistance with this stupid and contentious foreigner.

"Excuse me, ma'am!" the girl then said, in very clear pretty English, with just the hint of an accent. "Signora Neroni asks me to explain to you that only the *first* shawl on that rack is at the price marked; the others are more expensive."

"It is all a piece of barefaced deceit. Disgraceful! Outrageous! I shall certainly report it to the *polizia*. I shall tell the whole story to Mr. Wyndham, the British Envoy, with whom I am acquainted. The Grand Duke shall hear of this!"

The signora's derisive expression robbed these threats of their sting, and the girl remarked sympathetically, "I am afraid you would soon catch cold at that, ma'am. Signora Neroni is one of the best-respected traders on the Ponte Vecchio, and she is related to the Prefect by marriage."

"Her trade practices are grossly deceitful!"

"They are common practice in Florence, ma'am."

Angrily the lady, knowing this to be true, turned to reconsider the selection of shawls, while the girl, breaking into soft, fluent Italian, rapidly bought four white handkerchiefs from Signora Neroni.

"And how is your dear papa?" that lady inquired. "My husband says he has not seen him lately at the coffeehouse."

"He has had a bad cold, but he is better now, signora, I thank you, and is working hard."

"Always at the same business—*il re Carlo*?"

"Yes, signora."

"Better he should trouble his head less about that Carlo, and more about finding a husband for his own daughter!" grumbled the signora. "What can it matter about an old dead-and-gone, probably no better than he should be?"

"King Carlo was, on the contrary, a most excellent man!" flashed the girl. "He was devout—affectionate—and *very* handsome! If I ever do have a husband, I should wish him to be just such a person—"

Then she stopped, her mouth open. Out of the corner of her eye, she thought she had seen the tall foreign lady swiftly and unobtrusively slip one of the pairs of gloves off a small table and tuck them into her reticule. Or could she have been deceived? The movement was so rapid that her eyes might have been mistaken. She could hardly base an accusation on such insecure grounds. And Signora Neroni, apparently, had seen nothing. Moreover, the lady now walked forward with the coolest composure, and halted the girl with an uplifted hand as she was about to leave the shop.

"Excuse me, miss—one moment, if you please!"

"Ma'am?" The girl paused, with an inquiring expression on her small round face.

"You seem well acquainted with this town, young lady. I wonder if you can give me information as to the direction of an English gentleman—a writer—who, I believe, resides in this quarter."

At these words a veiled, cautious look descended over the girl's lively countenance. She had a wide, smiling mouth and large, dancing expressive eyes; but now the lids came down over these and she gazed pensively at the ground—not before, however, the visitor thought she had detected a swift exchange of glances with Signora Neroni. But the answer was quiet and civil enough.

"I will help you, ma'am, if I can. What is the gentleman's name?"

"I understand that he goes under the name of Mr. Charles Elphinstone. He is a writer of books. I have asked at the Envoy's office, but they seemed unable to help me," the Englishwoman said aggrievedly.

The girl looked up again. Now her face was quite devoid of expression. In a similarly colorless voice she replied, "I regret, ma'am. I fear that *I* am unable to help you either," and, turning, she left the shop with silent speed.

Something about the girl's tone—her look, her movement—aroused all the Englishwoman's curiosity, or suspicion.

"One moment! Miss! If you please!" she demanded in a loud peremptory tone, and she moved hastily to the shop entrance, looking out to see which way the girl had gone. But the commonplace gray cloak and the inconspicuous chip-straw hat were already lost in the crowd; gray cloaks and straw bonnets abounded among the shoppers and strollers enjoying the evening breeze along the Arno; the girl was nowhere to be discovered.

With an angry exclamation the Englishwoman stood still, staring around her, biting her knuckle; a bright spot of color burned on either high cheekbone, and she frowned, thrusting her long face forward in a curiously predatory and determined gesture; then, after a moment's indecision, she re-entered the milliner's shop, pulled out once more her slender knitted-silk purse, and started to interrogate the signora.

❧

Meanwhile the girl, after crossing the Ponte Vecchio in a northerly direction, threaded her way between bullocks and wine carts, and turned right, following the path beside the rushing Arno, which, now in early-autumn spate, had begun to dislodge the fishermen and mud diggers from its banks. Cautiously glancing behind her, the girl took a left turn and proceeded swiftly through a maze of little streets, going in the direction of Santa Croce. She seemed perfectly at home in the confusing network of alleys, occasionally nodding to people as she passed them, pausing here or there to buy fruit from the market stalls at street corners or in little piazzas. At last, reaching the doorway of a high, narrow house, she passed inside, and began going lightly and rapidly up the steep flights of stairs within.

On a landing two flights up she paused to let a fat old lady puff her way down.

"Good night, Signora Fontini. Thank you for seeing to Papa!"

"Aha, you are back, *bambina*! You are a good girl, you return swiftly. Your dear papa has been hoping you would soon be home—he says that he has many more words in his mind, ready to dictate. *Dio mio*, what a thinker! What a worker! Even when he is sick, he cannot rest for half an hour while his poor daughter takes the air! And he himself coughing and sneezing as if the devil had got into his chest! He should keep quiet and rest, I tell him, not talk away as he does, hour after hour."

"Poor Papa! He is so anxious to finish this book. Let us hope that these grapes and oranges will help his throat. Fruit is all he will take at present."

"Not good! Not good at all," muttered the old lady, continuing her way down the staircase. "Fruit is all very well for children. But a man, a grown man like the signore, needs good red meat and wine and a nourishing dish of pasta from time to time. I could bring him up a bowl of my spaghetti Bolognese. But it is no use talking! All the English are the same, mad as hares on the mountains. The signore Carlo is good and kind as a saint, but he is as crazy as all the rest."

"Is that you, Juliana?" called a man's voice as the old lady panted her way downward, and the girl ran on up the last flight.

"Yes, Papa!" she called, and entered a small but pleasant room. It was bare and clean, with a floor of polished red tiles, and a remarkable painted ceiling covered by heraldic devices in pink, blue, yellow, and red. The shuttered windows were closed against the evening chills and damps, and a small charcoal brazier gave warmth. Close to this, a tall man with a thin, lined face lay reclined in a basket chair. He was wrapped in a large knitted blanket, which, however, he had impatiently half tossed aside. His hair, tied back with a ribbon, was white, it seemed more from ill health than from age. His posture suggested a considerable degree of weakness, but the eyes were at variance with the haggard cast of his face: brilliant blue, they burned with intellectual fire.

"Thank you for being so speedy, my dearest," he said as the girl carefully shut the door behind her. "Your feet are shod with wings, I believe, like Hermes."

"However fast I may run," said Juliana, setting down her purchases on a small marble table and crossing the room to give him a warm hug, "I am quite sure you will have thought of another twenty pages while I have been gone! Old Annunciata said you had more work for me?"

"Well—it is true—I have planned out most of the chapter dealing with Charles's trial and execution—if you are not too tired, my dear child, after your shopping errands?"

A sneeze stopped him at this point, and Juliana said, "It is more of a question whether you are not too tired, Papa, for such an exertion, so low as you are with your cold. Do you not think your throat is too sore for dictation?"

"No—no!" he said eagerly. "I am most desirous of setting this chapter down on paper while it is yet clear in my mind. By the mercy of Providence, the more feeble my poor body becomes, the quicker my wits seem to work—a-a-a-tschoo!"

If Juliana was daunted by the thought of the probable hours of work that lay ahead, she gave no sign of it, but said cheerfully, "Very well, Papa, but just let me put these things away. And, first, here are your new handkerchiefs—you will certainly need them, if I am to understand anything at all of what you say. I will just hang up my cloak—so—and the hat on the peg—now I'm ready for you, Papa. Oh, but I had better pour a little more ink into the standish—if this is to be one of your *longer* chapters, we do not want to run dry in the middle!"

Having carefully decanted some black ink from a stone jug and supplied herself with a large heap of paper, she mended the point of her pen with a small

silver knife shaped like a fish, and then sat down at a
low table close to her father.

"You are certain that you are not too tired, my child?"

"Oh, what fudge! You know that I am as strong as
a pony, Papa!" Her mouth curved into its usual wide
smile, but she had to conceal an inward sigh at her
father's own reckless use of his waning strength.

While he vigorously blew his nose on one of the
newly purchased handkerchiefs, she remarked, "A
curious and somewhat comical episode occurred while
I was procuring those—but I will not distract you by
telling you about it now—that can wait until suppertime. Now, pray dictate, dearest Papa."

He had been waiting with ill-concealed impatience,
and the moment she had her pen dipped in the silver
inkwell, he launched into dictation as if the words had
been coiled up inside his head, and now flowed out
like a ribbon.

"On the twenty-seventh day of January, Charles,
again dragged before the Court, demanded to
be allowed to speak and defend himself before
the Lords and the Commons. Downes, one of the
Commissioners, thought that he should be permitted
to do so, but Oliver Cromwell turned on Downes,
exclaiming in fury, 'What ails thee? Art thou mad?
Canst thou not be still and quiet?' The Court then
retired to debate Charles's request *in camera*, and,
during the discussion that followed, Cromwell
called Charles 'the hardest-hearted man upon
the earth.'"

The girl's pen scratched busily, and her father,
who had been gazing with absent eyes at the painted

ceiling, lowered his gaze to inquire, "Do you have all that down, my dear?"

"Yes, Papa. Oh, how could they have so misunderstood his character? What a thick-skinned, bacon-brained numbskull that Cromwell must have been! Charles was *not* hard-hearted—only single-minded. Only bent upon doing his duty! Consider how he loved his wife and children! Consider how truly religious he was! Consider—"

"Hush, child!" said her father, laughing. "Who is writing this book, pray? Do not put yourself in a passion—due justice shall be done!"

"I am sorry, Papa! Only, when I hear him traduced, it makes me so wild! But I will not interrupt again—I beg your pardon!"

"Now, where was I?"

"Cromwell named Charles 'the hardest-hearted man on earth.'"

"Ah, yes. The Court, having refused Charles's plea, then reassembled, and Bradshaw made a speech in which he declared that the King, like all citizens, was subject to law, such law having been framed by the Parliament, which was the voice of the people... Have you that down, my dear?"

"Just a moment, Papa." The pen scratched. "Voice of the people—yes, I have it."

"Mind you write clearly, my love! It is but wasted labor if, after all, my words cannot be read."

"I am writing my *very* best," Juliana assured him stoutly.

"I did not mean to offend you, my dear—I know that I can rely on you. Oh," he sighed impatiently, "if there were but a machine into which a man might speak and his words be impressed upon wax!"

"Now who is being fanciful, Papa? That would be magic. And who needs such a machine, when he has a devoted daughter at beck and call?"

"Very true, my dear!—Charles made an attempt to speak in his own defense, but he was at all times an indifferent orator. The impediment of his speech which had troubled him so sorely as a child came back to plague him at such times of stress, and while he was stammering and choosing his words, Bradshaw shouted out, interrupting him: 'You have not owned us as a court! You look on us as a sort of people met together.'"

The girl wrote diligently, and, while he was waiting for her to reach the end of the sentence, her father observed her with absentminded affection.

She made a delightful picture as she sat with her feet curled sideways under her and one elbow resting on the table. Her gold-brown hair rippled about her face in natural ringlets, falling to the nape of her neck in front and caught up at the back in a Grecian knot. Her eyes, wide-set and almond-shaped, were dark brown, unlike those of her parent. A smudge of ink on the small chin only added to the charm of her face, which dimpled enchantingly as she looked up and smiled.

"'A sort of people met together.' I infer, Papa, that Bradshaw was employing the word 'sort' in the old-fashioned sense of a group, or number?"

"Yes, child… Bradshaw's speech continued, and terminated in a sentence of death."

Juliana sighed deeply as she wrote, but this time she ventured no comment.

"Charles again attempted to make a declaration in his own defense, but he was dragged out by the soldiers. He cried out bitterly, 'I am not suffered for to speak!'"

"It was *too* bad! Oh, if I had been there!"

"If you had been there, you, single-handed, would have vanquished Cromwell, Bradshaw, Cawley, and the rest of the impeachers!"

"I would have made *such* a speech!" Her fists clenched at the thought. Then she recollected herself, and said, "I beg your pardon, Papa! I will not interrupt again."

Nor did she. More than two hours passed by, during which her father dictated uninterruptedly and she, with tireless hand, wrote down his words. Occasionally, during the affecting description of Charles's final words and execution, she surreptitiously wiped a tear from her eye, with the hand that was not writing, but she made no complaint of fatigue, as the measured periods continued to flow from the author's mouth.

After the execution had been described in all its grim detail, Juliana did glance up hopefully, but, her father immediately proceeding to a discussion of the Martyr-King's character and difficulties, she obediently continued setting down his words. Only when he said, "Warwick informs us that Charles seldom ate of more than three dishes at most, nor drank above thrice, a glass of small beer, another of claret wine, and the last of water," did she remark, taking the opportunity to rub her right wrist, as her father's flow of speech was cut short by a coughing spell, "Papa, dear, let me pour you a glass of wine. Your throat must be dry with so much work. And I believe I had better light the lamp; I can hardly see what I have written."

"Very well, my dear. But no wine for me; a cup of water will be sufficient."

When the lamp was lit he proposed going on again, but his throat was now in reality so weary that the frequency of his cough finally obliged him to desist. Juliana carefully collated all her pages together, and put a book on top of them, choosing the heaviest from the large number of volumes that lay strewn about within reach of her father's chaise longue. His eye followed her actions wistfully, and he said, "I will read through those pages after I have rested for a moment or two. By the time I have perused them, I daresay I shall be fit to recommence."

"First you *must* take a little nourishment, Papa. No!"—as he protested. "You must, love, you must indeed! Otherwise I—I shall rebel! I shall refuse to take down your dictation. Look, here is a supporting broth which kind old Annunciata has left for you—let me but heat a little of it over the brazier."

He was very unwilling, but, presently recollecting that Juliana herself had taken no nourishment since breakfast, he at last permitted her to prepare a simple repast for both of them. While he was sipping the broth, he kindly inquired, "Did you have a pleasant outing, my dear? Were there many people abroad on the Ponte Vecchio?"

"Oh, a great many! Now try a grape or two,

Papa"—as he pushed away the half-finished broth. "The day has been so warm and pleasant," she went on, without betraying any hint of the fact that she might have wished to be out in it rather more than for one hasty trip to buy her father some handkerchiefs, "that multitudes of people were strolling by the river. Oh, that reminds me, Papa, of the amusing episode that I had intended relating to you." And she recounted, with considerable natural vivacity and many lively turns of phrase, the confrontation between the haughty but shabby lady traveler and the shrewd and redoubtable Signora Neroni. She omitted her only half-founded suspicion regarding the lady's theft of a pair of gloves, feeling that it would be wrong to blacken the character of someone who was not there to defend herself, and ended, "Now, Papa, was that not a diverting occurrence? Was it not singular that she should have applied to *me* for your direction? You see, your fame is being bruited abroad, and all Florence will soon know that it has a distinguished Englishman of letters living in its midst, despite kind Mr. Wyndham's being so obliging as to keep your address a secret!"

"You did not give the lady our direction?" her father interrupted. His tone was sharp. He had gone very pale—even paler than before.

"Now, Papa, you know me better than that, I should hope! I know your dislike of tuft-hunters and sycophants. I am fully aware of your desire for privacy and seclusion—I know you do not wish to be hunted out and toad-eaten by any sensation seeker who has read your books and wishes to sit at the feet of the author. I did no such thing, but, with the most poker-faced discretion in the world, replied, 'I am afraid, ma'am, that I cannot help you.' Did I not do right?"

He breathed a sigh of heartfelt relief. "Yes, my dear! Of course. I might have known that I could rely upon you."

After which he sat silent for many minutes, a half-eaten bunch of grapes dangling from his fingers, while he gazed ahead of him.

Juliana, too, had been pensive, chin on hand.

"It is a queer thing, Papa," she said at length. "I did not observe it at the time, but, recollecting that lady—something about her, I do not know what—perhaps the tone of her voice—has brought back to me an episode of my very early childhood—at least I am not fully certain that it happened at all—did I perhaps dream it? When we were living in Geneva—when I was very small—I seem to recall something that took place in a boat—was it in a boat? I can remember your shouting—you were very angry—and some person holding me up—you taking me from them—"

She had been saying these things in a musing tone, staring into the red heart of the brazier as she tried to piece together her early recollections, but now she looked up and, aghast, discovered her father white as a corpse, staring at her with dilated eyes.

"*Dio mio*, what is it, Papa?" she cried out, breaking into Italian in her agitation. "You look as if you had seen a ghost! What is the matter? For God's sake, tell me!"

"The Englishwoman!" he said harshly. "Describe her! What age was she? What was her dress? What did she look like?"

"Tall," faltered Juliana. "Decidedly shabby—I noticed a great darn in her glove, and a patch on the toe of her boot—long face like a horse—dark eyes, I think—her voice rather deep and loud—and I observed that she wore on her right hand, over her glove, a ring of white stone, shaped into the form of a unicorn's head. I observed that most particularly because it was so—*Papa!*"

A bitter groan had burst from him.

"It is she! God damn her, the fiend! I thought I had shaken her off at last. How has she managed to find out my whereabouts? I thought I was safe to end my days here!"

"Papa?" Juliana was trembling. "Who is it? Who is she? Oh, what is the matter?"

For he had sprung agitatedly to his feet and, with trembling hands, was attempting to assemble together some of the piles of books and papers that lay strewn about the room.

"We must leave instantly!" he ejaculated. "There is no time to be lost if that archdevil is in Florence. At any moment some unthinking person may betray my direction."

"Leave? Leave *Florence*?" Juliana stared at him in consternation. "But we have lived here for so long—ever since I was eight! You mean—go away altogether? Leave Tuscany? For good?"

"Yes, yes! Quick! Find the basket trunk! And the hamper and bandbox. And my portmanteau! I will go down to bespeak a chaise. Or, no"—recollecting. "Perhaps it is best if you go. But wear a cloak—a hood. Do you have a loo mask?"

"A loo mask, Papa?" she exclaimed in astonishment. "What ever should I want with such an article?"

"Then muffle the cloak around your face. Bid the chaise be here as soon as the horses can be set to!"

"But, Papa," said Juliana, wondering if her father had suddenly run mad, "pray consider! I doubt if any chaise may be had so late in the evening! Remember the hour! Will it not do if I go in the morning? Directly the sun has risen, if you wish."

"Very true—you are right," he sighed.

"And where are we to go?"

"To England."

"To *England*?" She could scarcely believe him. "But how are we to get there? A chaise will not take us to England."

"We will travel by stagecoach across France. Or, no"—recollecting. "I am so shocked I forget that France has declared war on England. As English subjects, that way is barred to us. We must go by sea, from Leghorn."

"All the way around Spain?" Juliana was horrified. "Papa, you *must* not! Do you not remember that Dr. Penzarro said a sea voyage was not to be thought of— that the pitching of a ship would be the worst thing possible—that time when you were wishing to go to Constantinople? Oh, I am sure you should not—I beg you not to think of it."

"Child, I *must* think of it. But it is true," he said, after a pause, frowning, "they say all the English are beginning to leave—embarking from Leghorn. *She* might, also. I must reflect. I will write a note to Mr. Wyndham—perhaps he may be able to help us. He has been a good friend. I shall be obliged, my dear, if you can summon young Luigi Fontini, and tell him that I shall require him to carry a note to the Envoy's residence—and, if Mr. Wyndham is not there, to seek him out."

"Very well, Papa," she said obediently.

"And, when you have done that, help me pack our possessions. *I* will attend to my papers—do you concern yourself with our clothes, and other belongings. Fortunately we have not much! We must, in any case, have left within a few months," he murmured to himself, and, to Juliana's inquiring glance, added rather hastily, "It is said that the French are certain to invade Tuscany."

With trembling hands he began inserting books into a canvas bag, breaking off to admonish Juliana, "If anybody knocks at the door—do not answer!"

"Oh, dearest Papa—truly I am not sure that you are well enough—"

"Hush!" he said, turning on her so terrible a look that without further question she set about doing his bidding.

Two

TWO DAYS LATER THE FATHER AND DAUGHTER WERE aboard a small packet boat in the Gulf of Genoa. Tuscany being neutral, shipping still plied to and fro between Leghorn and the French Mediterranean ports. By some mysterious means Mr. Wyndham, the British Envoy at the Court of Tuscany, a good friend of Mr. Elphinstone, had procured Swiss papers for the pair, and they traveled as Herr Doktor Eck and his daughter Johanna. Switzerland at that time was still on terms of uneasy friendship with France; therefore as Swiss citizens they might hope to travel through France unmolested, though Juliana worried privately as to what might befall them when they reached a Channel port and must take ship for England. However, that lay untold weeks ahead; no use to fret about it yet. There seemed little doubt that their journey across revolution-torn France must be far slower and more hazardous than it would have been in normal times.

Up to the moment of setting sail Juliana had not dared to question her father about their abrupt and unexpected departure—so harassed, apprehensive, and distraught had been his bearing, so impaired his state of health, so infrequent and nightmare-ridden his brief spells of repose as they journeyed across Italy in a drafty and rattling carriage. Sometimes, at posting stages, he had glanced back along the road, as if expecting to see the tall pale Englishwoman in pursuit, but, so far as Juliana was aware, and greatly to her relief, no further sign had been seen of this personage.

When they were safely afloat and, favored by a calm sea and following wind, were making northwestward, Juliana, observing with unbounded relief her father's happier look and somewhat easier deportment as the roofs of Leghorn fell away below the horizon, ventured for the first time to make an inquiry.

Little as she wished to worry her distressed parent any further by questioning, she felt it really incumbent upon her to do so. Beneath her youthful vivacity there lay a vein of sound common sense which told her that, reluctant though she must be to entertain the idea, her father's frail health and recklessly self-taxing disposition rendered it unlikely that he would live for many more years. Indeed, so exhausting had this hasty removal proved to his delicate frame that, she owned sorrowfully to herself, the period of life remaining to him might even have to be measured in months. If only he could be brought to follow medical advice! But he nurtured a barely concealed contempt for all Italian doctors and paid very little heed to their admonitions. Perhaps in England he might prove more biddable; this, Juliana thought, was one of the very few factors in favor of their removal.

She herself grieved at quitting Florence, in which

city they had lived for nearly ten years, and where
the climate appeared to agree with her father. They
had acquired few friends, however; Mr. Elphinstone
was of a reclusive temperament and seemed to shun
his fellow countrymen; their only connections were
his professional acquaintances, editors of journals for
whom he sometimes wrote articles or did translation, tradespeople from whom they purchased supplies, and the officials at the Envoy's residence who
were also glad sometimes to avail themselves of Mr.
Elphinstone's services as a translator. If her father were
to die, thought Juliana, she would hardly know to
whom she might turn; and so far as she knew, she had
no other relations. She had been vaguely aware that
their way of life—solitary, peaceful, hard-working—
was somewhat unusual, but she knew no other.

"Papa?" she ventured as, in the fresh autumn evening, they sat on deck wrapped in capes and watched
the sea turn from turquoise to a wonderful shade of
amethyst, while the sky's sharp blue faded to a trans-
parent green. "Papa, may I ask you some questions?"

She felt, rather than heard, the deep sigh with
which he received her words. But after a pause he
replied in a melancholy tone, "Of course you may
ask questions, my dearest child. Believe me, I am
fully aware of the self-restraint which has kept you
from doing so hitherto. But it is time, alas, that you
were informed, at least of such among our circumstances as are fit for your ears… How old are you
now, Juliana?"

"Papa! What a question to ask your own daughter!
I shall be eighteen on John the Baptist's Day."

"Eighteen…to be sure, that is not very old. Yet you are a sensible child. And—it is as well that you should be informed as to our plans. Ask, then, what you wish, my child."

At this permission, questions jostled together in Juliana's mind. She asked the simplest first.

"Where are we going to in England?"

"We are going to a house called Flintwood Manor, in the county of Hampshire."

"That is in the south of England, is it not?" Juliana inquired, after consulting a mental map.

"Yes, it is in a region known as the New Forest— though the forest has not been new for some five hundred years. We shall hope to take ship across the Channel to the port of Southampton, from where it is quite a short journey to Flintwood."

"You think that even in time of war ships will still be crossing the Channel to England?"

"Oh, I daresay there will always be privateers and freebooters," her father replied dryly. "At a price, doubtless a passage can be found. In my young days I know there was plenty of wool going out, and brandy coming in; I imagine it will still be found to be so."

"England!" said Juliana musingly. "I have imagined going there for so long! I have wondered so much what it was like, and wished to see London; especially Whitehall, where poor King Charles lived. Whitehall is such a beautiful name; I picture it all built in gleaming white marble, with orange trees and fountains."

"Do not get your hopes up too high," replied her father in a rather quelling manner. "It is not precisely like that; however, you will see it for your-self in due course, doubtless, and will be able to form your own opinions."

"Why are we going to this Flintwood, Papa? Who lives there?"

"Your grandfather, Juliana."

"My grandfather," she said wonderingly. "I did not know that I had one! He is your father, then, Papa?"

"My father, yes." His tone was far from enthusiastic.

"What is his name?"

"He is called General Sir Horace Tullesley Paget."

"Paget? Then why is our name Elphinstone?"

"Paget is our real name, Juliana. Elphinstone is the name under which I chose to write my books. I assumed it for—for various reasons."

"And why have you never spoken of my grandfather before?"

"Because we quarreled, my dear. We have not seen each other in a great many years—since before you were born."

"What was the cause of your quarrel?"

"There were various causes. First, he disapproved of my choice of profession. He wished me to purchase a commission in his regiment—as he had done, and his father, and all my uncles but one. My father could not understand my wish to study history and write for a living—it made him excessively angry."

"What a stupid reason!" said Juliana. "If *I* have children, I shall allow them to become writers or—or carpenters, whatever they wish."

"Ay, but you have been brought up in Italy, my little one. In English society, matters are more carefully regulated. And besides, this was twenty, thirty years ago. Children were obliged to mind their parents."

"Do I not mind you, Papa?"

"Sometimes!" he said, smiling. "But I am not near so strict with you as my father was with me."

"What were the other reasons for your quarrel?"

"Well," he replied, much more slowly, "the principal one was that your grandfather did not approve of the lady whom I wished to marry."

"My mother?"

"Yes, child. Your mother." His voice was hollow—heavy—he stared out over the darkening sea with a look of profound depression.

"Why did Sir Horace not approve of her?" Juliana wanted to know.

"First, because she came from a level of society which, he said, being lower than ours, was an unsuitable source for a partner: she was the daughter of an apothecary. He held that she was after nothing but my money."

"Your *money*? But we have so little money, Papa. Only what you earn from your writing."

"*Now* that is so—yes; but your grandfather was—is—quite a rich man."

"But if you had enough money, why did it matter that you wished to marry a girl who had less?"

"My father was certain that she did not truly love me; that she was merely after money and position. He said she was a sly, scheming, designing hussy."

Juliana thought about this for a little while. Then she said, "Was that true?"

Her father likewise waited a moment to answer. Then, sighing, he replied, "Yes, my dear. I fear your grandfather was in the right about her. At that time, though, I was but a romantic, idealistic young fool, with my head full of ancient history—notions about chivalry—gallant knights—beautiful ladies—and so on! Laura seemed my ideal of the knight's lady."

"My mother's name was Laura?"

"Laura Brooke." He paused, and then said slowly, "And she *was* extremely beautiful—tall, pale, dark-haired—like some queen from a legend of romance."

"Oh…" For some reason Juliana found that these words gave her a curious pang. After a while she asked, "But, in spite of my grandfather's opposition, you married her?"

"Yes, we married. I was of age, so he could not prevent me. But he could—and did—stop my allowance and cut me out of his will. He refused to support me or have anything more to do with me."

"What happened then?"

Next moment Juliana wished that she had not asked, for her father's face became so full of anguish that she could have bitten out her tongue. But his voice when he replied remained level enough.

"First, my dear, *you* were born—and have been my chief delight and comfort ever since. Then—what followed was precisely what your grandfather had foretold. Your mother, disillusioned by a life of poverty and scraping care, as I tried to earn enough with my pen to support us all, soon decided that—that she had made a mistake in thinking that she loved me. She found others—another, whom she preferred. And so she left me. And you too. You, of course, were only a baby then."

"So why did you not make up the quarrel with my grandfather?"

"He had said things that—that I could not forgive."

"And *you* were too proud to acknowledge that you also had been wrong," Juliana said in a reflective tone. "*I* know your nature, you see, Papa."

"Perhaps." There was a smile in his voice.

"Did you never see my mother again? Did she never wish to see *me*?"

She asked the question wistfully. It seemed to her incredible that another man could be preferred above her father—so handsome, clever, and sweet-natured as he was. And for a mother to go off and desert her own baby—that appeared hardly possible; it was the most strange, unnatural thing she had ever heard. She had always supposed her mother dead. She added tremblingly, "Did you *divorce* her?"

But to this question her father replied, "If you do not mind, my dear, that touches upon topics which are a cause of such anguish and horror to me that I prefer not to recall them. I would rather not speak any more on this subject at this time. In England—when we are rested from the journey—I will tell you the whole history."

"Oh, *dear* Papa! Indeed, I would not give you pain for the world! Pray do not think of—of telling me anything that you would rather not! I am only sorry to have distressed you so much as I have. I had thought that I ought to know something of our circumstances in case—in case you—"

Her voice faltered to a halt.

He said calmly, "You were very right. And I can tell

you also that a year ago—when France declared war on England—I wrote to your grandfather, explaining that—that I was not in the first degree of health, and that if I were to fall ill, or die, it would greatly relieve my anxieties about you if I could be assured that he might be willing to offer you a home—since you are the only thing in the world that I cherish."

"You wrote to my grandfather a year ago?" She was amazed. "You never told me!"

"There are many things that I do not choose to tell you, Puss." Her father pinched her cheek.

"And did my grandfather reply?"

"He replied—somewhat stiffly, which was to be expected, but without recriminations. He said that he was now alone, as your grandmother died five years ago—which I had heard—and that we might come to Flintwood—either or both of us—whenever we wished to do so. He was not cordial—he did not say that we should be *welcome*—his phrases were formal—but he said all that was proper, and intimated that we had a right to come; that he would not bar his door to us."

Juliana, with her chin propped on her fists, looked thoughtfully at her father.

"His letter was so unwelcoming that you did not wish to accept his offer," she deduced. "Or at least you wished to postpone accepting it as long as possible. Am I right, Papa?"

"You will think me selfish, my love, I fear, but I did greatly wish to complete my *Vindication of King Charles I* before removing to Flintwood. Your grandfather was always so wholly unsympathetic to my writing. And we have been happy in Florence, have we not? I know I should have been considering *your* interests—"

"*My* interests? What have they to say to anything?"

"Why, as a young lady of respectable birth, you should be learning to move in Polite Circles, instead of keeping house in a tenement and cooking on a brazier in Florence. Your aunt would be scandalized, without a doubt—"

"Oh, have I an aunt?" she said, all curiosity.

"My elder sister Caroline. She married a baronet and has two daughters; I daresay she will be prepared to bring you out in society, for she was used to go to all the *ton* parties; her husband, at one time, was on the fringe of the Carlton House set."

"What is that?"

"Oh, the Prince of Wales and his friends. My sister Caroline was always the most empty-headed fool possible; I doubt if time will have improved her. I believe her husband turned from fashionable circles to political ones—but with as little distinction, I imagine. He was always a dull stick."

Her father's tone was so impatient that Juliana did not pursue the question of her aunt's family.

"Does my grandfather know that you have written several historical works under the name of Charles Elphinstone? That your life of George Villiers received wide acclaim?"

"I fear, my love, that your grandfather is not to be impressed by the writing of books! He has rarely opened one in his life, unless it might be a history of some military campaign, or a treatise on strategy. He is a soldier first and last. Whether my books received acclaim or not would be of no account to *him*. But no, I have not told him. And I do not plan to do so. That is one reason why they have all been written under a nom de plume. I knew that your grandfather would detest the thought of the family name being used in such a context."

"I do *not* think that I shall like my grandfather," was Juliana's comment.

"I devoutly hope that you will endeavor to do so, my child! He is a man of just and upright principle, strict attention to duty, and impeccable religious beliefs. His military career was not marked by—by any outstanding success in the field—he commanded a brigade in the American war—but I understand that his careful regard to detail and his consideration for his men have earned him the respect of his peers."

Juliana did not voice her opinion that her grandfather sounded to her like a dead bore; instead she remarked, "I believe, Papa, that we should go below. The evening air is too cool for you. You are coughing a great deal, and that is bad."

"Yes, I fear that you are right, my dear. What should I do without my ministering sprite?" he asked playfully, as he rose with difficulty to his feet, supporting himself by leaning on her slight shoulder. Another violent fit of coughing shook him, and he had to clutch at the deck rail while the seizure lasted. His daughter watched, biting her lip with distress, unable to help or relieve him in any way, as he coughed and coughed, pressing a kerchief to his lips. A sailor passing nearby said in alarm, "*Il povero signore!* He should not be on deck—he should be in his bed!"

"Nothing—it is nothing!" Impatiently the sick man shook off the kindly hand laid on his arm, and began haltingly to make his way toward the companion ladder. But Juliana noticed with terror that the kerchief he had been pressing to his lips and now returned to his pocket was patched and stained with blotches of vivid scarlet.

❧

Six weeks later the travelers were approaching the port of St.-Malo in Brittany. Their journey across France had been slow and difficult enough to justify Juliana's worst forebodings. Sometimes she felt that it might even have been better to risk the effects of a long sea passage on her father's constitution; that way at least they might have been certain of a landfall. But now, although so close to the Channel coast, they still were not sure of being able to cross the narrow strip of water that lay so tantalizingly between them and England. And the weather had been bad, the roads had been vile, the transport had been uncertain; besides which, there were all the hazards of revolutionary officialdom. In these days of the people's government, every town gate and village tax office offered an obstacle, sometimes dangerous; the smaller the place, the more ignorant the natives, the likelier they were, in their new-found arrogance, armed with muskets and knots of red ribbon, to stop all strangers, cross-question them, inspect their papers, lengthily consult lists of proscribed persons in case the travelers' names might be found thereon, keep them waiting, and generally harass them in every way possible.

The journey had been a nightmare. On several occasions, furthermore, they had been obliged to stop at tiny places and stay in small country hostelries deficient in almost every convenience or amenity, because the sick man had been too weak to continue on the journey. Even then—lying abed in the dark chamber of some miserable little *auberge*—he could not bear to be idle, and demanded that Juliana find her pen, procure whatever ink and paper might be at hand, and continue to transcribe from his dictation. Obedient to his wishes, she therefore crouched by ill-placed windows to catch the last of the light, or knelt on the floor because there was no chair, by the light of guttering candles, setting down his final estimate of Charles's character, which was often dictated in a voice so faint with fatigue that she must strain her ears to catch its note. She herself would often be trembling with exhaustion after a day's travel, or shivering from the damp and chill of the inn bedroom; it was fortunate, she frequently reflected, that she was so strong, that her own health remained unimpaired and she was able to help her father with his book as well as ministering to his other needs, without succumbing to the strain of his unremitting requirements. Although the gentlest man in the world, he seemed unaware of how hard he was driving her.

Even in the diligence or stagecoach, as they rumbled on and on, over the monotonous and mud-covered French countryside, he would be thinking of new and important sidelights to the main thread of his book, and might require Juliana to take down notes, often greatly to the surprise, and sometimes suspicion, of their fellow travelers. Once a *douanier* in a small town demanded why, if Monsieur was a Swiss, as it said in his passport, did he dictate and require his young lady to write down in English, as one of their companions in the coach said he had been doing?

Juliana with great presence of mind explained that her father was a professor of English history, which necessitated his writing in English. The *douanier* scratched his head doubtfully at this, and she added with a stroke of inspiration, "My father, Citizen, is making a study of Cromwell's Glorious Revolution, and the execution of the renegade ci-devant Royalist usurper Charles Stuart—see, it is all written down here!" And she held out to him some of the pages that she had been writing.

"I do not read English, Citizeness."

"No, but you can read the names!" And she pointed out Cromwell, Downes, Cawley, Bradshaw, Charles. The *douanier* slowly peered his way from one to another, and at last said, "Good. The citizen-professor writes a history of the English revolution—very good. Too bad that revolution did not succeed! Ours is better. You may pass on your way, Citizens."

"Oh, Papa!" Juliana exclaimed that night in their damp, unsavory bedroom. "*Poor* King Charles! I felt the most wicked traitor to him—saying such things! I am sure he would never have forgiven me—*he* would never have told such a lie! But I was so afraid that if the man knew what your book really said, he might confiscate it, or tear it up."

"You did very well, Puss," her father said, smiling. "I should not have had such presence of mind. And I

daresay King Charles would condone your act—if he
wanted my book published, that is!"

"Of course—that is true. It will establish his good
name forever!"

The arrival within sight of St.-Malo was an occasion for joy. They stopped for the night in the small
fishing village of St.-Servan, where, for a wonder, the
inn they chose proved clean and comfortable. And on
that evening her father dictated his last paragraph to
Juliana, concluded his final peroration, and announced
with a sigh, "There! It is finished. And I fear a weary
work it has been for you, my pet! You have been
an angel—a rock—a monument of forbearance and
industry. How many pages of manuscript?"

"Six hundred and two, Papa," she said faintly.

"Hand me a sheet of paper, my love, and I will make
it six hundred and three by adding the title page."

With a weak and shaky hand he dipped his pen
into the standish, and wrote in staggering letters: *A
Vindication of King Charles I*, by Charles Elphinstone.
Then, underneath, he added, "This work is dedicated
to my Dear and Dutiful Daughter Juliana, without
whose untiring and faithful help its completion would
never have been achieved."

"Oh, Papa!" Reading over his shoulder, Juliana
could hardly see the words; her eyes were blinded
by tears.

But then he somewhat impaired her pleasure by
depositing the unwieldy bundle of manuscript in her
arms, and observing, "Now, as soon as you have made
a fair copy, Juliana—a task that should prove easy and
speedy once we are at your grandfather's, for there

will be no household duties to distract you from the labor—the book may be sent off to my publisher, Mr. John Murray. How long do you suppose the copying may take you, my love? Could you write as many as ten pages an hour?"

"I—I should rather doubt that, Papa," faltered Juliana—even her stout spirit was a little daunted at the prospect ahead, for the book was more than twice the length of any of his previous works. "For the first hour it is very well, but—but presently one's hand begins to tire! However, you may be sure that I shall do it as speedily as may be. You cannot be any more eager than I am to see it on its way to the publisher's. Only think! Instead of having to ask the British Envoy to undertake its dispatch, you may be able to travel up to London and leave it with Mr. Murray yourself."

"So I may," agreed her father, coughing.

At this moment they were startled by a tremendous noise of shouting, the clashing of sabers, and musket shots in the street outside their bedroom window.

"Mercy! What is it? What can be happening?" exclaimed Juliana in dismay, running to the window to look out.

"Have a care, my child. Do not let yourself be the target for a bullet. If there is a disturbance, it is best to stay out of sight."

But Juliana, reckless of his warning, struggled with the stiff casement, pushed it open, and hung over the sill.

"It is a mob," she soon reported.

"As usual," commented her father, who was lying on his bed. "Pray, dearest—"

"Men in red caps shouting, 'Down with the foreign spy!'"

"You do not think it is us they are after?" he said uneasily. "Are they coming this way?"

"No—no—they have got hold of somebody, but I cannot see who it is. Yes, they are bringing him this way. They are all dancing and yelling—it is like savages, indeed!" Juliana said, shivering. "They are shouting, 'To be the Tree, to the Liberty Tree! Hang him up!'"

"Poor devil!" said her father with a shudder. "But there is nothing *we* can do."

"Oh!" exclaimed Juliana in a tone of horror next minute. "It is the man who was so kind to you in the diligence, when you were sick! Oh, poor fellow, how terrible! How can they be such monsters?"

"Which man?"

"Why, our fellow traveler in the coach from Rennes—the Dane or German, or whatever he was, who gave you the cordial and was so kind and helpful when I was in despair because you seemed so ill I feared you were dying. Oh, how *can* they? I believe they do mean to hang him!"

"Well, that is very terrible," said her father, "but I fear there is nothing in the world we can do to hinder them."

Juliana thought otherwise.

"Well, I am going to try," she asserted, and without wasting a moment she ran from the room, despite her father's anguished shout of "*Juliana!* For God's sake! Come back! You can do no good, and will only place yourself in terrible danger!"

Running into the street, Juliana saw that the mob had dragged the unfortunate victim of their disapproval some distance along, to a small *place*, where grew a plane tree which, for the time being, had been garlanded with knots of dirty red ribbon and christened the Liberty Tree. Toward this the wretched man was being dragged by his red-capped assailants.

"Spy! Agent of foreign tyrants! Hang him up!"

The man, who had struggled until he was exhausted, was looking half stunned, and as much dazed as alarmed by the sudden fate that had overtaken him. He was a tall, thickset individual, plainly but handsomely dressed in a suit of very fine gray cloth, with large square cuffs and large flaps to his pockets, and a very high white stock which had come untied in the struggle. His hat had been knocked off—so had his wig—revealing untidy brown hair, kept short in a Corinthian cut. A noose had been slung round his neck, and the manifest intention of the crowd was to haul him up and hang him from a branch of the tree, when Juliana ran across the cobbled *place*.

"Citizens!" she panted. "You should not be doing this!"

Luckily her French, due to a childhood in Geneva, was perfect, but it seemed to have little effect on the crowd.

"Mind your own business!" grunted one of the three men principally in charge of the operation, but another explained, "Yes, we should, Citizeness! The man is a spy."

"He is not a spy—he is a doctor! And a very good doctor! He gave some medicine to my father that cured him of a terribly severe spasm. And my father is an important professor of Revolutionary History. Think if he had died, what the world would have lost. But this man saved him! Think what you are doing, Citizens! France cannot afford to lose a good doctor! Think of all the poor sick, suffering people!"

Juliana had raised her voice to its fullest extent in this impassioned appeal, and her words penetrated to the outer fringe of the crowd, which had come along mainly out of curiosity. She heard some encouraging cries of agreement.

"Ah, that is true! We can't afford to waste a doctor. There are plenty of sick people in this town!" "Let him cure my Henri, who has had the suppuration on his leg for so long." "My daughter's quinsy!" "My father's backache!" "Do not hang the doctor!" they all began to roar.

"Are you a doctor?" demanded a man who carried an enormous smith's hammer.

The victim's eyes met those of Juliana for a moment, and a curious spasm passed across his countenance; then he said firmly, "Certainly I am a doctor! If you have any sick people who need healing, I shall be happy to look after them. Just find me a room that will do as a surgery, and provide me with the materials I shall ask for."

This suggestion proved so popular with the crowd that in five minutes the man was accommodated with a small parlor of the same inn where Juliana and her father were lodged. A large queue of persons instantly lined up, demanding attention, but before he would even listen to their symptoms, the gray-suited man demanded supplies of various medicaments, such as rhubarb, borage, wine, brandy, oil, egg white, orris root, antimony, cat's urine, wood ash, and oak leaves. Some of these were not available, but others were supplied as circumstances permitted. He also asked for the services of "the young lady in brown" as a nurse and helper.

"You have gone halfway to saving my life, mademoiselle," he muttered as the crowd chattered and jostled in the passageway outside the door. "Now do me the kindness to finish your task and help save the other half."

"How do you mean, monsieur?"

"Help me devise some remedies for these ignorant peasants!"

"But—are you not, then—?"

"Hush! I am no more a doctor than that piebald horse across the street. But with your intelligent assistance and a little credulity from our friends outside, I hope that we may brush through."

The next hour was one of the most terrifying and yet exhilarating that Juliana had ever lived through.

"What are your symptoms, Citizen?" she would inquire as each grimy, limping, hopeful figure came through the door. "Sore throat—difficulty in swallowing—pains in the knee—bad memory—trouble in passing water—"

Then she would hold a solemn discussion with the gray-coated man—he told her in a low voice and what she had now identified as a Dutch accent that his name was Frederick Welcker.

"Sore throat—hmm, hmm—white of egg with

rosemary beaten into it—take that now, and suck the juice of three lemons at four-hourly intervals. Pound up a kilo of horseradish with olive oil, and apply half internally, half externally. A little cognac will not come amiss. Next?

"Toothache? Chew a dozen cloves, madame, and drink a liter of cognac.

"A bad toe? Wash it with vinegar, mademoiselle, and wrap a hank of cobwebs round it."

Combining scraps of such treatments as she could remember having received herself in her rare illnesses with some of old Signora Fontini's nostrums, remedies she had culled from *The Vindication of King Charles I,* and various ingenious but not always practicable suggestions provided by Herr Welcker, Juliana was able to supply each patient with something that at least, for the time being, sent him away hopeful and satisfied.

"Now what happens?" she asked breathlessly as the last sufferer (a boy with severely broken chilblains) hobbled away smelling of the goose grease that had been applied to his afflicted members.

"Now, mademoiselle, I have a moment's breathing space. And, with the French mob, that is often sufficient. They are fickle and changeable; in a couple of hours they will have forgotten me and discovered some other victim," replied Herr Welcker, washing off the goose grease in a finger bowl and fastidiously settling his white wristbands and stock.

"But what if the sick people are not all cured by tomorrow? They will come back and accuse us of being impostors," pointed out Juliana, who was beginning to suffer from reaction, and to feel that her actions had been overimpulsive and probably very foolish indeed. What had she got herself into? Her despondency was increased when her father burst hastily into the room, exclaiming, "Juliana! There you are! I have been half over the village, searching for you—I was at my wits' end with terror! Never—never do such a thing again! Rash—hasty—shatterbrained—"

"I am sorry, Papa! I am truly sorry!" Juliana was very near to tears, but Herr Welcker intervened promptly.

"I regret, sir, but I must beg to disagree with you! Your daughter's cool and well-thought intercession indubitably saved my life—for which I cannot help but be heartily grateful—and was, furthermore, the most consummate piece of quick thinking and shrewd acting that it has been my good fortune to witness! Thanks to her, I am now in a fair way to get back to England, instead of hanging from a withered bough on that dismal scrawny growth they are pleased to call the Liberty Tree."

"England?" said Juliana in surprise. "I thought you were a Hollander, sir?"

"So I am, but England is my country of residence."

Charles Elphinstone brightened a little at these words.

"If you are bound for England, sir—as we are, likewise—perhaps you can give me information as to what ships are sailing from St.-Malo?"

Herr Welcker looked at him with a wry grin.

"Ships from St.-Malo? You are hoping for a ship? I fear, sir, your hopes are due to be dashed. No ships are sailing at present. Those wretched devils of Frogs have closed the port."

"Then—" gasped Juliana's father. "My god! We

are trapped! Fixed in France! Heaven help us, what can we do?"

He tottered to a chair and sank on it, looking haggardly at the other two occupants of the small room. But Herr Welcker, strangely enough, did not seem too dispirited.

"Well, I'll tell you!" he said. "Damme if I haven't got a soft spot for you two, after the young lady stood up for me with such spunk. Pluck to the backbone you are, my dear. I'll take you both with me—though," he added puzzlingly, "it will mean throwing out some of the Gobelins, half a dozen of the Limoges, and most of the wallpaper too, I shouldn't wonder. Devilish bulky stuff!"

"Sir? I don't understand you."

"Walls have ears," said Herr Welcker. "Let us all take a stroll out of the town. And if you have any luggage that can be carried in a handbag, fetch it along. The rest will have to remain here."

"What?" gasped Mr. Elphinstone. "Leave my *books*? My Horace—my Livy—my Montefiume's *Apologia*— Dieudonné's *History of the Persian Empire* in fourteen volumes? Leave them behind?"

Herr Welcker shrugged.

"Stay with them if you please," he said. "Otherwise it's bring what you can carry. I daresay the innkeeper will look after your things faithfully enough if you leave a few francs in a paper on top—you can come back for the books when the war's over! Who wants a lot of plaguey books? The Frogs don't, for sure. Unlettered, to a man… Well, are you coming, or not?"

Anguished, Mr. Elphinstone hesitated, then sighed

and said, "Well, Juliana, my dear, if you will carry my own *Vindication*, I daresay I could make shift to bring along a few of my most treasured volumes. We shall just have to leave our clothes behind. I collect, sir, that you have at your disposal an air balloon?"

"You collect rightly," said Herr Welcker.

Three

By good fortune, the evening was a foggy one. Juliana, though apprehensive as to the effect of the moist, chill air on her father's delicate frame, could not but be grateful for the cloudy dimness as the three foreigners made their way, silently, and taking pains to avoid notice, toward the edge of the village. Herr Welcker walked a hundred yards ahead, not too fast, and Juliana and her father followed in a strolling, loitering manner, gazing about them at the cottages and the cabbage gardens and the wide bay of St.-Malo, as if their only intention were to view the scene and to enjoy the evening air. Luckily there were few people abroad in the street; most of the village population, it seemed, had repaired to the Liberty Tree to dance around it, drink cheap red wine, and sing revolutionary songs. The fugitives' exit from the village was achieved without mishap—due, partly, to the prudence of Herr Welcker, who led them away from the main road and onto a small muddy, brambly path which ran off between the vegetable plots and then up a wooded slope, the steepness of which made Mr.

Elphinstone pause, after a while, and gasp for breath, his hand to his side.

"Papa? Are you in pain?" exclaimed Juliana in an anguished whisper. "Here—let me carry your bundle. Pray try not to cough!"

"It is nothing, child—it will pass." And in a moment he continued on his way. Coming up with Herr Welcker at last, they found themselves in what seemed a large, saddle-shaped meadow at the top of the hill. They discovered him in low-voiced conversation with another man, a black-cloaked individual with a hood pulled low over his face. Juliana noticed also a cart, a tethered horse, and a complicated arrangement of guy ropes, dimly visible in the haze, wavering upward into obscurity.

"Deuce take it, there's very little wind," Herr Welcker was muttering discontentedly. "You do not think, Gavroche, that the plaguey machine will deposit us in mid-Channel? Or merely carry us up the coast to Normandy?"

"Have no fear, monsieur. There is a good southeast wind behind this fog—your craft will bear you to England swiftly enough. Only, make haste to embark! Your cargo is all packed in, and there is no time to be lost—at any minute a shift in the mist might render us visible to some native of the locality or fisherman in the bay."

"I have brought two more passengers," said Herr Welcker. "We shall have to remove some of the goods."

"Monsieur! Have you taken leave of your senses? After all the trouble you took to collect—"

"Hush! It cannot be helped. Without the aid of

these two, I should not be here at all. Quick, let us see what can be most easily displaced. The Petitot snuffboxes, for a start—he doesn't care for those above half—the smaller Buhl cabinet—some of the Gobelins—*not* the Sèvres—"

Arguing, the two men disappeared up a rope ladder into the gloom, leaving Juliana and her father below with the horse, which dropped its head and cropped in a dispirited manner at the poor pasturage, while the mooring ropes creaked and strained.

"Very good—I think that will do—"

Welcker was out of sight above, but he was evidently passing canvas-wrapped bundles to the other man, who, dangling on the ladder, received them from him; Juliana, running forward, called softly, "Pass them down to me, monsieur! I will catch them!"

"Mind yourself, mademoiselle! They are heavy. Above all, do not let them fall—though, what does it matter? Oh, the Limoges!" he exclaimed in anguish.

"When I think of the pains that Monsieur went to in order to acquire those—"

"Quiet, Gavroche!" A shift in the mist revealed Herr Welcker's round pink face looking authoritatively over the side of what looked like a very large laundry basket or vegetable farmer's hamper, floating above them in the haze. "Good, that will do! Tell the young lady and the gentleman that they may come up, and to make haste—I think I hear voices in the distance."

Juliana obliged her father to go first up the ladder, although he was most unwilling. The exertion of climbing up was almost too much for his strength, and the process took many precious minutes, while he clung to the ropes with shaking hands, gasping and coughing. Fortunately Herr Welcker, although so plump, appeared to possess a powerful frame; leaning over the side, at some risk to himself, he more or less hoisted the unfortunate Mr. Elphinstone bodily into the basket, assisted by the man Gavroche, who pushed from below. Then the bundles of books were passed up.

"Now you, mademoiselle—make haste! The voices are coming closer!"

Impelled by fright, Juliana tucked up her skirts and managed the undignified ascent as speedily as she could. Behind her she heard the vague shouts become closer and more menacing.

"Yonder! Ah, look yonder! It is the strangers—it is the spies! *A bas les scélérats! A la lanterne!* Quick, quick—they are attempting to escape!"

Careless of decorum, Juliana tumbled over the side into the basket. Louder than the voices of the mob, as she did so, came three sharp twangs from below.

"Good, Gavroche has cut the mooring ropes," remarked Herr Welcker, looking over the side.

"But what will happen to *him*? Is he not coming with us?" gasped Juliana.

"No. He will outdistance them easily enough—he has the horse, which was once the best of poor Chateaumacenay's stud—none of these ragamuffins has any beast that can possibly overtake him… Capital, he is away," he added calmly, and Juliana heard the rattle of hoofs across the turf. "Pity about the Limoges—never mind! But for you, miss, I should be dead as mutton by now, and I value my neck above a parcel of Limoges. Ah, there they come!"

Juliana by now had scrambled herself upright in the narrow, packed space available, and, looking over, she saw many dim figures with lanterns, and waving weapons, directly below where they themselves hung suspended. White faces gaped upward.

"'Send they have no muskets," Herr Welcker muttered uneasily. "One bullet through the envelope, and we should be laughing on the other side of our faces… Aha, though, Gavroche was right: here comes the breeze."

The basket that contained them tipped, swayed, and bore off in a northerly direction. Yells of baffled fury burst from the fog-shrouded group down below. Pikes and reaping hooks were shaken; a few stones whistled past and one or two fell in the basket.

Juliana's father let out a sharp cry as he was struck by a stone on the temple.

"Oh, dear Papa, are you injured? Here, let me see? Shut your eyes—I will bathe it—I have my vinaigrette in my pocket." Crouching by him, she ministered to him as best she could, wiping the wound with her handkerchief. It proved to be only a graze. There was remarkably little space for them all in the basket, which, perhaps four feet in diameter, contained, as well as themselves, a great number of canvas-wrapped packages of every shape and size.

"Pray observe particular care *not* to step on the ones marked with red chalk," Herr Welcker admonished his passengers. "They contain the breakables—the Lim—ah no, we have left that behind!—the Sèvres, the crystal lusters for His Highness's chandeliers, the Duc de Cévennes's Ming—"

"Are you, then, a merchant of china, sir?" Juliana asked curiously, attempting to accommodate her body to the awkward contours of the packages.

"I, ma'am? Indeed no!" He seemed quite affronted at her supposition. "I am a collector. I act as agent for my Patron."

"Your Patron is in England?" inquired Mr. Elphinstone weakly, reclining as best he could against a yielding bundle which appeared to contain brocade.

"Just so, sir."

"Not a very safe profession, yours, just at present?"

"Ah well, one must contrive as best one can. And it is gratifying to do what one may to rescue some of the treasures which these *canailles*, in their spite and ignorance, would probably smash, burn, or cut up to clothe their filthy brats. I have found priceless tapestries, sir, in hay barns, being used as sacks to hold potatoes. It is infamous! And of course in these times one may pick up a bargain here and there—which is quite an inducement with my Patron, I can tell you, hard put to it as he is, these days, for ready cash! They say his marriage to Princess Caroline will mend all, but for my part I take leave to doubt that."

"Your Patron is…?"

"Why, sir, His Highness! The Prince of Wales! I am surprised you did not know that!"

Since Herr Welcker seemed so surprised, Juliana made haste to pacify him. "My father and I have lived out of England for so long—I, all my life indeed! We are but now returning for the sake of his health… Oh, how beautiful that is!" she exclaimed in rapture as a division in the mist suddenly revealed to them the whole of the St.-Malo bay, with the shipping scattered about the estuary, the town of St.-Malo itself sitting snug on its island, surrounded by masts, and Dinard gleaming far away on the opposite shore. That they themselves were also seen from below was made manifest by various white puffs of smoke which blossomed out from the walls of the town and the quaysides and ships in the bay; they could hear the reports of the gunshots a moment or two after the puffs, but no shots seemed to come anywhere near them.

"We are already too high," said Herr Welcker with great satisfaction. He pulled on a string, and they went higher still.

Looking up, Juliana marveled at the great silken globe, wrinkling and straining over their heads in its network of cords. It seemed such a frail and delicate structure to carry them so far. It was colored gaily in red and yellow, and bore a crisscross design of harlequin checks.

"Is it filled with air? Why should it rise?" she wanted to know.

"No, it is filled with hydrogen, miss. Air comes cheaper, to be sure—but then you need a large bonfire to heat it in the first place, and a circular launching platform with a hole in the middle—that would never have served *our* turn, as we wished to leave quietly and escape notice."

Juliana would have liked to ask more questions about the nature and structure of the balloon, but she observed that her father, what with the high, frigid altitude and the swaying motion of the basket, was commencing to look exceedingly ill. Alarmed, she endeavored to make him as comfortable as possible in the bottom of the basket, and Herr Welcker administered another dram of the cordial which had proved so efficacious in the coach from Rennes. It was bright green, and very strong.

"Infallible stuff," remarked Herr Welcker with some complacence. "Monks make it—always carry a supply with me on my travels. Cure you of anything—except a bullet through the head!"

It certainly appeared to be a soporific; after a generous dose of it had been tipped between his lips, Juliana was relieved to see that her father appeared inclined to sleep, though he still shivered with cold. Juliana asked Herr Welcker if she might untie one of the parcels of tapestry to supply a coverlet for her ailing parent. Herr Welcker was at first extremely unwilling, but when she represented to him that there was very little purpose in saving a man from the French revolutionaries if he were then to perish from exposure to the elements, she finally received grudging permission, Herr Welcker himself selecting his most inferior tapestry for the purpose, and, soon after that, Juliana was happy to hear that her father's breathing had steadied into the rhythm of sleep.

For herself she saw no prospect of following his example. Obliged to remain upright on her feet, as was Herr Welcker likewise, she passed several weary hours as best she could, shifting miserably from one numb foot to the other, standing on one leg, leaning her hip against the edge of the basket, propping her elbows on the Buhl cabinet (when Herr Welcker was not looking), trying any position that might, briefly, give some relief to her cramped and frozen limbs. Never could she have imagined that aerial travel could be so uncomfortable! Regrettably, also, Herr Welcker and his assistant had neglected to provision the craft with any food, in the hurried departure. Hunger, therefore, soon added its pangs to the other vexations of the passengers, for none of them had taken supper before they embarked, and Juliana and her father had eaten no dinner either. She dared not inquire how long the passage was likely to take; for one thing, she had as soon not be told how many hours of this misery she might have to endure, and for another, she had a shrewd suspicion that Herr Welcker himself did not know the answer.

At least the night was clear; Juliana shuddered to imagine what their journey might have been like had a storm blown up. The keen steady wind blew continually from the southeast, carrying them, Juliana was gratified to think, much faster than if they had made their passage by sea; and innumerable large stars burned above them in the firmament, only obscured by the great circular globe of darkness directly above them that was the envelope of the balloon.

"If only some means could be achieved of guiding the vessel's *direction*," observed Herr Welcker, "this might indeed be a most practical and commodious method of travel. But I understand that neither oars, sails, nor traction by birds has yet proved efficacious in this respect."

"Traction by birds! I should think not, indeed!"

"And yet if only some *large* birds—say, swans—might be harnessed, one would almost think it practicable," sighed Herr Welcker. "However, such speculations are not to our purpose. And we appear to be making excellent headway—always supposing we do not drift too far to the west. Indeed I flatter myself that I might yet return in time to have the Sèvres delivered to the Pavilion for a dinner party that His Highness gives there in honor of Lady Jersey next Thursday."

"A Sèvres dinner service?" inquired Juliana.

"No, miss. *Pots de chambre*," Herr Welcker replied, employing the French term, presumably, out of a delicate wish not to embarrass the young lady.

Juliana, however, reared in Italy, where the most outrageous topics were liable to be discussed at the top of somebody's lungs in the street, at any hour of the day or night, was not embarrassed, but only curious.

"*Pots de chambre* for a dinner party? How singular! I do not precisely understand."

"Why, miss, where have you been all your life? In any English gentleman's establishment, it is the custom to keep a set of *pots de chambre* in the sideboard."

"Although born in England I have lived in Switzerland and Italy all my life, and I still do not understand. Why in the sideboard?"

"Why, for when the ladies leave the table."

Since Juliana continued to look baffled, he explained further.

"At the conclusion of any English dinner party, when the dessert is finished, the ladies quit the table and repair to the drawing room, leaving the gentlemen to their wine, their stories (unfit for the ears of ladies), and their *pots de chambre*."

"And what do the ladies do?"

"How should I know?" replied Herr Welcker. "I presume they, likewise, recount each other stories unsuitable for the ears of gentlemen."

"What a very uncouth custom! And how long do the gentlemen remain round the table drinking their wine and telling their stories?"

"As long as the wine holds out," replied Herr Welcker.

"So you are carrying a set of these toilet articles for the Prince of Wales?"

"Yes. He has several sets, of course; silver ones for travel and so forth; it was most vexatious: he had ordered this set from the Sèvres manufactory some while since, with his monogram and royal coat of arms. But then, of course, revolution broke out in France, and it was not possible to have them delivered. However, on my travels about France, I discovered that the set had, in fact, been completed, and I was able to come by them, on payment of various largesses. Only imagine my chagrin if, after all that, I had not been able to get them out of the country!"

"It would have been too bad, indeed."

"I may flatter myself that I have a most satisfactory consignment," pursued Herr Welcker, looking with complacence about his well-packed vessel. "I have, besides the Sèvres and the Gobelins, a table by Riesener (that was in the château of the unfortunate Vicomte de Boyenne), a marble bust by Coysevox, a Keller bronze, a candelabrum by Thomire, not to mention looking glasses, girandoles, two clocks, and some paintings by Greuze and Claude."

"How—how very gratifying," said Juliana faintly, shifting her feet and wondering if they were resting on the Claude—who was esteemed by her father to be one of the most superior French painters of landscape. "You may certainly congratulate yourself."

"I should say so! A pretty penny they have cost me too, from first to last! Come, give us a kiss, miss," said Herr Welcker, without altering his manner in the least particular.

Juliana stared at him in astonishment. His voice and expression were so perfectly matter-of-fact and unchanged from what they had been before that she could not at first believe she had heard him aright.

"I *beg* your pardon?" she said in a tone calculated, she hoped, to freeze out any encroaching pretensions.

"Come, don't be standoffish, miss! Give us a kiss? After all," said Herr Welcker, "who's to know? The old gentleman's fast asleep—if there are any angels flying around, they are the only witnesses. And *they* won't peach! And you can trust *me* not to cry rope on you at any later time. Bless my soul!" he added encouragingly, "I haven't run Prinney's errands all these years without learning to keep a still tongue in my head, I can tell you!"

"There will be nothing to keep a still tongue *about*, Herr Welcker!"

"Oh come, my dear! Don't be missish! After all, it isn't as if there were room for anything *else*," Herr Welcker pointed out with exactitude. "What's a mere kiss, after all? Situated as we are, there could be no thought of impropriety in a simple kiss, with that curst candelabrum sticking in between us like the sword of what's-his-name. So why not be friendly now, eh?"

"I am perfectly friendly, Herr Welcker. Indeed,

my father and I must be forever obliged to you! But I have not the least intention or inclination to kiss you. I should explain," said Juliana firmly, "that up to this day I have never kissed any male person, excepting my father—"

"God bless my soul!" he ejaculated involuntarily. "And you as pretty as a picture! What in the devil's name were all those Italians *about*?"

"It was not that they did not sometimes try," Juliana acknowledged. "That is why I always carry this extremely long pin in my fichu"—she drew it forth and exhibited it—"which I have been used to stick into any person who attempted to insult me."

"No, have you indeed?" he said, daunted, as she calmly returned the pin to its resting place. "Well, I'm blest if I understand you, miss, and that's a certainty! So pretty and lively as you are, with a cool head on your shoulders, worth a dozen fellows I can think of, a kind heart, anybody can see—and you boggle at a kiss. Now why, pray?"

"Why?" asked Juliana, wrinkling up her forehead thoughtfully. "It is because, Herr Welcker, I do not intend to kiss any male person—excepting relatives, I suppose," she added, thinking of her grandfather, "until I encounter a man who fulfills my ideal of what the perfect gentleman should be."

"Oh, indeed?" said Herr Welcker, with the liveliest curiosity. "And what might those ideals be, if I might inquire, miss?"

"He must be exactly like King Charles the First!"

"Good gad!" he said, really startled. "What a nature to wish on the poor fellow! If *that's* your ideal, I can't say I'm surprised that you haven't come across him yet—especially in Italy! Even in England you don't see replicas of Charles the First scattered all abroad."

"I daresay in England I shall be more likely to come across such a person, however," Juliana said with some confidence. "An English gentleman is said to be the flower of European civilization, is he not?"

"Is he? Being only a Dutchman myself, ma'am, I can't say."

"Certainly he is." Her confidence wavered a moment as she thought of the English dinner-party ritual just recounted to her by Herr Welcker; then she added firmly, "Think of Lord Chesterfield."

"Oh—why, yes, certainly, miss, if you wish," replied Herr Welcker, possibly asking himself whether she referred to Lord Chesterfield's precepts, or his practice. "I'll tell you one difficulty I see in your plans, though, my dear!"

"And what is that, Herr Welcker?"

"Why—you go to England—you look around you—by and by you meet this fellow who is the what-d'you-call-'em of European civilization and looks just like Charles the First—and what'll you do if he's married already, eh? Or if he don't seem inclined to look at *you*?"

"I shall never tell my love; but sit like Patience on a monument, gently pining away," said Juliana promptly. "But, if he is like Charles the First, he *will* look at me! He may not be free, of course," she acknowledged, "for life, as I already know, is full of such sad ironies, but he will *understand* me. One soul will reach to another. And I would rather love him in vain, from afar, than settle down in some stupid union with a more commonplace person."

And she regarded with indulgence Herr Welcker's round plump face and untidy brown hair, contrasting it with those angelically sad eyes, the silky beard and mustaches, the straight nose, curling locks, and look of mild, tragic gravity that characterized her hero. Herr Welcker, perfectly understanding the nature of her scrutiny, took such an estimate of his inadequacy in good part; there was absolutely no purpose, he acknowledged to himself, in trying to compete with somebody's ideal.

"Well, well!" he said good-naturedly. "I can see you have it all worked out, miss, and I'm sure I wish you well!" And I wish you joy of your ideal when you find him, he added to himself, for after ten years of serving the Prince of Wales, he was not apt to entertain visions of any Prince Charming.

"And I wish *you* well too, Herr Welcker," responded Juliana politely. "I hope that we reach England in time for you to provide the chamber pots for the Prince's dinner party." She gave a shiver, and a yawn. "*Dio mio*, but I am tired! I think if I were only a *little* warmer I might even be able to sleep for a short period."

She gazed hopefully at Herr Welcker, who, at this strong hint, could hardly avoid undoing yet another of his precious tapestries and passing it to her so that she might swathe it around her shoulders, which were indeed very inadequately protected by a worn old pelisse.

"*Thank* you, dear Herr Welcker. You are truly kind. Ahh…" She yawned again, and her eyes closed.

Herr Welcker regarded her with amiability mixed with exasperation; she seemed to have gone off into deep slumber on her feet, like a little pony, without the least difficulty; whereas he found himself totally unable to sleep, and was obliged to remain awake, shifting from icy foot to foot, while the remorseless hours slowly crept by, the stars moved across the sky, Juliana's father snored placidly in the bottom of the basket between the legs of the Riesener, and the balloon, it was to be hoped, wandered on its way toward the coast of England.

∼

When Juliana opened her eyes, several hours later, she was astonished to see broad daylight. The sun was not shining, however; indeed, thick gray cloud covered the sky, and a light rain was falling. And the reason she had woken was because Herr Welcker was shaking her by the shoulder.

"Miss! Miss! The Gobelins must *not* get wet. I must require you to pass it back to me, so that I can wrap it up in the sacking."

"What about *me*?" said Juliana rather resentfully, folding up the tapestry, however, as requested.

"You, miss, are young and strong, and have powers of self-regeneration not possessed by inanimate material," said Herr Welcker, whose amiability had been somewhat cooled by hours of cramped freezing wakefulness while his passengers slept. "I should be obliged if you would remove the covering from your father too, if you please."

"Certainly not!" said Juliana with decision. "My

father, Herr Welcker, is a very sick man. He is also a writer of international repute, and deserves the greatest care and attention."

Surprisingly, this reasoning appeared to weigh with Herr Welcker.

"Oh, a writer, is he? Prinney always had a regard for writers and such people. What is his name? What does he write?"

"He is a historian, and he writes under the name of Charles Elphinstone."

"Oh, ay, his name comes to mind. Life of the Duke of Buckingham, was that it? Ay, I mind Prinney thought highly of it."

"And he is in very poor health," Juliana said firmly. "He must *not* be uncovered. If you are anxious about your tapestry, Herr Welcker, the best thing you can do is to unwrap something else, that will not be hurt by a few drops of rain—such as the Sèvres—and lay the wrappings from that on top of the tapestry. Thus Papa will have an extra covering, which will be just as well, for I hardly think the Gobelin is sufficient to keep the damp off him."

"Oh, very well," grunted Herr Welcker, impressed in spite of himself by her practicality, and this was done. At first Juliana kept her gaze politely averted from the uncovered Sèvres ware, but as the long dull day wore on it proved impossible to maintain this attitude. Indeed, by dusk they were all three on terms of such intimacy that Juliana felt as if she had lived with Herr Welcker for years, and entertained toward him the kind of cordial boredom that is usually reserved for blood relations. They tried playing word games—at least Juliana did, and Herr Welcker did his best to comply; poor Mr. Elphinstone was too unwell to do anything but remain prone in the bottom of the basket, accepting gratefully, from time to time, a sip of Herr Welcker's cordial. At first Juliana asked Herr Welcker a great many questions about England, which he answered in a somewhat caustically objective manner, describing the Macaroni Club, the ways of *ton* society, Vauxhall gardens, King George III's erratic and irascible habits, Mr. Fox's amazing gambling losses, and other things that he thought might be of interest to her. Juliana said she thought England sounded a very singular place.

At last, hunger making them bad-tempered, they fell into a weary silence, and stared ahead with a longing that turned to hope and then to almost incredulous joy as the flat sandy coast of England finally crept into view on the gray and rainy horizon. More and more details gradually became apparent.

"Where are we, Herr Welcker, can you tell?" inquired Juliana, when waterways, chalk cliffs, and church steeples began to be recognizable as such.

"Ay, my dear, I am glad to say that the wind must have shifted round in the night, and has blown us due northward. I was afeared we might find ourselves down in Somerset, but that is the Isle of Wight we are now leaving to our right—I recognize the Needles lighthouse. So if I can procure some kind of conveyance to take me to Southampton, I may yet be in Brighton by tomorrow."

"Brighton? Is that where His Highness resides?"

"Yes, miss, mostly. He has built himself this great

Pavilion in the town, you know, and so long as one of his lady friends is there, he is content enough. Time was when it was Mrs. Fitz, but these days it is generally Lady Jersey; they say he has built her a special set of stairs."

"*Stairs?* What a singular present," said Juliana rather inattentively; her eyes were fixed on the scenery below. "*Dio mio*, but England is a gray, flat, dismal-looking country, Herr Welcker! Is all of it like this?"

"No, no, miss, some of it is well enough," said Herr Welcker tolerantly. "And Brighton, where His Highness resides, is as fine a town as you could wish to see."

"But, if Lady Jersey—Did you not say that His Highness was about to *marry*, Herr Welcker?"

"Marriage and love, miss, are two very different things."

"That will not be the case in *my* life," said Juliana very firmly.

As Herr Welcker had no reply for this, he inquired, after a pause, "Where is your destination in England, my dear?"

Since by this time Juliana had formed the opinion that Herr Welcker, though obliging, was a somewhat disreputable type of person, she decided that it might be best if he did not know their true name and direction. She therefore informed him merely that they were bound for a small place in the county of Hampshire, at no great distance, she understood, from Southampton.

"Oh, in that case you won't have the least difficulty, miss. By the look of our course, you will not have above forty miles to travel once we have made our landfall. And a good thing too, if you ask me," added Herr Welcker, with some concern, glancing at the sick man tossing restlessly at their feet. "I do not scruple to say, miss, that the sooner your papa is in his own home, and under the care of a good doctor, the better it will be." Since he was a kindly, though realistic man, he did not utter the thought that had come unbidden into his mind, which was that, considering Mr. Elphinstone's state of health and prospects of survival in Britain, he might as well have been left behind and the parcel of Limoges taken in his stead. But there was no use crying over spilt milk jugs.

"Yes; I am afraid you are very right," said Juliana, making him start slightly—but she was agreeing with his spoken comment, not his unspoken one. "Where shall we land, Herr Welcker?"

"On the first nice flat piece of land that we spy, my dear."

He pulled a string that let out some of the hydrogen gas, and the balloon sank slightly, wrinkling and swaying as the air hissed from the valve. Juliana, who had been mending a small rent in one of the tapestries—for she carried a housewife full of needles and thread in her reticule and hated to be idle—bit off her thread, folded the material carefully once more, and rewrapped it in its sacking cover.

"Are we nearly home?" said Mr. Elphinstone faintly. His mind had wandered at times during the day; Juliana thought that he believed himself a boy again, returning from school for the Christmas holiday.

"Yes, dearest Papa! Soon we shall be there!" She

crouched down to embrace him and smooth his hair. Herr Welcker pulled the string again, and the balloon descended even lower. The blue of dusk was beginning to enshroud the countryside below; when next Juliana looked over the side she could see, among the bosky woods and little, hedged-in fields, that here and there a solitary light was beginning to shine faintly in the twilight. It seemed a very quiet, unpeopled landscape.

"Ah, there's a clump of lights ahead," Herr Welcker said with satisfaction, and opened the hydrogen valve once again. "This is not a part of the country I know well, but that looks like a decent-sized place where one would hope to be able to hire a conveyance. Heaven send they are not as suspicious as the French, take us all for a parcel of spies, and cast us into jail!"

"What recourse have we if they do so?" inquired Juliana rather hollowly. She did not relish the thought of spending her first repatriated night in an English jail.

"Nay, never trouble your pretty head, my dear. I carry letters of authorization from Prinney himself—enough to get us all out of the Tower of London should we chance to land in there. Now—here's a big meadow—slow and steady does it—we don't want to hit a hedgerow at this juncture and break all those pots we have brought so far at such trouble!"

Considering that he had never navigated an air balloon before, Juliana could not but admire his dexterity, as, little by little, he reduced the quantity of gas in the envelope, so that the great unwieldy craft sank lower and lower, not too fast, not too slowly, while it continued to glide northward on the light wind. The ground moving past below them was very close now; Juliana, looking down, could see with disappointment that English grass looked much like French or Italian grass. English cattle, though, she was interested to note, seemed decidedly fatter than French cattle, as, bellowing with fright, they bolted heavily away from the descending aerial monster.

"Now, miss! When I say 'Hold,' will you please endeavor to hold that tall pile of packages in place? For I am afraid that when we touch the ground there may be some considerable bump, and it would be too bad if everything should fall about and get broken at this stage."

"Besides falling upon Papa, which would also be too bad," agreed Juliana.

"Hold!" he cried, and she did her best, as requested, to keep the cargo in position by wrapping her arms and body around as many bundles as she could, and clutching the edge of the basket with both hands.

There was a violent thump, and poor Mr. Elphinstone cried out with alarm and surprise.

Herr Welcker let out a most appalling oath, fortunately in Dutch.

"Oh, what is it?" cried Juliana, terrified. "Is something broken?"

"No," he growled. "You have stuck your *verdoemde* bodkin into the side of the basket, and it has run very nearly right through my thumb!"

"Oh, I am *sorry*!" she exclaimed repentantly. "It is a dreadful fault I have, I know! I am always sticking my needle into the arms of chairs. Papa has scolded me for it, times out of mind. Are you very severely hurt, dear Herr Welcker?"

"No, it is nothing," he said with a fair degree of calm, pulling out the needle, which he threw onto the grass, and wrapping a handkerchief round his bleeding thumb. "And, look, here we are in England without a bone broken—or even a crystal from the candelabrum—"

"And there are some English coming to meet us," said Juliana, looking eagerly toward the end of the field, where running figures with lanterns and pitch-forks could now dimly be discerned.

Four

EARLY NEXT MORNING, JULIANA AND HER FATHER SET off once more.

Herr Welcker had not lingered a moment; as soon as his letters of authorization had satisfied the English villagers that the balloon party were not French spies, he had bespoken the only carriage available in the place—it turned out to be a small hamlet of half a dozen houses named Burley Heath—loaded up his consignment of goods, and, after a hasty farewell, had departed at speed for Southampton, recommending that Juliana and her father should rack up for the night at the village inn.

"I am obliged to be in Brighton by tomorrow if I can arrange it, but the old gentleman would do well not to travel further at this hour."

Juliana could only agree, and as they were assured that the chaise would be back by the following morning, and they might have the use of it next day, she was relieved to see her father comfortably established in a warm bed, with a basin of soup, at the Fox and Grapes. She herself was so tired, cold, and stiff that

she was soon happy to follow his example and retire
to bed, although it was some time before she was
able to sleep. Despite the fact that she lay on a soft
feather mattress, under a sloping cottage roof, she still
seemed to feel the lurch and sway of the balloon's
basket as it bore them across the sky, and, looking up,
she expected to discover the innumerable stars still
above her.

On the following day Mr. Elphinstone was feverish
and weak; his features seemed to have sharpened in the
course of the journey, and his eyes had sunk back in
their sockets. He was frighteningly pale, and his hands
shook badly; Juliana was divided between a certainty
that he should not be allowed to leave his couch, and
the knowledge that nothing would satisfy him but to
be once more within the confines of his own home.

"Come—make haste—let us be on our way!" he
urged as soon as Juliana had eaten a morsel of bread
and butter and drunk a little coffee—he himself would
touch nothing but cold water. "My bones ache to be
at home—I shall not be comfortable until we are at
Flintwood. Old Mrs. Hurdle will look after me there;
I daresay she will soon put me to rights with one of
her possets."

Juliana devoutly hoped that old Mrs. Hurdle—
whom she took to be the housekeeper—*was* still
presiding in her grandfather's house.

Fortunately for the pair, Herr Welcker, although
he had been in such haste to be off on the previous
evening, had taken time to consider their welfare.

"Reckon you won't have any English money
about you, miss, hey?" he had inquired as he stood

superintending the transfer of his cargo from the balloon into the chaise. "And in a little hamlet like this they won't thank you for French louis or Italian lire; different if you'd landed at a port where there'd be a changing house. Best let me loan you a few guineas—a—a—now don't come missish over me again, I beg!" as Juliana began to protest. "Don't forget, you pulled me out of a scrape, for which I'm vastly obliged, as I value my skin highly. Pish, what's a handful of coins? Bless you, where I'm going, Prinney would fill one of these to the brim with gold guineas, if I asked him"—and he flourished one of the Sèvres pots.

Realizing that her scruples were indeed absurd, Juliana had accepted the loan, promising to repay it as soon as she was established at her grandfather's.

"No need, my dear—but still—if you insist—very well, then! Adieu! And thanks for the pleasure of your company—convey my best respects to your papa—" He bowed and sprang into the chaise, with surprising agility, considering the long, hard twenty-four hours he had just undergone.

Thanks to him, therefore, they were provided with funds to pay their shot at the inn and hire the chaise in which, immediately after breakfast, they set off once more. They were a bedraggled-looking pair. Without nightwear or toilet articles, Juliana had been obliged to sleep in her shift and borrow a comb from the landlady to bring some order into her tangled curls. Her old brown worsted dress and pelisse were damp and travel-stained from the journey. She was divided between anxiety for her father, despair at the first impression her grandfather was likely to receive of her, and lively interest at the scenes through which they were passing.

"Oh, Papa, it is all so pretty, is it not? A thousand times prettier than the countryside in France! I wonder that last night I thought it all so flat and gray. The meadows are so green! And the little gardens are so trim—oh, Papa, look, there are still roses, though it is so late in the year. And the little thatched houses are so delightful! Do but look at that pair! Oh, see the wild horses, Papa! And the deer! Do the horses belong to nobody? May they roam where they please? I knew of the wild horses in the Camargue, but I never heard there were wild horses in England also."

Her father smiled faintly at her enthusiasm as he reclined in his corner of the carriage, but he was too ill to sit up and appreciate any of the objects that attracted her interest; he said that he must be content with her descriptions. Indeed, after giving detailed directions to the driver concerning their route, he lay back, for the most part, with his eyes closed, and, since he had passed a very bad night, Juliana, hoping that he might sleep a little on the way, wrapped round him a traveling rug which the landlady had thoughtfully supplied, and endeavored to suppress her exclamations of wonder.

She reflected that it was as well he had been able to instruct the driver as to their direction, for the way seemed very tortuous. The road, often no more than a sandy track, wound through long stretches of wood-land, where the trees grew huge and massive, most of them leafless now, though here and there a great oak still kept its bronze foliage. Now the road climbed over heathery moorland, becoming even narrower and more stony; sometimes they must splash through a ford, or scrape along a narrow, deep-banked lane. The forest hamlets through which they passed grew more and more infrequent; their pace was necessarily slow, and, as the hour of noon came and went, Juliana began to feel quite hollow with hunger, for she had been too tired to eat much on the previous evening, and had taken very little breakfast.

She would have liked to ask the driver if he thought they were nearly at their destination, but she did not wish to risk disturbing her father, who had fallen into a kind of restless sleep, twitching and moaning in his corner.

At last, when they reached a woodland crossroads, she was delighted to observe a signpost which said on one of its arms: "Flintwood 2 miles." A mile, she recalled, was somewhat less than a league, so they must be fairly close to the end of their journey. Presently the road began to improve. The banks were trim, the surface was well kept, and soon they drove between a handsome pair of gates and, coming out through a grove of large beech trees, found themselves within sight of a house—a château, Juliana thought it might have been called in France; not a castle, nor exactly a mansion, but a largish rambling, comfortable-looking gentleman's residence built in rosy, ancient brick, with tall twisted chimneys.

"That'll be Flintwood Manor," called back the driver, evidently quite as relieved as Juliana to come within sight of his goal. "Reckon 'ee'll be glad enough to jump down and stretch your legs then, missie!

Massy me, I niver did goo to such an out-o'-the-road
spot—I reckon myself a New Forester born an' bred,
but I niver set foot here in my life afore. Time an' agen
I made sartain we was lost."

He cracked his whip to encourage the horses to
trot forward in style. The approach to the house lay
over a stretch of rough, grassy parkland, sparsely set
with clumps of large trees, over which the road ran
straight and unfenced, so that they must be observed
from the windows of the house, if there were anyone
at home. While they traversed this stretch of road,
Juliana had ample opportunity for many conflicting
anxieties: suppose her grandfather should be ill, dead,
away from home, the house empty? General Paget
might have died during the year since his son had
written to him. Or, on the other hand, he might be at
home—indeed, a blue thread of smoke ascending from
one of the chimneys certainly suggested that *somebody*
was there—but he might be entertaining fashionable
company—dozens of elegant strangers—not at all disposed to welcome the sudden arrival of his ill, weary
son and dirty, travel-worn granddaughter. Or perhaps
he had sold his ancestral home to strangers, on whom
the travelers would not have the slightest claim...

The chaise pulled up beside a wide flight of shallow brick steps which led up to the main entrance—a
massive oaken door set in under a round archway. To
Juliana's mingled relief and apprehension, a black-clad
manservant appeared in the doorway, descended the
steps as the carriage rolled to a stop, and came to open
its door.

"Good day. I am Sir Horace Paget's granddaughter,"

Juliana informed the man, in her pretty, accented English, thinking to herself how strange the words sounded. "I am come with my father—Mr. Charles Paget—we have just arrived from France. I believe my grandfather is expecting us?"

"Yes, miss," said the man, whose expressionless face gave no intimation as to whether he meant that Juliana and her father were indeed expected, or merely that he had heard and understood what she said.

"My father is—is not quite well," Juliana went on hurriedly. "The journey has fatigued him dreadfully—he is sleeping at present. I think it—it might be best if you could summon assistance—perhaps he could be carried in a chair—and taken straight to a bed?"

"I will apprise Sir Horace of your arrival, miss, and instruct some of the footmen to assist Mr. Charles and see to the disposal of your baggage," said the expressionless major-domo. "Would you care to step this way, miss?"

Juliana, however, did not like to leave her father, or rouse him until more practical help was forthcoming, and so she waited beside the carriage, feeling very uncomfortable, and very conspicuous, as if all the diamond-paned windows of the house were holding her under observation. She was wretchedly conscious of her hair, which hung in rat's-tails, for any order achieved with the aid of the landlady's comb had long since been deranged by the jolting of the carriage. The inn mirror had told her that she was pale and holloweyed. As for our baggage, she thought, no doubt the revolutionary mayor of St.-Servan has long since confiscated it. I only hope that one of my grandfather's housemaids is somewhere near my size, so that I can borrow a nightgown from her.

"Papa," she said tentatively through the open carriage door. "I—I believe this must be Grandfather coming to greet you."

A tall old man was slowly descending the shallow steps, with the aid of a cane. She had time to observe his likeness to her father was very pronounced. He had the same classic regularity of feature, the same clear blue eyes. But his face lacked the gentleness and kindliness of her father's: it seemed stern, set in austere and humorless lines. He wore a somewhat old-fashioned costume of black frock coat, knee breeches, silk stockings, and buckled shoes. He wore a wig, but his eyebrows were frosty white.

Juliana walked forward to meet him and curtsied.

"How do you do, sir?" she said. "I—I believe I cannot mistake? Are you not my grandfather?"

He quickly withdrew his hands behind his back, looking at her without visible pleasure, and ejaculated a loud "Humph!" After a moment's frowning survey of her, with his lips pressed together and jaw thrust forward, he remarked, "At all events, you don't appear to favor that designing hussy. Don't know who you *do* favor! Not anybody in *my* family. Well, don't stand there mum, girl! Where's your father?"

"He—he has been sadly indisposed, sir," Juliana said, greatly taken aback by this brusque greeting. Her heart sank; as on several occasions during the course of the journey, she passionately wished herself back in Florence. "He has been sleeping on the way hither, and I waited to rouse him until I was sure that—"

A flash of some unrecognizable emotion lightened momentarily her grandfather's bleak countenance. Juliana was not sure what it expressed. Pleasure at his son's safe arrival? Concern? Regret? Next moment it had passed and, scowling as before, muttering, "Damned young fool to have left it so late," he pulled back the carriage door, saying gruffly, "Well, Charles! Home at last—and not before it was time, eh?"

"Why—Father—is that you?" Charles Elphinstone murmured faintly, and he endeavored to rise from the coach seat, pushing himself up with his thin hands.

"Take care, Papa—let me help you!" exclaimed Juliana, moving swiftly forward. "He is grievously weak, sir," she added in an undertone to Sir Horace.

"Very well—very well," replied the latter testily, extending his left arm. "*I* can help him, girl—I am not in my grave yet! Come along, my boy—lean on my shoulder—that's it!"

Swaying with weakness, Juliana's father was assisted from the vehicle, the driver coming round to take his other arm. A little group of liveried footmen now appeared at the head of the steps and stood awaiting instructions.

Charles Elphinstone took a deep breath and looked all around him, at the mellow brick house, the green grass, the leafless trees.

"Very—very beautiful!" he said unsteadily. "Just the way—I remembered it—many and many a time—my dear father!" and he swayed forward out of his father's grasp, and pitched onto his face on the steps, and lay still.

Juliana gave one short cry—"Papa!"—and then

stood, with her hands pressed to her breast, as they carried him carefully into the house, two footmen on each side.

Sir Horace limped alongside the little cortege, furiously shouting instructions.

"Put him in the morning room—lay him on the sofa! Fetch brandy—cordials—a hot brick—tell Mrs. Hurdle—send Will on Firefly for the surgeon—no, for Dr. Garrett. Damme, has no one any sense round here?"

Numbly, Juliana followed the procession into a stiff, old-fashioned room, with furniture primly aligned against the walls, where her father was laid down upon a narrow couch, and his head was supported by a stiff bolster. Juliana went and stood by him, looking down into his face.

Then she looked up at her grandfather.

"He is dead," she said quietly.

The old man stared at her angrily, his face working.

"Nonsense, gal! Stuff and nonsense! How can he be dead? I never heard such tomfoolery! A drop of cordial, and he'll be as fit as fivepence."

Juliana shook her head. But the effort to convince him seemed too hard for her to undertake. Her throat was clogged; she could find no more words. Dimly, beyond her grandfather, she noticed a group of females: a plump lady, pink-faced, fashionably dressed, with a profusion of golden ringlets; and beyond her, staring eagerly past her shoulders, a pair of girls in striped dresses who, to Juliana's clouded, bewildered vision, appeared indistinguishable; they swam together, they separated, they were the same person, but divided into different places…

The lady let out a slight scream. "Charles! Oh, my poor dear brother—"

"He is dead," Juliana repeated hoarsely, and slid to the floor in a deep faint.

◦❧◦

She came to in a dusk-filled room, hours or even days later, it seemed. A sense of terrible anxiety possessed her.

"Papa?" she cried out confusedly. "Are you there? Do you wish to dictate? I am sure I could write—the balloon does not sway too badly—"

"Ah, poor little dear," a voice remarked. "She does not remember. And who's to tell her? Eh, mercy me, what a journey she must have had of it, with him. Best she remain abed until after the funeral."

Funeral? Juliana's mind came together, and she remembered.

"Papa is dead—is he not?" she whispered.

"Yes, my poor dearie—but try not to think about it," answered the voice. "Just you drink this and lay down easy now. You're a-going to be took care of, and there's naught to worrit ye."

She looked up into a round pink face, set in a huge white frill of cap. A firm, plump arm lifted her into a reclining position, and a cup was held to her lips.

"That's the dandy," said the voice encouragingly. "Just you drink old Hurdle's posset—white wine whey wi' a drop o' summat extry in it—and that'll settle ye comfor'ble fo' a twelve hours' sleep."

Drinking down the potion, Juliana remembered in a vague way that Mrs. Hurdle was her grandfather's housekeeper. Her father had said, "Old Mrs. Hurdle will look after me…"

Two tears forced their way out of her eyes and down her cheeks.

"Nay, now!" said the voice reprovingly. "Niver waste yourself wi' grieving, but put your trust in Him above as has fetched ye here, and holds all in His hand."

Juliana nodded weakly, as she felt herself laid back on the pillows.

In a dim way, at some distance, she noticed once more the plump ringleted lady, and two pairs of staring eyes behind her.

"How does she go on, Hurdle?"

"Eh, poor little thing, my lady, she's fair wore to a raveling. 'Tis early yet to know whether it be but the journey weariness, or whether she've brought one o' they contiguous fevers from furrin parts."

"Gracious me, Hurdle! A fever? Do you think it possible?"

"Who's to say, my lady? Desperate mortial fevers they do have over yonder—mayhap 'twas one o' them as fetched poor Master Charles to his end."

"Lud save me! If you really think that possible—! Girls, leave this room directly! Go and begin putting your things together—order Ringmer to pack your bags without delay. Hurdle, instruct Liphook to have my carriage in readiness to return to Weybridge; we shall leave at noon! I must go and inform Sir Horace immediately—we cannot stay here if my niece is suffering from a putrid fever!—Well, girls, what are you waiting for?"

Two complaining voices cried, "Oh, but, Mama, may we not just look at her?"

"And perhaps catch your death from her? Indeed you may not! Do as I bid you!"

Juliana heard the rattle of curtain rings, the soft click of a door closing. She slept.

The next few weeks passed, for Juliana, in a strange confused procession of dream-haunted nights and feverish, restless days. Sometimes she thought she was back in Florence, trying to run home to her father, who needed her badly. But the streets were full of angry strangers, standing in her way, preventing her from passing. Sometimes the tall thin English lady was there, hungry-eyed, calling out in her loud harsh voice, like a bird's shriek, "Where is he? Where have you hidden him? I shall find him yet—and then he will be sorry!"

"No, you will not! You will never find him!" Juliana shouted, and woke herself.

"Now, dearie, you're having the nightmare again," Mrs. Hurdle's voice would say, and Juliana would find herself sipping a spoonful of medicine, sweet and stupefying.

"Just like Herr Welcker's cordial…" she murmured. "Oh, I owe him some money! Eight golden guineas, to be sent to Brighton. I promised, I promised…"

"Never worrit, dearie, we'll see that ye keep your promise. Just you be a good girl now, and go to sleep for old Hurdle."

Sometimes they were in the coach crossing France and her father was dictating.

"Wait, Papa, wait! I cannot write so fast! I have not

all Charles's speech written down yet! Oh, why did he have to make such *long* speeches?"

In her dream, sometimes King Charles and her father were the same person. She would wake shrieking, "No—no! They are cutting Papa's head off! Oh, stop them, stop them!"

"Now, that's enough of that, child!" Hurdle's voice, firm and comforting. "'Tis naught but the nasty nightmare. Nobody's head be a-going to be cut off in *these* parts."

At last the fever receded, and Juliana lay weak, aching in every limb, but whole and calm once more, able to take stock of her situation. She saw for the first time that she occupied a four-post bed, in a large pleasant chamber, with a fireplace oddly set in an angle of the wall, a few pieces of old-fashioned furniture, and two windows looking out at the tops of trees. She was in her grandfather's house, and her father was dead. All her old life lay behind her, and ahead of her was a blank, an empty frightening void. Limp and docile, she allowed herself to be washed, combed, fed, taken up and laid down, but daily gained a little in strength.

At last there came a day when she could pull herself up, to sit against her pillows.

"Ay, that's more like it!" said Mrs. Hurdle encouragingly, giving her a basin of gruel. "Now ye're able to feed yourself, we'll soon have ye as plim as a pippin! Swallow that down, my dearie!"

Then, a week later, there came an evening when her grandfather climbed the stairs to visit her.

He was wearing formal evening dress, and stood

black as a pillar between Juliana and the fire. His face, she thought, was set in even more rigid lines of disapproval than when she had first laid eyes on him. He cleared his throat.

"Well, child—how do you find yourself going on now, eh?"

"Much better, sir, I thank you," Juliana said faintly. "I am sorry to be such a trouble on your household for so long." She tried to smile. "I am used to look after myself, and after my f-f-f…" Her voice failed, and she had to take a breath, but added, "I shall soon be about again, on my feet, and hope to make myself useful in some way."

"Useful? Humph! What could you do? Females cannot hope to be useful," he said dryly, more to himself than to her, but then added, as if he meant to do his best to cheer her, "No, no, when you are better, and your cheeks have filled out a bit on Hurdle's gruels—for at present you look like a little starved lapwing—you may post up to town, to your aunt Caroline, who will rig you out in fine feathers, and take you about to all the gaieties. She and those two noddlecocks of hers will soon cheer you up, I daresay." He turned to the fire muttering to himself. It seemed to Juliana that he said, "And then doubtless you will catch a husband, and then you will be off my hands," but she was not certain of this.

"Sir," she said, "I thank you—and my aunt Caroline—for the thought, but I do not wish to go up to town."

"Hey? What's this? Not go up to town? You will do as you're told, miss, and no disputing!"

He wheeled round again, leaning on his cane, and Juliana saw the look that must often have struck dismay into the heart of her father as a boy—a blue, fierce flash of the pale eyes, a grim set of the jaw as he glared at her, thumping his stick on the boards for emphasis.

"Sir," she protested feebly, "I am still in mourning for my father—who was the best and dearest parent a daughter could hope to have. It is too soon to think of—of fine clothes and gaieties."

"Well—well," he conceded, with a little less severity in his tone, "true, it is early days yet, I acknowledge, to be thinking about town fripperies. Hurdle says you must get your strength back yet awhile. Country food and country air. But what will you do with yourself in this old house? There's naught here to amuse a wench. Only the garden and the forest. *I've* no time to entertain ye."

"Or inclination, either," he muttered to himself.

"Pray do not trouble yourself on that head, sir. I shall find plenty to occupy my days. Firstly, I must make myself some black clothes."

"No need for that," he said. "Your aunt Caroline will attend to it—Hurdle gave her your measurements before she went off. Totty-headed woman, with her silly notions about foreign fever—but at least it got rid of her and her two nincompoops five days before the end of their visit! And now Hurdle tells me she's sent down a whole bale of furbelows from some warehouse."

"That was very kind in my aunt," Juliana said, somewhat surprised. Kindness had not been the chief impression she had carried away from her two brief glimpses of her aunt Caroline; she had not seemed the kind of person prepared to be so obliging. But most probably the General had given orders for her action. Vaguely wondering who had paid for the clothes, Juliana was reminded of something else.

"Oh, sir, there is a man to whom I owe money. He—he very kindly lent eight guineas to my father and myself when—when we were destitute on arrival in England. I have his name and his direction at Brighton, if—"

"Silence, child!" said her grandfather, very pale about the lips. "I do not, at any time, wish to hear any details about your father's last months of life—or about your life in Italy—or that disastrously ill-considered journey. Any details whatsoever! I do not wish to hear! Had matters been managed otherwise—had he had the sense to come sooner—he—he might perhaps still be with us. It does not bear thinking of! You will oblige me by never again referring to it. You arrived here, sick, starving, indigent—he, dying—can you expect that I should wish to be reminded of *that*?"

"No, Grandfather," said Juliana, trembling, "but it is not—we were not—"

"Silence, child! Such shame and wretchedness must be forgotten—thought no more of—utterly buried. Do not speak of it again!"

"No, sir—but the debt—"

"You may speak to Clegg, my steward, about it," he said, turning on his heel. "I will see that he is instructed to present himself when you are able to rise from your bed. He will undertake to discharge the debt."

"Thank you, sir," Juliana said, but her grandfather was already out of earshot. And, on the whole, as she lay in bed, turning over the strange, dreamlike details of that last journey in her mind—already they seemed to have receded into a past which lay separated from her by great misty gulfs of distance—she began to believe that it was just as well if her grandfather preferred not to know what had happened. So strict and straitlaced as he appeared to be, Juliana could not believe that he would approve of their wild mode of transport—of Herr Welcker, or his balloon—still less of his consignment of tapestries and *pots de chambre*. If Sir Horace chose to imagine that they had come over in a smugglers' vessel with a cargo of run brandy, let him continue to do so!

I will ask Clegg to send off the money to Herr Welcker, Juliana thought to herself. He need not put any address in, or say where it comes from; Herr Welcker will guess that soon enough. And, fortunately, he never learned our real name. In any case, it is in the highest degree improbable that I shall ever come across him again.

So thinking, she rolled over, and went peacefully to sleep.

Five

ABOUT A WEEK AFTER THIS CONVERSATION WITH HER grandfather, Juliana was pronounced well enough to get up in the afternoon for a short spell, and to leave the chamber that she had occupied for so long.

Abigail, one of the maids, a young, round-eyed country girl, helped her dress in some of the clothes that Lady Lambourn had sent down. These, though they were, of course, all in the severest unrelieved black, were far superior in style and material to any that Juliana had ever possessed before: she tried on a silk dress, high-waisted, with a double ruffle running down the front of the skirt, a V-necked bodice with a fichu round the shoulders, and sleeves tight to the arm, ending in a frill round the wrist. It was, however, a very indifferent fit; either Mrs. Hurdle's measurements had been inaccurate, or Lady Lambourn had paid very little heed to them; knowing Mrs. Hurdle by now, Juliana was inclined to the latter conclusion. However, calling for a needle and thread, she was able, in the course of an hour's stitching, and much to Abigail's astonishment, to remedy the worst of the deficiencies.

"You are so thin, miss," said Abigail, hooking the dress over her petticoat at the end of this time. "Mrs. Hurdle says you must eat bread and honey at every meal. There! Now let me just curl your hair into ringlets, and you will look quite the thing. 'Tis too bad there's no gentlemen to see ye."

Juliana, however, had not the slightest wish for gentlemen. As soon as she had been well enough to sit up, she had called for the canvas bag with its oiled silk lining that contained her father's precious manuscript, and, lying weakly in bed, she had beguiled the long hours with reading slowly through it, marking with faint crosses in pencil at points where she knew that her father, on a second reading, would have been inclined to amend his text in order to avoid repetitions, or to make the style run more smoothly. Now she greatly wished to begin transcribing the book, making a fair copy for the publisher.

"Would you be so kind as to bring this manuscript downstairs, Abigail," she said. "It is a little heavy for me, still. And I shall be wanting paper, ink, a pen, and a large table where I can do my writing undisturbed."

"Massy me, missie!" gasped Abigail. "You bain't niver going to write? Writing be men's work!"

"Indeed I am going to write," said Juliana. "My father wished me to copy out this book for him. It was one of his last requests."

Large-eyed, Abigail helped her down the stairs and across a stone-paved hall.

"Mrs. Hurdle have had a fine big fire kindled for ye in the drawing room—for Sir Horace niver goes in there, so ye won't fratchet him. But there beant no

big table in the drawing room… I dunno what's best
to do, miss."

Glancing through an open door as they passed it,
Juliana inquired, "What is that room?"

"'Tis the library, miss."

"Does Sir Horace spend much time in there?"

The library appeared just right for her purposes; it
had tables, ink, pens, paper, and, no doubt, dictionar-
ies and maps, all of which she would be needing.

"Now-an'-now he does, miss, but niver for very
long together. Mostly he talks to Mr. Clegg and sees
the criminals in the Estate Room."

"*Criminals?*"

Sir Horace, it appeared, was a justice of the peace,
who, since the nearest court was many miles off,
mostly interrogated accused persons in his own house.
He also spent many hours a day riding over his estate,
talking to tenants, inspecting crops, hedges, water-
courses, bridges, barns, and livestock; he was a careful
and vigilant landlord, and had not exaggerated when
he said that he would have no time to spend on his
granddaughter. During the hours of daylight he was
rarely to be seen within the house, and, when Juliana's
request was put to him, he fortunately raised no particular objection to her sitting quietly writing away at
a large table in a corner of his library. He, like Abigail,
deemed writing no sort of work for women, but, as he
said to Clegg, "So as it keeps her out of mischief, she
may as well continue. I see no great harm in it; soon
enough, when she has her strength back, she will be
wishing for livelier employment."

He displayed not the slightest interest in the work

that Juliana was transcribing, and, when she mentioned that it was a book by her father, said impatiently, "Spare me, spare me, child! I had no time for your father's scribbling—I told him so often enough! Let me hear no more on this subject, pray!"

Juliana, accordingly, said no more, but held her peace, and continued to write undisturbed. Nor did she again attempt to allude to the circumstances of their escape from France.

December, January, and February of a bitter winter passed by. Snow fell, and more snow; sometimes no sound could be heard for hours together, from the big house, but the sigh of wind in branches, of the soft thud as a lump of snow fell from an overweighted bough. Flintwood Manor, though cut off, sometimes for days, was well provisioned, and warmed by massive logs burning in every hearth. Juliana wrote on.

At last in March the cold broke; warm winds melted the last drifts, and snowdrops began to shine where the drifts of snow had lately rested. Sir Horace said to Juliana, "It is time you went to London, child."

"Why, sir? I have not been plaguing you, have I?"

"No," he said stiffly, and not with complete truth—he wished very much to have his library to himself again—"but you should be with young company. Your aunt Caroline writes that she is hiring a house in Berkeley Square until July; you may as well visit her and go to the Assemblies and ridottos with her gals."

"But I am in mourning, sir."

"Time you came out," he said impatiently. "Three months is enough, at your age. I shall write and tell

Caroline to buy you some half-mourning—lavender, gray, such stuff—it's enough to give one a fit of the dismals to see you creeping about all the time like a little black crow."

Encouraged by what seemed almost a conciliating mood in the General, Juliana wondered if she had courage enough for a question that had been on the tip of her tongue many times in the past months, as they shared awkward, silent repasts, or sat together for the reluctant few minutes that Sir Horace considered it proper to spend with his granddaughter in the evening, until he felt able to excuse himself and go off to take snuff in his Estate Room.

"Sir?"

"Hey? Well? What now? You are wondering who's going to pay for the new clothes? Well, I will send you up with fifty pounds to give to your aunt—that should see you fitted out respectably."

"No—no, sir, I was not wondering that—though indeed I am not unmindful of your bounty, and most grateful for it."

"Fustian!" he muttered. "What d'you expect? Let you go about in rags, hey? Can't depend on much of a bride portion, from me, though, I might as well warn you here and now. So you may tell *that* to any pretendants who come dangling around. You can tell them that your face is your fortune—nothing is to be expected from me! D'you understand?"

"I would not dream of assuming otherwise," Juliana said firmly. "In Italy I had expected to be under the necessity of earning my own bread, and I should be happy to do so here likewise."

"Oh, indeed?" He shot her a sharp look from the cold blue eyes. "And how, pray?"

"I could teach French or Italian; I could do translation work."

"A fine thing for my granddaughter!"

Juliana did not trouble to point out that his attitude was somewhat inconsistent; she sat calmly with her hands folded in her lap while he pished and pshawed, and finally grumbled, "Well, well! We shall have to see! It is by far the more likely that—but time will show!"

Juliana said, "It was not about money that I was going to ask you, sir—"

"Eh? Well? What *was* it, then?"

"Sir, is my mother still alive, can you tell me?"

The moment these words had left her lips, she was sorry she had uttered them. For one frightful instant she really believed that the General was going to have a seizure. His face turned the most alarming shade of blue-purple, his eyes bulged, his veins knotted, he almost frothed at the mouth.

"Never mention that woman's name in this house!" he spluttered at last. "D'ye hear me? D'ye hear me?" he roared again, as she stared at him, frozen with astonishment.

"Y-yes, sir!"

"When I think of the harm she did—the trouble she brought—of her utter depravity and rapacity—I can only hope that the harpy has gone to her just deserts—or is starving in a stew!" he declared, and, in much agitation, strode from the room, leaving Juliana to deduce that her mother *was* probably still alive, if

the General had no information to the contrary—
though how somebody could starve in a stew, she did
not perfectly comprehend. However, it seemed plain
that further application to the General for news on this
subject would be worse than useless, so Juliana put that
idea aside.

Another four weeks elapsed before circumstances
rendered it convenient for Juliana to be transported
to London, and by that time she had her own reasons
for wishing to go. In April her aunt's husband, Lord
Lambourn, who owned a borough nearby, came
down to canvass on behalf of a candidate he was putting up for a parliamentary seat that had fallen vacant,
and spent a night at Flintwood on the way back.

Lord Lambourn had two daughters of his own, and
was heartily bored by schoolroom chits; he inquired as
to how Juliana did, at the outset of his visit, and after
that paid no more heed to her, until it was time to ask
if she had her box packed and was ready to go.

The General's farewell to his granddaughter was
brief and curt.

"Be a good girl, now, miss! Mind what your aunt
says, and don't get up to mischief."

"Good-bye, sir. Th-thank you for all your kindness
to me." She would have liked the courage to embrace
him, to say, "Won't you miss me in the slightest,
Grandpapa?" but his aspect was so very repellent,
and it was so plain he only wished her to be gone,
that the courage failed her. She climbed submissively
into the chaise of her uncle, who at once immersed
himself in business papers and ignored her. Juliana was
not disposed to be resentful at this treatment, for she

found Lord Lambourn a very uninteresting man; he was inclined to paunchiness, had a florid complexion and bulbous gray eyes, receding hair, and a loud, self-satisfied voice. He appeared to disapprove of almost everything in the country excepting Mr. Pitt. Juliana remembered some of her father's strictures on the subject of his sister's husband, and agreed with them. She very much preferred to look out of the window at the forest scenery, which gradually changed, as they drove along, first to bare grassy hills, and then to well-watered farmland. They halted briefly at Winchester to change horses, and Juliana would have liked to get out, stretch her legs, and inspect this handsome lively town, with a little river running busily beside its great wide street, but Lord Lambourn said there was no time to be idling about if they were to reach London by evening. They did pause at Farnham for a brief nuncheon of cold meat, fruit, and cake, and here Lord Lambourn unbent so much as to ask Juliana what she thought of England, hey? She replied politely that it seemed very pretty. Indeed, her chief impression was of trimness, prosperity, and extensive cultivation, compared with the ragged poverty of the French countryside through which she had traveled with her father. But how much a more pleasant journey that had been!

Dusk had fallen by the time they reached London, and Juliana, who, for the last hour and a half had been huddled in her corner listening to Lord Lambourn's snores, was heartily glad when at last the horses stood still, and a footman came to open the door and let down the step. Juliana climbed out stiffly, and followed Lord Lambourn up a flight of steps and into a hall that seemed ablaze with candles reflecting lights from a myriad polished surfaces. She glanced around her, blinking in the dazzle. The place seemed to be packed with people and she could hear a babble of voices exclaiming and chattering.

"My dear husband, how do you come to be so late? We have been expecting you this age—remember we go to Almack's this evening! How did you leave my father? Did he send any messages?"

"Papa, Papa, have you brought us anything, Papa?"

"No, what should I be bringing you from Hampshire?" said Lord Lambourn impatiently. "I have brought your cousin, that is all. Why do you not take her upstairs and make her welcome?"

Juliana, her eyes becoming accustomed to the bright light, now recognized her plump aunt Caroline, who gave her a scented, inattentive kiss, and said, "Dear me, child, I daresay you will be quite fagged out from the journey. I trust you are quite recovered from your indisposition and that there are no contagious aftereffects? Girls, why do you not take your cousin Juliana upstairs and see her bestowed. You had best tell Partridge to help her with her dressing, and remind her not to loiter. We dine at seven, Juliana."

This late hour somewhat startled Juliana, accustomed to her grandfather's country habit of dining at four, but she was hungry, and glad of the prospect of a meal.

Her cousins accompanied her upstairs, talking volubly.

"La! So you are taller than us. Who would have guessed it? When you was laid down in a faint you

looked so much smaller! Partridge will be surprised,
she said she dared say you would be small, being as you
grew up in Italy, where they eat nothing but grapes
and fish and macaroni."

"Well, that is hardly true," said Juliana, laughing.
"They do have other things to eat—"

"Partridge said you very likely would not speak
English correctly—"

"Or have any accomplishments—"

"Can you play any instrument?"

"Do you know how to dance the gavotte, cousin
Juliana?"

Both talking together, the two girls led her into
a smallish room on the third floor, which was to be
hers, it seemed. There Juliana was able to take stock
of her cousins, and now she understood the strangely
nightmarish impression she had received of them
when she was barely conscious. For they were as
alike as two peas—freckled, stocky, bony girls, with
light-brown hair, sandy eyelashes, their father's protu-
berant gray eyes, and also, alas, extremely prominent,
irregular teeth, which seemed to show from ear to
ear when they laughed, which they did a great deal.
They were dressed very fine, in embroidered gowns
of Spitalfields silk, which did nothing to ameliorate
their plain looks.

"You are twins!" said Juliana. "How shall I ever tell
you apart?"

"Nobody can—only our maid, Partridge. I am
Fanny," said one of them.

"And I am Kitty," said the other.

"I shall be able to tell *you*," said Juliana, whose

quick eyes had detected a difference. "Your little finger is slightly crooked."

"Very few people notice *that*," said Kitty, not pleased.

"Does your hair curl naturally?" said Fanny.

"How tall are you?" said Kitty.

"Did you have any beaux in Italy, cousin Juliana?"

"Were you not bored to death, all alone at my grandfather's? La, he's a sad old stick! I was never so pleased as when Ma said we was to pack up and go, for fear of catching your contagion. He does nothing but bawl at us and scowl at us."

"Lord, cousin, how thin your wrists are!" cried Kitty.

At this moment a tall, thin, sour-visaged female came into the room, who said, "You'd best leave Miss, now, young ladies, while I help her to dress, or you ma will be displeased. You know how much your pa dislikes unpunctuality. Come, miss, make haste," she added, and bestowed a somewhat frowning glance upon Juliana, who immediately said, "Thank you, but I am very well accustomed to dress myself."

However, Partridge the maid insisted on helping her into an extremely ugly, overtrimmed, and ill-fitting dress of white muslin with lavender ribbons that lay ready waiting for her. Juliana could think of half a dozen things that could be done to improve the dress, but there was no time to do anything but scramble into it.

She felt herself at a loss to account for Partridge's manner of scowling disapproval, unless it was that she felt herself put upon at having a third young lady to look after.

As soon as Juliana's hair was arranged, and her

sleeves buttoned, she thanked Partridge, and ran down the stairs to the saloon on the first floor, where she had been told the family assembled.

She found them all there waiting—her cousins, her aunt, Lord Lambourn, who had changed into evening dress with knee breeches, and an elderly lady with a hooked nose, a very high-colored complexion, hair dressed with feathers, and a somewhat old-fashioned gown with panniers and a sacque, who at once inspected Juliana through a quizzing glass and remarked, "So that's the gal, Caroline? Lord, I thought you said she was a plain-looking starved little piece. Why, she's as pretty as a picture—she'll mighty soon cast your two into the shade! If she were better dressed, there'd be no holding a candle to her!"

Looking extremely irritated, Lady Lambourn made haste to cut short this comment by saying, "Cousin Honoria, let me introduce my niece Juliana. Juliana, this is your uncle's cousin, Miss Ardingly."

"I am happy to make your acquaintance, ma'am," Juliana said, curtsying.

"Well, well?" exclaimed Lord Lambourn impatiently. "Why does not that fool Fitton announce dinner? I am so hungry that I could eat an ox."

During dinner two things became perfectly apparent to Juliana. One was that her aunt had received her only with the greatest reluctance, almost certainly due to pressure from Sir Horace; it was very plain that, left to herself, she would never have bestirred herself in the matter. And it was also evident that Miss Kitty and Miss Fanny were not in the least gratified to have their cousin's company inflicted on them; as they sat eating their dinner they cast looks at Juliana that were full of ill-concealed hostility. She felt very forlorn, and heartily wished herself at Flintwood again, where, if not exactly welcome, she was at least left in peace, and was not the target of direct animosity.

After dinner the ladies prepared themselves to go to Almack's Assembly Rooms.

Juliana begged to be excused, pleading the fatigue of the journey.

"Lord!" cried Kitty, staring. "Why don't you want to go? There's beaux and dancing, and Ma has procured you a voucher from Lady Jersey—you'll never catch yourself a husband if you stay at home and mope!"

"La, sister, if our cousin don't choose to come along, do not tease her to do so!" cried Fanny.

"Quiet, girls!" cried their mother, giving them a quelling look. "Catherine, I do not like to hear you speak in that vulgar manner... Well, Juliana, if you do not wish to go I suppose you must stay at home, though it does not show a very becoming spirit of gratitude in you."

"Another night, ma'am—" faltered Juliana. "Another night I shall be most happy to accompany you."

"Oh, very well! Come, girls—come, cousin Honoria"—and the ladies departed with Lord Lambourn, who, Juliana gathered, would do no more than escort them to Almack's and would then repair to his club, White's, where he proposed to spend the rest of the evening. Juliana was therefore left to her own devices. She discovered a harpsichord in the saloon and spent some time playing it with pleasure, for she had taken lessons from a music professor in Florence; then she went up to her room and put in two hours' work on the lavender-and-white dress; then, feeling more homesick for Italy than she had for several months past, she retired to bed.

Next morning she found herself alone in the breakfast parlor with Miss Ardingly; the other ladies were still sleeping after a late night, it seemed.

Miss Ardingly, after again thoroughly scrutinizing Juliana through her glass, at once opened fire: "So, miss, you have come to London to catch yourself a husband, hey?"

"I do not know if that was my grandfather's intention for me, ma'am," replied Juliana, helping herself to chocolate, "but it certainly was not *mine*."

"What *was* your intention, then, child, in heaven's name?"

The old lady's tones, though brisk, seemed not unfriendly, and Juliana replied, "My purpose was twofold, ma'am. I wished to deposit my father's last work at his publishers'—and I was in hopes of finding myself some congenial remunerative occupation, since I do not at all wish to be a charge upon my relatives."

"Hey-dey! What kind of remunerative occupation could a gel like yourself find to do, pray? No—no— take my word for it, that is not to be thought of. In any case, now that I see you I am certain that Caroline will not have the slightest difficulty in making a good match for you—despite all that old tale about your mother! Nobody will give a rush for *that*. I daresay it will be best for Caroline to marry you off directly, so as to get you off her hands—for sure she won't wish to take you about for longer than she can help it alongside those two plain wenches of hers, showing up all their imperfections!"

And the old lady let out a malicious cackle.

Startled and dismayed at this sharp estimate of her situation, Juliana nevertheless felt her curiosity aroused by one part of Miss Ardingly's remark.

"Pray, ma'am, what was the tale about my mother? What *did* she do? And—and where is she now? My grandfather will tell me nothing on the subject—and nor would my father. He promised to do so before he died—but then—but then—"

Juliana was obliged to come to a stop.

"Lord, child, if your grandfather will not tell you, it is best I should not! Besides, the tale is hardly fit for your ears. Your mother tossed her bonnet over the windmill with a vengeance. Prospered exceedingly for a time, too. But I believe she ended up in Queer Street. Found herself at Point Non Plus."

"Where is she now, ma'am—do you know?"

"Haven't a notion, child. She was established in Paris for some time, that I do know. But I daresay when the Revolution came she was obliged to decamp, like all the other English."

No further questions from Juliana could elicit any information from Miss Ardingly; she said, "Now that's enough on that head, child, don't tease me. I certainly shan't give you details which your grandfather thought improper to impart. Wait till you are married!—But tell me about this work of your father's. What is it, pray, and who are his publishers?"

This Juliana was very ready to tell her, and she listened with acute interest.

"A life of Charles the First, hmm? Had your papa written other books?"

"Oh yes indeed, ma'am, a life of George Villiers, and one of Thomas Wentworth."

"Strange that I never came across them. I read a great deal of history. He did not write under the name of Paget?"

"No, ma'am, he assumed the nom de plume of Charles Elphinstone."

"*Elphinstone*, why did you not say so before? Lord yes, I have read all *his* works, any time these last six years! He wrote very well, very well indeed. But did your grandfather not know this?"

"I do not think so, ma'am. My grandfather was—is very reluctant to listen to anything at all concerning my father's writing. My father may have written to him about it—I am not certain."

"I'd not wager my diamond eardrops on it," remarked Miss Ardingly. "I knew your father when he was a young man—the dreamiest, most head-in-the-clouds young fellow I ever came across! He was no more fit to look after himself than a cherub on a tombstone! No wonder he—eh well, that's all water under the bridge now. And as for your grandfather— the most obstinate, cross-grained old curmudgeon. Deaf to all he does not choose to hear!—And so who *was* your father's publisher, miss?"

"Mr. John Murray, ma'am. I was in hopes that my aunt or one of my cousins would tell me how to find my way to his offices in Albemarle Street."

"Tilly-valley, child, they'd not thank you for dragging them to such a fusty spot! I can just imagine those twins' faces in a room that was all filled with books. It is as much as they can do to read the words of a song. But I don't mind giving you my company there—'tis but a step to Albemarle Street, and I can buy myself a new pair of mittens on Bond Street on the way back."

Accordingly, when Juliana had fetched her precious manuscript, now all rewritten in her most exquisite handwriting, and Miss Ardingly had provided herself with her pattens, her parasol, and her calash (a most amazing structure of silk and whalebone, carefully disposed over her high-piled hair, which was dressed in the old-fashioned manner with powder), the two ladies set out together.

Juliana was all interest, as she gazed about, and found herself bound to admit that the elegant shopping streets of London were quite the equal of the Ponte Vecchio or any of Florence's most fashionable thoroughfares.

Mr. Murray himself was not in his office that day, when they reached the publishing house in Albemarle Street, but an elderly clerk, who introduced himself as Mr. Twining, greeted the arrival of the manuscript with evident delight.

"Mr. Murray will be overjoyed—overjoyed!" he said several times, gazing at the title page as if a lost child had been returned to him. "We were so afraid that possibly the script had been destroyed—these troubled times, you know, such dreadful happenings in France—and Mr. Murray's last letter to Mr. Elphinstone was returned to us with the words 'The English gentleman has gone away' written across the superscription. I do sincerely trust that no misfortune has overtaken Mr. Elphinstone?"

"I am afraid it has," said Juliana sadly. "The journey to England, after all the hard work on his book, was too much for my father. He is no more, sir."

Mr. Twining's face conveyed his sincere sorrow and shock at this. He expressed his deep sympathy with Juliana.

"Mr. Murray will be very grieved, very grieved indeed… And so this is Mr. Elphinstone's last work," he said mournfully. "Well, we must do it justice in our production. The very best gilding and binding! You will be your father's executor, miss, I daresay? You were his only child, I apprehend? Then Mr. Murray will be communicating with you presently as to terms. Perhaps you would be good enough to give me your direction?"

Juliana felt that it might be imprudent to give Lady Lambourn's residence as her direction; she had a presentiment that her aunt would not be in the least degree gratified to have such low-class persons as publishers sending communications to her house.

"I am paying a visit to my aunt in Berkeley Square at present, sir, but I believe it will be better if I give you my grandfather's address; pray, therefore, write to me in care of Sir Horace Paget, at Flintwood Manor, Hampshire."

She then bade Mr. Twining a civil good day, and he assured her of his best attention and respects at all times.

"You have some sense, I see," commented Miss Ardingly when they were again in the street, Juliana with a sense as of an immense load off her heart. "Your aunt Caroline is a very silly woman," the old lady went on. "Still, she can't help but see that you take the shine out of those hen-faced gals of hers; I'll wager she soon finds some excuse to ship you back to Flintwood, unless she is able to marry you off in the next six weeks. I would place small dependence on her hospitality, child!"

The old lady's tone was so tart that Juliana remarked thoughtfully, "Since your opinion of my aunt seems to be so low, ma'am, I wonder that *you* chose to avail yourself of her hospitality!"

"So you've a tongue in your head, miss, have you?" retorted Miss Ardingly, not ill pleased. "That was well said—at least you are no mincing mouse. Sometimes you have a look of your grandfather. Well, child, when you are at your last prayers, as I am, a roof in town and a chance to see my old friends and mix with the *ton* is not to be sneezed at. And Caroline is glad enough to have me stay with her; she knows I can be depended on to chaperone those silly chits to Almack's when she has an invitation to a house where the entertainment is too lively for young girls; Caroline has a great fondness for the gaming tables, as you will find out; and I don't sit in her pocket, but take myself out a fair deal; so we contrive to brush along. But you, I fancy, will soon find yourself uncomfortable enough in her house… Now, here is Poltagrue's. I mean to buy myself a new cap for tonight's Assembly at Lady Bethune's. We are all bidden there, you as well."

"Who is Lady Bethune?" inquired Juliana as they

stepped into the milliner's shop full of silks and gauzes and smirking, finical assistants.

"Lady Bethune? Married to Lord Bethune—Tom Ellesmere. He was one of the Carlton House set—the most good-natured fool in town. His sons and daughters are mighty close with your cousins because they are all as dull as each other... Now you may give me the benefit of your advice, if you please!"

This request, Juliana soon discovered, was intended as the merest formality; what Miss Ardingly really wished was to have her own taste endorsed; which, as she persisted in preferring a spangled headdress adorned with a profusion of imitation fruits and puce-colored feathers, could hardly be done with truth. Juliana contented herself with saying, "You must be the judge, ma'am; I prefer this charming Valenciennes lace."

The old lady darted a very shrewd glance at her. "Well, well, you are an honest chit! But you must know that when a female reaches my degree of years, the only way to attract notice is by eccentricity. It answers delightfully"—and she bought the cap with the purple feathers.

This done, they returned to the house in Berkeley Square, where Juliana received a trimming from her aunt, now taking breakfast in a satin wrapper and a fretful temper.

"Here have I been this half hour waiting to escort you to a silk warehouse to buy you something for Lady Bethune's Assembly—for if I am to take you about you must dress fit to be seen—and what do I find but that you are gone jauntering off heaven knows where, without any consideration for *my* convenience."

Juliana was somewhat surprised, since her aunt hardly looked dressed for an excursion to a silk warehouse, but she apologized very humbly.

"Well, it is too late now," said Lady Lambourn. "You must wear the dress you put on last night, for the girls and I are engaged to go to an auction this noon."

Juliana said she was sure it could be of no consequence what she wore, since she was acquainted with nobody in London. But this reply did not please Lady Lambourn.

"Certainly it is of consequence, miss! You forget that you are *my niece*!" and she departed to dress for her auction, leaving Juliana to regret the solitude and tranquillity of Flintwood.

She soon found that the servants in Lord Lambourn's house treated her with ill-concealed contempt; she was made to feel the evils of being a poor relation at every turn. If she rang the bell in her room, nobody answered it; no coals were brought to replenish the miserable fire in her grate, and her washing water, tepid when it arrived, remained unemptied for half the day; no nuncheon was brought her, her aunt and cousins being out; and in the evening when Partridge came, obviously at her mistress's bidding and with the utmost reluctance, to help her dress for the Assembly, she showed her dislike and scorn by frizzling Juliana's hair with unmercifully hot tongs, pulling and tweaking it, and jerking her into her dress as if she would have liked to throttle her. The dress itself was plainly a surprise to Partridge, for Juliana had passed some more hours of the afternoon at work on it, altering it to a better fit, removing most of the ugly trimmings, and moderating its harsh colors by an overdress made from a length of gauze bestowed on her by Miss Ardingly.

"Thank you, Partridge, that will do," Juliana said at length. "I am sure my cousins have need of you," and Partridge withdrew, giving her a malevolent look. Juliana surveyed herself doubtfully in the glass. The dress was now well enough, but it seemed to her that the maid had turned her into a figure of fun, by teasing her dark-gold hair into a beehive erection, supported on woolen pads, which looked lamentably old-fashioned. I fear I shall be a laughingstock, thought Juliana, and she did her best to reduce the high tower of hair, taking out some dozens of black pins and the cushion that Partridge had inserted, brushing back the hair, and finally pinning on a charming fall of lace which Miss Ardingly had also brusquely given her that morning. The result seemed to her a decided improvement, and she wrapped herself in her shabby pelisse, and ran down to join her aunt and cousins. The latter greeted her with cries of derision.

"Why, cousin, what in the world have you got on your head? You look a fright—does she not, Mama? People will take you for a quiz—they will wonder where in the world you came from!"

Juliana could not see that their headdresses were in any way superior: their lank brown tresses were elaborately tortured and frizzed up into Grecian crowns, interspersed with ribbons and feathers, which only served to emphasize the awkward configuration of their jaws and teeth. However, dressed alike in striped sarsenet with embroidered sashes and Norwich shawls, they were evidently quite satisfied with their appearance.

Lady Lambourn only said, "Well, it is too late to remedy Juliana's hair now, for Thomas coachman has been waiting these ten minutes; therefore let us be off without any more delay," bestowing an irritable glance upon her niece.

The ball at Lady Bethune's house in Grosvenor Square was, Juliana soon realized, a very grand affair. Bethune House had its own courtyard, and they were obliged to wait quite fifteen minutes while their coach crawled along in a waiting line of other vehicles, until they arrived at the awninged and carpeted front steps. When they had ascended the stairs that led to the Assembly Rooms, a succession of brilliant saloons lay open to view.

Once having paid their respects to Lady Bethune, a tall gray-haired personage with a magnificent pearl tiara and an absent eye, Lady Lambourn made directly for the card room, and Miss Ardingly for some cronies of her own, while the twins were greeted by Lady Bethune's daughters, the Misses Ellesmere, whom they hailed as if they had been parted for untold years, though in fact, as Juliana discovered, they had all met at the auction and were in the habit of meeting almost every day.

"Oh, by the by, this is our cousin Juliana," Kitty introduced her casually. The young ladies favored Juliana with very cursory glances and slight bows, then turned back to Kitty, who was exclaiming, "My dearest Jane! Where did you find that gauze? It is beyond anything sweet, it becomes you vastly. I declare if I can't get one just like it I shall die of disappointment."

Rather ill at ease, Juliana glanced about her,

wondering if she should join her aunt, and, as the four chattering girls took no further notice of her, she presently went in search of that lady, whom she found seated at a card table playing silver loo with some other ladies and gentlemen.

Juliana positioned herself nearby until Lady Lambourn looked up peevishly and remarked, "Pray, Juliana, do not tease me by hanging over my shoulder. Why do you not divert yourself with the young people? There is no sense in coming to a ball to dawdle in the card room all evening."

Thus adjured, Juliana went off with some reluctance to seek her cousins again, but the orchestra had now begun to play and dancing had commenced; she could not find them.

At this moment a voice in her ear said, "Pray, my pretty miss, will you favor me with the honor of your hand for this set?"

Juliana turned, and saw an elderly man regarding her in a somewhat quizzing and supercilious manner. He was dressed very foppishly in a gray satin coat and smallclothes, striped stockings, a pink embroidered waistcoat, and very elaborate lace ruffles at his throat and wrists; his hair was heavily powdered, unlike that of the younger men, who wore theirs plain; his skin was red-mottled and patchy, deeply pocked here and there, which imperfections were disguised very imperfectly with a kind of paste, painted red over the cheekbones. His eyes were moist and rheumy, his lips were cracked, and the numerous large flashing rings he wore served merely to draw attention to the palsied shaking of his hands. There was something feverish and rather avid about his air and manner which did not at all suit Juliana's taste. She therefore replied politely, "Thank you, sir, but I believe you must hold me excused. I am not acquainted with you, moreover I do not intend to dance at present."

"What? Come to an Assembly and not dance? Here is a piece of absurdity! Do not be so cruel to the male sex, I beg of you!" And he poured out a profusion of compliments which were as flowery as they were insincere, ending, "As for being acquainted, I know that you are Caroline Lambourn's niece Miss Paget, for it was Caroline who sent me in search of you—a vastly rewarding search by heaven!" and he continued urging and pestering Juliana to dance with him, eyeing her meanwhile in a most disagreeable way, until she was fain to return to her aunt, finding no other help at hand—for she now perceived her cousins dancing with a red-faced young man apiece, from their resemblance evidently the brothers of the Ellesmere girls.

"What, child, is it you again?" exclaimed Lady Lambourn, not at all pleased. "What is it *now*? Cannot you find a partner?"

"There is a gentleman pestering me to dance with him, aunt—I need not if I do not wish to, need I?"

At this moment the gray-satin gentleman arrived in pursuit.

"Hey-dey, Caroline! Will you not make intercession for me with this hard-hearted young lady of yours?"

"*Not dance?* I never heard such nonsense in my life," said Lady Lambourn, very angry indeed, directing a formidably quelling glance at her niece and, at the same time, administering a sharp pinch to her arm. "Not dance when Sir Groby Feverel does you the honor to request your hand? Be off with you at once, miss, and let us hear no more of such nonsense, I beg! Juliana is quite new to our London ways," she apologized smoothly.

"My dear ma'am, a little innocence and rusticity only make the young lady appear to greater advantage," he replied, smiling, in a tone that horrified Juliana by the lewdness and depths of innuendo contained in it.

"I must rely on you, Sir Groby, to instruct Juliana how to go on in our society," Lady Lambourn said.

"It will be the greatest pleasure, ma'am"—and, smiling still, he led the reluctant Juliana to the ballroom. There he insisted upon not one dance but three, from which Juliana could not escape, being acquainted with nobody else in the room. By the end of the third dance she was half fainting from the discomfort of his hot, feverish grip on her arm, the need to make some kind of civil rejoinder to the inanities he kept pouring out, and the highly unpleasant fetid odor of his breath as he leaned close to whisper his compliments.

At last suppertime drew near, and, with great presence of mind, she exclaimed that a ruffle had come unstitched on her gown, and so succeeded in making her escape to the ladies' robing room. There she would gladly have remained for the rest of the evening, despite suspicious glances from the maidservant in attendance, but, a group of other ladies arriving, she was obliged to return downstairs. She perceived Sir Groby watching out for her, but managed to slip past him concealed behind a group of other persons and, in the dining room, was lucky enough to find her cousins sitting with the sandy-haired Ellesmere girls and their red-faced brothers. Thankfully she joined them, though greeted with unwelcoming looks from Kitty and Fanny. The young men, however, seemed glad of her company and began asking her how she liked London; was this her first visit?

She explained that she had seen nothing as yet.

"What? Not seen the Pantheon? Nor Vauxhall nor Bagnigge Wells, or the lions at the Tower? Nor visited Drury Lane nor Ranelagh nor the Haymarket? This must be remedied, bigod!"

"Our cousin is but now come from the country, and before that from foreign parts," explained Kitty sourly, adding in a low voice, "And it's no manner of use dangling after her, Hugh, for Ma says she hasn't a penny to bless herself with."

"And with looks like hers, what need?" he answered cheerfully, at which Kitty's expression became even more disagreeable.

After supper several more young men came up and asked to be introduced; Juliana did not lack for partners, and began to feel more comfortable, though her cousins' looks of sulky ill will greatly reduced her enjoyment, and she was in continual apprehension of being pounced on again by Sir Groby, whom she noticed on various occasions eyeing her from the side of the room. Twice more she was obliged to escape him by retiring to the cloakroom. Altogether it was a relief to her when carriages were called, and the evening ended, although she had to bear some spiteful remarks from her cousins on the ride home. Lady Lambourn, who had won fifteen pounds at silver loo, was in placid good humor and slept all the way back to Berkeley Square, as did Miss Ardingly.

Next day Lady Lambourn somewhat irritably took Juliana shopping to various silk mercers and milliners' establishments. Since the twins were allowed to come too, and to buy such garments as their fancy dictated, the excursion put them in a better frame, and they became lively and voluble.

"Lord, cousin, why'n't you buy this amber satin, why must you stick to such sad colors?"

Juliana pointed out that she was mourning.

"Oh dear, who cares about that? Not a soul in town knew your pa, so it can't signify—what does it matter when he died?"

"Don't be ridiculous, child," said Lady Lambourn sharply. "Juliana is in the right. It would not be at all becoming in her to wear that amber."

Juliana soon perceived that if she bought ready-made dresses, or even had them made up, her uncle's fifty pounds would go nowhere; indeed, a sad hole had already been made in it by Lady Lambourn's purchase of the lavender-and-white-striped dress; she therefore resolved on procuring several lengths of jaconet, mull, crepe, gauze, and muslin, so as to make her own garments; now that she had been given an opportunity to study what was being worn by ladies of *ton*, she felt quite confident of being able to fashion herself some gowns that were fit to be seen, for the modes worn that season were exceedingly simple, straight, slender, and high-waisted. Fanny and Kitty stared at such a notion, but their mother, for once, seemed quite approving of Juliana.

"Your cousin cannot afford, as you can, to be buying gowns from fashionable houses, so it is fortunate that she has learned some skill with her needle—and it will give her a useful occupation indoors. I daresay, if you ask her, she may be pleased to alter such of *your* dresses as have something amiss with them or need mending."

"Oh, yes," said Kitty directly. "There is my jonquil crepe that has a great rent in it; Juliana will be able to mend that for me, I daresay, and I shall be very glad, for it is my favorite and then I could wear it to the Gazehams' ridotto."

Juliana felt somewhat dismayed at the prospect of continual darning that seemed to lie ahead of her, but if this was the way to earn her cousins' goodwill and make life more comfortable in Berkeley Square, she supposed she must be glad of it.

Indeed, as she sat and sewed that afternoon on a half dress of fine silvery-gray sarsenet, ornamented with a small glossy spot, which was to be worn over a robe of white silk, her cousin Fanny appeared and in a manner that was half commanding, half cajoling, exclaimed, "Dear cousin Juliana, I *know* you can somehow contrive so that this nasty spot does not show on my pink velvet! Partridge says that it is not worth the trouble, but I am *so* fond of this habit!"

"Oh, I believe it could be managed," said Juliana. "The skirt is so full that we can take in the front breadth and so remove the spot… But why are you not gone to Cox's Museum this afternoon with cousin Kitty and my aunt?"

"I am sick to death of Cox's Museum—I have seen it above a dozen times, and do not at all admire mechanical music and pineapples full of singing birds! So I told Ma that I had a headache and must lay down on my bed—and now I have stolen a fine march on Kit, for I know she has several dresses that she wishes you to improve for her... Ay, that is famous," Fanny exclaimed approvingly, as Juliana, by taking a tuck in the material, managed to conceal the offending grease spot. "I was sure you would know how to put it to rights."

The doorbell rang downstairs, and she went to the window and peered out.

"Now it rains—*how* glad I am that I did not go out with Mama and Kit! Oh, there is that odious old cull, Sir Groby, come a-calling! I quite detest him, with his poxy skin and his mincing nasty ways and his foul breath—I pity his next wife... No, Fitton, we are *not* at home," she added as the butler came to inquire if the young ladies were ready to receive company. "My cousin Juliana has better things to do with her time than receive the addresses of that old monster— besides, I wish to wear my rose-colored habit in the park tomorrow morning." Fitton retired again, and Fanny went on, "Ma intends you to have Sir Groby, I know, but it won't hurt the old toad to be kept wondering a while longer. I know he's a monstrous fine catch, for he has fifteen thousand a year, but he has buried three wives already—Lucy Ellesmere says he starves them to death—so he can just wait a while!"

"You mean your mother intends that I shall *marry* Sir Groby?" faintly inquired Juliana.

"For sure she does! And you might as well make up your mind to it, for Ma always has her way in the end. I daresay it may not be so bad," said Fanny encouragingly. "Once you are married, you know, you may have any number of lovers and cicisbei—though they *do* say Sir Groby has a very jealous disposition. But then you are quite likely to outlive him, you know, and may be a rich widow."

"I have not the least intention of marrying him," said Juliana, very decidedly.

"Mercy! You had best not let Ma hear you say that," said Fanny, staring. "Or she will very likely have you on bread and water in the attic, as she used with me and Kit when Miss Lurgashall said we would not learn our lesson. Well, I would not care for him myself, I allow, but beggars in your position, you know, cannot be choosers. You have no portion, after all."

Juliana said that she could think of many alternatives to marrying Sir Groby.

"Not for *you*," Fanny told her earnestly. "Besides, your mother was so very scandalous that Ma says you must be thankful for any eligible connection."

"What did she do?" Juliana could not resist inquiring.

"Oh Lord, *I* don't know! It was all long ago—when I was in my cradle."

When Lady Lambourn returned and was informed by Partridge that the young ladies had had themselves denied to Sir Groby, she was exceedingly angry, and visited her displeasure immediately on her niece, storming and railing at Juliana until the latter felt quite sick and weak.

"Obstinate, ungrateful girl! You will receive his

attentions with complaisance, or it will be the worse
for you! Why do you think I took Kitty off to Cox's
Museum? You need not think you can afford to be picking and choosing. What is wrong with Sir Groby, pray?"

Juliana, battered beyond endurance, could only
retort, "He lacks the least resemblance to King Charles
the First, ma'am!" before, with tears starting from her
eyes, she ran away to her own room.

She was not to be left in peace for long. A message
came to her by Partridge that she must dress herself in
readiness to accompany her aunt and cousins to the
Pantheon Rooms for a concert that evening.

Juliana would rather have done anything else, but
she saw no help for it; she therefore bathed her eyes,
and put on the gray sarsenet dress.

"You want I should do your hair, miss?" inquired
Partridge sneeringly.

"No, thank you, Partridge, that will not be necessary," replied Juliana, and bound it up herself with a
ribbon of gray material left over from the dress.

"Miss is so clever that she might as well be a lady's
maid herself," was Partridge's parting salvo as she
flounced out of the door.

The Pantheon, Juliana discovered, was a large,
impressive concert hall which had something the
appearance of a chapel. It was much ornamented
inside, with vaulted arches, pilasters, and many statues.
To Juliana's dismay Sir Groby appeared almost immediately, and sat down beside her at the beginning of
the concert. Her pleasure in the music—a Coronation
anthem by Handel—was quite spoiled, the more so
as the rest of the audience talked loudly all through

the playing. Sir Groby was no exception, plying her with his fulsome compliments, admiring her hair, her gown, and everything about her, pinching her arm, and squeezing her hand.

"Sir, I infinitely prefer the sound of the music to that of your voice!" she exclaimed impatiently at last, and reduced him to an affronted silence. She thought she saw his eyes flash vengefully at her boldness, but his silence was so grateful to her ears that it seemed worth his hostility.

After the concert they strolled about the hall, meeting numerous acquaintances of Lady Lambourn and the twins. Sir Groby accompanied them. Presently they went below to the tearoom, which was in the basement. Here they had to wait for a table some little while, and Sir Groby beguiled this time with knowledgeable gossip about Court circles.

"They say the King rewards his mistresses with sweepstakes tickets," he remarked with a titter. "Is he not a famous old miser?"

"And, pray, how do you reward yours?" Kitty muttered under her breath.

"When he becomes angry he takes off his hat and wig and kicks them about the room! It is said that he is very angry indeed at the Prince's reception of Princess Charlotte. Prinney must marry her, of course, or his debts will never be paid, so he might as well do it with a good grace."

"Is the Princess really such a sloven?" inquired Fanny.

"Indeed, yes!" cried Kitty. "Hugh Ellesmere, whose mother went down to Greenwich with Lady Jersey to meet the Princess, said that she smells like a stable, and cannot even put on her stockings right side outwards. Poor Prinney!"

"And he so used to have nothing but the best about him!" Fanny giggled.

Juliana thought, for the first time in weeks, of her odd traveling companion, Herr Welcker, and his cargo of rarities for the Prince. Had he arrived in time for his dinner party, and been adequately rewarded?

"Ah, there is a table free," said Sir Groby, and secured it, by sticking his elbow sharply into the side of a young gentleman who was just about to sit down there. The young gentleman threw him an angry look, and then his eyes widened as he glanced past Sir Groby and saw Juliana. He gazed at her with unconcealed admiration. She gave him a slight, commiserating smile, at which his expression lightened; he made a half bow to her and moved away while the Lambourns, with Sir Groby, arranged themselves round the table and called for tea and refreshments. Juliana, who had been most favorably impressed by the young man's air and appearance, followed him with her eyes to the other side of the room, where she saw him take the arm of a tall woman and move away; they presently found seats quite at the other end of the room. Juliana could not see her companion's face or form any conclusion as to her age.

Meanwhile the Ellesmere girls and their brothers had come gaily up and contrived to squeeze round the table, which was only intended for four or five persons. Sir Groby was evidently displeased at this, but it gave him an excuse to squeeze very close to Juliana and slide his arm round her waist.

The others were conducting a cheerful and preposterous conversation about the mixtures used by ladies to improve and preserve their complexions.

"I know for a fact," cried Hugh Ellesmere, "that my aunt Cholmondelay lays a pound of minced veal on her face every morning for an hour, to remove blemishes and imperfections. And afterwards it is given to her pug for his breakfast."

"Ma uses cucumber water and lemon juice, don't you, Ma?" cried Kitty. "And shall I tell you what cousin Ardingly uses for a lip salve?" She lowered her voice to a carrying whisper, and hissed out, "Cat's piss, boiled with loaf sugar! Did you ever hear anything so nasty in your life?"

"Grandmother Bethune uses cat's dung to remove hair," countered one of the Ellesmere girls. "Mixed with vinegar."

"I wonder what your beau puts on his complexion?" whispered Fanny in Juliana's ear. "It puts me in mind of a graveled road!"

"Who would want to remove hair, anyway?" demanded one of the boys, carelessly glancing at Sir Groby's scanty locks. "Most people would rather wish to grow it."

"Not Granny Bethune! She has the longest beard in Berkshire."

Sir Groby, looking with dislike at this rowdy company, suggested to Juliana that if she had drunk her tea, he and she should take a turn about the room together. She would gladly have declined, but a savage glance from Lady Lambourn, and a sharp kick on her ankle, persuaded her to be conformable, and so, very reluctantly, she stood up and moved away with Sir Groby.

The room was now very crowded, and they had to edge their way slowly along; while waiting for a group of gaily dressed personages to walk by, Juliana saw again the young man who had been elbowed aside by Sir Groby. He was seated, talking earnestly to his female companion. When Juliana had seen him for the first time, there had been something in his countenance that struck her as strangely familiar; now she understood the reason for this. He had a rather grave air, and wore luxuriantly curling beard and mustaches, unlike the generality of other men in the room, who were clean-shaven. His eyes were shadowed and thoughtful, his hair and beard of a darkish brown, inclining to chestnut. And what gave him his appearance of familiarity was his striking resemblance to King Charles the First! Juliana could not help being struck by it. She would have liked a friend to be near, with whom she could laugh and exclaim over the coincidence; she could not help remembering Herr Welcker's comment: "Even in England, you don't see replicas of King Charles the First scattered all abroad." For a moment she wished that Herr Welcker was at hand. There would be no use in remarking on the odd resemblance to Sir Groby; she felt quite certain of that.

The press of people around them increased, and Juliana found herself thrust in a different direction from Sir Groby. At that moment she observed an expression of extreme annoyance, and something else—what, she was not quite sure—calculation? spite?—come over his unprepossessing countenance.

"Wait here a moment, child," he said sharply, and thrust his way through the crowd toward where the young man was sitting with his companion.

Juliana, impelled in a different direction by the crowd, was now too far off to hear what ensued; she saw the young man jump to his feet with what looked like a flush of rage; then several more persons pushed by, and Juliana had much ado to keep her feet. She resolved to retrace her way to where Lady Lambourn sat with the girls, but, to her extreme chagrin, when she reached the table where they had been, she found it now occupied by strangers. After seeking vainly about the tearoom she returned to the upper concert hall, where the crowd was now thinner, but her relations were nowhere to be seen.

Juliana stood still in some distress, wondering what was best to be done. After waiting a while for her aunt and cousins, she began to believe that they must have started for home without her, perhaps assuming that she could return under the escort of Sir Groby—a thing she was most anxious to avoid doing.

But she had no money on her to pay for a hackney cab or sedan chair; and, moreover, on going to the entrance, she discovered that the rain poured down violently; it would be impossible to walk, and in any case she had no very clear notion of the way, only that it had taken about half an hour in her aunt's carriage. While she stood hesitating, biting her lip, she heard again the hateful accents of Sir Groby.

"There you are, my pretty runaway! Did you think to give me the slip, my little charmer? But you are justly served for your unfriendliness," continued he, looking out at the rain, which continued to beat down on the cobblestones, "for unless you intend to arrive home looking like a drowned mermaid, you must e'en put up with my company. I will call for my chariot directly."

"Indeed, sir," said Juliana most earnestly, "I would be infinitely more obliged to you if you would but order me a hackney carriage, so that I need not trouble you."

"Unthinkable!" he croaked, giving Juliana a look of malicious relish which made her shiver at the prospect of being shut up in a carriage with him. "No, no, my dear enchantress, wait you there a moment while I summon my conveyance"—and he limped off.

At this moment a voice behind Juliana inquired in the most solicitous tones, "Madam, may I ask if that old gentleman is annoying or distressing you? If so, I shall be most happy to send him to the rightabout! Only give me your commands."

Juliana turned herself round in mingled amazement and relief—to see the young man whose resemblance to King Charles the First had so forcibly struck her!

He was looking at her with what seemed the most earnest kindliness and solicitude; he added, "Forgive me, ma'am, for importuning you in what must seem a strange manner—but I could not help observing your looks of distress. And I believe that shared feelings of animosity towards a common object may, perhaps constitute a bond between us? If I am wrong, a thousand pardons! But if I am right, I shall be happy to do whatever lies within my power to help you."

"Oh, sir!" exclaimed Juliana, too much relieved to

mince her words. "Indeed, indeed you are not wrong, and I shall accept your help with the most heartfelt gratitude. If you could but order me a chair, I should be infinitely obliged."

For she had recollected that, once arrived at the house in Berkeley Square, she could very well instruct her aunt's porter to pay the chairmen.

"That will be the easiest thing in the world, ma'am," said the young man with a graceful bow, and he was as good as his word. In a moment he had somehow contrived to summon a chair from the seething crowd outside the Pantheon building, and soon saw Juliana bestowed in it. She was too happy at this swift rescue to object to the fact that the chair was quite sodden from rain inside and smelled most dismally of damp burlap and wet horsehair.

"Would you please direct the men to take me to number forty, Berkeley Square?" she asked her rescuer, and, as he was about to turn away, she inquired, "To whom, sir, may I address my thanks for this most welcome assistance?"

He made her a low, graceful bow, and as the chairmen began to move away, she just caught the words, "My name, ma'am, is Davenport—Captain Francis Davenport."

Six

ON THE MORNING AFTER JULIANA HAD GIVEN SIR Groby the slip and returned home from the Pantheon without escort, she naturally expected a severe trimming from her aunt. But, strangely enough, her escapade went unrebuked. Possibly, she thought, Sir Groby had been too mortified at his prey's having eluded him to make any public complaint about it; and perhaps he had not been aware of the young man's instrumentality in the matter. Juliana, when questioned by her aunt, said merely that, having become separated from her party and being in considerable distress and agitation, she had been befriended by a stranger who had procured a chair for her in which she had returned home alone; a fact readily confirmed by the porter who had paid off the chairmen.

Lady Lambourn did scold her for her carelessness, to be sure: "We were looking all over the room for you, were we not, girls? And sent Sir Groby in search of you, for our coach was blocking the way and we must needs be off. It is strange that Sir Groby did not find you. Let this be a lesson to you, miss, to keep your wits about you and be less shatterbrained in future!"

Juliana privately resolved that it would indeed; she did not intend to be left alone again with Sir Groby if she could possibly help it.

The following day dawned brilliantly fair. Fanny and Kitty were invited to ride out in Hyde Park with the Ellesmeres; since Juliana possessed no habit, and had not been offered the use of a mount from her uncle's stable, and, in any case, did not know how to ride a horse—she suggested to Miss Ardingly that, if the latter had nothing better to do, they might take the air together on foot. Miss Ardingly readily agreed to this.

"We may as well go to St. James's Park; I have not been there this age."

On quitting the house they had not walked above fifty paces when Juliana observed in the distance the very same young man who had come to her rescue at the Pantheon. She recognized him at once. He, approaching, bowed very gracefully, and said, "Pardon my seeming presumption, madam! I had had the intention of calling to make inquiries as to your welfare—as to whether you had returned safely to your friends' house after your misadventure."

Juliana, eagerly thanking him yet again for his timely help, begged leave to introduce him to Miss Ardingly, who, meanwhile, had been surveying him with a very shrewd and piercing eye.

"This is Captain Davenport, ma'am, who was so very kind as to procure me a chair when I was all alone at the Pantheon Rooms."

"Davenport—hmm," said that lady. "Are you related to Sir Marcus Davenport, of Kettering?"

"My uncle, ma'am," said the young man, with another bow.

"And how is it that I have not seen you about town before this?"

"I have been abroad, ma'am, the last five years— attached to the British Embassy in Rome, from where I am but just returned."

Juliana was enchanted to discover that he had been in her beloved Italy. As Miss Ardingly appeared to find the young man unexceptionable enough, when he begged to be permitted to escort them on their prom-enade, saying that he had come to that part of town with no other object but to satisfy himself of Miss Paget's well-being, she gave him gracious permis-sion to bear them company as far as St. James's Park. Walking with them, accordingly, along Piccadilly and across the Green Park, he conversed in such a well-bred, sensible, and spirited manner, his air and address were so open, amiable, and engaging, that Juliana, already half won by his resemblance to her hero, could not but acknowledge to herself that he was the most interesting and agreeable man that she had ever met. Even the critical Miss Ardingly seemed greatly taken with him, for he addressed his conversation equally to both ladies, and there could be no doubt that the escort of such a personable and gallant young man must give them consequence in the Mall. Juliana found herself greatly disappointed by this much-spoken-of walk—it was a long, straight road of dirty gravel, very uneasy to the feet, with houses at either end. Nothing remarkable about it whatever! But she was bound to admit that the company abroad upon it was very fine: the day was so clear and warm and the personages strolling to and fro were so numerous and so gaily dressed that she would not have changed her situation for the world.

After walking for above an hour and conversing on general topics—about Italy, the Prince's forthcoming wedding, the entertainments to be enjoyed in town—they returned to Piccadilly and parted from Captain Davenport, he bowing gracefully once more, and begging that he might do himself the honor of inquiring after Miss Paget's welfare again at some future time.

"Well, miss, you seem to have lost no time in finding yourself a beau," remarked Miss Ardingly, observing him through her quizzing glass as he walked away. "And indeed he seems a monstrous fine young man! But it will be of no use hoping for anything to come of his addresses, I must warn you, for none of those Davenports have a penny to bless themselves with—it is pockets to let with all of them—and I doubt if this one is any exception to the rest. So far as I can remember, his father was quite burnt to the socket with gambling losses, and had to retire to the Continent. However, at least it must be said for this young man that he appears to have found a respectable means of earning his living. And his air and address are very pretty. But do not place any expectations on him, child! Your aunt would never countenance such a connection."

"Why, ma'am!" cried Juliana, coloring up. "How can you be so—how can you make such a suggestion?

I am sure the young gentleman was only prompted by true politeness and solicitude."

"In course he was!" remarked Miss Ardingly in a dry tone, sharply observing Juliana, who, with flushed cheeks and sparkling brown eyes, showed more animation than she had done since arriving in town.

"Besides," she argued, "what can his father's financial affairs—or his own—signify, if he is of good family and truly a gentleman?"

"You will have to ask that question of your aunt," tartly replied Miss Ardingly as they re-entered the house.

The afternoon was spent by Juliana in devising for herself an elegant evening robe in cream-colored muslin, low on the shoulders, with a fichu gathered on the breast, and a black-edged frill running down the front of the skirt. It was modeled on the satin gown of a lady whom she had carefully observed at the Pantheon. The latter's dress had been embroidered with beads of jet round the hem, but as time was short, Juliana substituted for the embroidery a decoration made from knotted black ribbon, which also adorned the fichu.

"Why, cousin, I wonder you do not set up as a modiste?" exclaimed Kitty, arriving with her arms full of garments in need of repair. "I daresay you would make your fortune. And perhaps that would be best, for Sir Groby has not called today, but Ma has had a note from him, and is looking monstrous grave. I'll wager he is about to sheer off, on account of the trick you played him... Now, do, dear cousin Juliana, please contrive to have my azure silk fit to wear by this evening, for we are all to go to Almack's, and Hugh

Ellesmere has promised the first dance to me. *You* may not dance, of course!"

"Oh, indeed?" inquired Juliana, biting off a thread. "And why not? Because I am in mourning?"

"Lord, no, what does that signify? No, but you may not dance until the Patronesses give you leave to do so."

Juliana was later glad that her cousin had bestowed this caution on her, for by some oversight Lady Lambourn neglected to do so that evening when they arrived at Almack's Assembly Rooms. Juliana was briefly introduced to the Patronesses, Lady Jersey, Lady Alvanley, and Mrs. Drummond-Burrell, who scrutinized her with care, and then gave her cool nods. Lady Lambourn, as was her custom, made direct for the card room, leaving the girls to their own devices. The Ellesmere boys were there, however, with some friends, and Juliana had no lack of partners. On the music striking up, however, mindful of Kitty's warning, she took a seat near the wall, and resolutely refused all offers.

A plump man who had just arrived stood conversing with the Patronesses. He was neatly dressed, without ostentatious parade, but in the most elegant good taste. Glancing around the room, he said to Lady Jersey, "Pray, who is the young lady in the cream and black who is seated yonder?"

Lady Jersey, turning her lorgnette onto Juliana, replied, "That is Miss Paget. She is newly come to town to stay with her aunt Lambourn—who, silly, feather-headed woman, seems to take precious little care of her. But the gal herself seems pretty-behaved enough. Her mother, of course, was another matter. You remember Laura Paget?"

"Oh, dear me, yes," replied the gentleman, who spoke with a slight foreign accent. "Laura Paget, *lieber Gott*! However, *that* cannot be laid to the child's account. Will you introduce me to her, Sally?"

"Why, certainly, if you wish it," replied that lady, giving him a needle-sharp look, "though it is a new thing in you, Frederick, to be concerning yourself with schoolroom misses!"

Accordingly Juliana, listening with some envy to the lively beat of the music, was surprised to be approached by the august Lady Jersey herself. At first she could hardly believe that she was the lady's object, but then rose and curtsied, full of confusion.

"Miss Paget, allow me to present Count Fredrick van Welcker, who is solicitous of obtaining the honor of your hand for this dance."

Looking past Lady Jersey, Juliana only just managed to suppress a gasp of astonishment, and then, snatching hold of her presence of mind, said a little breathlessly, "The Count does me great honor—but—do you permit it, ma'am?"

"Certainly child—go and dance with the Count before the set is finished."

"So we meet again, miss!" remarked Herr Welcker, leading her off into the middle of the room. Like many plump men, he was extremely light on his feet, and a very graceful dancer.

"Oh, sir, I am so delighted to meet with you again! Tell me, did you arrive in time for the Prince's dinner party? And was he pleased with what you brought?

Did all the articles arrive in good condition? Was anything broken?"

"Yes, yes, and no," he replied, laughing. "I did arrive in time, and the Prince was delighted—poor fellow, he is in need of anything that will serve to cheer him up at the moment, with his wedding so imminent! And the only thing that got broken was one of those tedious Sèvres articles that took up so much room. But tell me about yourself, Miss Paget—at last I know your name! Did you find your grandfather's abode without too much difficulty? And how does your father go on? Is he better from his illness?"

"Alas, sir," said Juliana sadly, "as you may see by these"—she touched her black ribbons—"I have suffered from a bereavement. He is no more. The journey proved too much for his waning strength. Oh, how I miss him!" she added from her heart. It was the first time she had been able to confide her grief to anybody.

"Poor child," said Herr Welcker sympathetically. "I feared it might be so, but hoped otherwise. And so you were cast all friendless upon a foreign shore. I trust that your grandfather received you kindly?"

"Well," said Juliana with truth, "he did his duty by me. But I think he did not like me—he seemed glad enough to get rid of me—to dispatch me to my aunt Lambourn. Where my cousins look down on me because I have no portion."

"Ay, is that so? And how does your aunt use you?" It was so novel to encounter a friendly face and a sympathetic ear that Juliana could not help disclosing some of her troubles. She was quite surprised at her own pleasure in meeting Herr Welcker again. He seemed very different from her fellow traveler in that uncomfortable basket—he was cheerful and friendly, instead of being rather short-tempered. And, in place of the untidy brown coat, he was now most correctly dressed in a black superfine tailed coat, knee breeches, and silk stockings. His cravat was tied by the hand of a master, she could see; it differed completely from the laboriously tied neckcloths of the Ellesmere boys and their friends.

"My aunt, sir, is not precisely unkind to me, but she makes me feel an encumbrance. And she seems to think herself obliged to find a husband for me—when all *I* want is some unexceptionable means of earning my own living."

"An encumbrance!" he ejaculated. "With your looks, and your story? I'd have thought you'd be the heroine of the hour, my dear!"

"You mean, because I escaped from France in your balloon?" inquired Juliana. "But, you see, nobody knows that, sir."

"What? You never told anybody?" He was astonished. "Not even your grandfather?"

"He did not wish to hear about our journey. And nobody else was interested enough to inquire. Also I—I felt that it was not my secret—that perhaps you might have reasons for not wishing your method of exit from France to be divulged."

He burst out laughing. "Why, Miss Paget, you are a regular nonpareil! If they had men of your discretion in the government, my dear, this country would have won the war by now! But you are hiding your light under a bushel. Allow me to rectify that!"

And, indeed, when the dance was over, he led Juliana back to Lady Jersey, saying, "Ma'am, I daresay you have heard me a dozen times over extolling the pluck and coolheadedness of the unknown young lady who with such presence of mind saved me from the French mob near St.-Malo. Now you must allow me to present her to you, for this is she!"

"What, indeed, is that so?" cried the lively Lady Jersey, all curiosity at once. "Well, you are a sly dog, Frederick—no wonder you were taking such an interest in Miss Paget! And so, my dear, you were the heroine who bade the bloodthirsty revolutionaries stop when they were about to suspend Count van Welcker from a tree?"

"Oh, it was nothing, ma'am," said Juliana, rather confused at so much attention, for several other persons, hearing Lady Jersey's exclamation, had begun to gather round. "Indeed, I gave poor Herr Welcker a great deal of trouble, for I told the people that he was a doctor, and so all the sick persons in the village came flocking to him for remedies."

"Ay, and a fine partnership we made of it, Miss Paget and I," declared Count van Welcker. "We were at it for three hours together, I believe, handing out tinctures and poultices, before they would leave us alone."

"And do you mean to tell me that you then escaped with the Count in his air balloon, you intrepid girl?" demanded Lady Jersey, her face all sparkling with inquisitiveness and mischief.

"What else could I do, ma'am? My poor father was grievously sick and longing to make his way to

England before—before it was too late," Juliana said in a faltering voice. "No ships were sailing and—and—and since Herr Welcker had been so kind as to make the offer—"

"Well, it is the most romantic thing that I ever heard," pronounced Lady Jersey. "A veritable case of a *deus ex machina*—though whether the Count is the *deus*, or you, my dear, are the *dea*, I am not quite certain."

Juliana was not certain whether to be glad or sorry that Count van Welcker had recognized her and made public her story to the society gathered at Almack's. To be sure, it was very agreeable to see him again—but all the attention now focused on her made her uncomfortable. From this moment on, she was the undoubted success of the evening. Partners clamored for her hand, so many that she was obliged to refuse a great number. Young men vied for the privilege of bringing her lemonade, tea, and orgeat. Lady Lambourn, secluded in the card room, remained unaware of her niece's sudden popularity; but Fanny and Kitty soon discovered that Juliana was always the center of an enthusiastic group, and cast her many sour looks of envy and dislike, especially when the red-faced Ellesmere boys asked them why they had never divulged that their cousin was such a bang-up heroine.

During the ride home, a prickly silence prevailed in the carriage. Next morning the hall of the house in Berkeley Square was half filled with bouquets; a stack of cards and invitations had arrived for Miss Paget. Lady Lambourn, by now apprised, through several notes from dear friends, of her niece's sudden fame, took Juliana most severely to task over the whole affair.

"I was never in my life so mortified! Reckless, foolish girl! To have traveled in an air balloon at all is bad enough—a wholly capricious, unladylike thing to do!—but to have done it with Count van Welcker, of all people! A most notorious rake! One of the Prince's associates! Nothing could be more unfortunate. I daresay your uncle may feel that, having compromised you to such a degree, van Welcker should make an offer for you and what kind of a match would *that* be?"

"Why should he do any such thing?" exclaimed Juliana. "Besides, he has not compromised me in the least. My father was present throughout—what better protection could I have?"

"Your father—tush! And why, in heaven's name," said Lady Lambourn, changing to another tack, "why, when fortunately nobody knew about it, could you be so disastrously foolish as to make public the whole history?"

Juliana felt herself ill used.

"I would never have spoken of it, I assure you, ma'am. But what could I do if Herr—I mean, Count van Welcker—himself told the tale to Lady Jersey?"

"We shall be the talk of the town," said Lady Lambourn, wringing her hands. "What your uncle will say, I shudder to contemplate."

The front doorbell rang, and Fitton came to say that Count van Welcker was below, inquiring as to whether he might take Miss Paget driving in the park.

"Tell him, certainly not!" said Lady Lambourn sharply to Fitton. "You may say that my niece is not going out today." And to Juliana, she said, "You had best remain indoors, miss, and not show your face abroad until this undesirable commotion has died down. Good God, what will Sir Groby say to it all?"

Juliana had not the slightest wish to speculate upon what Sir Groby might say. Regretting the lost excursion with Count van Welcker, she retired, as bidden, to her room, where she spent the morning in the occupation of altering a dark-blue velvet riding habit that Miss Ardingly had given her. One breadth was very worn, but as it was by far too large around the waist, that was easily remedied by taking it in.

Then Kitty arrived, carrying a walking dress of striped poplin.

"Cousin Juliana, I hope you ain't too high in the boughs now to help me mend this robe? There's something amiss about the bodice—it has never sat on me as it should, and I depend on you to set it to rights, for Fan and I mean to go walking in Kensington Gardens at noon with the Ellesmeres. The boys wished for you to come too, but Ma says you must keep your chamber," she added without visible signs of regret.

"You will have to put the dress on," Juliana said, "or I can't see what is amiss."

"Oh, Lord, must I? Very well," exclaimed Kitty, yawning, and dragging her other gown, a loose morning robe, over her head.

While Juliana unstitched, and pinned, and turned Kitty this way and that, the latter, after yawning some more and gazing vacantly about the room for a while, said, "Shall I tell you a secret, coz?"

"Not if it is no concern of mine," replied Juliana.

"Ay, but it is! I'll tell you, for it is a prime joke. Sir Groby means to have you, after all, in spite of the prank you played on him the other night. Mr. Throgmorton, his man-of-business, sent Pa a note about a marriage contract. Indeed, *I* believe he offers for you out of spite, for he was vexed beyond anything at your giving him the slip! He was downstairs, half an hour ago, talking with Ma in the breakfast parlor; I happened to be passing the door, which was not fully closed, and I heard her say, 'My niece shall have you, Sir Groby, if I have to discipline her on bread and water, and I am only sorry she is so contumacious and ungrateful.' And he said, with that nasty, spiteful laugh he has, 'Why, pray don't regard it, ma'am. I like a little spirit in a chit; it only makes it the more amusing to break 'em to bridle…' Why, cousin! Mind what you are about! You stuck a great pin right into my back!"

"But why in heaven's name should your mother encourage this odious man?" demanded Juliana, when, with shaking hands, she had removed the pin.

"Oh, I can easily tell you *that*," replied Kitty blithely. "Ma owes Sir Groby a monstrous deal in gaming debts—I believe it is as much as four or five thousand pounds. She does not dare let my father know about it, but Partridge told Fan and me, for Ma was wondering if she dared sell some of her jewels— only, if Pa found out about that, she would never hear the last of it. I daresay Sir Groby had promised to let her off the debt if he marries you."

"Oh! How wicked!" gasped Juliana. "How can she strike such a shameful bargain?"

"Lord, what's wrong with it?" said Kitty, staring. "She has her debts settled and you off her hands—Sir Groby has a smart young wife, which the old goat

fancies will add to his consequence—you get a rich
husband. Why, many girls would give their ears for
such a match! Good heavens, cousin, ain't you finished
yet? You have been poking and stitching this age, I
do declare!"

"There—it is done—look at yourself in the glass,"
said Juliana rather hastily, and Kitty, after looking and
declaring with approbation that she was now as smart
as sevenpence, danced out of the room with her other
robe on her arm, leaving Juliana a prey to the most
dismal reflections.

That her aunt was a silly, lazy woman, Juliana had
long understood—that she could be so venal, and
completely, callously indifferent to the thought of
her niece's inevitable misery as the wife of Sir Groby
came as no particular surprise. What recourse did
Juliana have? She could write to her grandfather—but
supposing he took her aunt's part? Suppose he considered Sir Groby a suitable match? Living secluded
in Hampshire, wholly remote from town gossip, as he
did, he might not know Sir Groby's evil reputation.
Or perhaps, thought Juliana wretchedly, he might not
care; he might not regard it, in his anxiety to get his
tiresome grandchild settled and off his hands.

If only I could run away! she thought despairingly.
But where should I go? If I went back to Grandfather,
he would not be at all pleased to see me. Furthermore,
she recollected that she had hardly any money left;
and she thought with regret and impatience of her
grandfather's fifty pounds, disbursed on dress lengths
and trimmings, besides some absolutely necessary
shoes, stockings, and underwear. As she had brought

to England only the clothes she stood up in, her wardrobe was sadly deficient even by the meanest standards. She still must make do with her shabby old pelisse, both for morning and evening wear, and she had only two guineas remaining in her purse, which would not get her to Flintwood, she knew, for the fare from London to Winchester on the common stage was one pound and sixteen shillings, and from Winchester she would have to hire a chaise.

What was to be done?

She had reached no conclusion when she was summoned downstairs for another interview with her aunt.

Lady Lambourn, like many lazy people, could only exert authority when she had put herself into a rage, which she had now done.

"Listen to me, miss. I want no nonsense or missishness from you, no more heedless folly! You are a very lucky girl, let me tell you—considering the gossip that must now be spreading about you, very lucky indeed! Sir Groby has this day made your uncle a formal offer for your hand, which I have accepted on your behalf."

"Then, madam," cried Juliana desperately, "I fear you must reverse your answer, and decline it again, for I will not have him. I will never have him!"

"Insolent, ungrateful girl! You will accept him if I have to drag you to the altar. Sir Groby has behaved in the most magnanimous way possible—he is prepared to ignore the imprudence of your behavior in riding with Count van Welcker in his air balloon; he is prepared to turn a deaf ear to the scandalous stories going round town; he is prepared to overlook the undesirable connection with your scandalous mother—indeed, he has very obligingly saved your uncle the task of warning your mother to leave the country—"

"*What?* He has warned my mother?" gasped Juliana, overcome with amazement. "Do you, then, mean to tell me, madam, that my mother is in this country, and I never knew it? Suppose I wished to see her?"

"Good heavens, child, are you quite out of your senses? See her? I should think not, indeed! To be acquainted with *her* would be to damn your chances entirely. I trust by this time she has taken heed of Sir Groby's warning, and quitted these shores."

"But why? Why should she leave? What has she done?"

"Why should she leave? Because if she remained she might be cast into prison, miss! Now, let me hear no more on this head, but prepare yourself to receive Sir Groby's addresses with a proper complaisance," cried Lady Lambourn, who was by now worked into a high degree of irritation. "Tonight he takes us to Ranelagh, and I wish you to be as pretty-behaved as possible."

"I make no promises, ma'am," declared Juliana, and ran from the room.

She went directly to Miss Ardingly and asked for her help and intercession, but this proved wholly unavailing.

"Lord, child, what could I do?" said that lady. "You ain't *my* niece, after all, and I am but a cipher in this house—of no consequence, save as a convenience. But why make such a coil? It is nothing new, after all, for young ladies to have advantageous matches arranged by their friends—it happens every day of the week. I fear you will just have to make the best of it."

"But he is *odious*, ma'am—and—and diseased, and wicked!" cried Juliana, utterly cast down by these words of cold cheer. "Could I not appeal to my mother? Do you not know where she is to be found?"

"Your *mother*, child—what put that maggot into your head? How did you know she was even in England, pray?"

"Sir Groby has seen her, my aunt said."

"Has he, indeed?" said Miss Ardingly, inquisitively. "I wonder how that came about? But, no, child, an appeal to Laura Paget—or whatever name she goes under now—would be quite useless, would only do you grave disservice; bless you, *she* would never help you, she never lifted a finger to serve a soul but herself; and association with her could do you nothing but harm."

Discouraged, Juliana went away to her own chamber. She meditated an appeal to Lord Lambourn; strict, he was, but he was also very respectable; could he really know what kind of a man had offered for his niece? Unfortunately he was hardly ever to be found at home, dividing his time between White's Club and the House of Lords. And even if she had managed to obtain an interview with him, she had little expectation of winning his sympathy: his opinion of his wife and daughters, and, consequently, of the whole female tribe, appeared to be a mixture of boredom and contempt.

Juliana dressed for the party to Ranelagh in the most dejected frame of mind. She put on a rather old-fashioned black silk sack dress, draped at the back, with a full skirt, dropped shoulders and gold-embroidered sleeves, which Lady Lambourn had worn in mourning for some bygone aunt, and had long since discarded as being quite out of the mode. What does it matter how I look? thought Juliana dismally. Indeed, it would be better if I looked a fright, only to discourage that old monster. In fact, the draped elegant lines of the dress charmingly set off her long neck, gold-brown hair piled high, and small piquant face. But she was in no mood to study her glass.

During the carriage ride to Ranelagh she formed various wild resolutions for escape—she would run away from her party and appeal to some benevolent-looking stranger; she would write a beseeching letter to Lady Jersey asking for her intercession; she would slip out next day to one of the milliners patronized by Lady Lambourn and ask if she might take a position as a seamstress. But she feared that Lady Jersey would never take her part against her aunt, and she knew the latter project would be ineligible, since she had no money to pay for apprenticeship indemnities. There seemed no way out of her predicament.

Arrived at Ranelagh, she had little enthusiasm for the beauty and magnificence of the rooms, the brilliancy of the lights, or the fantastic decorations which made the whole place appear like some enchanted palace from a fairy tale. Sir Groby was waiting for them, looking, in his pale-green satin evening dress, even more like the ogre of the fairy tale. He greeted them with suave civility; Juliana received a particular greeting, a smile that combined triumph with malice.

He had already procured a box for them—as the arched recesses were called, where parties sat to partake of refreshments. Lady Lambourn and the twins were all delight at the thin-shaved ham, the rack punch, ratafia, jellies, creams, and confections of fruit and sugar that were brought to their table. Juliana ate but little.

When they had finished eating they listened to a concert, and Sir Groby contrived to sit beside Juliana, squeeze her arm in a pinching, vise-like grip, and murmur in her ear, "My lovely little charmer, I am the happiest man in London, for your aunt has informed me that she has persuaded you to listen to my addresses with indulgence."

"I fear, sir, that my aunt has misled you," replied Juliana, "for I will never, never do so!"

He cast her a glance whose malignity terrified her, and, gripping her wrist so tightly that she cried out, murmured, still in the same undertone, "Ah, but I think I may be able to make you change your mind, my pretty one."

Juliana shuddered, and, turning her head away so as not to see his loathsome countenance, to her astonishment caught sight of a friendly face: in the crowd of persons at the end of the row, standing because they had been unable to procure seats, she observed the handsome figure of Captain Davenport. He had been looking in her direction—his eyes met hers—and she found in them a look of such grave compassion, such true sympathy, that her heart swelled within her.

Oh, what a difference it makes, she thought, to encounter just one person who might feel for me in my plight. That gives me courage! Now I feel that I shall be able to take a firm stand against Sir Groby and my aunt.

When the music was finished, she looked about again for Captain Davenport, but he was nowhere to be seen. Sir Groby hurried his party out into the gardens, for a spectacle of fireworks was now preparing, and they must hasten to secure good places. The gardens, at this season of early spring, had but little to show by daylight; however, by night they appeared bewitched, with garlands of lamps hung between the trees; there were pools, fountains, and cascades illuminated by colored lights, and the trees and shrubs were festooned with artificial flowers. The fireworks, too, were prodigiously handsome, depicting in lights the tale of Cupid and Psyche; but Juliana had little attention to spare for these wonders. She was too uneasy, for Sir Groby, keeping a tight clutch on her arm, was all the time insensibly drawing her farther and farther away from Lady Lambourn and the girls. She tried to detach her arm from his grasp, but without the least success; at all her efforts he only chuckled maliciously and grasped her the tighter.

Then, at the climax of the fireworks display, there suddenly came a tremendous clap of sound, and a flash of fire; taking advantage of the screams, shouts, and general alarm and commotion occasioned by this unexpected explosion, Sir Groby fairly dragged Juliana away from the crowd, and hustled her off into a dark alley between high hedges.

"Now, my charmer," he said, "that accident has given me just the chance I was looking for; now is the time for you to give me your answer; and I should warn you that I am an ill man to flout! But your aunt promised me that she would persuade you, and so I am prepared to believe that your previous rejoinders were merely pieces of maidenly coyness. I am assured that I need have no real apprehensions. Come, tell me, is it to be yes?"

"No, Sir Groby," Juliana answered with tolerable firmness, though her teeth were chattering from fear, from pain as he drove his nails into her wrist, and from the chill night air. "I have to tell you that I would not marry you if you were the last man left alive! And however many times you ask me, my answer will still be no, unalterably no!"

She could guess the intensity of his rage from the hissing breath he drew; in the dim light from a distant lamp she could see his lips draw back from his teeth. He ground out a savage oath, and then muttered, "On your own head be it, then, girl!—for I warn you, if I can't have you by fair means, I shall have you anyway—I'd just as soon—and then you and that precious aunt of yours may weep and pray to no avail!"

So saying, he pulled a whistle from his pocket and blew on it shrilly; then he began dragging Juliana as fast as he could toward the end of the hedged alleyway, where there appeared to be a gate leading out onto an unfrequented street. Now Juliana was truly terrified, for she thought she could see a carriage waiting beyond the gate; she struggled desperately, she attempted to shriek, but a second man, appearing beside her, clapped his hand over her mouth and silenced her.

"Tie her hands," said Sir Groby. "Have you a bag to put over her head?"

"Ay, sir."

Juliana had given herself up for lost, when a loud voice exclaimed, "Leave that young lady alone, you villains! Let her be! Unhand her, or, by all that's sacred, I'll dash your brains out!"

A violent blow sent Sir Groby staggering to one side; a second laid the other man senseless on the gravel. Sir Groby soon recovered; his false teeth had been knocked out by the blow, so, uttering imprecations which were all the more fearful for being incomprehensible, he dragged a thin evil-looking sword out of the cane that he carried. But the newcomer, who had seized a garden stake out of the hedge, knocked his blade aside and succeeded in felling him with another stunning blow.

Then, approaching Juliana—who, during this rapid reversal, had stood petrified and paralyzed with astonishment—the man who had intervened so opportunely took her arm with the utmost solicitude, exclaiming, "Thank God, madam, that I have been the means of preventing such a brutal abduction! Pray allow me to restore you to your friends! I trust that you have sustained no injury?" Then, looking closer, in a tone of the most profound astonishment, "Good God! Do my eyes deceive me, or is it—can it be Miss Paget?"

It was Captain Davenport.

"Oh, sir!" exclaimed Juliana. "How inexpressibly thankful I am that you chanced to come this way at that moment!"

"You cannot be more thankful than I am myself!" said he. "I shall never cease to rejoice and to congratulate myself on the fortunate circumstance that, low in spirits, weary of the bright lights and loud noise, I chose to retire from the tumult to this peaceful glade, and therefore was enabled to be the instrument of rescuing you from those abominable ravishers!" And he led the shaken Juliana back to the rows of seats from which the audience had been observing the fireworks display.

There, fortunately, order had been restored, and they found Lady Lambourn, who, decidedly impatient, was urging Fanny and Kitty to look sharp and see if they could not spy out Sir Groby and their cousin, since the entertainment was now at an end and the night grew chill.

"*There* you are, miss!" Lady Lambourn exclaimed as Juliana approached her. "But"—with a sharp look— "who is this? And where, pray, is Sir Groby?"

During the brief walk from the alley Juliana had come to the hasty decision that, to avoid the public shame which must accompany a disclosure of Sir Groby's baseness, she would not immediately divulge his part in the affair. She therefore said, simply, "Two wicked men tried to abduct me in a dark alley, aunt, and this gentleman was so very kind as to come to my rescue."

"Lord, what next?" exclaimed Lady Lambourn, and Fanny and Kitty burst into loud cries of amazement.

"Why, cousin, what ever was you doing in a dark alley?"

"Where, pray, was Sir Groby?"

"What did the men look like?"

"La, coz, what an adventure!"

"Where is Sir Groby now?" demanded Lady Lambourn again.

"I do not know, ma'am," replied Juliana. "I have not seen him since the occurrence."

"He must be sought!" began Lady Lambourn, but Captain Davenport, with the most respectful, though mild authority, said, "If you will forgive me, ma'am, the young lady who has suffered this misadventure should instantly be taken home; she is half fainting, and it is not to be wondered at, after such a shocking occurrence. Shall I call her a chair? Or will you permit me to summon your conveyance?"

Recalled thus to her duty as a chaperone, Lady Lambourn fretfully said, "Oh, very well—we had best all return home, I daresay, for the girls have been complaining of cold this half hour. I shall be obliged, sir, if you will call our carriage."

Bowing, Captain Davenport went off to do so, and soon returned to say that it was waiting for them at the front entrance. He had behaved, throughout, with the most striking dignity, propriety, and concern. His eyes had hardly met those of Juliana. But, on seeing them into the carriage, he bowed again and, taking her hand, just carried her fingers to his lips. Then he wished them all good night, promising himself the honor of coming to make his inquiries after Juliana on the morrow.

Lady Lambourn was still restlessly looking about for Sir Groby.

"Did you know that young man, Juliana?" demanded she as soon as the carriage was in motion.

"Yes, aunt. I had met him when out walking with Miss Ardingly. He is a Captain Davenport; he was the same person who was so kind as to procure me a chair at the Pantheon the other evening."

"Very singular!" remarked Lady Lambourn, fixing her niece with a most suspicious eye. "Strange indeed that he should be on the spot to assist you on two occasions!"

"Cousin has found herself a beau!" The twins giggled.

"Hush, girls! I trust that Juliana has a better sense of duty than to encourage any pretensions which would run so completely counter to my wishes for her!"

Juliana made no reply. She was, in truth, so shocked and agitated still by what had passed that her mind was in confusion; had Sir Groby, she wondered distractedly, planned the whole abduction from the start? She could not help hoping that the blow with the hedge stake had deprived him of any further wish or ability to continue his pursuit of her; indeed, she could not but pray that it had put an end to his odious existence. She was too tried and distressed to be drawn into an argument with her aunt, and remained silent for the rest of the journey back to Berkeley Square.

As she fell asleep she could not help reflecting, as her aunt had done, on the coincidence of Captain Davenport's having twice come to her rescue within such a short space of time; she wondered if he had, perhaps, observed her being drawn off by Sir Groby, and whether he had followed with the intention of intervening? If so, what did that mean? Was it possible that he felt an interest in her—an attraction toward her? Or were his motives simply those of friendship?

But if he had known her identity, why pretend surprise on recognizing her? Perhaps he had too much delicacy to wish his interest to be suspected at such an early stage of the acquaintance?

Exercising her mind on these speculations, Juliana became less agitated. And the image of his grave, concerned face—so like that of Charles the First—the brief touch of his bearded lips on her hand—these were the last things she thought of before she fell asleep.

Seven

NEXT DAY NO WORD CAME FROM SIR GROBY, AND Lady Lambourn, Fanny reported, was in a rare taking, beyond all reason cross and twitty.

Juliana dreaded a summons from her aunt; if interrogated, she must tell the whole tale, she had decided, and she was utterly cast down at the thought of the scene that must follow. But no summons came. Lady Lambourn was said to be laid down upon her bed with the headache, and did not appear until a late hour.

Meanwhile, more and more cards and invitations arrived for Juliana; she did not know what to do about them. All were from complete strangers.

Captain Davenport called to inquire after Juliana's health and spirits, and she received him in the breakfast parlor, suitably chaperoned by Miss Ardingly; he stayed no longer than the ten minutes enjoined by ceremony, and his remarks did not pass beyond polite commonplace, but the look in his eyes told another tale.

In the afternoon Count van Welcker likewise called, and, since Lady Lambourn was not about to deny him admission, he invited Juliana and Miss Ardingly to come for a drive in his curricle.

"What do you think, ma'am?" Juliana asked Miss Ardingly. "My aunt did not wish me to go out yesterday—?"

"Lord, she can't keep you mewed up in the house forever," said the old lady robustly. "I don't know—I see no harm in it, I must confess!"

Plainly she was much taken with the prospect of the drive herself, so with this encouragement, Juliana was glad to accept, and greatly enjoyed the pleasant airing. Count van Welcker's cheerful company and friendly conversation were exceedingly soothing to her distressed spirits. He chatted on a variety of amusing topics: told how Lord Rockingham and Lord Orford had made a match for five hundred pounds between five turkeys and five geese to race from Norwich to London—"Who won?" inquired Juliana. "A fox got two of the geese, ma'am so the bet was called off"; how Thomas Whaley had betted that he would jump from his drawing-room window into the first barouche that passed, and kiss the occupant; of the special costume worn by gamblers at Almack's.

"They remove their evening dress, ma'am, and put on frieze greatcoats, or turn their coats inside out for luck. They tie up the lace ruffles at their wrists and leather thongs, and, to guard their eyes from the light and keep their hair from falling forward, they affect high-crowned hats with broad brims, adorned with flowers and ribbons."

"How very singular!" exclaimed Juliana, who could not help being diverted, despite her low spirits.

"But I forget, Miss Paget, your aunt is an habituée of the rooms, and no doubt has told you these things."

"No, indeed she has not," said Juliana.

Miss Ardingly spied innumerable acquaintances out walking or riding, and wished to speak to somebody every two minutes; consequently their progress was at a dawdling pace. During one of these interludes, when Miss Ardingly was occupied in absorbing conversation with a Mrs. and Mr. Chumleigh, Count van Welcker remarked to Juliana, in a low tone, "I am glad to have this opportunity of speaking to you, Miss Paget. The *ton* gossip has it, my dear, that your aunt plans to marry you off to Sir Groby Feverel. Is this true, by any chance?"

"Oh, sir, not if I can help it! I have the utmost detestation for Sir Groby, and would do anything not to be married to him!"

"I should have thought as much," said he.

"Sir, what can I do? My aunt assures me that no one else will offer for me, since I have no portion, and because my mother disgraced herself in some dreadful way, and—"

Juliana could not bring herself to reveal Lady Lambourn's abominable bargain with Sir Groby, and stopped short.

A look of astonishment came over Count van Welcker's round, good-natured face. "Nobody offer for you!" he ejaculated. "What a simpleton your aunt must be! Why, I know at least half a dozen young fellows who are dying of love for you at this very moment, after a single meeting! You are the Toast of the Town, my dear! Your aunt must be quite totty-headed. Why, for the matter of that—"

He checked himself as Miss Ardingly turned from her conversation. They had no more chance for private talk on that occasion, but Juliana was happy to think that in the Count she might have found a friend and partisan. But of course he was very much occupied and might have no time to spare for her problems. The Prince of Wales was about to marry his imported German princess, and, as one of the members of the Prince's entourage, Count van Welcker must have a hundred tasks to perform.

That evening Lord Lambourn, for once, had undertaken to escort his family to the theater—a rare favor to which, Juliana discovered, neither his wife not his daughters looked forward with any pleasure at all.

"Pa always thinks it his duty to go with us at least once in a season," Fanny told Juliana, who was remodeling for her the sleeves of an evening gown of pink-and-green-striped tabaret silk. "Otherwise he is afraid the *ton* will begin to say that he and Ma must have quarreled since they never go anywhere together. Pa cannot abide scandal. So he takes us to Drury Lane to be bored by some horrid tragedy… Is my dress finished, coz? Do you not think it vastly smart?"

Juliana though it hideous, but was too civil to say so. She was wondering whether it might be possible to make an appeal to her uncle during one of the intervals in the performance.

Lord Lambourn did not accompany his family in the coach to Drury Lane, but met them there, having dined at his club. He had procured a stage box for his party, and immediately sat himself down at the back and immersed himself in a newspaper, while the twins hung over the front of the box, waving to their friends.

"We had best amuse ourselves while we can," said Kitty, "for the piece is that horrid *Hamlet*, the most dismal fustian, with a story that nobody could follow, and the hero dies in the end; I have seen it before. Never mind! I see the Ellesmeres in their box, so we can go round in the first intermission for a fine frolic."

That will be my time, thought Juliana, for her aunt was already absorbed in conversation with some card-playing friends. Juliana herself glanced about the theater in mingled curiosity and apprehension, hoping to see Captain Davenport, fearing to see Sir Groby. She wished she had thought to mention to the Captain, that morning, that they were to go to Drury Lane in the evening. But still, what difference would that make to him? She discovered neither the Captain nor Sir Groby, but she did see Count van Welcker, in the opposite box, with a party of very fashionable people. He, likewise, observed Juliana, and gave her a low bow, making a gesture to signify that he wished to come round in the interval to pay his respects. Juliana was obliged for his politeness, but, there goes my chance to be alone with my uncle, she thought.

"Why, cousin Jule," said Fanny, "there's your beau!"

"What beau?" said Juliana, with suddenly quickened breath.

"What beau? Why, the monstrous fine young man who saved you at Ranelagh—there he is—see—with a quiz of a woman, old enough to be his mother!"

"Perhaps it is his mother," suggested Juliana. "Where do you see him?"

"There—see—in the gallery—no, he is gone. But you may see the lady, still there, with a blue gauze scarf and a spangled fan."

Before Juliana could locate the lady, however, the lights went down, and the curtain rose. Juliana found herself moved and absorbed by the play, but her cousins fidgeted and whispered throughout, Lord Lambourn continued to peruse his paper by the light of a lamp that burned at the back of the box, and Lady Lambourn maintained a conversation in low voices with a card-playing crony. Judged as family entertainment, Juliana decided, the occasion could hardly be called a success.

The moment the curtain came down for the interval, the twins darted off to visit their friends; Lord Lambourn moved out into the corridor to discuss politics with two parliamentary acquaintances; and Count van Welcker arrived to pay his respects. He begged leave to present Juliana to some of his friends who were desirous of meeting her. But Lady Lambourn, giving him a cold look, said sharply, "I regret, sir, that my niece is promised in Lady Bethune's box. Come, child," and she almost dragged Juliana away; all the latter could do was give Count van Welcker a regretful and apologetic smile. On the way back from the Ellesmere box (where Juliana had nothing to do but listen in boredom to a lot of vapid chatter) they encountered Captain Davenport. They were hurrying, for the curtain was about to rise; so was he; he seemed greatly startled at meeting Juliana there—said he had not anticipated the pleasure of seeing her at the theater that evening, since it had not been mentioned that morning—but his whole expressive, manly countenance was overspread with such a glow of delight at sight of her that Juliana, though frustrated in her plan to speak to her uncle, still could not but feel an elevation in her spirits.

She sat through the remainder of *Hamlet* in a happy dream, and sustained the worst of its vicissitudes with composure.

After the main performance a farce was to be shown entitled *The Deuce Is in Him*; however, to the astonishment of the whole party, Lord Lambourn, who had again been conversing with his colleagues in the second interval, suddenly re-entered the box and, in the most peremptory manner, ordered his family to make ready for departure.

"But, Pa!" exclaimed Fanny and Kitty in horror. "We have not seen the farce! And that's the only part of the whole entertainment that's worth watching! We can't go home *now*!"

"Be silent!" said Lord Lambourn, and escorted his family down to the carriage with such a black countenance as allowed of no argument. He accompanied them in the coach, but maintained a thunderous silence during the whole journey; it was not until they were all assembled in the saloon in Berkeley Square that he revealed the cause of his vexation.

"Madam!" he said, addressing his wife, but giving Juliana a very angry look. "At the theater tonight I have learned of two circumstances which have filled me with the gravest displeasure and apprehension. The first concerns that depraved woman—with whose name I prefer not to sully my lips—I refer to my niece's female parent; that woman, madam, is in town; was, indeed, in that very theater—!"

Juliana gave a gasp, but her uncle continued, without heeding her astonishment.

"And my second reason for bringing you away so speedily was that I discovered, and I cannot describe what chagrin—what horror—from some of my acquaintance, that my niece—that this young girl—due to her disastrously ill-judged association with Count van Welcker—has become a Toast—a *Toast!*—among Macaronis and Corinthians, among park saunterers and counter coxcombs; she has become a Byword; she is referred to by the sort of person who would never be invited to enter this house as—as the Balloon Belle; or, even worse, as—by a sobriquet with which I prefer not to sully my lips—it refers, madam, to a *domestic utensil!*"

Though she could not help being amused at the difficulties to which her uncle was put in order to avoid sullying his lips, Juliana was greatly abashed at this, and colored deeply. The twins, though gazing awestruck at their father, could not forebear a titter; Fanny whispered to Kitty under her breath, "*Miss Potts!*"

Lady Lambourn gave a faint scream and sank into a chair, fanning herself.

"How comes it, madam," thundered Lord Lambourn, "that this has been allowed to occur?"

"I am sure it was none of my fault, Lambourn," whimpered his wife. "How could *I* help it? Juliana had undergone this disastrous adventure before she ever set foot in my house. Was it *my* fault if Count van Welcker recognized her at Almack's?"

Lord Lambourn was not to be appeased.

"You should have kept a closer watch on her, ma'am, and not encouraged the attentions of such a person. You should have anticipated something of the sort! Now our family is disgraced! My *own daughters* must also, by polite society, be associated with this outrageous vulgarity! I must request that the young lady leave our house at once—she cannot remain any longer beneath my roof. She must return to Hampshire directly!"

"But she promised to trim the neck of my costume for the Masquerade!" wailed Fanny.

"Quiet, child! She must leave tomorrow," Lord Lambourn said to his wife.

"But, Lambourn, how can she? *You* cannot escort her to Hampshire. And I most certainly cannot!"

"I? No, indeed! Your maid Partridge may accompany her as far as Winchester; and I will send an express to your father, requiring him to have a carriage meet her there."

"Papa will not be best pleased—" began Lady Lambourn, and then she gave a scream and said, "*Send Partridge?* Are you out of your mind, my lord? I cannot possibly spare Partridge tomorrow."

"Why not?" snapped her husband.

"Have you forgotten *everything*?" demanded Lady Lambourn tragically, sniffing at the wrong end of her vinaigrette in her agitation. "Tomorrow is the night of our Masquerade—! I cannot possibly allow Partridge to be absent. Juliana will have to stay here until the following day. Besides," she added practically, "even if you sent an express, it is odds that it would not reach my father in time, and Partridge can hardly leave Juliana on her own in Winchester. And I cannot possibly spare her for upwards of twelve hours."

Lord Lambourn was obliged to concede to this, but he laid the most strict injunctions on his wife that Juliana was not to stir outside the house in the meantime, and that she must leave at daybreak on the following day.

Juliana, who had hardly been addressed during this scene, crept away like an outcast, and retired to bed in a mood of mingled relief, resentment, and melancholy. Relief predominated. The thought that she might now be free from Sir Groby's odious advances—for it seemed improbable in the highest degree that he would trouble to pursue her to Hampshire—was inexpressibly comforting.

What matter that she would, on her return to Flintwood, almost certainly have to endure her grandfather's displeasure? That would be much easier to support, she thought; and she might perhaps, in course of time, make herself so unobtrusively useful that he might be persuaded to allow her to remain in his house.

She could not help feeling somewhat unjustly used, however. It was no fault of hers, after all, that her name was being bandied about in Corinthian circles; why should she be debarred from social intercourse on account of such a misadventure?

Nor could she deny to herself that she felt a pang at the prospect of leaving London without seeing Captain Davenport again. She would have liked to thank him once more for his unbelievably opportune intervention at Ranelagh. If he had not come along just then, where would she be now?

Shuddering at the horrible thought, she drifted off into sleep.

Next day from dawn to dusk the whole house in Berkeley Square was in turmoil and confusion while the servants made ready for Lady Lambourn's masquerade party that evening. Errand boys ran in and out with deliveries of food, of flowers, great baskets of napery and hired glasses, hampers of wine; carpenters hammered, putting up an awning, and also erecting a gallery in the ballroom, which Lord Lambourn said was a perfectly foolish and unnecessary expense; upholsterers were at work laying carpets, and florists' men contrived bowers of blooms and greenery. Lord Lambourn irritably conferred with his butler and steward. He was perfectly aware of the necessity to give a large party at least once in the season, but he considered that his wife's choice of date was ridiculously early.

"But, Lambourn, then everybody we invite is obliged to invite us back!"

"And why, of all idiotic forms of entertainment, must you choose a Masquerade? It invariably gives rise to horseplay and ill-bred behavior!"

"The girls enjoy dressing up," said their mother, without going on to add the obvious rider that such a plain pair were seen to best advantage in fancy-dress costumes and loo masks.

Juliana, though vaguely aware of the party's imminence, had given little thought to it. She had helped her cousins with their costumes, but had not troubled to try to provide herself with one; and now she was glad she had spared herself the pains, for it was made plain to her by her aunt that, being in disgrace, she was not expected to attend. This was no particular blow to her, since she was very certain that neither Captain Davenport nor Count van Welcker had been invited, and if Sir Groby were recovered enough to be present, she had no wish to encounter him.

She passed the morning of that day tranquilly enough, in a small chamber known as "the young ladies' music room," embroidering fleurs-de-lis on the costume of Miss Ardingly, who had chosen to attend the Masquerade in the character of Jeanne d'Arc—a singularly unsuitable choice, reflected Juliana, for a lady who was in her sixties, and had a nose and chin like a pair of nutcrackers. Miss Ardingly occasionally stepped in to see how Juliana was progressing, but was called away with equal frequency to give advice about floral arrangements, write the place cards for the dinner before the ball, and attend to numerous other details.

A Court hairdresser had been bespoken, and was passing the day at the house; Lady Lambourn, Miss Ardingly, and the twins each spent several hours under his ministration, and emerged, Juliana thought, resembling the elaborately caramelized and confected creams that had been served at Ranelagh. Once coiffed, they did not dare move about too much or take part in any activity, but were obliged to retire to their chambers and lean against wooden backrests.

"When I was young all ladies had their hair done once a fortnight," sighed Miss Ardingly reminiscently.

"And then you had to *sleep* on a wooden backrest, so as not to disarrange your coiffure, and you scratched your head with a hooked ivory rod. Fleas were the main problem."

"I should think they must have been," said Juliana thoughtfully, rethreading her needle.

"You had a paper cone for your face and cotton jacket for your shoulders."

"Why was that, ma'am?"

"To keep the powder off you, of course, while you were being powdered! We had blown-glass ornaments in our hair, and flowers in containers of water."

"You must have looked delightfully, ma'am."

Then Miss Ardingly was summoned by the hairdresser's assistant, and hastened away.

Juliana, having finished the Jeanne d'Arc costume, was about to take it to Miss Ardingly's chamber when, walking out into the upper hall, she was astonished to observe the plump elegant form of Count van Welcker ascending the staircase at a leisurely pace, and glancing about him with the most amiable interest.

"Ah, good morning, Miss Paget!" he remarked, executing a graceful bow when he perceived Juliana. "The very person I wished to see. I am so delighted to encounter you! I observe that this house is at sixes and sevens! Nobody was in the hall to inquire my business, but the portals were wide, as they were laying down a piece of carpet on the steps, so I ventured to walk in. Ah—Lady Lambourn's Masquerade tonight, I apprehend?"

"Why—why, yes, sir," replied Juliana, a little embarrassed because of her certainty that he had not been invited. Stammering a little in her confusion, she said, "W-won't you step in here, Count?" and retreated to the little music room. "Though I should inform you," she added, recollecting, "that I am in disgrace and not allowed out, and I daresay that also applies to receiving visitors."

"That is the reason why I am here, Miss Juliana," he replied unexpectedly. "I heard from a friend of mine, Sir Miles Beaumont, who is acquainted with your uncle, that Lord Lambourn was very displeased to learn of your fame as a balloonist and heroic rescuer; Sir Miles told me that Lord Lambourn proposed to *rusticate* you, and perhaps visit you with other penalties? Which is why I came here, to ask if I may help you, or in any way avert his displeasure, for I feel sadly instrumental in this undeserved disgrace that has fallen upon you."

Juliana was greatly touched at this consideration. She felt tears prickle in her eyes.

"Dear sir, this is extremely kind in you. But to tell you the truth, I am not yet so addicted to London that I feel any great distress at the prospect of being sent back to Flintwood. And I am in hopes that my retreat to Hampshire may at least rid me of my unwelcome suitor."

"I would not be too sure of that, ma'am," said the Count. "I hear that your seventy-year-old beau is hobbling about with a plaister on his head, a new and very ill-fitting set of porcelain teeth, and a vengeful light in his eye. True, once you have left town it may be out of sight, out of mind—but I would not depend upon it. I am wondering if another solution to your problem might not prove more satisfactory and permanent."

"What might that be, sir?" inquired Juliana, surprised, and greatly dismayed to learn that Sir Groby was so soon recovered. She wondered very much what other solution the Count might have in mind.

To her astonishment he now went down upon one knee.

"Ma'am, I fear that this proposal does not come amid the romantical circumstances which I know you prefer, and indeed deserve," he said, taking Juliana's hand in his, and casting a hasty glance back over his shoulder to make certain that the door was closed, which it was. "But believe me, my dear child, although aware that I cannot in any way aspire to your ideal of the English gentleman—of which I recall the description most vividly—yet I have so sincere a regard for you, and so keen a sympathy for your situation; I so deeply admire your amiable virtue and the elegance of your mind—not to mention the inexpressible charm of your air and countenance—damme, I have lost the thread, where was I?"

Juliana, though exceedingly astonished, could not help laughing.

"You have so sincere a regard and keen a sympathy for me," she said obligingly, "that—?"

"Ah, yes, thank you, that was it. That, in short, Miss Juliana, I think you the most charming of your sex, and, although you may have heard that I am not a marrying man, I find myself impelled to consider changing my state, and must now hazard my fortune in one momentous question. Dear Miss Juliana! I believe that through life, as in that damned uncomfortable balloon, we should deal extremely together.

May your devoted servant have the honor to shield
you from further harms and difficulties—to nourish
and cherish you—in short, to call you his own? Will
you be mine, Miss Paget?"

Juliana would really have preferred to put a period
to this speech the moment she saw whither it was
tending, but it had been impossible to interrupt the
Count, once he was in full flow; she had not had the
heart to cut him short.

But now she quickly said, "Dear sir, you are all
goodness—all consideration! I cannot express to
you how deeply I feel your generous kindness. But
although I look upon you as one of my most trusted
friends, I do not entertain for you those sentiments
which—which I would wish to feel towards the man
I married. You are not—you are not—"

Count van Welcker—he was still upon one knee—
looked up at her resignedly, with a rueful grin upon
his good-natured countenance. He heaved a sigh.

"*I* know! I know how it is! You need not be at the
pains of explaining to me, Miss Juliana. I do not in the
least resemble King Charles the First—is not that it?"

Laying a hand upon the arm of a chair that stood
beside him, he had begun helping himself to his feet,
when he suddenly let out such a furiously loud yell—
"*Godverdomme!*"—that Juliana started back in horrified
amazement, and Fitton, the butler, who had been
passing the door with a tray of cut-glass decanters,
dropped the whole load upon the stairway. Servants
came dashing from all directions, and two footmen
burst open the door.

"Oh, sir! What can be the matter?" exclaimed Juliana.

"What's going on here?" cried one of the footmen, regarding the overturned chair, Miss Paget pale and startled, and the foreign gentleman furiously wiping his bleeding hand.

"What's going on? Why, nothing, nothing at all," replied the indignant Count. "Only Miss, here, as usual, has left her bodkin sticking in the arm of the chair, and it has run halfway through my palm. Here—pull this out, will you?—the damned needle is so slippery with blood that I can't get any purchase on it!"

A footman's kid-gloved fingers soon had the offending needle removed. Juliana, overwhelmed with penitence and contrition, offered to bind up the wound, but the Count, whose feelings had been considerably ruffled by the occurrence, merely wound his hand in his kerchief, and then said he had better get out of there before he fell prey to some other hideous mishap. Juliana begged his pardon over and over, thanked him for his good opinion of her, and bade him a most friendly farewell. "Indeed, I cannot apologize enough, sir!"

"No, indeed you cannot!" he replied.

"My grandfather also complains of the fault."

"You would certainly have to shed *that* habit before I married you, I can tell you! But now, my dear Miss Juliana, will you do me a kindness—will you make me a promise?"

"Anything that is within my power, sir."

"If you are ever in difficulties—remember that you can always turn to me. I mean this seriously: I am your friend, and will stand by you in need."

"Sir, you are truly kind, and I *will* remember—I will seek your help if it be necessary. Only, where should I apply to you? What is your direction? Suppose you are abroad again, seeking more treasures for His Royal Highness?"

"I shall not be doing that for some months after the wedding," he replied. "Prinney will want his friends about him then, if I know anything of the matter! So you may apply to me at the Royal Pavilion in Brighton; and a letter addressed to me there will always be sent on to me."

"I will remember—and I thank you again, sir. There is, perhaps, one kindness," said Juliana hesitantly, "which you might possibly be able to do for me—yet I hardly like to ask it—"

"What is that, my child?"

"Why," she said, rather embarrassed, "are you by any chance acquainted, sir, with Captain Francis Davenport?"

"Davenport, Davenport—to be sure, the name does ring a bell—is he a member of my club?" the Count wondered. "What does he look like—what age of man is he?"

"I suppose, sir, in his mid-twenties; he has a beard, and he—and he looks very much like Charles the First," Juliana faltered.

The Count shot her one very sharp look. "*Does* he indeed? And what is your wish, in respect of this Captain Francis Davenport?"

"Only, sir—that if you *should* come across him—you might, perhaps, very kindly mention to him that I—that I am obliged to go out of London quite suddenly."

All the Count replied to this was "I see!" in very pregnant accents. He then bowed briskly, and was out of the door and down the stairs, just as Lord Lambourn, whose attention had been attracted by the shout and the crash, come to inquire into what was going on. Juliana would have incurred a rare scold for illicitly entertaining a visitor, had not her uncle been too preoccupied in discussing with his butler the catastrophic breakage of his best six Waterford glass decanters.

Juliana slipped away to her chamber and spent the rest of the day musing over this strange proposal. How kind the Count was! For she was sure that he had made the offer only from feelings of obligation: he felt that her name was compromised because he had related her story. He had said that he was not a marrying man, and by now Juliana had heard enough about his reputation to be aware of the truth of this statement. "A delightful cicisbeo, a charming quiz," Miss Ardingly had said after the drive, "but just like the Prince his patron—light-skirts—high flyers— ladybirds—dozens from the muslin company, but never a serious attachment. Once a rake, always a rake, I fear. So there would be no purpose in setting your cap at *him*, child."

"I would not dream of setting my cap at him, ma'am," Juliana had answered indignantly.

Recollection of this conversation made her aware that she had not yet taken Miss Ardingly her costume, and she now made haste to do so. She found the old lady reclining against her curved wooden backrest, laughing to herself over a scandalous novel from France. Her face was covered by a leathern visor to reduce wrinkles, her forehead was wrapped in a bandage steeped in mud and vinegar, for the same purpose, and her eyebrows were thickly smeared over with an unguent of mixed gall water, green vitriol, and gum arabic. She was able to thank Juliana only with the greatest difficulty, since her teeth were covered in bleaching powder; she smelled strongly of Spirits of Ambergris, Otto of Roses, Aqua Mellis, and Cordova Water.

Having no maid of her own, she was happy to accept Juliana's offer to stay and help her dress for the party.

"It is certainly rather hard that you may not attend it yourself, you poor little Cinderella," she remarked, having rinsed her mouth with a breath-sweetening tincture of wine, bramble leaves, cinnamon, cloves, orange peel, gum, alum, and honey infused in hot ashes. "Especially as everybody will be masked. What difference could it make whether you were there or not? Nobody would recognize you!"

"Oh, I do not regard it at all, ma'am," cheerfully replied Juliana. "I am to travel all day tomorrow, so may as well go to bed early. Besides, nobody will be there that I wish to see. And if Sir Groby is present, I had very much liefer *not* see *him*."

"Augustus is in a fine fret," confided Miss Ardingly, "for it seems the Duke of Clarence has intimated that he may drop in for half an hour—they are neighbors down in Surrey, you know, for Bushey ain't so far from Weybridge, but Augustus would never have dared risk a snub by inviting Clarence—and he is not at all gratified by the honor, I call tell you!"

"Is the duke not respectable, then?"

"Aha! I see you have gauged your uncle's nature to a nicety! No, the duke is *not* respectable—or not above half. He lives with his mistress, Mrs. Jordan, who has four children by previous lovers, besides two or three of his—there never was such a scrambling household!"

Apart from a certain curiosity to see this younger brother of the Prince of Wales, who, Miss Ardingly informed her, had spent most of his life at sea, and made some very extraordinary speeches in the House of Lords, defending the slave trade and urging a speedy end to the war with France, Juliana was not at all sorry to miss the party. Since she was also debarred from the dinner before it, she resolved, once she had seen Miss Ardingly totter off, equipped with fan, handkerchief, snuffbox, patch box, perfume container, head scratcher, and cane, to seek her own chamber and not leave it again. Listening to sounds of laughter and talk downstairs, she occupied herself by packing up her clothes, in readiness for her departure early on the morrow.

Presently the strains of music came up from below. Juliana decided that she might as well go to bed; the music, she hoped, would lull her to sleep, and assuage the pangs of hunger which she had been feeling for the past hour.

But just then there came a tap at the door. Juliana called "Come in!" thinking that perhaps one of the servants might, at this late hour, have remembered her and thought fit to bring her a tray of supper.

Greatly to her astonishment, however, it was Fitton, the butler, with a message: "His Lordship wishes you to attend him in the Blue Saloon, miss."

"Good gracious, whatever for?" exclaimed Juliana, in the liveliest astonishment.

At this moment Fitton's stately form was pushed aside by Lady Lambourn herself, looking exceedingly put out; she carried a dark-blue domino with a half-mask over her arm, and exclaimed, "It is the *most* vexatious thing! If I had had any notion Clarence would take such a quirk into his head, I should somehow have contrived to have packed you off today; here, child, put this on—for it will look excessively odd that you should be in day dress when all the world is dressed up for the Masquerade," and she proceeded to drape Juliana in the domino, before giving her a push and saying crossly, "There, run along now! Make haste!"

"But why, ma'am?"

"Never mind—go to your uncle!" Still wholly puzzled—and very apprehensive that this might have some connection with Sir Groby—Juliana ran down the stairs to the first floor, where the ballroom and reception rooms were situated. The whole house throbbed with music from the band of the Grenadier Guards, Lord Lambourn's old regiment. The rooms were all illuminated by colored lamps, which made the variegated costumes of the guests appear even wilder and more grotesque. Juliana saw Spaniards, chimney sweeps, Turks, night watchmen, orange girls, gypsies, devils, harlequins, haymakers, milkmaids, and Sultanas, strolling, dancing, promenading, and posturing.

On her way along to the Blue Saloon, as she passed a dimly lit alcove, she was suddenly riveted by hearing the tones of a voice that, in some curious, tantalizing

way, seemed to recall her past life, Italy, her years with
her father in Florence.

"If you do not do it tonight, I shall think you abominably poor-spirited!" this voice was saying harshly.
"Why do you delay? All circumstances favor you!"

"Hush! It is too soon!" protested the second voice,
in a much lower tone, hardly above a murmur. "To
press on too fast now might ruin all—besides, it would
lack artistry."

"*Artistry?* Numbskull! Who asks for artistry?"

"I require it," murmured the other voice, soft and
dulcet. "Besides, if I go there—"

"If you go there—*I* know why you wish to go
there! To see that Tillie, or whatever the creature calls
herself—" Juliana moved on, wondering why the first
voice, with its harsh, angry cadences, had struck such
a chord of memory; it seemed connected in her mind
with some sad occasion, some time of crisis…

Lord Lambourn met her in the doorway of the Blue
Saloon. He was not in masquerade costume, but clad
in the most formal black evening dress.

"*There* you are, child! Why in the name of heaven
have you been such an age? His Royal Highness
wishes you to be presented to him—!"

Utterly astonished at this unlooked-for occurrence,
Juliana advanced into the room, where a small group
of persons surrounded a fat, red-faced figure wearing a bottle-green-and-claret-striped silk jacket and
breeches, silk stockings, a dazzlingly embroidered
waistcoat, and such a profusion of epaulets and medals
that the upper part of his dress seemed quite smothered
in gold.

Dropping into her best curtsy, Juliana noticed that one of the royal stockings had a great rent in it.

"Hey-dey! So this is the little miss—the dauntless lass who's the toast of the town?" said a loud, cheerful voice. "Well, well, missie, let's have a look at ye— push back your hood, let's see the cut of your jib!"

Rising up and obeying this instruction, Juliana was just able to observe, from the corner of her eye, Lord Lambourn's expression of icy outrage, but most of her attention was concentrated upon the Duke of Clarence. She could well understand how he had earned his nickname of Old Tarrybreeks, for he did have the look of a red-faced sailor; but there was something open, honest, yet gay and mischievous about his round weather-beaten countenance which she could not take in dislike.

"By gob!" he exclaimed, inspecting her up and down. "She's a well-favored little craft, i'n't she, Lambourn? Casts those bucktoothed, potato-jawed twins of yours into the shade, hey? Here, you"—he broke off to say to a footman—"scamper off and bring me a glass of champagne, I'll drink Miss's health. And—hearken—bring a glass for Miss too! So, I hear, miss, that you saved my brother's equerry, van Welcker, from a deuced near squeak with those Frenchies? Hang me! I wish I'd been there to see! It sounded like a monstrous fine lark. And then you flitted across the Channel together like a pair of stormy petrels, ha, ha! My brother is much beholden to you for saving van Welcker, lassie! He could ill afford to lose a friend like Frederick, let alone as pretty a set of Sèvres chamberware as I've seen this seven year. He'd be delighted to see ye at Carlton House, I dare swear! And, bless me! You must come down to us at Bushey! I'll get Mrs. J. to send you an invitation."

Lord Lambourn's face set into a rigid mask at this suggestion, but Juliana, curtsying again, replied. "Your Royal Highness does me great honor, but I believe I must forgo the pleasure. My visit to London terminates tomorrow."

"What? When you've not seen half the lions?" cried the duke. "Bigod, Lambourn, this is a devilish misman-aged affair! Why does not Miss remain longer?"

At this point the champagne arrived, and the duke gulped down a glassful, saying to Juliana, "Here's to your bright eyes, midear!"

"Thank you, sir," said Juliana, sipping from her own glass.

"Your Highness," said Lord Lambourn in a stran-gled voice, "my niece's grandfather has need of her. She is obliged to return to Flintwood."

"Hang me, why can't the old gentleman manage on his own? Where does he live—Hampshire? Oh well, I daresay Miss could put on sail and tack over to Brighton for a visit—or to Bognor—George spends a deal of time there with Lady Jersey!"

Endeavoring to suppress his evident feelings as to the utter ineligibility of this scheme, Lord Lambourn signaled with a motion of his head to Juliana that she should now withdraw. She therefore curtsied a third time and bade His Highness good evening.

"Burn me, but she's as neat a little pinnace as I ever set sail in, Lambourn," exclaimed the duke loudly, before Juliana was half out of the room, "and, now

I've seen her and can describe her to George, I'll be hoisting anchor myself, for I promised to look in at the Charlevilles' ball. Here, you! Run and see for my carriage! Where are all my rascals of servants? I shall be devilish late. But I will take another glass of champagne before I go."

Pulling the hood of her domino over her face once more, to avert the possibility of being seen by Sir Groby, supposing him to have come to the Masquerade, Juliana slipped unobtrusively through the laughing, jostling, masked crowds, and made her way toward the supper room. It had occurred to her that, since plainly no servant was going to be bothered to attend to her this evening, if she wished to avoid going hungry to bed, she had best forage for herself. No doubt there would be a tart or cake, something that she could carry up to her chamber.

The supper hall, in normal times the family dining room, lay ravaged and empty, its candles guttering in their sconces. Carcasses of turkeys and geese were picked clean, crumb-strewn plates were scattered everywhere, the great dishes that had contained jellies and syllabubs now held hardly a drop. Searching through the debris remaining on the white-spread tables, however, Juliana was able to find a small but sufficient repast—a roll, a chicken leg, a few grapes; and, having piled these on a plate, she was retreating through a service door and about to slip up the back stairs to her room, when she was startled by the sight of the masked figure of a lady wearing a Spanish costume with mantilla, comb, and fan, who had glided silently into the supper chamber and, thinking herself unobserved—for Juliana was in a distant and shadowed corner—moved swiftly to the mantelpiece, where she proceeded calmly to take from their velvet-lined case six little gold-framed miniatures, which, Juliana was aware, were among the most prized of Lord Lambourn's possessions. The unknown masked lady briskly dropped them into her reticule and then quitted the room again in the same speedy and silent manner.

Juliana gasped with horror. Setting down her plate, she ran after this audacious thief, and was in time to see her descending the main staircase. Coming up the stairway at the same moment was Fitton, the butler, and Juliana immediately accosted him.

"Fitton—oh, Fitton!" Remembering that she was disguised, she pushed back her hood. "It is I—Miss Juliana. You see that lady at the foot of the stairs, dressed as a Spaniard? She is just going into the ballroom. Two minutes ago I saw her take my uncle's little Fouquet miniatures from their case! She has them hidden away in her reticule!"

At first Fitton was suspicious, doubtful, very unwilling to believe Juliana, but when she showed him the empty velvet case he muttered, "Mercy on us, miss! What's to be done? I can hardly accost the lady—His Lordship cannot abide any to-do or scandal."

"No, but I think you must tell my uncle, Fitton—I am certain he would be in flat despair at the loss of his miniatures. I have heard him say he values them above everything in the house. You had best inform him directly, in case the lady slips away before the end of the ball."

"Yes, miss," said Fitton, looking at Juliana with a certain respect, and he hastened off to find his master. Juliana, having done what she could but hoping not to be involved in the distasteful business, turned back toward the supper parlor, intending to retrieve her plateful of food. She had gone but a few steps when she heard herself addressed in soft but urgent accents.

"Miss Paget! Miss Juliana! May I have the honor of a word with you?"

Glancing round in surprise, momentarily forgetting that she had again pushed back her hood, she saw a black-visored chimney sweep, carrying his sack and brushes.

"Why, I thank you, sir," she said, laughing, thinking that it was some young gentleman who wished to dance with her. "But I am in no need of having any chimneys swept and must hold myself excused!"

So saying, she pushed her hood back into position and was about to run up the stairs again when he caught her by the hand.

"Pray, pray, hear me but one moment!" he begged, and, leading her aside into a niche at the head of the stairs, he slipped aside his mask for a moment and revealed the handsome features of Captain Davenport. "Why!" she exclaimed. "Captain Da—!"

"Hush!" he adjured her. "I am trespassing on your aunt's hospitality, for I received no invitation to her Masquerade. Yet, hearing that you were so soon to be cruelly reft away from us, and returned to rustic seclusion, I could not forbear coming to make my farewells!"

"Oh!" cried Juliana, now somewhat confused and embarrassed, for, thinking the matter over during the day, she had come to the conclusion that she had acted in a rather forward and improper manner in sending a message by the Count. "You have seen Count van Welcker, then?"

"I have. He sought me out at the Cocoa Tree and imparted the sorrowful news that you were to leave tomorrow shortly after dawn. I felt I must take this chance of seeing you. But tell me, Miss Juliana, only give me one hope—may I, should occasion arise, may I come to pay my respects to you at your grandfather's residence? Will you permit me to do that?"

"In Hampshire?" Joy and astonishment made her heart beat fast. "But, Captain Davenport, what possible occasion could you have to visit Hampshire?"

"Oh, I have friends residing in Southampton," he replied. "It is the most likely thing in the world that I might have occasion to visit them. Indeed, business affairs may very probably call me thither at no very distant date. In which case it would give me inexpressible pleasure if—do you think your grandfather would permit me to wait on you at Flintwood?"

"Truly, sir, I cannot say for sure—" But, Juliana thought, why should her grandfather bar his door to this perfectly unexceptionable young man? "I believe, if you had come so far, he could hardly deny you," she added hopefully.

"Miss Paget, you give me hope again! London will seem—will seem a dark desert without your presence," he murmured in a low, constricted tone. "But if I may entertain the possibility of calling on you in the country—then there will be a star in my darkness!"

And, carrying her hand to his lips, he saluted it in

the most respectful way—looked in her eyes for a brief instant—then, picking up his brushes, he hurried away down the staircase—Juliana, looking after him, saw him walk between the footmen and out through the front door.

She stood for a moment with her hands clasped together, then, very slowly, began to move toward the upper stairs. But she had ascended one flight only when she heard what sounded like a commotion down below in the entrance hall. There were angry cries, a woman's shrill exclamation, a man's shout, the slam of a door.

Turning in sudden irrational anxiety—what if Captain Davenport had been detected and accosted?—forgetting that she had seen him make a safe departure—Juliana ran back to where she could see the entrance hall over the baluster rail. Guests were now moving toward the main doors, ready to depart, and others, in cloaks and pelisses, were waiting for their conveyances.

The scene that met her eyes at the foot of the staircase was so brief, so swiftly terminated, that, a moment later, she might have thought she had dreamed it—except that she knew she could never have imagined such a tableau.

Fitton, the butler, stood close to the front door, which was shut. Her uncle Lambourn, tall and severe in his black evening dress, was halfway between the door and the stair, holding a black mask in his hand; his whole posture and countenance denoted outrage, disgust, and contempt. In a defiant attitude, facing him, stood a tall woman in black Spanish costume;

Juliana could not for a moment think why her face seemed so familiar; then: "Why—it is the woman from the Ponte Vecchio!" she said to herself in astonishment. "That was the harsh voice I recognized upstairs! It was *she*!"

Next instant the scene had dissolved. The woman, with a glance of loathing at Lord Lambourn, and with some low-voiced remark which made him redden up to his ears, had pulled a handful of objects out of her reticule and cast them scornfully on the floor; then, turning swiftly on her heel, with an imperious gesture to Fitton to stand aside, she had pulled open the front door and was out through it before anybody had time to prevent her departure, even did they wish to do so. But Fitton, with a cry of distress, had gone on his knees to collect the fallen treasures; Lord Lambourn swung round and strode up the stairs without a word. The look on his face terrified Juliana. She glanced around, to make certain that Captain Davenport had not been involved—but there was no chimney sweep in the entrance hall. Then, petrified at her uncle's expression, congested with rage, she turned and silently fled up to her own room. Lord Lambourn had not noticed her; nobody had. As she hurried up the stairs, she could hear a buzz of amazed discussion break out among the departing guests who had witnessed the incident. Juliana had no wish to hear what they said. She had no wish to hear any talk at all about what had happened. If she could have locked her door she would have done so. But no member of the family came to disturb her further that evening.

A horrible thought absorbed Juliana as she made her preparations for bed; how it had arrived, whence it had come, she did not know, but a complete certainty had taken possession of her mind.

"That woman was my mother," she repeated to herself, over and over. "I am sure, I am sure that she was my mother!"

Eight

IT WAS IN VERY SUBDUED AND DEJECTED SPIRITS, NEXT morning, that Juliana started out on her journey back to Flintwood. None of her relatives had thought fit to see her off or say good-bye to her, but this, considering the earliness of the hour, was hardly to be expected. She and Partridge left Berkeley Square at first light, traveling in one of Lord Lambourn's smaller chariots. It was hoped that in this conveyance they would be able to reach Winchester by noon, so that Partridge might be restored to her mistress that evening.

Juliana very much wished that some other escort than Partridge might have been selected for her, since it was very evident that the lady's maid considered it wholly outside the sphere of her activities to be obliged to travel with a penniless, disgraced niece of her mistress, and she lost no time in making the disagreeable nature of her task as plain as she could in every way. Her aspect combined contempt and resentment in equal parts; she adopted a lofty, scornful tone whenever she had occasion to speak to Juliana, and grumbled continually to herself in a monotone, muttering various pejorative remarks about indigent hangers-on, inching place-seekers, grasping toe-lickers, and people who were no better than they should be, all under her breath but just loud enough to be heard.

At last Juliana, thoroughly irritated by this snapping and sneering, said clearly, "Partridge, I assure you that I have had no more pleasure in residing at my aunt's house than you have taken, apparently, in my presence there. I am only too delighted to be returning to Hampshire, and I assure you it was by no request of mine that you were obliged to accompany me. I would far rather have traveled unescorted. I must ask you to be silent."

At this the maid's dislike and resentment broke into active manifestation. "Ho! So you're glad to leave, are you, miss? Well, there's some might believe that, and there's others as mightn't! Trying to creep into your cousins' good books by darning their gowns—I could see through your nasty toad-eating ways!"

"Oh!" exclaimed Juliana, really angry now. "How dare you! As if I *cared* what my cousins thought about me! I did it merely to while away the time."

"A likely tale," muttered Partridge. "Like mother, like daughter, *I* say. And, Lord knows, she was a right slimy twisty Serpent, who'd creep into your bosom and kiss you one moment and bite you with her poisoned teeth next minute as soon as look at ye. Massy me, I don't know how my lady had the heart to let you in the house, with *that* one in London. She'd never 'a done it if the General hadn't given her money. I could have said how it would end! Never did I think to see one day when Master 'ud let that one go free, after what she done—*and* after what she done afore!"

"You mean," said Juliana with a beating heart, "that it was *she*—? Partridge, was that my mother last night in the front hall, with Lord Lambourn?"

She felt she would rather have asked any other person than Partridge, but she had to know.

"That one as swiped Master's pictures?" said Partridge with grim relish. "Ah, that it was! I wonder that you can hold you head up, miss—I do indeed. Lucky for you, you was just leaving!"

"My mother is a thief," whispered Juliana, half to herself.

"She is that—and worse! She's a heartless, wicked Deceiver—throw over one poor fool so soon as she's used him, and on to the next. Not only that—a Murderer, too!"

The emphasis with which Partridge brought out these words was truly frightful.

"A *murderer*?" Juliana faintly said, feeling weak with horror at such terrible disclosures. "Oh no—surely not, Partridge! Murderers are ha—are hanged—she wouldn't be walking around free—"

"Nor should she if she had her just deserts," pronounced Partridge. "Often and often I've heard my lady say, 'That heartless Fiend nearly done in my poor brother—only by the grace of Providence he found out in time.'"

"*What?* How?" faltered Juliana. "How did she do it?"

"Antimony," said Partridge somberly. "Antimony in the poor gentleman's gruel, and he, dear soul, all the time doubled up with gashly pains, never guessing what ailed him. There's naught more diabolicular, to *my* mind, than a wife what tries to kill her husband so she can go off with another man."

"Who did she want to go off with?" wretchedly inquired Juliana. Partridge threw her a baleful look, which also contained a kind of pitying scorn.

"Didn't your pa never tell you *nothing*?"

"No, he did not," said Juliana, with more firmness. "He found it too distressing—he did not wish to talk about her."

"Well, and who's to blame him?" Partridge muttered. "*He* were a decent-enough gentleman—though weak as water, if you ask me. Why should *he* be the one to skulk i' foreign parts?"

"Well, and why should he?" inquired Juliana, drawn, in spite of her own doubts and scruples, to apply for information to this apparently brimming source.

"Why? Acos she were arter *you*, that's why! She'd run off and left you—how flesh an' blood could *do* sich a thing passes all understanding!—then, in course, when matters went awry for her, it came into her head as she'd lost summat as had value, so she was bound she'd get you back."

"Value?" Dismally Juliana recalled Lady Lambourn's disreputable bargain with Sir Groby over the gaming debts. "You don't mean she realized she *loved* me?"

"*Love?* Laura Brooke?" Partridge gave a derisive sniff. "Her heart was as hard as her head—an' *that* were like a chunk o' Stonehenge!"

"Did you *know* my mother, then?" asked Juliana curiously.

"Did I know Laura Brooke? Her an' me went to

the same dame school in Cadnam—only she allus gave herself superior airs, nose in the sky, acos her pa were the apothecary. Then I went to be lady's maid to your auntie, at Flintwood House, while *she* sat in her pa's parlor, too good to work—took singing lessons—went to the Ringwood Assemblies—and that's how she catched your pa, a-singing of a ballad about a saucy sailor lad."

"Yes, he always did love singing," Juliana murmured.

"And *then*, when he'd wed her an' she found there was no money to be wrung outa your grandpa—off with His Highness."

"*What?*"

Forgetting all decorum, Juliana gaped at Partridge, open-mouthed.

"Didn't you know *that*, miss?" Partridge stared back, equally astonished. "Don't you know nothing at *all*?"

"I most certainly do not!"

"Eh, well…" Partridge surveyed her in almost friendly commiseration. "Your pa were such a delicate, thoughtful nice gentleman—ah, he had a sweet nature, he did—" She sighed, and for a moment Juliana wondered bemusedly whether the young Ann Partridge had been jealous of Laura Brooke's fine catch. "I daresay he thought it best to bring you up iggerant of it all—though how a gal as knows naught is fit to deal wi' the world's wicked ways, never ask me! But doubtless that were why he saw fit to live abroad—where you'd not get to hear the talk."

"What—what happened?" Juliana asked nervously.

"What happened? Your pa and ma went to live i'

Lunnon, where your pa might get writing work for newspapers; your pa were friendly wi' Lord Maldon, as had been at Oxford College wi' him, Lord Maldon were a bosom beau o' the Prince's, an' the next thing were, your ma were a-casting out her lures at Prinney, an' the next were, she were a-sitting in his pocket!"

"You mean the Prince of *Wales*?"

"Who else? Handsome young swell he were in those days—'seventy-nine, it would be, the year the twins was born. *You* were in your cradle, wi' old Bessie Hedger, Abigail's auntie, a-looking arter ye. Prince Florizel, they called Prinney in those days, handsome as a picture he were. Now, they say, he weighs sixteen stone!" She gave her sniff again. "I heeard as how he writ your ma eighty-ought letters afore she'd let him have his way—*an'* sent her a lock of his hair. So, in the end—arter she'd tried to kill your pa, an' he'd escaped her wicked wiles—she hitched up her skirts an' off she went."

"With the Prince?"

"None other. Set her up in a house at Kew, he did. *But*, arter a few months, he grew tired of her; that was allus his way; then, 'twas said, she had the devil's own job to wring a settlement outa him— even in those days he were a mean, clutch-fisted cheeseparing niggler—in the end she thought herself lucky to get five thousand down, an' five hundred a year pension."

"Good God," murmured Juliana. Then a horrible thought struck her. "Is there—could there be any possibility that I am—could be—his daughter?"

Partridge surveyed her candidly.

"Well, miss, o' course that's what everyone were asking theirselves."

Uneasily Juliana remembered Lady Jersey's interested scrutiny—Miss Ardingly's sharp stare—Sir Groby's disagreeably probing look—was *that* why the Duke of Clarence had wished to see her—because she might have been his brother's child?

"But now I know ye," Partridge went on, "I be inclined to think that ye favor your pa. O' course ye have brown eyes, an' hisn were gray—but you get your eyes from your ma, Prinney's eyes are gray-blue an' he's very fair-complexioned. They say Madam Dalrymple Elliott's daughter is his child—Miss Seymour—and she bain't o' your complexion—not a bit."

Somewhat relieved, Juliana inquired, "So what did my mother do then? When—when the Prince left her?"

"Took up wi' Colonel Fotherby—an' various others," said Partridge circumspectly. "Then, when the Colonel left her an' the lease o' the house at Kew run out, she went to France an' got her claws in one o' they Frenchy marquees. But she were allus bound to have you back, if she could; several times she applied to my lady for your pa's direction—even writ to your grandpa, I did hear tell—but o' course they wouldn't demean theirselves to answer such a creature's letters. 'Sides, mostly even my lady didn't know where your pa had got to, he never wrote to her above once a year… Once he writ an' said she'd tried to snatch you."

"You mean," Juliana gasped, "my mother tried to *make off* with me?"

Partridge nodded. "Ay—'twas when your pa wore

in Swisserland—she tracked him down an' hired kidnappers to abduct you. But he were too many for her—he took you back."

Dimly Juliana remembered that far-off, long-ago scene—in a boat, on a lake, with mountains all around.

"No *wonder* poor Papa seemed so hunted—so distressed," she murmured, more to herself than to the maid. "And then—and then she arrived in Florence—and he must have known that he was near death—he was afraid that she would assume authority over me after he was gone—oh, what dreadful mischance can have brought her there at such a time? Partridge, I do believe that I am the most unfortunate young lady alive! And *poor* Papa!"

"Fiddlestick, miss," said Partridge bracingly—her feelings for Juliana seemed to have undergone a trans-formation during the unfolding of this tale of vice and treachery—she now appeared quite amiably disposed. "Do not be putting yourself in such a pucker! For sure, you're best out o' Lunnon, in case your ma might try to snatch ye again, but down at Flintwood ye'll come to no harm—the old General will see arter ye, till ye're of age, an' by an' by some decent young gentleman'll come a-courting."

"But—to have such a dreadful parent—to be uncertain, even, of one's paternity!"

"Pish!" said Partridge. "Who cares for that? Why, half her ladyship's acquaintance have misbegotten children. Look at Lady Melbourne! A different father for each child! Look at that lot in Devonshire House! Who knows which belongs to whom? Lunnon society don't concern itself wi' such stuff."

"But my mother is also a thief!"

Partridge scratched delicately at the frizzy hair under her white ruffled cap. Then she said, in a reflective voice, "Ay, she's a thief. But I reckon she steals what she believes she've a right to. She went off wi' a ruby ring o' Prinney's that were worth ten thousand pounds—she said he'd promised her twenty thousand pounds an' she were obliged to take what she could get—Lord! what a rare kick-up about that ring, there were! But he decided he wouldn't prosecute, so it blew over."

"But my uncle's miniatures—?"

"Ah, well—" Partridge rubbed her nose. "There *were* a time—after the twins were born, her ladyship were sickly-like an' poor-spirited for a two, three years—when his lordship an' your ma was monstrous great together—it didn't last, acos she didn't like his pinchpenny ways; she allus said as he promised her more than she ever had of him."

"Good God!" Juliana muttered. "My own uncle! No wonder he was not anxious to have me in his house. Poor man! I am amazed that he—or my aunt—could be prepared to countenance my presence there at all."

"Oh, he be wholly wrapped up in his politics these days," Partridge said disparagingly. "He takes precious little heed o' what goes on about him; an' nothing at all o' the female sect! While as for my lady, if the General was willing to give her five hundred pounds, so she could pay off some of her debts, I believe *she'd* be willing to give houseroom to King Lucifer hisself... But now, here we are, coming in to Winchester, miss; Jem coachman have made famous time, I declare! We shall have a tiddy while to wait, I dare swear, afore the carriage comes from Flintwood, for 'tis not yet noon, so we mid as well please ourselves and have a bit o' nuncheon at the King's Head tavern."

"Good gracious, are we arrived already? I had not thought the journey could pass so quickly," said Juliana.

She gave Jem coachman a crown, and laid out some of the rest of her last guinea on a meal at the inn: a leg of mutton, a boiled batter pudding, a rabbit smothered in onions, and an apricot tart; of which delicacies Partridge also deigned to partake. Then, observing her grandfather's carriage pull up outside the King's Head (which was also the designated place of assignation), Juliana impulsively gave all the rest of her money to Partridge, and thanked her for her company.

"I am sorry to have been the cause of your being obliged to take such a long, tedious journey, Partridge; and I wish you as speedy a one home again."

To her astonishment, Partridge gave her a hearty kiss.

"Bless your thoughtful heart, miss! And I'm sorry I was a mite twitty at first set-out. Now, don't you put yourself in a pelter about what's past, but mind what your grandpa says, and comport yourself like a pretty-behaved young lady, and you'll do well enough."

With which parting advice she skipped up onto the box beside Jem coachman, and the Lambourn chariot, with fresh horses, was soon on its way back toward London.

Juliana reflected that Partridge was the only member of her aunt's household to have bade her a friendly farewell; indeed, the only one who had troubled to say good-bye at all.

Abigail, the little maid from Flintwood, had been dispatched to bear Juliana company, and seemed unaffectedly delighted to see her again. "'Twill be a pleasure to have you back, miss; the house have been uncommon quiet since you went away!" she said.

"How is my grandfather?" Juliana nervously inquired. "Did he seem very angry when he received the news that I was returning?"

"Well, miss, I believe he was in a bit of a taking; thumped upon the table, and vowed his family would all drive him mad among them; but do not you be downhearted, miss, he will soon come about, I am sure."

Juliana devoutly hoped so; and in the meantime she endeavored to restore her spirits by gazing out at the countryside, which became more beautiful with every mile they traveled. Soon they were among the noble trees and great rides of the New Forest; and well before dusk they had arrived at Flintwood.

Juliana, looking out as they drew up before the house, could see no one waiting to receive her on the steps, but she had hardly expected a welcome, and knew she must not repine.

Mrs. Hurdle, the housekeeper, came bustling along to greet her in the hall, however.

"Well, there, miss! Lunnon have put roses in your cheeks, to be sure! Still, Sir Horace is bound you'll be tired arter your journey, so you're to have supper on a tray in your room, and he'll see ye tomorrow. I've a nice broth for ye, and there's a pan of coals a-warming your bed this very minute."

Which Juliana took to be an intimation that the

General could not be bothered with her that night. She did feel tired and stiff, after her early start, and was not sorry to postpone the interview with her grandfather until the following day. Thankfully she partook of Mrs. Hurdle's venison broth and apple pie, bathed in a tub before the leaping flames of her bedroom fire, and slipped between the deliciously warm sheets.

It was plain, next morning, that Lord Lambourn must have written a fulminating letter about the troubles attendant upon Juliana's visit, for the confrontation with her grandfather was every bit as disagreeable as she had feared. The General made no attempt to conceal his displeasure at Juliana's return to Flintwood.

"A fine mull you have made of it, my girl, you and your cork-brained aunt; I might have known I could not entrust such a business to Caroline. Lambourn tells me you have properly disgraced yourself—made yourself the talk of the town. And then that diabolical woman had to turn up—it is the outside of enough. It would serve you justly if I was to wash my hands of you, let me tell you! Going for balloon rides with one of the Prince of Wales's cronies—in heaven's name, gal, what persuaded you to such a piece to folly?"

"Sir, it was the only thing to be done. It was on the journey from France, and my father—"

"Don't tell me about that!" he said very unfairly. "You know I have said I do not wish to hear. Nor about this Macaroni, Count van What's-his-name, who has made your name a nayword!"

"Sir, the Count is not a Macaroni, but a man of sense and feeling. He—"

"Hush, girl! Not a word from you. Hold your

tongue and listen to what *I* have planned for you. I should have handled the business from the start. That notion of your aunt's to marry you to Feverel was quite ineligible—can't imagine why she encouraged *him*. A man of my age—*he'd* never keep you in order! Why, you'd have the poor fellow worn to a raveling inside of a month. No, no, that would never have done."

Relieved that her grandfather was at least in agreement with her on one point, if for the wrong reason, Juliana remained silent as he took a turn about the room, with his hands clasped under his coattails, then stopped to announce, "Since your aunt has failed to find a respectable husband for you, and in order to keep you out of your rapacious mother's clutches, I have resolved to marry you to a man of *my* choice."

Juliana opened her mouth to protest, to object, to bring up the name of Captain Davenport—but her grandfather's look was so threatening, with compressed mouth, flashing blue eyes, and jutting white eyebrows under knotted brow, that, for the moment, she held her peace. And, after all, what had she to say about Captain Davenport? All she possessed were hopes.

The General continued. "There is a distant connection of mine—a widower—son of my cousin Hortense by her first marriage. He was my aide-de-camp in the American war—and *that* was a cursed mismanaged business if ever there was one," he broke off to mutter irrelevantly. "However! I have not seen the fellow since then, but he was a very decent sort, and I believe he has done tolerably enough in government service. He will be just the husband for you, miss! Old enough to stand no nonsense from you—a steady, settled sober man of middle age."

"But, sir," replied Juliana, so firm in her intention of not acceding to her grandfather's plan in any way that she did not trouble to inform him what a very repulsive picture he was painting of this eligible suitor, "if you have not seen this gentleman since the American war, which took place nineteen years ago, how do you know he has not remarried?"

"Amn't I *telling* you? Do not be continually interrupting me, miss! He was married at eighteen— wife died of typhoid fever—striken with sorrow— wouldn't look at another woman—vowed never to marry again."

"Then—if he has taken so firm a resolution—how can he possibly be brought to marry *me*—someone whom he has never even laid eyes on?"

"Don't you worry your head—*I'll* soon persuade him!" growled her grandfather. "I daresay he'll heed what I say soon enough. Always had a regard for the young whelp, and he for me…"

Sir Horace heaved a sudden sigh, thinking of those far-off times in the American war, and for a moment he looked a much young man.

"What is this gentleman's name? And where does he reside?" coldly inquired Juliana, thinking how unlikely it was that by any persuasions a confirmed and disconsolate widower should be brought to marry again. Her grandfather would be disillusioned soon enough; the man was certain to object to the plan; as Partridge had said, there was no need for Juliana to put herself in a taking.

"His name is Augustus Arpel. And as for his residence, I do not know it; I told you, he is working for the government as a courier; they will know where to find him at the Foreign Office. He always had a clever head. Ay, ay, he'll do famously," Sir Horace muttered to himself. "I'll invite a letter to him directly, before I set out for Beccles."

"Beccles, sir?"

"Ay, miss, Beccles. I was to have set off today—a fine deal of trouble you have put me to. On account of your cantrips I was obliged to defer my departure by a day, which was not at all convenient, let me tell you."

And Sir Horace informed Juliana, who listened in some dismay, that Lord Lambourn's express had caught him on the eve of his annual departure to visit his estates in Norfolk, where he proposed staying for five or six weeks.

She was not at all happy at the thought of remaining at Flintwood alone.

"Oh, sir! May I not accompany you?"

"No, you may not, miss! Are you clean out of your wits? A fine time of it I would have with you along, getting in my way at every turn. No, no, you must bide here, sew your sampler and mind your book—learn to ride on horseback—occupy yourself somehow—you had best get Hurdle to instruct you in her housekeeping ways. You have only yourself to thank, after all! Had matters been otherwise you would have been in town accompanying your cousins to all their ridottos."

And the General bustled off to harry the servants about his packing, insult Clegg by rechecking all the meticulously arranged estate papers which he would take with him, and give Mrs. Hurdle unnecessary instructions as to the huge hamper of provisions with which he was equipped for the visit to his manor house at Beccles. Juliana discovered with relief that he would not be passing through London, but would travel by way of Oxford and Cambridge, where he proposed to spend nights with old friends; so that at least he would not hear any more tales of her own and her mother's misdoings in the metropolis.

His train of two carriages, one for himself and one for servants and baggage, departed before noon, and Juliana was left to her own devices in the house, which suddenly seemed singularly large and empty, and notably silent, once the General's energetic presence had been removed from it.

However the sun shone; the birds sang; daffodils were tossing their yellow heads in the formal garden to the side of the house; it would be folly to spend her first day restored to this beautiful spot in entertaining dark thoughts of kidnapping, adultery, theft, and attempted murder; instead Juliana ran upstairs and put on Miss Ardingly's renovated velvet riding habit, then repaired to the stable, where she told Goatcher, the head groom, that she had her grandfather's permission to learn to ride on one of the quieter horses, and asked which he would recommend.

"Bless you, missie, the powny that rolls the lawns and drives 'ud carry you a fair treat while you're a-learning, and he's mild an' biddable as an old kitchen table. I'll have him saddled up in the shake of a lamb's tail."

So the pony was brought out, and Juliana happily spent the rest of the day walking, trotting, falling off, laughing, and remounting; by dusk she had three times risen to the trot, and was stiff, triumphant, and exhausted.

"We'll have ye out cubbing, come autumn time, missie," said Goatcher. "Now you'd best go and have a bath and ask Mrs. Hurdle to put some of her bean-flower essence in it, else you'll be eating your breakfast off'n the mantelshelf!"

While Juliana was eating her solitary supper that evening, Mrs. Hurdle said, "There, missie, I clean forgot, in all the scuffle of Master's going, there's been a letter as came for ye two days agone; since you was expected home, we kept it for you."

Captain Davenport! was Juliana's first hopeful, joyous thought; but when she opened the folded paper she saw that it was signed "*John Murray*" and was from the publisher's office in Albemarle Street. The writer expressed his great regret at having been absent from the office on the occasion of Miss Paget's visit, and his grief at the news of her father's untimely death; went on to praise *The Vindication of King Charles I* in terms of the most unqualified enthusiasm; hoped that if Miss Paget herself ever considered taking pen in hand to formulate some literary or historic essay, she would honor Mr. Murray by allowing him to be its first reader; and lastly begged her to accept the enclosed draft, which was moneys outstanding on the last book by Mr. Charles Elphinstone; the advance of the new book would be prepared and ready for forwarding during the next few weeks. "Your esteemed father's life of Villiers sold very well," Mr. Murray concluded, "and I am very certain that this new work will do even better."

Out from between the pages fluttered a draft for eight hundred pounds!

Juliana was so astonished by this that she sat for many minutes regarding it in silent amazement. Was this, she fleetingly wondered, the reason for her mother's persistent interest—the wish to profit from her ex-husband's works? But, no, that seemed too improbable. She showed the note to Mrs. Hurdle, who presently came to take her tray.

"Look at this, Mrs. Hurdle! It is money that my father earned by his book writing!"

"Well, there, miss, fancy that! He always was a clever one, the young master. Mr. Clegg will cash that for you, I daresay, and then you can buy yourself a new pelisse. I wonder that your auntie never saw you properly fitted out while you was in town."

"Oh, my old one will do for down here," said Juliana.

However, she did take the draft to Clegg, who promised to cash it for her at a bank in Winchester, and meanwhile gave her fifty pounds on account.

"Though what I will do with fifty pounds down here," Juliana said, laughing, "it has me in a puzzle to imagine!" However, she tucked the notes into a pocket which, country-fashion, she wore under her skirt.

Several days now passed in peaceful occupations: Juliana continued with her riding lessons, helped Mrs. Hurdle mend the household linen and make new aprons for the maids, picked spring flowers in the garden, walked in the forest, and read extensively in her grandfather's library. She could see, now, where her father must have acquired his taste for history; the library at Flintwood was singularly well furnished in that respect; some historically minded member of the family must have expended great pains in acquiring an impressive number of volumes, and Juliana happily spent her evenings in this room, climbing up and down the steps, candle in hand. The only volumes lacking from the collection, she sometimes sadly thought, were her father's own works.

On the fifth day, as she was trotting the garden pony across the grass sward at no great distance from the house, and was endeavoring, without success, by means of thumps from a hazel wand, to persuade him to change his heavy trot to a canter, she noticed a horseman coming up the drive. He came closer; she could recognize him now; it was Captain Davenport! Seeing her, he took off his hat and waved it; then turned his horse in her direction. So they met in the middle of the grass.

"You see me as yet a very indifferent horsewoman!" Juliana said, laughing, to cover the excited thumping of her heart. "However, I persevere, and my *will*, at least, is quite as strong as the pony's; I am in hopes that after a few months I shall make him mind me well enough to canter... But, Captain Davenport, what brings you here? I had thought you fixed in London."

"*You* bring me, dear Miss Juliana," he replied, his ardent gaze fixed on hers. "I felt that in London, without your nearby presence, I was but half alive; so I posted down to visit my friends in Southampton, and have lost no time in riding over to see how you did.

Tell me your news? Were you kindly received by your grandfather? Was he displeased at your return? Will he receive *me*, do you suppose?"

Juliana explained that her grandfather was from home, away in Norfolk. Captain Davenport's face fell very much at this intelligence.

"In that case," he said doubtfully, "as you have no chaperone, perhaps it will not be correct in me to call on you?"

"Well, I can see no harm in our riding up and down here," said Juliana hopefully. "I daresay all the servants have their eyes glued to the windows, so they can see that we are behaving with perfect propriety."

A smile touched his features; but faded again. "Dearest Miss Juliana! I love your sportive wit," he said. "But, in truth, I deeply regret the General's absence. I had hoped—I had planned to speak to him—" He paused, looked at Juliana, and said simply, "My most earnest wish was to ask your grandfather if I might be permitted to pay my addresses to you. It cannot have escaped you, Miss Juliana, that I entertain those sentiments towards you which—which are not sufficiently nourished by friendship alone! My feelings are of a deeper nature! I had wished to ask for your hand in marriage."

Juliana blushed rosily. The fact that she was on horseback when she received this declaration, however, helped her retain command of her feelings, which might otherwise have become tumultuous. She drew a deep breath, shortened her reins, and said after a moment, with a fair assumption of calm, "Sir, you do me great honor. And—I cannot deny—that for myself I would be happy to receive your proposals in the most favorable spirit! But I am afraid that with my grandfather it might be otherwise. He has announced his intention to marry me off to a distant connection of his, a widower."

"Damnation!" cried Captain Davenport. It was the first time she had seen him lose control of his temper; she liked him for it. "To marry you—*you*, peerless in your youth and beauty, to some ageing, gouty, snuffy dotard—how *can* he perform such a heartless act?"

"Oh, very easily, I fear," said Juliana. "He is only too anxious to get me settled and off his hands."

"But in that case, do you not think that, if he knew of it, he might be favorable to my suit? If his principal aim is to see you settled?" Captain Davenport asked earnestly. "If I were to write to him, for example?"

"You *could* do that, I suppose," Juliana said, a note of hope in her voice.

"I will do so directly!"

"But I am bound to tell you, Captain Davenport, that I am not at all certain of his approval. He is not disposed to regard me with any favor at the moment, and I think the very fact that you—that you are so obliging as to wish to offer for me—might be enough to put him against the match."

He looked dismayed, but said, "No matter. Perhaps he is not so hard-hearted! I will write forthwith—if you will be so kind as to give me his direction in Norfolk?"

Juliana had been forwarding her grandfather's letters for some days; she said, "It is the Manor House, Staitheley, Beccles."

"I go to write on the instant," said Captain

Davenport, and turned his horse about. Then he paused, took Juliana's hand, kissed it, and inquired with the most respectful devotion, "Until I hear from him—may I continue to visit you? Flesh and blood would find it hard indeed to be so near and remain away!"

"I do not see any objection to your coming," she said after thinking it over. "We can ride here, in the park; there is surely no harm in that?"

"Those words make me the happiest man in Hampshire," he said, and put spurs to his horse.

Juliana rode slowly toward the stables.

During the next three days, Captain Davenport's handsome figure and his dapple-gray horse became a familiar sight in the park at Flintwood. For hours together he and Juliana rode slowly to and fro under the spreading oaks, or across the sheep-cropped turf, to and fro, to and fro, talking about places in Italy that they both knew, about books they had read, poems and plays and writers they admired. Juliana told him about her father's writing, and about the money she had received from John Murray; she discovered that "Charles Elphinstone" was a writer Captain Davenport had long admired, and, while not depreciating the eight hundred pounds, he trusted that she might receive considerably more for the next work, which he was sure deserved it. They discussed the revolution in France, and its effects on the people there. They talked about London society, and about each other: an inexhaustible topic.

On the third day Mrs. Hurdle said rather doubt-fully to Juliana at breakfast time, "Lord knows, miss, I don't wish to pry, nor to deprive you of any harmless diversion, for you seem to me as decent and sensible a young lady as ever stepped, but does Master know of this young gent as keeps coming a-calling? Clegg and me was wondering if it is right for him to be coming here day after day in such a regular manner, with Master away."

"I think we are doing no harm," Juliana told her, "for the gentleman came to my aunt's house in London—and also he has written to my grandfather asking if he may pay his addresses to me." She felt, a little guiltily, that she was prevaricating somewhat here, but the housekeeper's brow cleared at once.

"Sure if the young man's known to Lady Lambourn and has writ to your grandpa, that's quite another matter, miss! I only thought it best to ask, seeing how mighty great you and the gentleman seemed to be becoming with one another. You'll pardon the liberty, miss, I'm sure."

"Indeed I will. You did very right, Mrs. Hurdle," said Juliana, feeling even more hypocritical.

However, later that morning Captain Davenport arrived with a very long face. Juliana could see at once from his bearing that something was greatly amiss.

"Oh, what is it?" she cried, when their horses met, halfway up the drive.

"It is all over!" he groaned. "My hopes are at an end!"

"Why, what has happened—has he answered your letter?"

"He has written—in *such* language—utterly withholding his consent to my desires—to my presumptions, as he calls them; he has pronounced my doom in no uncertain terms; oh, how can I endure it?" he cried out in anguish, and he clasped his head in his hands, but, his steed becoming restive, he was obliged to lay hold of the reins again.

"My grandfather gave you no hope at all?" said Juliana, aghast.

"None—none! He is unalterably set on your marrying this elderly acquaintance of his; he has no pity at all for our youth and our tender affections."

"It is strange—it is very singular that he has not written to me also," said Juliana.

"He has done so, my dearest love; doubtless you will receive the epistle tomorrow; in my letter he said that he had written you in the most peremptory terms, bidding you abandon all thought of marrying me and cease having any communication with me. You are to dismiss me from your thoughts."

"Heaven help me, how am I to do that?" cried Juliana. "I must be obedient to my grandfather—I owe him my physical duty—but my thoughts, my affections, are my own, and they will forever be yours, my dearest Francis! Even wed to another, I shall never, never forget you."

And she fixed her eyes upon his grave and handsome features, as if determined to learn them by heart. A miserable silence ensued, of no short duration.

"There is but one thing," said he at last, in a hesitant manner, "that we might do—but no, I dare not suggest it."

"What is that?" she asked eagerly.

"You may not like it, my dearest—indeed, I am sure you will not—but I see no way out of this coil otherwise. *You* will be married off to this aged stranger, and *I*, for the rest of my days, must eat out my heart with longing for my lost love."

"What are you suggesting?" said Juliana with a beating heart.

"Why, that we should travel to Scotland and be married there—that we should elope."

"Elope!"

"I do not, in the general way, approve of such head-strong, indecorous, precipitate behavior," said he gravely, "but in the present circumstances, what other course have we? Your grandfather is not to be persuaded! Yet, after all, I am engaged in a respectable calling—I come of an old and well-established family; I am able to support you; there can be no real objections to our marriage; and, once it is an accomplished fact, I hope that the old gentleman may be brought to accept it readily enough. It is only that he has taken this obstinate notion into his head—as old men will!—that he wishes you to marry this friend of his, I daresay a most unsuitable *parti*; once he is obliged to set this scheme aside, there is no reason in the world why he should not countenance our connection."

"No, you are in the right," said Juliana after some reflection. "Little though I like it, I fear that an elope-ment is the only solution for us."

Captain Davenport's eyes sparkled. He said, "You agree? You really mean that? Too good—too excellent creature! I am unworthy of you, indeed! This readiness to take a step which must affront you—which must be abhorrent to your sense of propriety—makes me admire you—nay, worship you—all the more!" And he raised her hand to his lips.

"But how should we set about it?" Juliana inquired,

doubts and scruples now beginning to rear themselves in her mind. "Is it, for example, really necessary to travel all the way to Scotland?"

"I fear it is—for you are a minor, my love, are you not?—and no marriage performed in this country without your guardian's consent will be legal. I know, my sweetest angel," he said, "you are distressed as to the impropriety of our undertaking such a long journey together before our marriage—and indeed, it is not at all what I like myself. Every feeling must be offended at the thought."

"I own, it *is* that aspect of the scheme that troubles me," Juliana said. "My grandfather would be so afflicted if I committed such an impropriety, and I cannot bear the thought of his distress. Already he deems me a hoyden, and this would confirm his worst misgivings about me—might, indeed, incur his lasting displeasure. Which would grieve me, I must confess! If only there were some lady, some person of repute and discretion, to whom we might confide our problem; in whose company I could make the journey north, and then meet you at Gretna."

She thought wistfully of Miss Ardingly. But Captain Davenport exclaimed, "Why, what a muttonhead I am! My sister! She would answer capitally."

"Your sister? I did not know that you had a sister."

"Oh, she is the very pink of married sobriety—I hardly ever see her! She lives with her husband at Horsham. I will take you there, you may remain with her as long as it takes her to ready herself for the journey north, and then we may all three travel to Scotland without the least indelicacy."

"Yes, that would certainly answer," said Juliana, her hopes beginning to rise. But then she added in a graver tone, "Only, do you think your sister would be willing to set out for Scotland at such short notice?"

"To be sure she will! She delights in a frolic."

"What about her husband—her children? She can hardly leave them so suddenly."

"Children she has none, and as for her husband, he is a sad stick, and spends all his time cultivating his fields—he will hardly notice her absence."

This plan certainly appeared to resolve all their difficulties, and, once agreed on, it only remained to fix on the time and decide the details.

"I can hardly drive up to the door for you in a chaise and pair," said the Captain. "How would it be if you were to walk a short way into the forest, tomorrow morning, and meet me at the stone cross which lies a mile to the north of here, on the Winchester road?"

Juliana knew the spot, and agreed that this would be an excellent scheme.

"For I am out-of-doors a great part of the day in this weather, walking and riding and sitting in the garden, so that the servants may hardly notice my absence until suppertime."

"By which hour you may be safe under my sister's roof, if we leave early," Captain Davenport said in a triumphant tone.

"What is your sister's name?"

"Bracegirdle—Amelia Bracegirdle. But now I had best leave you, my own love, and make arrangements to hire a chaise… One last thing—do you think it might be possible, my dearest, for you to assume some slight disguise—say, the garb of a milkmaid or servant girl? Then, if we should be observed along the way—if any inquiry is set on foot regarding your departure—"

"Nobody will connect the milkmaid in the mobcap with the missing young lady from Flintwood," said Juliana, laughing. "That will be the easiest matter in the world, for I have been helping Mrs. Hurdle make new mobcaps and aprons for the maids, and I may carry a pair into the garden without the least difficulty, as if I intended to do my sewing here."

"Capital! Till tomorrow then—at ten sharp—by the stone cross."

"One thing—" said Juliana diffidently. "I do not quite see how I can bring my baggage with me; a cap and apron may be tucked into my pocket, but if I were to walk into the forest carrying a cloak bag, the servants would think it decidedly strange."

"Oh, do not trouble your pretty head about that!" cried Captain Davenport in a buoyant manner. "My sister can lend you what you need for a night—you and she are much of a size—and after that, it will be my delight to rig you out in the first stare of the mode! Adieu, my dear, dear girl—until tomorrow!"

Kissing his hand to her, he galloped away at full speed.

Left to herself, Juliana could not but feel some doubts and qualms—some pangs of conscience and anxiety. If only it might have been possible to marry with her grandfather's consent and approval! If only he could have been brought to meet Captain Davenport and see how exceptionable he was. She was distressed at the thought of her grandfather's disgust. And she detested having to deceive Mrs. Hurdle and the other servants at Flintwood, who had all been most uniformly kind to her.

She spent the evening rather unhappily, composing two notes, one for Mrs. Hurdle, saying merely that she had been called away by a sudden emergency, and one, written and rewritten many times, for her grandfather. This she left in Clegg's office for him to send with the rest of the estate papers.

My dear Grandfather:

It fills me with the deepest Sorrow to be obliged to pen these lines. Only the knowledge that you have already written to Captain Davenport, refusing his suit in such severe and unqualified terms, has brought me to a Step which I must regret even more keenly than you, for besides deploring its Impropriety, I am aware of what Pain it will give you. Tomorrow I set out for Scotland to marry Captain Davenport. Truly, dear Grandfather, he is the most Excellent young man, and if only you could have brought yourself to meet him, I am persuaded that you would have thought so too! I need not refine upon the Respectability of his Connections or station in Life, since he assures me that he gave you all this information in his letter to you. I do most Sincerely believe that, once you have abandoned your scheme for marrying me to your friend, you will find Captain Davenport a perfectly unexceptionable match in every way, and I am in Hopes that you will be prepared to extend your Forgiveness and Blessing to your distressed but ever-hopeful Grandchild.

Grandfather will think me just as headstrong and foolish as my father, she reflected sadly, as she laid this epistle upon Clegg's desk. But at least *I* have not made such a disastrous choice as poor dear Papa! And when my grandfather discovers what a noble and eligible character Captain Davenport has, he must surely relent.

Juliana rose early next morning, but found it hard to partake of any breakfast; a cup of chocolate was all that she could swallow.

"You've no appetite, miss," said Abigail. "You was up too late a-poring over them books in the library. I saw your candle shine! You'd best take a nice walk in the forest—look for white violets and primmyroses."

"Yes, that is an excellent suggestion," said Juliana, feeling that matters were being made almost too easy for her. She put on her worn old pelisse, over the brown worsted dress that she had worn all through France, which was by now quite shabby enough to belong to a milkmaid. In her pocket she tucked an apron and mob-cap, she hung a small basket over her arm and, so equipped, left her grandfather's house.

It wanted still nearly two hours to ten o'clock, but she was far too restless to remain within doors.

The forest calmed her, as she walked quickly and lightly northward along the Winchester road. Tiny vivid leaves were uncurling on the oaks and beeches; the pale yellow of primroses gleamed among mosses and last year's leaves at the side of the track. Birds were shrilling and chattering overhead, and she sometimes caught a glimpse of distant deer and fawns slipping silently between the bushes.

Half an hour's walking brought her to the stone cross where four ways met. Consulting her father's watch, which she wore pinned to her belt, she discovered that she had nearly an hour and a half to wait, so, in order to avoid notice, she retired some distance from the road, and sat herself on a grassy bank, where she could inhale the sharp cool fragrance of the primroses. For half an hour she was very happy in the dappled sunshine. Then, unfortunately, the sun retired behind a bank of cloud, and Juliana began to feel rather chilly. Presently rain set in; a gentle spring rain at first, which increased by degrees to a drenching downpour. By the time Captain Davenport's carriage came into view, Juliana was decidedly damp, for at that time of year the trees afforded but little shelter. However, her lover's face was so radiant at the sight of her standing by the roadside that she had not the heart to point out that he was quite half an hour behind the time specified. He was driving the chaise himself, and jumped down from the box to greet her.

"My dear, dearest creature!" He wrapped his arms round her and swung her off her feet. "I had such a fear that you would not have come, after all! I cannot describe how rejoiced I was to see you here!" He set her down, not appearing to notice how wet she was. "At last we are truly alone together!" he murmured, gazing deep into her eyes, and he set his lips on hers. Juliana could not help being startled, and a little disturbed, at the violence of his kiss. It seemed so unlike him! She had experienced nothing like this! Would Charles the First, she fleetingly wondered, have thus saluted his soaking-wet ladylove in a storm of spring rain, on the high road, at a time when it was critically necessary that they should leave the vicinity without delay? As Captain Davenport's lips explored hers with greater and greater urgency, Juliana, out of breath and swayed almost off her feet, could not avoid the feeling that Charles the First would have comported himself far otherwise. Captain Davenport, she was obliged to admit to herself, seemed today in some way different from her previous imaginings.

At this moment—perhaps fortunately—the passionate embrace was interrupted by a shrill, indignant voice from the inside of the chaise, which called out, "*Do* not do so! How dare you do so!"

"Oh, devil take it!" exclaimed Captain Davenport, relinquishing his hold of Juliana.

She, greatly shaken, turned to see a small dirty face, framed in pale flaxen curls, gazing disapprovingly out of the carriage window. It appeared to be that of a child of three or four years old.

"Who in the world is *that*?" demanded Juliana, in a tone of the liveliest astonishment.

"Deuce take the brat!" he growled. "I had almost forgot her. I thought she was sleeping. Quiet, you!" he called to the child.

"But who is she?" inquired Juliana. "And why have you brought her along?"

"Why," he said, "do you not think it is a clever notion? Persons along the way who see a couple with a child will never think that we are eloping!"

"No—that is true," Juliana was obliged to acknowledge. However, it seemed to her that the complications of traveling with such a small child might well outweigh the advantages. "Whose is she? How did you come by her?"

"Well—in point of fact," he admitted in a lower tone, "I did not bring her expressly for the purpose of deceiving onlookers; she is the offspring of—of a servant of my friends in Southampton who suffered an accident and was unable to look after the brat; so, as I was coming in this direction, I agreed to convey the child as far as Petworth, where some uncle or cousin is supposed to take her off me and carry her to the farm of her grandfather, which lies thereabouts."

"I see," said Juliana. "That was very good-natured of you. But should we not be on our way? The rain is rather heavy; also it grows late, and I am a little afraid of being observed by some of my grandfather's people along this portion of the road."

"Oh, very well," he said rather shortly. "It is not my fault! I was delayed—the roads are so miry that the horses made wretchedly slow work of it. I suppose you had best travel inside the carriage—why in the world did you not provide yourself with a thicker pelisse? Did you remember to bring a cap and apron?"

"Yes—I will put them on," she said, somewhat chilled by his tone.

"Do it in the carriage—if you are so anxious to be off!"

He opened the door for her, slammed it when she had got in, sprang to the box, and lashed up his pair of horses into a quick canter. Juliana, feeling a little low-spirited, sat herself down inside and, with some difficulty, due to the swaying motion of the carriage, discarded her soaked pelisse, and drew from her pocket the cap and apron she had purloined. She tucked all her hair inside the cap, pulled the strings tight, and tied them in a bow on top of her head. The ample cotton apron covered her gown and reached to her ankles.

All of her actions were studied with what seemed acute hostility by the child, who sat curled up in one corner, with her arm tucked through the seat strap. She was a skinny little creature, thin-faced and freckled, neatly enough clad in a gingham dress, white cotton stockings, buckled shoes, and a sunbonnet, but she looked somewhat puny and underfed, and was evidently suffering pain from a spot on her sharp little nose, a large inflamed red carbuncle which looked excessively sore.

"What you doin' that for?" she presently demanded with scorn as Juliana put on the apron. "You can't sweep in here. There bain't a broom." Her accent was somewhat rough, though she spoke clearly enough.

"I am putting these things on in exchange for my pelisse, which was wet," Juliana replied, hanging the latter garment from a hook. "What is your name, my little girl?"

"Shan't say" was the reply, accompanied by a very disagreeable grimace.

"Don't be saucy to the lady," called back Captain Davenport sharply—he could hear their conversation, for the slide window was open. "The child's name is Prue," he told Juliana.

"How old are you, Prue?" Juliana persevered, hoping to overcome the little girl's unfriendliness, but all she had in reply was an outstretched tongue and the words "Shan't tell *you*!"

Captain Davenport, evidently irritated, lashed up his horses to a yet faster pace. The carriage swayed about so much that the child was presently dislodged from her perch and thrown to the floor, where she banged her nose and wept exceedingly. Nonetheless, she furiously repulsed Juliana, with small dusty fists, when the latter would have attempted to comfort her.

"Go 'way! I don't like you! Go 'way!"

"I believe it may be better if you do not drive quite so fast," Juliana suggested to Captain Davenport.

"What now?" he demanded angrily. "First you complain because I am late; and now you say do not go so fast. There seems to be no pleasing you!"

Nine

JULIANA, THOUGH FAR FROM WELCOMING THE PRESENCE of a rude, unfriendly little girl on what ought to have been her romantic elopement, nonetheless felt sorry for the child, and somewhat concerned about her. Plainly some of these repulsive manners might be due to anxiety about what was to happen to her, missing her mother, or pain from her injured nose.

"I daresay you will enjoy visiting your grandfather's farm," Juliana told her hopefully. "Have you been there before?"

"Shan't say."

"There may be ducks and geese; perhaps lambs and pigs—shall you like to play with them?"

No reply—unless a very vulgar noise could be counted as one.

"I am sorry that your mama is ill," Juliana persevered. "What is the matter with her?"

"Tillie? She fell downstairs and broke her leg," called back Captain Davenport, who appeared to be following the conversation with a close ear. "She will be laid up until it mends." He sounded as irritated as if the wretched Tillie had done it on purpose, or as if he himself had undergone the mishap. Juliana supposed that he was now greatly regretting the good-natured impulse that had prompted him to bring the child. He continued to whip along his horses at a punishing pace. The carriage, an old, hired one, was exceedingly drafty; rain and wind blew in through various cracks, as well as through the sliding panel that gave onto the box. Juliana, in her worsted dress, felt decidedly chilly, and was of the opinion that the child, clad only in gingham, must be half frozen.

"Have you no cloak, my dear? I do not believe you should be out driving in just that thin dress and pinafore."

Prue made no reply to this until asked twice over, but at last she answered sulkily, "*Have* got a cloak."

"Where is it, then? It is best that you put it on."

Prue unwillingly pulled it from under her; she had been sitting on it in order to give herself height to see out of the window. Searching about, Juliana discovered an old horsehair-stuffed cushion under the seat, which she substituted for the cloak, earning a scowl, perhaps of surprise, from the child, who muttered, "I ain't a-going to put on that cloak, not whatever you says. That be all torn—and it don't fit me neether."

It was, in fact, not a cloak but a pelisse. Since it was nowhere near Prue's size, and was, moreover, in a sad state of disrepair, Juliana inferred that it had been hastily acquired and thrust in at the last minute.

"Well, it certainly is torn, and much too large for you as well, I can see," she agreed, critically holding it up. "But I believe these faults can be remedied. How very lucky it is that I always carry a needle and thread in my reticule. If I take large tucks down the seams—like this and shorten the sleeves by turning them up at the cuffs—so—and move these buttons across the front—and turn up the hem—which, by good fortune, does away with the worst of the rents—I think it may be made to fit you quite tolerably."

She was accompanying her words by taking the appropriate measures. At first the child deliberately ignored her, turning a hostile shoulder and staring out of the window at a line of grass-covered hills which they were now passing on their left. But presently she wriggled round, and began to watch what Juliana did with a kind of amazed attention.

"Those hills are the South Downs," Captain Davenport called back after a while. He sounded more cheerful. "Now we are in Sussex! Soon we shall come to Chichester, and then it is only fifteen miles or so to Petworth."

"What happens at Petworth?" asked Juliana.

"That is where we leave Prue."

Juliana was relieved that he seemed in better spirits. She had been much afraid that his curt manner meant he was now bitterly regretting the whole adventure but could see no honorable way of going back from it.

However, beyond Chichester—a pleasant old town with red-roofed houses, a tall-spired cathedral, and a market cross like a little round chapel where the four main streets met—his spirits unfortunately received another check. They had been obliged to slow to a walking pace in order to negotiate the cobbled streets of the town, and when Captain Davenport attempted to whip up his horses to their previous brisk speed, one of them made no effort to obey the lash, but continued at a plodding pace, forcing its companion to a similar dawdling progress. A man by the roadside called out, "No use larruping that 'un, measter! 'E be dead lame, surelye!"

Cursing, Captain Davenport descended from the box, and discovered the truth of this statement.

"God rot the swindling scoundrel that hired me this wretched turnout!" he exclaimed in a passion. "Now what's to be done?"

Juliana, who had just hastily finished cobbling together little Prue's pelisse by turning up the hem with very long basting stitches, now laid the coat on the seat, opened the stiff door with some difficulty, and, joining Captain Davenport, agreed with him that the horse was not fit to go any farther.

"But look," she said, "is that not an inn, a little farther along the road? Yes—I can see a sign, the Coach and Horses. Surely they might be able to furnish us with another horse? How fortunate we are that the mishap occurred so close to a source of help."

"True—I suppose they may have a horse," agreed Captain Davenport, slowly and doubtfully. He turned to look at Juliana. For the first time in several hours, his engaging smile lightened the harassed, irritable expression that had overhung his countenance. "But—the difficulty is—you will think me a wretchedly unhandy conspirator, my dear, by the fact is that it is pockets to let with me—I used up my last five guineas hiring this accursed rattletrap and spavined pair, and shall not be able to lay my hands on any more blunt until we reach Pet—until we come to my sister's."

"Oh, if *that* is all your worry," Juliana said, relieved, "you may set your mind at rest, for I have some money on me, enough to hire another horse, I am sure."

"You have?" His face cleared wonderfully. "My dearest angel, I might have known that I could depend upon you!"

The matter was soon arranged. Captain Davenport led the equipage, at a walking pace, as far as the inn, where the landlord engaged to supply them with another horse in five minutes; there was one out at pasture, he said, that would take the gentleman fifty miles without turning a hair. The new horse having been brought and put to between the shafts, they were soon on their way again.

Hitherto they had traveled in an easterly direction, along the coast, but beyond the Coach and Horses they turned north, inland, and soon began to ascend the grassy gentle slopes of the South Downs. After climbing several moderate hills, they reached one that was decidedly steep; Captain Davenport requested that, in order to spare the horses, his passengers should get out and walk up. This Juliana was very ready to do, for the rain had now ceased, and she welcomed the prospect of a walk to warm her up. Little Prue, however, was very reluctant to get out. She did, indeed, agree to put on her mended pelisse, and even surveyed herself with some approval, but at the order to walk she cried and whimpered and screamed that she did not wish to walk, hated walking, detested walking!

"What difference can her small weight make? Let her stay in," suggested Juliana, but the exasperated Captain Davenport, muttering something about spoiled brats, forcibly dumped her in the road, whereupon she sat down, flatly refused to stir a step, and had to be dragged to her feet with a box on the ear by the furious captain. He then stamped away to lead the horses, leaving the disciplining of Prue to Juliana, who, by alternate cajoling and sternness, by telling stories, lavish promises of sugarplums when they should reach Petworth, and an occasional sharp reprimand, finally managed to persuade the child as far as the top of the hill.

There, jigging about uncomfortably on one leg, she complained that she wished to go to the closet.

"Well, there's no closet here," said Captain Davenport impatiently. "You will just have to go behind a bush. Run behind one of those bramble clumps over there. Hurry up!" He pointed to a green slope set about with may trees in blossom. "Heaven deliver me from ever again traveling with a child," he growled as Prue went off in a dawdling, reluctant manner, with many suspicious glances back over her shoulder.

"Poor child, she probably fears that we may go off and abandon her," said Juliana.

"I would like nothing better! Hey, but I'm weary," he added, throwing the reins over a signpost that stood where four white chalky tracks met on the hilltop. "Let us sit in the carriage until that ill-conditioned imp reappears."

Juliana would have preferred to look about her at the grassy, bushy slopes that curved away in every direction around them, but Captain Davenport, taking her hand, assisted her into the carriage. He jumped up beside her and enveloped her in a passionate embrace, pulling her down beside him on the seat.

"Stop—stop—oh, pray, stop!" gasped Juliana, hardly able to catch her breath between his kisses.

"How *can* I stop? It is driving me mad—being so close to you and yet prevented from showing what I feel," he muttered, clasping her so tightly that she feared her ribs might crack.

"Sir—Captain Davenport—"

"Francis, my angel—call me Francis!"

"I do not think we should be doing this until—until we—"

"Hush! How can I help it?" He covered her mouth with his.

In vain did Juliana try to thrust him away. And she was becoming seriously alarmed at what seemed a total inattention to their situation on his part, when help arrived, in the form of a small human whirlwind. Crying, "Do not do that, do not do so!" little Prue scrambled back into the carriage and forced herself jealously between the pair, pushing and hammering at Captain Davenport with her fists.

"Oh, confound you, you hell-begotten little pestilence! Get out of the carriage and stay out!" he growled.

"No, I will not! You are not to kiss that lady!"

"She is in the right—and we should in any case be on our way," hastily agreed Juliana, who had had time to withdraw into a corner of the carriage, retie the strings of her mobcap, and shake her dress into order. "Did you not say that Prue's relations were to receive her at midday? And it is already long past that hour. It is nearly three!"

"Damn them, they will just have to wait!" But receiving a somewhat quelling look from Juliana, he at last jumped sulkily out of the carriage, gathered up the reins, and returned to his box. Juliana had barely time to close the door before he cracked his whip and the carriage started with a jolt.

Now their way lay downhill, down a slope which soon became much steeper than the one they had slowly and with such difficulty ascended. Captain Davenport was soon obliged to put on the drag, to prevent the carriage rolling down on top of the horses, who snorted nervously and slipped on the smooth chalk track. Captain Davenport was too preoccupied with reining back his team to address any remarks to Juliana, who, in any case, was not in a mood for conversation. In fact, she found herself momentarily more distressed and concerned at her situation. She began to ask herself whether she had not committed a terrible blunder in agreeing to this elopement. Captain Davenport seemed to be turning out such a different person from what she had supposed him! Gone were the polished manners, the elegance of mind, the respect, the tender consideration! And I fear it is my own fault, Juliana thought miserably. I myself have wrought this change in him, I have forfeited his respect. How can he look up to someone who has agreed to such a scandalous breach of propriety?

But then she thought: Perhaps he is merely worried and put out by so many things going amiss; when we reach his sister's house, I daresay he will recollect himself, and all will be as before.

She told herself this, but in her heart she was not

certain that she believed it. One fact that dismayed her very much was that she found she could not enjoy Captain Davenport's embraces. Loving him as she was sure she did, she had felt certain that being kissed by him would be the summit of bliss; but it was not. Rather, as she owned to herself ruefully, it was like being gnawed by a hungry dog. But how can this be? she asked herself. Why do I find it so disagreeable? I love him, do I not?

Or do I?

Absorbed in these disconcerting reflections, she hardly observed the couple of small hamlets and smooth green farmland through which they had been passing once the Downs were left behind. But now they came to a narrow stone bridge over a little river, and Captain Davenport, pointing with his whip, called in a relieved voice, "Yonder lies Petworth— see the church spire? A mile up this lane, and we shall be there."

"How far is it from Petworth to Horsham?" Juliana inquired.

"Horsham?"

"Is not that where Mrs. Bracegirdle resides?"

"Mrs. Br—oh, *Horsham*, yes. It is about another ten miles."

Prue, who had relapsed into silence, now complained that she was middling hungry and wanted her dinner.

"Be *quiet*, you!" Captain Davenport said to her, slewing round with such a savage face that she shrank back into her corner, quite cowed. He must have noticed Juliana's expression, for he added more mildly,

"Forgive me, my angel. I am afraid I have been acting like a bear with a sore head. The truth is, if you must know, that ever since we left the Downs, one of my teeth has begun to ache most confoundedly, and I can hardly stand the pain."

He laid a hand on his jaw, wincing, and Juliana realized that his face did indeed look somewhat swollen.

"Oh, how shocking for you!" she exclaimed in the liveliest sympathy. "Poor dear, and you have had so many difficulties to bear! I am so sorry for you. But surely there will be a surgeon in Petworth—it looks like a good-sized little town. Do you not think that you should have the tooth drawn without delay? I am certain that you should not be driving in such a state."

"Well, perhaps you are right," he owned, wincing from another twinge. "I will inquire at the inn where we are to meet Cox—where Prue's uncle is to pick her up—if there is a tooth-drawer or barber in the town."

"Yes, I am sure you should do so," said Juliana warmly. Poor dear, how I have been misjudging him, she thought to herself. If he has been in pain all this while, it is no wonder that he has seemed a trifle surly. The only wonder is that he should have wished to kiss me!

After about ten minutes' more driving, Captain Davenport arrived in the main square of Petworth, which occupied an irregular, sloping space round a central town hall, and contained three inns, the Bull, the Half-Moon, and the White Hart. Of these the White Hart seemed the largest; Captain Davenport drove around it into a fair-sized yard at the back, demanded a feed for the horses, and then disappeared into the inn, to make inquiries about surgeons.

Juliana, who had noticed that some kind of entertainment was taking place in the square, suggested to Prue that they should walk round and see what was going on. They discovered half a dozen morris dancers in the middle of a performance, watched by an admiring crowd. Prue's complaints of hunger were soon appeased by the gift of a large hunk of gingerbread off a pie stall, and she stood eating this contentedly enough, watching the antics of the dancers, who wore ribbons on their hats, bells tied to their legs, and held staves which they clacked together loudly as they danced. Twenty or thirty people had by now assembled, and Juliana said, "Look out for your uncle among these people, Prue, my child, and tell me if you see him."

Prue gazed about her rather blankly and shook her head.

Presently they saw Captain Davenport in front of the White Hart, and made their way toward him. He wore a much more cheerful expression, and said, "They say there is a barber and surgeon up the hill in Church Road—a man called Goble. I shall go up to him directly. Can you find some amusement about the town until I return? I daresay it will not take many minutes to have my business attended to. Walk about—look at the shops—watch the dancing. Oh, but could you oblige me with a little more money, my dear?" he asked Juliana. "I daresay a tooth will not cost above a shilling or two."

"Of course," she said, pulling out her purse, and,

with a nod of thanks, he took a handful of money and hurried off.

"What about Prue's uncle?" she called after him, but he did not hear.

"You said as how you'd buy me sugarplums in Petworth," Prue reminded Juliana, tugging at her hand.

"So I did—let us go down this little street, and perhaps we may find a baker's, or a cake shop."

Petworth seemed to be a very small town indeed, set around the top of a hill. Three or four streets leading irregularly out of the central square soon petered away into fields and farmland. The shops were not many or at all elaborate; however, they found a baker who had some toffee apples, and were returning, with Prue wreathed in sticky bliss, toward the main square and the morris dancers, when a voice hailed them.

"Hillo, Prue, my sweetheart! So we meet again!"

Glancing up, startled, for the voice was an educated one, Juliana wondered if *this* could be Prue's uncle. Surely not? The young man who had accosted them wore the uniform of a naval lieutenant; he had a pink face, a merry eye, and yellow curly hair.

"Where's Davvy, then?" he inquired, falling into step beside them, and giving Juliana a friendly grin. He took a large bite from the side of Prue's toffee apple, which made her scream with indignation. She made no answer to his question, so Juliana replied for her.

"He was afflicted with severe toothache, and had to go to a surgeon," she explained.

"Was he, though, poor old fellow? He always has the most confounded ill luck," said the lieutenant, bursting into a fit of laughter. "Oh, well, an aching tooth is soon mended! Hope the barber doesn't have to trim that beard he was at such pains to grow! In the meantime, allow me to introduce myself—Lieutenant Cox, Tom Cox at your service! Prue knows me already, don't you, Prue, for we met on the docks in Southampton last week when you were out with your papa. And *you* must be Tillie," he added, turning to inspect Juliana's apron and mobcap. "Devilish good taste Dav always did have—no wonder he calls you his Sussex Rose—remind me to congratulate him, my dear! But where's the heiress—did she not come up to scratch? Don't tell me all Dav's playacting has been in vain?"

"The heiress?" inquired Juliana, puzzled.

"Why, Miss Moneybags—what's her name, Paget? Don't tell me after Dav grew that Charles the First pair of mustachios and went to so much trouble, that you have not brought her along, just when I've cozened my captain into granting me three weeks' leave, so that I can help you carry her off to Scotland?"

He mistook the stunned look on Juliana's face for one of chagrin, and added kindly, "I'm sure your nose need not be out of joint, my dear, never look so glum! I dare swear Dav will always love you best, but he could not have married you, after all! This will only be a marriage of convenience, though. Even the Prince of Wales does it, so why should not Dav? Once he has his hands on the lady's fortune, and has paid her half to old Madam Horse-face, the mother, I daresay he will be ready to set you up in fine style— you and little Miss Prue, here. Do you fancy a house in Chelsea—or one at Richmond? Hey, sweetheart?

You will be riding behind a team of six gray horses in a few months! But where is the young lady? Did you manage to bring her as far as this without raising her suspicions?"

Finding her voice with an effort, Juliana replied, "Oh, yes. She suspected nothing at all. She is resting—in a private parlor at the inn. The large one in the square—the White Hart."

"What about Davvy's cattle?" Lieutenant Cox wanted to know. "Are they good for another hundred miles or so? Or should I pay them off? I've found a couple of prime steppers at the Bull. But I've no dibs on me, and the old lady would not pay out a penny until she was assured that we had her daughter safe under hatches."

Juliana felt her knees almost failing under her, so faint with horror did Lieutenant Cox's artless disclosures make her. She managed to say hoarsely, "The pair we have come with—are not very good. Perhaps you should take a look at them. They are in the White Hart yard. Pray, where—where is the old lady?"

"Oh, *she* was taking a nuncheon at the Bull," he said blithely. "I told her she had best remain out of sight lest she should scare the bird from covert… Very good, I shall go and cast an eye over Davvy's hacks. Do you come up to the Bull in ten minutes or so, and we may discuss our plan of campaign when old Dav comes from his tooth-drawer."

And, chuckling again at his friend's misfortune, Lieutenant Cox swung off in the direction of the White Hart.

Without waiting an instant, Juliana started away in the opposite direction. She was dazed, almost witless from shock. Her main impulse was that of an animal—to escape from the scene of so many horrifying revelations, to go to ground. Without any conscious plan, she walked up a short street, took a left turn, then a right one, along a grassy track which seemed to lead downhill, out of the town.

"Where you goin'?" grumbled Prue, who had at first been too absorbed in her sweetmeat to pay much attention to their route, but was now approaching the core of the apple, and becoming dissatisfied.

Juliana glanced down. She had almost forgotten Prue, whose hand she still clasped. Now, jerked into awareness, she observed for the first time a strong similarity between the child's eyes and those of Captain Davenport; there was an equal likeness in the structure of brow, nose, and temples.

"Captain Davenport is your father, is he not?" she demanded.

Prue nodded.

"And Tillie—Tillie is your mother? Did she really break her leg?"

"Ay. The doctor set it with a splint. An' Ma cried wi' the pain, an' Davvy was mad-angry, acos she said she was blest if she'd be plagued wi' me when she were laid abed, an' he must bring me with him."

"Do you really have a grandfather in Petworth?"

"Ay, Grandpa Strudwick, over to Hoghurst. 'E beant *in* Petworth… Where we goin'?"

"Out of town… I suppose your father told you not to tell me anything?"

"Ay. 'E said 'e'd larrup me if I so much as opened my gob."

No wonder the child had resented her father making love to Juliana!

Faced with evidence of a deception which must have been carefully laid, going back weeks, if not months—those Charles the First mustachios!—Juliana felt as if the ground were crumbling beneath her feet, as if she were walking in a quaking bog.

He must have planned this all along, she thought. From before our very first meeting. How can I have been such a gull—such a simpleton? How he must have laughed at me up his sleeve!

Her cheeks burned at the thought; she clenched her hands. If Captain Davenport had come in sight at that moment she would have flown at him like a fury.

The most horrible feature of the whole business was that Juliana's mother was also involved. She had supplied the funds for her own daughter's abduction! But why? To what possible end? To extract money for her dowry from Sir Horace? They would soon catch cold at that, reflected Juliana. She was willing to wager that her grandfather would never part with a single penny. His runaway granddaughter had made her bed, he would say, and she must lie on it.

Oh! Juliana thought, clenching her hands again at the thought of his anger—his disgust at the scrape she had got herself into. He would say, "Like father, like daughter," and he would be right! How could she have been such a goose as to let herself be taken in by Captain Davenport?

Now he seemed a hollow sham, through and through.

I must make a plan, she thought feverishly; I must consider what to do.

Instinctively seeking peace and quiet, she had followed the lane that seemed to lead toward the fields. It was wide enough for a cart track and ran between high stone walls. Now Juliana realized with a sinking heart that it was not a way out of the town, but merely led to a house—a fairly new house that must have been built perhaps some ten or fifteen years ago, a little secluded, some five minutes' walk out of the town center. In fact, as they passed a pair of carriage houses and reached a gateway, Juliana discovered that the house was not yet finished: the main, central portion was complete, but scaffolding still enclosed a side wing, and workmen were wheeling barrows of bricks to and fro.

The house faced out over a grassy shelf, beyond which lay a deep green valley. It would be a pleasant place to live, Juliana thought dismally; so close to the town, yet private, with a wide prospect of countryside in front, and a spacious plot of land surrounding it. A formal flower garden had been laid out in part of this area, which was enclosed to the rear by another high stone wall, and lay open to the valley in front. Looking down into the valley, Juliana noticed a path, which led to a bridge over a brook at the bottom. If we could get to that path, she thought, we could leave the town quite unobserved; but how to reach it? A ha-ha wall protected the garden on the valley side; only a couple of feet high inside, it gave onto a ten- or twelve-foot drop beyond.

"Want to see the dancing men again!" whined Prue.

"Hush. I am thinking."

"Want another sweetie! Want to find Davvy!"

"Do not forget," Juliana reminded her, "that Davvy forbade you to tell me anything. When he finds that I know he is your father, he is liable to be very angry."

Prue's face fell. She said, in a quelled manner. "When Davvy larrups, 'e fair lays on. What'd we best do, then?"

"I think I had best take you to your grandfather's house. I shall ask one of those workmen how to find it."

Having reached her decision, Juliana approached the workmen, who now, since it was nearly the end of the day, were beginning to stack their tools and tidy up for the night. She had made up her mind only just in time; another five minutes and they would all have been gone.

"Pray can you direct me to Hoghurst Farm?" she asked the man who looked like a foreman—a stocky, grizzle-haired individual wearing a carpenter's apron over his smock and carrying a bag of tools.

"Hoghurst? Nay, you graveled me there, lass; I'm a Midhurst man myself." He spoke in a friendly tone, but without any particular deference, and Juliana recollected that she was still disguised in the maid's apron and cap. He turned to his mates. "Anybody here know o' Hoghurst Farm?"

"What be farmer's name?" someone asked.

"Strudwick—old Mr. Strudwick."

"Arr! Owd Strudwick's place. A tidy step that be from yurr, maidy!"

"Never mind. If you will tell me how to find it, I shall be very much obliged."

The man who knew the way led her to the garden wall overlooking the valley.

"Fust you goos down an' across Rectory Brook at bottom. Then you goos up the Gog—yonder hill wi' the liddle coppice atop; then you goos down t'other side an' up Lovers' Lane into the Dilly woods yonder." He waved toward a thick mass of woodland which was discernible on the high land beyond the valley. "Then you goos on, a two, three hours' doust, up along through the 'oods, an' ye'll come to a droveway. Goo along it for a spell, while ye can say Our Father three times, slow-like. Then ye must clim up through an oak hanger to your right hand, till ye come atop the hill, an' maunder along, eater-wise, for half a mile, till ye come to a bramble crundle an' two cuckoo gates, set middling close. Goo through the second cuckoo gate, an' along the headland, an' ye'll come to Owd Strudwick's place. 'Tis a liddle daggly owd cottage wi' a mort o' stinging nettled round about."

"I—I see," said Juliana, not a little daunted by these instructions.

"Have ye got it arl queered out, maidy? Now, mind you dooant goo astray in the Dilly woods by the part-ways o' the forrep-land; 'tis easy done; an', atop o' the packway, goo ye *straight* into the hurst, whurr thurr's two-three fodroughs; facing ye; take the one as is dead ahead. Otherwise ye'll be as lost as Owd Lawrence! Will ye mind that?"

"Oh, indeed I will," said Juliana, hoping there would be somebody else to advise her when she had reached this part of the journey.

She glanced across the valley. Already blue dusk

had begun to enshroud the woodlands beyond the little hilltop which her adviser had referred to as "the Gog"; by the time she and Prue were in the woods, true dark would have come. A two- or three-hour walk through the woods, in the dark, with little Prue no doubt whining and complaining every step of the way? Was it feasible? She hardly thought so.

Very unexpectedly, at this point, a new voice accosted her, which inquired in not unfriendly, but authoritative tones, "*Qu'est-ce qu'il y a? Qu'est-ce qui se passe?*"

Juliana and her informant were standing on a broad grassy path, bordered by a yew hedge, which ran alongside the low wall overlooking the valley. At each end of this path lay a small pavilion-like building, and from one of these buildings a lady had emerged; it was she who had called out the question as she approached them.

She was a tall, well-built personage, not in her first youth; she wore a white muslin garden dress over a blue silk under-bodice; a broad-brimmed straw hat was tied under her chin with a blue silk scarf. Under the hat she also had a green silk eyeshade, and she wore long blue gloves and carried a basket of narcissus. She had remarkably thick and handsome auburn hair, braided up into a massive chignon; her eyes were brown, and her strong-featured face, which at present wore an inquiring expression, showed traces of what must, twenty years ago, have been great beauty.

The man who had been advising Juliana turned and explained.

"'Tis the young maid yurr, Mis' Reynard. 'Er wants

for to get to Hoghurst Farm. You goo out by yonder
gate, maidy, that'll take ye down the dene"—and he
pointed to a gate by the pavilion from which the lady
had come. "That is, if Mis' Reynard don't mind ye
a-crossing her garden."

"I—I beg your pardon, ma'am," said Juliana,
abashed to discover that she had strayed into occupied and private property. "I had thought—as the
men were still building—that nobody lived here.
Otherwise I would not have trespassed—"

"*Chut, chut! N'importe pas*," said the lady. "I will show
you the way down. Good night, Boxall. *A demain!*"

"Good night, missus," said the man, pulling his
forelock, and he hurried after his mates, as the lady
turned to escort Juliana to her back gate.

The lady seemed, for some reason, slightly disappointed, and her next words explained why.

"You did not, then, come about the position? I was
so hoping you had!"

"Position, ma'am?"

Juliana had been rather desperately wondering
whether to confide her story to some total stranger.
"I am running away from my mother, who is at the
Bull Inn, and has hired two men to abduct me." How
implausible did that sound! The most likely reaction
would be to hand her over to her mother forthwith.
But at the lady's question her hopes suddenly rose.

"Why, my advertisement for a lady's maid. I was in
hopes, when I saw you, that you were an applicant."

Mrs. Reynard, as the man had called her, spoke
with a slight but unmistakable Parisian accent. Juliana
wondered how a lady from Paris should have taken

up her abode in such a tiny place; but no doubt she, like so many others, was a refugee from the terror in France.

Juliana looked up at the lady's face, and, encouraged by something she saw there—a mixture of humor, experience, and tolerance manifest in the broad brow, wide mouth, strong cheekbones, and twinkling brown eyes—she suddenly came to a decision.

"Madam," she began, speaking rapidly in French, "may I please tell you a little of my story? Will you have the goodness to listen to me for two minutes?"

"*Mais, mon dieu!*" exclaimed Madame Reynard, overjoyed. "Here is somebody who speaks French in the midst of all these peasants. And with a most beautiful accent too! Speak what you wish, my child. I shall be enchanted to listen."

Thus encouraged, Juliana swiftly poured out an abridged version of her tale. She did not mention the names of any persons, but simply explained that she had run away from her grandfather's custody, and discovered by chance that her supposed lover was no lover at all, but had been paid by her mother to abscond with her.

"*Nom d'un nom!* But it is a melodrama! Never did I think to hear such a tale in Petworth." Madame Reynard pronounced it "Petvurrt."

"Now, madame, I was wondering—I have no experience as a lady's maid, it is true, but I know how to do hair, and I am quite skilled with my needle—I would be happy to do anything you asked me, if I might stay with you for a few nights—until you find someone more suitable—and until—"

"Until the *maman méchante* and the false lover take themselves away from this town, *hein*?" said the lady, laughing. "Just now, *sans doute*, they are scouring the streets for you, and may very likely have the constables out searching; better you should come into my house directly, I think, eh?"

"Oh, madame! You will take me? Oh, I do not know how to thank you—"

"*Et la petite ici?* You wish me to take her in too? Or shall we turn her out into the town to starve?" Madame Reynard inquired cheerfully, pinching the cheek of Prue, who had stood scowling like a thundercloud while this incomprehensible conversation had gone on.

"It is a shocking imposition, ma'am, but if you could have her for tonight, I could take her to her grandfather's tomorrow. It seems to be above a five-mile walk from here—I think it would be too far for her tonight."

"So! We decide about that in the morning. For now, come inside, *tous les deux*."

Without further ado, Madame led them round to a side door and into the main part of the house.

"We goin' to stay wi' this lady?" whispered Prue.

"Yes. It is too far to go to your grandfather's tonight," replied Juliana.

Madame Reynard led them into a spacious, handsome room with a semicircular window looking out onto the garden and valley. The furniture was scanty, but French, and very elegant. Looking at it, Juliana was reminded of Herr Welcker, as she continued to think of him. The memory gave her a sudden queer

pang. For who but he could have advised Juliana's
mother to find a decoy so closely resembling Charles
the First? He must have been in the plot too. Oh,
what a blind, naive, gullible simpleton I have been!

The weakness she felt at this disagreeable thought
made her realize, all of a sudden, how extremely tired
and hungry she was; sheer terror and the need to
escape had hitherto borne her up, but now that she
was, temporarily at least, in shelter, she found herself
almost on the point of fainting. It seemed an eternity
since the first hopeful, happy sortie through the forest;
an eternity without any breakfast or dinner in it.

"*Vous avez faim?*" inquired Madame Reynard,
reappearing with wine and biscuits. "Here—a little of
this will do you good. I am happy to say that French
wine still finds its way to Petworth—up the Rectory
Brook." She gave a chuckle. "Now, Berthe will take
the little one down to the kitchen and take care of her.
She is not of you?"

"Madame? No, *indeed*!" said Juliana, taken aback at
this sharp question.

"No, *enfin*, you look too young to be her mother.
Va, Berthe, take *la petite*, and stuff her with *tartines* and
sugar cakes and put her to bed."

Prue was at first highly reluctant to be parted from
Juliana, in whom, by now, she had acquired a certain
degree of trust; but Berthe was such a fat, friendly,
smiling dumpling of a French cook, who pulled a
handful of sugar candy out of her pocket and said,
"*Viens avec moi, p'tite!*" that without the need for any
linguistic exchange, her fears were allayed.

"I have been thinking!" said Madame Reynard,

seating herself comfortably on a handsome ottoman and swinging her feet up with a flash of Valenciennes. She helped herself to a glass of wine and continued. "It would not be at all sensible for you to take Prue to her grandfather's tomorrow."

"Why, madame?"

"Why, what kind of a plotter are you? That is the first place where they will look! But see how fortunately it falls out! They will be asking for a young lady round the town. They may approach some of my workmen. Yes, we will say, a strange young lady with a child was seen; she asked her way to Hoghurst Farm (brr, what a name!). So you must on no account go there."

"I suppose that is true," acknowledged Juliana. "But what is to be done? You cannot wish to keep Prue here, madame. She is the most disagreeable child!"

Madame Reynard laughed. "Oh, well, in that case I will take her over to her grandfather's tomorrow, in my carriage. I can make up some tale—that I found her wandering, that you went up to London on the stagecoach. The main thing is that you should stay close in my house until we are sure your pursuers have left the district."

"Your servants—?"

"Both French. They do not mingle with the townspeople. After a week or two we will let you out—*quite* changed in appearance—take off your cap, child!"

Juliana did so, and Madame remarked thoughtfully, "It may be best to change the color of your hair. Perhaps we turn you into a chestnut-head, like me. Then I tell everybody that the Free Traders have brought over my niece, from Rouen, who has come to live with me."

"Oh, madame, you are too kind. I—I wish that I *was* your niece!"

"*Il n'y a pas de quoi!* I have not been so well amused for years; since Milord Egg began growing old and thinking of nothing but his oxen and his brown bread and vaccinations, my life has become *bien ennuyante*, I assure you. I am enchanted to have you, my child, and mean to enjoy your company to the full. Tell me, how comes it that you speak French so well? Most young English misses do not."

"I was brought up in Geneva, madame, and then in Florence."

"So? You speak Italian too?" she asked in that language.

"Certainly, signora," Juliana replied in the same tongue.

"But this is famous! Milord Egg will want you for a *gouvernante* for his children, but I shall not part with you. You shall be my *dame de compagnie*. We shall read Dante and Molière, and in course of time you shall tell me your whole history—with the names left out, of course, if you prefer it," she said, suddenly changing her lively tone for one of the most kindly solicitude. "You have had a long, fatiguing, and distressing day— all men are deceivers, we know it, we know it, but *tout de même*, each time one of them is caught out in his deceit, we must suffer the same shock and chagrin! Come along, I show you your room, and presently old Berthe will bring you a bowl of tisane. Then you weep away your troubles and sleep, and tomorrow you will be better."

Setting down her wineglass, Madame rose and escorted Juliana upstairs to the next story, where she was accommodated in a neat little room which just had space for a bed, a chair, a closet, and a fireplace.

"Milord Egg built me this house," Madame explained somewhat enigmatically. "When he was young, he was the most extravagant man in the whole world—I had a gilt coach, diamonds, six racehorses of my own! But as we grow old we grow prudent. By the time he came to build my little nest, his spendthrift days were over. That is why I am now adding a new wing... Now, sleep well, my child, cry for your faithless lover and then forget him. Here is a night robe of mine—it is too large, but you will not regard that!"

With her engaging chuckle she handed Juliana a wonderfully frothy pile of gauze and tulle. Juliana accepted it with a smile and a quick stab of pain, remembering Captain Davenport saying, "My sister can lend you what you need for a night—after that it will be my delight to rig you out in the first stare of the mode." No doubt the sister was all invention. Never, never again will I be so deceived by *anybody*, she resolved.

Old Berthe arrived with a steaming tisane and the welcome news that little Prue, after eating an enormous meal, had fallen asleep on a makeshift cot in the housemaid's room and seemed likely to sleep the clock round.

Juliana, having finished the tisane, blew out her candle, fully prepared to follow Madame Reynard's direction and cry her eyes out. The grave, handsome face of Captain Davenport, as he had been when he first rescued her at the Pantheon Rooms, did dangle tantalizingly before her in the darkness. How perfect he had seemed then. A tear or so trickled down. But either because the perfect image was now overlaid by what had happened today, or for some other reason not understood, her grief seemed to be for something else. She wept, but she did not know why. Her tears did not last very long, though. Very soon she followed little Prue's example, and drifted off into oblivion.

Ten

WHEN JULIANA NEXT AWOKE, SHE FELT INSTANTLY IN her bones that it must be very late, and this, consulting her father's watch, she found to be the case: exhausted by the agitations of the previous day, or lulled by some soporific in Berthe's tisane, she had slept until almost noon. She started up in bed with an inarticulate exclamation, and then discovered that she must have been roused by a sound from outside the room, for immediately afterward Berthe tapped on the door, and entered, bearing a tray which had on it a cup, a little silver pot of chocolate, and a crescent-shaped roll.

"*Bonjour, mademoiselle,*" she said cheerfully. "'*S avez bien dormi!*"

"Oh, *mon dieu!*" Juliana exclaimed in horror. "Poor Madame! That terrible child! I should have been up long ago, and occupying myself with her."

She had fallen naturally into French, since Berthe had spoken it.

"Don't disquiet yourself, mademoiselle. The little one has been no trouble to anybody. She got up, ate a big breakfast, played with Madame's monkey, and now Madame has taken her in the carriage to seek for her grandfather's farm."

"Good God! And Prue did this without disobedience—without making any complaint?"

Berthe shrugged. "She did not wish to go in the carriage, it is true; she wished to remain and play with the monkey. But when Madame intends a thing to be done—one does it. Madame does not like to waste time."

Of this, Juliana soon had evidence: when, having drunk her chocolate—which was very good—she wished to get up, Berthe said, "A moment, mademoiselle. I call Rosine."

Rosine, the housemaid, almost as elderly as Berthe, equally plump and friendly, arrived with a basin, a steaming kettle, and various mysterious little bags of dried roots and petals.

"Madame left instructions that, before coming downstairs, Mademoiselle's hair was to be recolored, as a precaution," she explained, tipping the contents of the bag into a jug and pouring hot water on top. "Mademoiselle's hair is so pretty that it is almost a pity to alter it, but—we shall see—perhaps with chestnut hair she will be even more beautiful, who knows? And the color is not fast—it can be changed back later."

Rather nervous and reluctant nonetheless, Juliana wrapped herself in a calico peignoir, and submitted to the ordeal of having her hair washed and immersed in Rosine's mahogany-colored tincture. Apart from a natural anxiety as to the possible results, she also found herself entertaining some alarms about the ménage in which she now found herself—last night, Madame had seemed likable, trustworthy, a real friend in need; but might Juliana have entirely mistaken her nature, as she had that of Captain Davenport? Tales related by Fanny and Kitty and their friends came back to her: tales told with bated breath and round eyes, of innocent young girls stolen away—snatched in the street, abducted from respectable homes, drugged, spirited off into houses of evil fame, hideous bordellos, where, once deflowered, such girls were lost forever to decent society, could not even escape, for their families would not receive them back, they had nowhere to go, and so must resign themselves to a life of shame, almost inevitable disease, and probably early death. Was this to be her own fate? Had she walked into such a place?

However, Petworth seemed an unlikely location for a bordello, and it was difficult to sustain these terrors in the amiable presence of Rosine, who chattered away all the time she was rubbing Juliana's head, about her home on a farm in Normandy, her father's cider press and herd of cows, and how Madame intended to return to France for a long visit, as soon as the present war was concluded.

"For, although she loves Milord Egg very well, Petworth, as you may figure to yourself, is not too amusing."

"Who is Milord Egg?" asked Juliana, remembering that this name had come up once or twice on the previous evening.

"Milord Egg? Why, he is Milord Egg. He is the Sieur de Petvurrt!" Rosine seemed astonished that everybody did not know about this personage, who lived in a huge house close by "*un château, alors*" and indeed owned the whole of Petworth and all the country for miles around. "And he is a Comte—but it is different in England—it is called an Errll."

Juliana hardly liked to ask what was the relationship between Madame Reynard and Milord Egg; it seemed all too obvious what it must be. Instead she inquired how long Madame had resided in Petworth. Rosine, counting on her fingers, replied, "Oh, it is now a long time. Nearly twenty years."

"*Twenty years?*"

"*Mais oui.* It was in 1774 that Milord first met my mistress in Paris—in those days she was the friend of the Duc de Chartres. But she liked Milord Egg better, so she came to England with him, and they led a very gay life. At that time, Milord was a great Macaroni! He dressed all his postilions in white jackets trimmed with muslin, and he gave Madame so many diamonds that she had necklaces made even for her cats. And Milord was the friend of Monsieur Fox and the Prince of Wales—they spent more time in London then, at Milord Egg's house in Piccadilly. But now Milord prefers to look after his oxen and plow his park, and gives prizes for work done by widows— the life he leads is altogether bourgeois! Still, he is a kind man, Milord Egg, and a good landlord—he has much *bonté*."

"Did they have any children?" Juliana asked, fascinated.

"*Mais oui, bien sûr.* Two boys. Both are now in the *corps diplomatique*, in America. Madame did not wish it that they fight in the war, for which side could they be on, English or French? But they write her long letters; they are good boys. Milord, too, misses them very much. But he at least has the other children to console him."

"Other children?"

"*Georges et Henri et la petite Fanny*. And Madame is now again enceinte; it will be a charming family."

Juliana was startled. Since Madame Reynard was plainly *not* enceinte—having, indeed, long passed the age of child-bearing—she could only assume that some other Madame was in question.

"Milord Egg has a wife?" she inquired cautiously.

"*Mais non, jamais! C'est sa belle-amie, Madame Iliffe*—" Rosine pronounced this name "Eeleef"—"a lady in the highest degree kind, charming, and agreeable. She and Madame Reynard are the closest possible friends."

"Then are he and Madame Reynard not friends anymore?" Oh, dear me, Grandfather would *not* approve of my asking these questions, Juliana thought; in fact, he would be quite horrified to discover the company I have fallen into, and so would Papa!

"But, of course they are friends!" said Rosine, shocked. "Milord comes to visit Madame every afternoon of his life, and she gives him very good advice about his family and his lands, for she is *tout à fait pratique*—her father was the Duc de Maçon, and she knows all there is to know about running a big estate... Now, if Mademoiselle would be so kind as to sit up straight, I am going to give her head a great rub."

Juliana submitted to the great rub, and subsequently to having her hair blown partially dry by the bellows. Then Rosine anointed her dyed locks with a delicious-smelling dark-green lotion which she said was essence of rosemary, and sat her by a sunny window which looked out over an orchard, handing her a large hairbrush. "*Alors*, if Mademoiselle will give herself the trouble of brushing her hair five hundred times…"

Brushing away dutifully, Juliana presently heard the sound of a carriage, and voices. To her surprise, shortly afterward, she saw little Prue run across the orchard, bowling a hoop under the apple trees. Had Madame Reynard, after all, failed to find the farm of old Mr. Strudwick?

She was rising to go and inquire, and make her apologies for oversleeping, when Rosine reappeared.

"Madame asks you to remain upstairs a little longer. She is closeted with her notary, and thinks it best that he does not see you. Only figure to yourself, mademoiselle, here is a placard up in the square of the town relating to a lost young lady who is sought by her mama, and the town crier was proclaiming it, and a constable was here this morning, inquiring, also!" Rosie chuckled comfortably.

"What was the constable told?" Juliana inquired with some anxiety.

"*Eh bien*, one informed him that yesterday evening a young lady came inquiring the way to Hoghurst Farm, and that without doubt she had become lost in the forest. Those woods on the other side of the valley extend for many leagues, and it is well known that they are full of ferocious animals, foxes and weasels; most probably the young lady will never be seen again! Now I devise a new coiffure for Mademoiselle."

Rosine had brought in a large glossy switch of chestnut-colored hair, no doubt made from the combings of Madame Reynard, and, pinning it among Juliana's own locks, which were now exactly the same color, she constructed an elaborate chignon, after the style of Madame's own headdress.

"It is entirely elegant," she said, admiring her own handiwork. "Now Mademoiselle appears altogether a different person."

Juliana was indeed startled at her own image in the glass Rosine held up to her; she hardly recognized herself. The different color and style of hair had apparently altered the shape of her face. I look so much older; grown up, she thought. She was not sure that she liked the change. But certainly as a disguise it must be considered admirably successful; even Papa would hardly know me now, she decided, rather sadly.

Madame Reynard appeared, walking along the flagged path below the window with a small, round-faced, short-sighted-looking elderly gentleman, and Rosine, touching a finger to her lips, drew Juliana back out of sight. "*C'est le notaire—M. Trockmorrton!*" she whispered. "In one minute he will be gone—then Mademoiselle may descend."

Indeed, shortly after, farewells were heard, then Madame's voice was heard calling, and Juliana ran down, to be greeted with a cordial handshake and a kiss.

"*Alors*, here is my dear niece!" Madame said, laughing. "*Dieu de dieu*, what a transformation! Rosine is an artist! Now, the next thing is to find you some clothes. For today I fear you must endure to wear a dress of mine when I was younger—I was thinner then, so it will be not too bad a fit—and, most fortunately, *les gentilshommes* visited us last night, when there was no moon, so today we have a fine bundle of beautiful Lyons silks to make you a new outfit."

"The gentlemen, madame? Who are they?"

"*Chut!*" Madame Reynard held up a warning finger. "Everyone knows about them—even Milord Egg—but no one must speak of them because of course they are breaking the stupid law. They navigate by boat up the Rectory Brook as far as Haslingbourne Mill, and then they come up the valley and leave their goods in my little *kiosque*, before taking his wine and tea on to Milord Egg by way of the subterranean route."

"Good God!" said Juliana, greatly startled. "You mean that Milord Egg"—*surely* that could not be his real name?—"makes use of smuggled goods?"

"But naturally!" said Madame, raising her brows. "*Everybody* does. How else could Milord afford to build all the hospitals he does, and repair the jail, and construct almshouses, and effect so much good among the poor? Why, remember that tea costs ten shillings a pound, and Georges is *so* fond of his tea! Do you now know that, out of thirteen million pounds of tea drunk each year in this land, only five million have paid duty?"

Juliana did remember some indignant pronouncement of Lord Lambourn's upon the subject. But *he*, of course, had strongly disapproved of smuggling.

"Madame—" she began, thinking it best to change the subject.

"I think you must learn to call me Tante Elise, my dear. And I shall call you—what?"

Juliana, remembering her assumed identity on the journey through France, said that she had sometimes been known as Jeanne.

"Jeanne—*très bien!* My niece Jeanne Duthé. Duthé was my maiden name."

"Tante 'Lise, why have you brought back little Prue? Could you not find her grandfather's farm?"

"I found it, my child, but what a pigsty! One could not condemn a child—even the naughtiest—to live in such a spot! And there was no *fermière*—she must have died—only the most evil old wretch, who snarled at me that he wished to have nothing to do with his daughter's infant of shame. So I have brought Prue back again. And if the constable goes inquiring to the farm, I am sure he will get no help at all."

"But, good heavens, madame—" Juliana had not considered the possibility of such a refusal. "Now Prue is on your hands! What can be done with her?"

"You do not know where to find her mother?"

"All I know of her is that her name is Tillie, and that she is in Southampton with a broken leg, and sent her child away to the grandfather."

"Oh, well, perhaps Milord Egg will be able to trace her." Madame appeared to have complete faith in the ability of this nobleman. "In the meantime she may go to live at *la grande maison*, where she will have plenty of other children to play with."

"You mean the workhouse?" Juliana said, rather troubled.

"*Mais non! Chez Milord Egg!*"

At this point little Prue herself appeared, bowling her hoop along the path and demanding to play with

the "pussy," so Juliana felt it would not be proper
to ask any more questions just then, though by now
she was feeling the liveliest curiosity regarding this
mysterious character.

Little Prue, after the manner of children, had
completely habituated herself to her new surroundings; two good meals and a night's sleep had done
wonders for her. The swelling on her nose had abated
somewhat, helped by a dab of bright-red Pimpernel
ointment applied by Berthe. She grabbed Juliana by
the hand, crying, "Miss! Miss! Come see the pussy!"

The "pussy" proved to be a small gray pet monkey,
a present, it seemed, from Milord Egg. Its name,
Madame said, was Mistigris, and it lived in a cage near
the Rumford stove in the kitchen. Prue demanded,
and was given, permission to take him out into the
garden on his leash. The day being Sunday, there were
no builders working on the new wing of the house,
and, as the garden was completely enclosed, Madame
said she saw no reason why Juliana should not take the
air in it also. "But do not stray into the street! When
the inquiry for the lost young lady has died down
and been forgotten, you shall be my dear niece, who
escaped across the Channel with the gentlemen; such
crossings are not uncommon."

Accordingly, attired in an old blue muslin robe of
her hostess's, Juliana sat out on a bench, watching Prue
scamper up and down the long grass alley between
the two little garden pavilions, alternately bowling the
hoop and chasing the monkey. The sun shone warmly
on the innocent scene, and Juliana looked out over the
valley, wondering where her mother was now. Would

she still be in the town, searching for her daughter? Or scouring the countryside round about? What was the relation between her and Captain Davenport? Was I very cowardly, Juliana wondered, not to confront her? But if she had exerted her parental rights, and made me marry him? How strange to think that, even yesterday, that was the thing of all others that I wanted to do!

For the first time Juliana wondered why, if her mother had been party to the scheme, it had been thought needful to go all the way to Scotland. Surely, with parental consent, a marriage would have been possible anywhere? Perhaps it never *had* been intended to go to Scotland? And this brought her back to the original question, why had the plot been formed in the first place? For whose gain? If Captain Davenport had no money, how could her mother stand to benefit by it? Or how could he?

Baffled by these insoluble problems, Juliana glanced after little Prue, who had disappeared with Mistigris into the left-hand pavilion, a small stone building, with glass doors and windows, built as a continuation of the wall that overhung the valley. Below it the ground dropped sharply away, so that its windows commanded a handsome prospect.

At this moment Prue came dashing out of the open door, screaming agitatedly, "Miss! Miss! Come quick! The pussy's gone down the 'ole!"

"What is the matter?" Oh, mercy, Juliana thought; if the child has contrived to lose Madame's pet, we shall hardly be welcome guests.

She entered the little pavilion, which was

furnished with a rustic table and chairs, and a cane chaise longue.

"There—see—the pussy went there!" exclaimed little Prue, clutching her by the hand and pointing to the corner. Here, Juliana was disconcerted to discover a square hole in the floor, with a trapdoor standing open, and an iron ladder leading downward into a deep dark cavity, from which a strong smell of wine rose up. An icehouse—no, Madame's cellar, was her first thought—how singular to have it so far from the house—and then she remembered Madame's remark, "They leave their goods in my little *kiosque*." There must, perhaps, be a second entrance to the underground chamber, leading out into the valley.

"The pussy went down the 'ole," repeated Prue fearfully, clinging to Juliana's hand.

"Well, I will go down after him," resolved Juliana. "But *you* had best not."

"Oo, *no*! I'd be frit to death." Prue let go her hold, and, rather nervously, Juliana climbed over the edge of the trap, and let herself down the ladder.

"Be you all right, miss?" Prue called. "Can you see Misty?"

"I am still climbing down the ladder," Juliana called back.

She had to descend some fifteen rungs, widely spaced apart, and then stood still a moment, while her eyes grew accustomed to the dim light, which came only from the opening above her. When she began to see, she discovered, as she had expected, that she was in a brick vault, surrounded by a number of casks, and a powerful smell of liquor.

The errant Mistigris was sitting on one of the barrels, but as soon as Juliana made for him, he swung
himself down and scampered away into a dark corner.
Going after him, she was discouraged to find an opening, apparently the end of a passageway, into which
the monkey had disappeared.

I cannot follow him in *there*, she thought at first,
panic-stricken, for the passage looked dark as a chimney; but then she thought of what she owed Madame
Reynard and resolved to try. Luckily she now
observed a flint and steel, and a bundle of rushlights,
lying on a ledge in the brick wall.

"Miss! Miss! Where be you?" Prue called anxiously.

"The monkey has run into a hole. I am going after
him!" Juliana called back. "Do you stay there, and let
us hope that I can catch Misty before Madame knows
that he is lost."

"I'm afeared," whined Prue dolefully. "Suppose
there's summat *bad* down there!"

Stifling feelings of a similar nature, Juliana told her
not to be a goose, and lit one of the rushlights. This
disclosed a narrow rock tunnel, which was evidently
much-used, for there were many trampled footprints
in its clay floor. Of Mistigris there was no sign, but
she started resolutely along the passage. After walking some distance, she began to feel more and more
nervous; there was still no trace of her quarry, and she
wondered where the passage could possibly be taking
her; she must by now have traversed several hundred
yards, and still there was no end to it! Several times she
was on the point of turning back, but she could not
bear to admit defeat and the loss of the monkey; so she

kept on. At last she was rewarded by a glimmer of light ahead, and came to the foot of a flight of stone steps.

It was from a half-open door at the top of the stairs that the light emanated; to Juliana's joy she now perceived the monkey crouching in the doorway and looking back at her as if teasing her to follow. She ran up the steps and thought she had him, but he slipped through the door just before her hands had closed on him, and darted across the room beyond, which was a vaulted brick chamber like that below Madame's summerhouse, except that there were no wine barrels in this room. More steps led up out of it to another door, also slightly open; and the exasperating Mistigris bounded up the steps and through the crack of the upper door with Juliana in eager pursuit, so sure she could catch him that she never stopped to wonder where the chase was leading her, until she was fairly through the second door, when she was suddenly brought short by a man's voice exclaiming, "God bless my soul! Who the deuce have we here?"

Juliana came to an abrupt halt, looking around her in astonishment and confusion. She now found herself in a most extraordinary room, which seemed at least a hundred feet long. Its width was about a third of its length and the walls were painted black. White lines were described in a regular pattern on both walls and floor. A gallery with a sloping roof ran around three sides of the room; it was netted over, as if to keep in prisoners, and a strip of netting about three feet high ran across the middle of the room from side to side. Two men clad in trousers, white shirts, and waistcoats stood regarding Juliana with expressions of considerable surprise; one of them was middle-aged, the other younger. They held long-handled racquets in their hands, and, now that she had collected herself enough to think rationally, Juliana realized that by some extraordinary means she had blundered into a tennis court—though how a smugglers' passage should lead into such a place, she found it hard to imagine!

The wayward Mistigris, who seemed perfectly at home here, had snatched up a ball from the stone floor, and, holding it in his paw, was swinging across the dividing net in the center.

"Mistigris I know," said the older man, who was standing nearer to Juliana, "and, seeing him, I understand why you are here—try if you can catch him, Socket!—but who *you* can be, my dear, has me in a fair puzzle! Do enlighten me, I beg!"

"Truly, sir, I beg your pardon," Juliana said, rather breathlessly—his amused glance made her feel like an untidy, blundering child. "I—I am Madame Reynard's niece! And, as you see, I was trying to recapture Mistigris—I had no notion that the passage led into your tennis court, or I would not have trespassed. I must apologize again."

"Madame's *niece*? Well, by all that's famous! Here have I been acquainted with her these twenty years, and never even knew that she *had* a niece. What reserve! I see very little resemblance," he added, studying Juliana with twinkling eyes, "though it's true that you are of the same coloring; but your features, my dear, are cast in a more delicate mold. Well, well! Only to think of 'Lise having a niece. And how did you arrive, my child?"

"Well, sir—" began Juliana, blushing and confused.

The gentleman, on observing her hesitation, misunderstood the cause and said kindly, "No, no never mind! I can guess without your telling. You came along with Ebenezer Lee—not to mention my burgundy and claret and my half-anchor of rum and the Hyson tea that Madam can't be without—that's it, eh?"

Juliana curtsied without replying. By now she had guessed that her interlocutor could be none other than "Milord Egg" and she studied him with as much curiosity and interest as he was giving her. She saw a medium-sized man, in his mid-forties, with a trim, well-knit figure. He had a long, hawk-like nose, a long upper lip, a fresh-colored complexion, and a look of quiet humor, derived from the set of his eyes, which tilted down at the outer corners, and a slight quirk at the corner of his mouth. His hair was cut short and his dress very plain, though of superior quality. His neckcloth, though snowy white, was somewhat carelessly tied.

"Do *you* think that Mam'selle has a look of Madame 'Lise, Socket?" he asked the younger man, who, having at last caught the monkey, now approached them.

"Well—perhaps—just a little," said the latter, rather doubtfully. "The shape of the head is similar. Here is your aunt's pet, miss. Would you like me to carry him home for you?"

"Ay, see her back along the passage, Ned; we are used to it, but the young lady is not," said Milord Egg. "In the circumstances, it was very brave of you, my child, to chase after that naughty beast. One of these days it will get stuck up a tree that nobody can climb, and I for one shan't weep millstones. Give my respects to your aunt, my dear, and tell her that I shall give myself the pleasure of calling in this afternoon to improve our acquaintance. Good-bye for the present!"

"Good-bye, sir—and my apologies again," Juliana said, curtsying.

"Think nothing of it—we use that corridor all the time, don't we, Socket?"

But Socket, a fair-haired, stolid-looking young man had already descended the steps, holding the indignant Mistigris, who chattered and screamed with annoyance all the way back.

"I am glad my pupils do not make such a row," Socket observed as they emerged into Madame Reynard's vault.

"Are you a teacher, sir?" Juliana inquired.

"Why, yes; I tutor Lord Egremont's sons," the young man replied. "Shall you be all right now, miss? Then I will return to his lordship, for he does not like to stop in the middle of a game. Good-bye!" He carefully handed her the monkey and turned back into the dark passage, which he negotiated with as much ease and familiarity as if it had been lamplit all the way along.

Juliana climbed the ladder in a very thoughtful frame of mind, only just in time to reassure the frantic Prue, who was beginning to believe that some underground Troll-king had swallowed her and that she would never be seen again.

"Wherever *was* you, miss, for so long?"

"I had to run a very long way after the monkey,

Prue; and now I think we had best go back to the house, for very likely, after all that chasing, he will be wanting his dinner."

"I wants mine, I knows that," said Prue, and she ran on, calling to Berthe, who had come into the garden to pick a bunch of parsley, "The pussy went down the 'ole, and Miss had to fetch 'im."

"Oh, what horror!" said Berthe cheerfully. "Come, little one, there is a great bowl of soup for you!"

Juliana followed more slowly. Lord Egremont, she was thinking, why, of course! Why had his name not occurred to me? For she had heard various tales, while in London, of this eccentric peer, who had won the Derby several times with his racehorses, who had been a notable member of the Macaroni Club, yet never drank or gambled, who had had the most ravishing mistresses, yet was reputedly very shy and disinclined for society, who had been engaged to Lady Maria Waldegrave, but broke it off and never married anybody else. Miss Ardingly said he had been Lady Melbourne's lover and was the father of one of her children. He was a friend of Charles James Fox, he was averred to be highly cultured, lively-witted, well grounded in the classics, keenly interested in the arts, yet chose to retire to his estates in Sussex and was hardly seen in London above once every two or three years; when he did come he brought his own drinking water because he said London water tasted disgusting. Lord Lambourn—who had once been to stay at Petworth on some business connected with the Sussex Regiment—said the house was the most uncomfortable he had ever visited—damp sheets, no bell, and nothing but rustic impertinence from the servants. When he had asked for a glass of water and wine after supper, a footman told him the butler had gone to bed...

Juliana's thoughts were interrupted by the voice of Madame Reynard, who was sitting out-of-doors on a cushioned chaise longue, writing slowly in a large leather-bound volume—for the day had turned out a hot one.

"*Malepeste!*" exclaimed that lady, in a kind of cheerful indignation, as she surveyed Juliana's absent, dreamy demeanor. "I can see all too well what has happened to *you*! Mistigris went into the wine tunnel, is it not so? He always will, if we forget to shut the trap. And you went after him, and of course you encountered Milord Egg, playing tennis, and now you have fallen head over ears in love with him, am I not correct? He had only to cast his eye on a *jeune fille* and down they all go like bowling pins. Oh, it is too bad! Now we shall never have any peace!"

Juliana burst out laughing. "No, no, Tante 'Lise," she said, "it is not so bad as that, I promise! Milord Egg does have a great charm, I can see that, but, after all, he must be at least twenty-five years older than I."

"What is that to the purpose?"

"No, madame, truly, you mistake. I have been looking all my life for somebody like Charles the First, and Milord Egg, though, I am sure, very delightful, does not resemble Charles the First in the slightest degree."

Eleven

LORD EGREMONT CAME TO CALL, AS HE PROMISED HE
would, later on that day; but Juliana did not take
this as any particular compliment to herself, since
Rosine had said that he visited Madame Reynard
every afternoon. However, when he did come he was
dressed very handsomely in a black coat of superfine
cloth, skintight pantaloons, and exquisitely polished
boots; his neckcloth was most correctly tied, and he
brought a charming bunch of hothouse flowers "for
the young lady from over the water." The effect of all
this formality, however, was somewhat marred by the
fact that he came along the underground passage, and
ascended the ladder just as Juliana, who was playing
hide-and-seek with Prue, had concealed herself under
the table in the summerhouse.

"This young lady has the most unusual habits,"
Lord Egremont remarked to Madame Reynard, who
was also in the summerhouse, reclining on her chaise
longue. "First of all she arrives in my tennis court as if
the Militia were after her; now I find her sitting under
a table. It is most singular!"

"Do not be absurd, Georges!" replied Madame Reynard, giving him her hand to kiss without getting up. "She is playing *cache-cache*, that is all. It is entirely your own fault, for arriving unannounced in this way, that you find her under the table. You should have come round correctly, by the road."

"That way is so much farther," he complained, sitting down and fanning himself with his hat. "Besides, then I must be civil to ever so many people all the way through the town."

Juliana, who had wondered whether the passage had been constructed more as a convenience for smugglers, or for Lord Egremont's private visits to his *chère amie*, now correctly concluded that it was almost equally employed in both capacities. Having stood up to curtsy and receive the flowers, she retired under the table again, just in time for little Prue to discover her with a loud cry of "Got you, then, miss!"

"Who is this?" inquired Lord Egremont, inspecting the child through his quizzing glass. "*Another* niece of yours, my dear 'Lise? Or a great-niece?"

"No, Georges, how can you be so foolish? She is a foundling, at present deserted by her parents," explained Madame Reynard in a low voice, having instructed Prue to "run to Berthe and ask her to bring a glass of lemonade for the gentleman."

"And do you propose to keep her?"

"Why, no," said Madame Reynard calmly. "I was about to ask if you could find a niche for her in your establishment, my friend. It would be so much more amusing for her there."

"Oh, by all means," he replied with the utmost

amiability. "Send her round whenever you like—Lizzie will stuff her with sugarplums, Mademoiselle Lord will weep over her orphaned state, Conrad Leidenberg will bake her a cake on her birthday, and Mrs. Garland will hem her pinafores for her. There can be no difficulty. I daresay she will get on excellently with little Henry—he is always saying that he needs an ally because Georgie bullies him."

"*Bien*, then that is settled. I will bring her round tomorrow—not through the subterranean way. I shall be glad to see my dear Liz. How is she?"

"She feels the heat—she finds herself troubled by nausea and backache; you know she is always so at such times… But tell me about this delightful young lady," he said affably. "It is news to me, dear 'Lise, that you possess a niece. You have been very silent about her all these years!"

"Why, she is not precisely a niece, but a kind of cousin," explained Madame Reynard placidly. "You remember my cousin Raoul Duthé?"

"Ah, I see. His daughter? Yes," observed Milord Egg, bringing the quizzing glass into action once more. "Yes, now I examine her closely, I see she has quite a look of Raoul… And how is your father, my dear?" he inquired suavely of Juliana, who cast an anguished glance at Madame Reynard. That lady shrugged her shoulders in a particularly Gallic manner, and made a significant chopping gesture with the side of her hand.

"Alas, sir," faltered Juliana, "he, like so many others—"

"No, guillotined, was he, poor fellow? Too bad, too bad. And that reminds me, God bless my soul,

'Lise, *what* do you think is all the crack now among the *ton*, up in London? Throgmorton was telling me, and I was never so shocked in my life. All the ladies go to balls with a band of red velvet ribbon round their necks, to represent the victims of Madame Guillotine. I call that abominably vulgar—quite the outside of enough! By the by, did Throgmorton carry out your business for you all right and tight, my dear?"

"Yes, I thank you, Georges. It was just to note down the additions to my house on the title deeds, and to make an inquiry about the Glebe Path."

"The new wing looks well," he remarked, turning to inspect the almost completed addition. "I told you Jem Bowyer would do a good job... Ay, Throgmorton's an excellent attorney; I find it is better to have him down from London once in a while than to entrust my business to local fellows. They mean well, but they know about as much law as my horse Fingal. Now, old Throgmorton is a close-mouthed, quiet old stick-in-the-mud, but he's fully up to snuff; knows all the tricks of the trade; I shouldn't wonder but what he has the family history of every member of both Houses of Parliament at his fingertips. I daresay there's many a man who will breathe easier when old Throgmorton's gone to his fathers and taken his secrets with him... Talking of secrets, I see that young Cox is back in town on furlough, which does not much delight me."

"What, the son of your tenants over at Newgrove? But his father and mother have gone to Bath."

"All the more reason why I hope that he leaves

Petworth again soon. Alone, he is more prone to get up to mischief."

"And what kind of mischief do you have in mind, *mon ami*? Every young man will flirt."

"Of course; but the last girl that your Cox flirted with—that pretty Rosie Tanner, the baker's daughter—was found dead up in Bedham Woods last January, if you remember."

"Georges! You do not think—?"

"I don't like young Cox. At best he is a puppy. At worst—I don't know what. I shall be glad when he returns to his ship. He has gone with the Free Traders, too, on several occasions, it's said. To purchase a dallop of tea from them is one thing—to accompany them on their runs is something quite else, and unbecoming to a gentleman."

This conversation was making Juliana uncomfortable; and besides, she felt that Lord Egremont and Madame Reynard must have many private matters to discuss. So she politely excused herself and returned to the house. Looking down from her bedroom window later, she saw the two of them pacing slowly along the grass walk, arm in arm, their heads bent together in conversation. How very strange! she thought. They seem like a married pair—indeed, far more attached to one another than my aunt and Lord Lambourn. And yet he is not married to her—not married at all! People, she concluded, are not in the least the way that I was led to expect. Now, Papa, and my aunt, and Grandfather were all persuaded that for a man and woman to love when they are not married is disgraceful and scandalous; even wicked; but I am sure that Madame Reynard is not wicked. I think, on the contrary, that she is probably very good. As for Milord Egg, I am not so sure about him. But no, I do not believe that he is wicked.

As for Mr. Cox, she tried not to think about him at all. Like Lord Egremont, she hoped that he would soon leave the town again.

She began trying to frame a letter to her grandfather.

> *Dear Grandfather:*
>
> *The Excellent young man mentioned in my last letter to you turned out, on closer acquaintance, to be a Snake in the Grass, and a complete Charlatan and Deceiver. Having discovered this sad fact only after our Elopement was under way, I have now escaped from him and taken refuge with a most Estimable lady, the erstwhile Mistress of the Earl of Egremont; he, too, is a very Pleasant and Polished Person, and I understand, an excellent landlord...*

Discouraged, she abandoned the attempt. She was obliged to admit to herself that she would probably never be received by her grandfather again. It had been just possible that, if Captain Davenport had turned out as respectable as he seemed, Sir Horace might in the end have been brought to countenance the match, but in the present circumstances he could only consider Juliana utterly disgraced; compromised by her elopement, by its equivocal ending, and by her present company. There would be little use in attempting to state her case. Sighing, she abandoned the effort of composition (in any case, there was no paper in her room) and, as she now observed from her window that Lord Egremont had quitted his hostess after bestowing on her an affectionate kiss and a polite bow, she went downstairs to ask in what way she might make herself useful.

She found Madame Reynard equipping herself with a large basket containing many small bottles and packets, and what looked like a large pot of raspberry jam. Then she wrapped herself in a cape. "I go to visit the poor," she explained.

"Are there so many poor?" Juliana was surprised. Petworth had seemed a particularly trim, prosperous little town.

"In effect, no; but there are always some unfortunate through illness or accident. And the English notions of doctoring are barbaric! An infection of the eye they rub with a black cat's tail—still attached to the cat! And to cure a case of ague, the wretched sufferer is filled up with Geneva and then thrust into a horse pond, imagine it! When you have been here long enough to be accepted as my niece, you may accompany me on my rounds."

"I shall be very happy to help you, ma'am, and to learn your methods of medicine," Juliana said, smiling as she remembered her agitating experiences with Herr Welcker and the inhabitants of St.-Servan. The smile changed to a sigh. "But in the meantime, Tante 'Lise, what can I do to assist you?" she asked.

"Do you write a clear hand, child?"

"Why, yes, ma'am. I have always—" Juliana checked herself. "I have always been used to copy out my father's manuscripts," she had been going to say. She changed it to "I have always been accounted to write a legible script," and Madame Reynard said, "Excellent. In that case, I shall be infinitely obliged if you will undertake the task of making a fair copy of my memoirs."

And she handed Juliana the large leather-bound volume in which, earlier, she had been writing.

Settled at an elegant escritoire, Juliana could not avoid some amusement. Here she was, in such different surroundings, required to carry out the very same task that she had so often performed for her father. The substance of what she had to copy was, however, she very soon discovered, of a very different nature. Madame Reynard, the illegitimate daughter of a duke, had moved in aristocratic circles in Paris of the 1770s, and wrote of the people she had known with tolerance, intelligence, a discerning eye, and a devastating wit. Petworth must indeed seem quiet to her after Paris, Juliana thought, scratching away with her quill. She found herself becoming more and more fascinated by the scene revealed, and presently could not resist turning ahead, to see whether the reminiscences continued on to cover Madame's London life with Lord Egremont. They did; and Juliana was much tempted to read on in hopes of discovering some mention of her own parents; but Madame's writing was very spiky and hard to decipher; Juliana decided that she had better proceed in a regular manner, and not allow herself the indulgence of reading the later pages until she came to them, or the work would proceed too slowly.

She had transcribed some twenty pages by the time Madame Reynard returned. That lady put off her cloak and hat, and sank with a sigh of exhaustion onto her chaise longue, calling to Berthe to bring wine and biscuits.

"*Pouf!* Those obstinate English peasants! If they were dying in the desert, and you offered them a glass of the best wine in France, they would scowl in your face and say, 'Dunno as I want it, missis, 'taint noways what I bin used to.'" Her imitation of the rich Sussex accent had the skill of long familiarity and exasperation. "It is no wonder that you will never have a revolution in this country! If one came suggesting they should rise and take away his wealth from Milord Egg, they would say, 'Nay, dunna mek such a fanteague, old Lordy baint so bad. Things be best left the way they be!' and that would be the end of the matter. Thank you, Berthe! Pour a glass also for Mademoiselle Jeanne... Have you managed to interpret much of my scribble, child?"

"I'm getting on famously, Tante 'Lise, and I find it beyond anything interesting!"

Madame Reynard chuckled and said, "I fear you will discover some matters that are not usually disclosed to an English *jeune fille*, but in my opinion the sooner some facts are known, the better; I do not approve of keeping young girls in total ignorance of the world. There was a sad case not long ago of a German princess who became pregnant by her footman simply because she was too ignorant to realize that what he was doing to her would lead to such a condition. Imagine it!"

"I am sure that you are right, ma'am," replied Juliana, thinking of her experiences in London.

When Berthe had withdrawn and the door was closed, Madame Reynard remarked, "Well, my child, I have discovered, as I expected to, that your mother is still in the town, staying at the Bull. Nothing like taking round medicines to people's houses for learning all the talk of the place! Setting a chambermaid's sprained thumb, I learned that the lady was very miserly with her vails; doctoring an ostler's mother's rheumatism, I heard that the bearded young gentleman who has escorted the lost young lady here is gone off, it is thought up to London to fetch the Bow Street Runners, for he has bespoken a room at the Bull again for two nights from now. And their friend Lieutenant Cox still remains at his family home in the town; he comes from a respected Petworth family, but he is not a shining example of it."

"Oh, good God," said Juliana, trembling. "My mother still in the town! Do you suppose she can have got word of my whereabouts, ma'am?"

"No, I do not. The general opinion seems to be that you must have been lost in the woods, which are very extensive; and that you are now dead of cold and hunger! And I am very much afraid that your mother hopes that is the case. 'Not a bit of proper feeling about the poor young lady did she show,' my chambermaid told me with the utmost indignation. 'Just wished to know if a-many folk died in those woods, and how long might it take to discover the young lady's body, happen she had died in there.' I greatly fear, my dear, that your mother believes it would be in her best interests if you were dead."

"But why? Why?" Juliana murmured, utterly puzzled and distressed.

"My dear, in a case like this, with characters such as that, there is only ever one motive. Money. It must be that you are entitled to moneys of whose existence you are not aware and that your mother stands to inherit. This must be the explanation."

"Perhaps you are right," Juliana said thoughtfully. She remembered Lieutenant Cox saying, "But where's the heiress—Miss Moneybags—?" She had thought at the time he was speaking ironically. But perhaps he was in earnest?

"I wonder how I could find out," she said slowly. "If I am entitled to money, I would very gladly give some of it to my mother." She remembered the angry, hungry look of the woman on the Ponte Vecchio; her acquisitive, resentful stare round Lord Lambourn's dining saloon. Juliana could not like what she had seen or heard of her mother, but she found that she felt deeply sorry for her. "If only my grandfather would tell me! But if he knew—he seems to have taken pains to keep me in ignorance."

"It is a pity *cher Monsieur Trockmorton* has gone back to town," Madame Reynard said. "We could have asked him to discover whether you are the heiress to a fortune that nobody has thought to inform you of! Shall I write to him and inquire?"

"Oh, no, ma'am—thank you for thinking of it, but no," Juliana said hastily. "For how could you divulge your interest without betraying your knowledge of my whereabouts?"

"True," said Madame Reynard. "And—I must

now tell you, my dear, that, without setting out to do so, I have learned your identity. You see, I saw your mother coming out of the Bull Inn, and I remembered her. I have encountered her in London, many years ago."

Juliana was a little dismayed, but, rallying, said, "I am sure you will not betray me, ma'am, however!"

"Most certainly I will not, child. You need have no anxiety on that head."

"My—my mother did not recognize *you*, ma'am?"

"She showed not the slightest sign of having done so. All she will have seen is an old country woman with a basket."

"Hardly that, dear ma'am," said Juliana, looking with affectionate admiration at the handsome countenance of her hostess. She was beginning more and more easily to comprehend how Lord Egremont's regard had endured for twenty years.

"Did—did you know my mother, ma'am—in the days when she was married to Papa?"

Next moment it occurred to Juliana that her question had been tactlessly phrased; it seemed possible that Madame Reynard had had more chance of meeting Laura Paget later on, in the brief period when she had been mistress of the Prince of Wales, as Elise Duthé had been of Lord Egremont. But Madame answered, quite unperturbed, "I did meet her a few times in those days. But she was never one to make friends with her own sex; she was of a haughty, cold disposition, always striving to be queen of whatever company she found herself in. To tell truth, I did not like her. You are very different from her, child."

Juliana would have liked to ask more questions, but Berthe came in to announce that supper was waiting for them, and the subject was dropped. Never mind, Juliana thought comfortably, Tante 'Lise does not seem to object if I ask her questions, and I have all the time in the world to do so!

And, in fact, next day Juliana found an opportunity to ask Madame Reynard why there seemed to have been such terrible enmity between her parents—why her father had been so distraught to learn that his wife was seeking him in Florence.

"Revenge," Madame Reynard said slowly. "She had a very revengeful nature. She could not bear to be slighted. *She* must be the one to do the spurning! And when your father divorced her, it made her dreadfully angry—she longed for the means to hurt him. I am afraid, my child, that your mama is not an agreeable character."

"Did you know my father, madame?" Juliana said wistfully.

"No, my dear, I never had that pleasure. His books, yes. I know them!"

During the next few weeks, life at the Hermitage—which, Juliana discovered, was the name of Madame Reynard's dwelling—settled into a surprisingly placid routine. Little Prue was taken over to Petworth House on the day following her arrival, and, although she set up a great uproar at the prospect of being parted from Juliana and Mistigris, Madame reported that, when she discovered that she was to live in an establishment where there were untold cats, dogs, parrots, pet rabbits, other children, ponies to ride, a park full of deer,

and even an orangery where the children were sometimes permitted to pick the fruit, her spirits underwent
a mercurial change, and she was so enchanted by her
surroundings that she hardly troubled to say good-bye
to her conductress.

"Are there so many children about the house,
then?" inquired Juliana. "Whose are they all?"

"Oh, well, two of them—*Guillaume et Marie*—are
by another lady, a previous mistress of Georges, who
left him some twelve or thirteen years ago to marry
somebody; then there are some little nephews and
nieces—Georges has three brothers, you know, Percy,
Charles, and William—then, also, Georges is a great
patron of the arts, and you will always find writers
about the house, or painters, working away at their
easels, and they are quite likely to bring their children
with them if they come for a long stay."

"Good gracious! And does Lord Egremont not
object to all these children about the place?"

"*Mais non, pas du tout!* He is the most amiable man
in the world. A friend of his said that the quality in
which he excels above all others is 'put-up-ability.'"

"Well, he will need it with little Prue," Juliana said.

In the mornings Juliana wrote letters to Madame's
dictation, or sewed, or read aloud; the afternoons
were devoted to the transcription of her memoirs;
and in the evenings, when the workmen had
departed, Juliana was encouraged to go out into the
garden for air and exercise. Madame insisted that this
was a time for recreation, since Juliana was kept so
hard at work all day, and she was ordered to swing
in the swing that hung from the walnut tree, or play

at long-bowling or Dutch rubbers or quoits with
Lord Egremont; but Madame Reynard herself was a
notable gardener, and Juliana often chose to help her
in the long light evenings. Truly, she often thought,
it was a happier existence than any she had known
for years, since her father's illness had begun robbing
him of strength and spirits, and filling his daughter
with anxiety and apprehension.

Several times, also, Juliana paid informal visits
to Petworth House, escorted by Madame Reynard
through the underground passage, and she found, as
she had been told, that it was the most unceremoni-
ous establishment in the world, certainly like no
other house that she had ever been in. The original
foundations were very ancient, but the house had
been rebuilt, about a hundred years previously,
by the Duke of Somerset, and was of a large size,
over three hundred feet long, Juliana was informed,
with fifteen or sixteen rooms on the ground floor
alone, full of handsome furniture and interesting
works of art; one room lined throughout with
the most remarkable wooden carving, done with
exquisite skill; these rooms, as Madame Reynard
had described, were occupied by a heterogeneous
throng of visitors, poets, established at desks in the
throes of composition, artists at their easels, nurses,
children, girls playing pianos, boys playing tennis on
the enclosed court or comparing the merits of their
fowling-pieces, ladies drinking endless cups of Hyson
and gossiping over their embroidery. Lord Lambourn
had objected to the lack of order and comfort, and
the bucolic ways of the servants, but Juliana found the

free-and-easy atmosphere delightful, the master of
the house wandering about, his hands in his pockets
and his hat on his head, inquiring after everybody's
well-being. Juliana had not yet met the enceinte
Madame Iliffe (or Ayliffe), who had taken to her bed,
being afflicted with cramps and backache, but she
became fast friends with young George and Henry,
aged respectively eight and five, who had received
little Prue very good-naturedly, and by their broth-
erly example were greatly improving her peevish
ways. Juliana also liked the older children, William
and Maria and enjoyed the company of the equable
Mademoiselle Lord, their French governess, who
might have been expected to become quite distracted
at the succession of pupils who slipped in and out
of her jurisdiction, but who took their comings and
goings with remarkable calm. Juliana was encouraged
to perform on any of the pianos or harps whenever
she wished, go riding with the girls in the extensive
park (which Milord Egg had done much to reclaim
from wild woodland), make use of the library, or
stroll about admiring the many fine pictures by
Van Dyck, Gainsborough, Reynolds, and Holbein,
besides many more modern painters. It was very
agreeable to be made free of such a treasure-house of
people and things—and it was very agreeable, also,
to return from it to the calm, orderly ménage of
Madame Reynard.

"I hope Georges is not throwing out too many lures
at you?" that lady one day inquired. "I am afraid he
can hardly help it, when there is a charming young girl
at hand—he is the most confirmed gallant!"

"He does throw out a lure or two," Juliana was obliged to acknowledge. "But so far I have been able to repel them without hurting his feelings, I think."

"The feelings of Georges are never hurt," Madame Reynard said. "He merely bides his time and waits for a more favorable occasion. But if you tell him a really firm no, then he will accept it. There is not the least particle of harm in him; he is the dearest man! And so thoughtful—did I tell you how he once had all the people of Petworth vaccinated?"

"No, ma'am—vaccinated against the smallpox, do you mean?"

"Yes. It was five years ago." Madame Reynard began to laugh. "He had been trying to persuade them all to eat brown bread, because he read that was better for their health than white flour. But try to change the habits of the English laboring classes! They would not—they preferred their white flour. So then Georges decided that at least he could prevent their dying of the smallpox, and he sent for a supply of serum from Monsieur Jenner at the London Smallpox Hospital. But, unfortunately, by some mischance, the wrong kind of serum was supplied, and a number of people fell ill. So Georges had fourteen of them brought into Petworth House to be nursed, and one of them died—*eh bien*, it took him a long, long time to live that down here. 'Owd Lordy an' 'is pathery ways,' they all said. 'If 'e dunna roil us in one way, 'tis in another. But, scamble-'eaded as 'e be, 'e be middling good-natured.'"

"I am amazed at how well you speak the Sussex dialect, Tante 'Lise!"

"I should be able to, after taking salves and simples to them for nineteen years. Apropos of which, my ostler's mother tells me that the young man with the beard was returned to Petworth accompanied by two unmistakable Bow Street Runners, who are scouring the forest for dead bodies. So it will be necessary for you to keep indoors for the next day or two, my dear... It is a pity I am not the owner of Newgrove, where the bad young Cox's parents reside."

"Why is that, ma'am?" asked Juliana, who had gone rather pale at the mention of the Runners.

"Why, because in Newgrove House they have a secret room, where people were used to hide Royalist sympathizers."

"A secret room! Perhaps Charles the Second hid in it when he was escaping from the Roundheads. Did he not travel through Sussex?" Juliana asked hopefully.

"Don't ask me, child. I always confuse those Charleses and Jameses. Was Charles the Second the one who believed that, because he was King, everything he said must be true?"

"No; that was his father, Charles the First."

"A most boring, bigoted man! He quite deserved to have his head cut off."

Juliana opened her mouth to speak, then shut it again, as Rosine came in to say there was a message from George Barrett, the steward at Petworth House, that a party of gypsies were encamped on Hampers Green, the common to the north of the town, and that Madame had best watch out for her poultry; all landowners with houses on the edge of the town were being advised to take extra precautions.

"The gypsies will be clever if they can get into my garden," said Madame, "with walls on three sides, and a steep drop on the fourth. But I thank Barrett for his thoughtfulness."

As if to remind them of the warning, an old gypsy woman came to the Hermitage on the following afternoon, selling clothes-pegs and birch whisks for beating eggs, and remedies made from wild plants. Madame Reynard was out at the time taking a bottle of foxglove tea to a dropsical publican, but Juliana, on her behalf, bought a flask of Pimpernel water, for she knew that the household supply was running low; and she hesitated over some cobweb pills, which the old crone claimed were a sovereign cure for asthma and consumption; but as they looked decidedly unsavory, and cost a penny apiece, Juliana did not in the end buy any; cobwebs, after all, were common enough, and Madame Reynard could compound her own pills, were she minded to try them as a remedy.

"You have a lucky face, my dearie," said the old woman, fixing Juliana with a sharp eye, as she accepted a shilling for six pegs and the Pimpernel water. "But you should beware the wiles of fine gentlemen, and I see danger for you high in the air."

"Thank you, old mother," Juliana said, laughing. "I have already discovered the truth of your first warning, and the second one even more so—being high in the air has brought me nothing but trouble!"

When Madame Reynard returned from her charitable mission, which had included a call on her friend Liz Iliffe at Petworth House, she had much of interest to relate.

"I hear that your mother and the bearded young man are in difficulties at the Bull," she reported. "Monsieur Rapley, the landlord, began to suspect that they had not enough to pay their account, and demanded some money from them, and they made him a great scene, my chambermaid told me. Perhaps they have used all their funds to pay the Bow Street Runners, who have so far found nothing. I think it unlikely that your *maman* will remain here much longer."

"I hope not, indeed," Juliana said fervently.

"Also Milord Egg plans to hold a Cuckoo Fete, a fair in Petworth Park, on John the Baptist's Day."

"June the twenty-fourth? Why, that is my birthday," said Juliana. "But why is it called a Cuckoo Fair?"

"That is supposed to be the day when the cuckoo ceases calling. Georges has invited the Prince of Wales to come from Brighton; he intends to hold a great dinner, and there will be a feast in the park for the townspeople. Georges has commanded one thousand yards of tablecloth and two hundred dozen mugs from London. And there will be sports and games and archery contests, and naturally all the country people wish for bullbaiting and cockfighting, though Georges does not approve of those sports. He is always trying to persuade the farmers to use oxen to pull their plows, for oxen cost only half the price of a horse, but of *course* they will not listen to him."

"Poor Lord Egg," said Juliana, laughing. "I hope very much that my mother will have abandoned the search and left Petworth by the day of the fete, for I should like to see it."

Two days later there was a very disconcerting

occurrence. Berthe came home after buying fish in the market to report that the whole band of gypsies had been arrested and were being held in the Town Hall (where the stocks and other instruments of correction were kept) under suspicion of having made away with the lost young lady in the woods. The Bow Street Runners had laid an accusation against them.

"But this is dreadful!" said Juliana, horrified at the news. "Of course they are innocent! Is Lord Egremont the magistrate here? I must ask him to let them go at once. May I go over to Petworth House, ma'am, and inform him of the true state of affairs?"

"I suppose you must," agreed Madame Reynard. "It will, I fear, entail telling him a portion of your history, but, to be honest, I fancy he guessed from the outset that you were not my niece. Very well, then, run along, my child."

Juliana accordingly hastened by the underground passage to Petworth House, and demanded of George Barrett where Lord Egremont was to be found.

"'E be in the picture gallery, reckon," a footman said, after some inquiry. "I fancy 'e be a-talking to one o' they poetical gentlemen."

Following this advice, Juliana discovered Lord Egremont and the poetical gentleman seated on two half-unpacked wooden crates; by the casual eye they might have been taken for workmen, as they were both in shirt sleeves and surrounded by wood shavings and several stone busts. The poetical gentleman—a strongly built muscular man with a wild visionary light in his eye—was reading some lines from a notebook which he held in his hand:

> *"The lark, sitting upon his earthy bed, just as*
>   *the morn*
> *Appears, listens silent; then springing from the*
>   *waving cornfield loud*
> *He leads the Choir of Day; trill, trill, trill, trill*
> *Mounting upon the wings of light into the great*
>   *expanse.*
> *Re-echoing against the shining blue and lovely*
>   *heavenly shell—"*

He broke off to say, "There is something about those lines, Lord Egremont, that does not quite sit as it should, but I am foxed if I can discover what it is."

"Why, my dear Mr. Blake, it is those trills, to be sure! Trill, trill, trill, trill! You cannot put that into a serious poem. Four trills, indeed! It is the outside of enough!"

"But, sir, the lark invariably trills four times. One must be exact."

"No, no, my dear fellow, the line would be a great deal better if it read, 'He leads the Choir of Morning: trill, trill, trill!'"

"My dear Lord Egremont, you oblige me to believe that you have the ear of a penny ballad-monger. 'Choir of Morning: trill, trill, trill,' indeed! *That* sounds downright ridiculous! Besides, I used the word 'morn' two lines above. No, no, that will not do—I must think again…"

He sat frowning and nibbling at his quill.

Lord Egremont looked up and saw Juliana, who had hesitated, not liking to break into their discussion.

"Why," he said, with lifted brows and his endearing

crooked smile, "it is the charming Mademoiselle Jeanne! How can I serve you, my dear child, on this delightful summer morning which has just been so accurately described by our friend?"

"If I might have a private word with you, sir?"

"By all means." Lord Egremont glanced around, then led the way round a corner into an annex of the gallery where one immense stone statue was transfixing another with a spear. "Now, what is troubling you, my dear? Why this agitated air?"

"Sir—those gypsies who have been apprehended on suspicion of making away with a young lady—"

"Yes, my child?"

"Well—you see—" Juliana nervously adjusted her fichu and then looked up to see that Lord Egremont was observing her with a twinkling eye.

"I collect that you wish to inform me you are the young lady in question, so it is not possible that they can have murdered you? And that therefore they should be released without delay?"

"Yes, sir, that is it exactly," she said with an unbounded sense of relief. "But will it be necessary that I should appear in court, or give evidence? For I am, just at present, extremely anxious—"

"To lie low, is it not so? Well, I see no difficulty here. I shall send a note to say that, in my opinion, there is not enough evidence to bring a case against them, and give orders to let them go immediately."

He summoned a footman and did so.

"Oh, sir, I am *exceedingly* obliged to you," said Juliana, with such heartfelt gratitude that Lord Egremont, laughing, pinched her cheek and said it was a good thing she did not sit on the bench with him all the time, or there would be no prisoners to put in his comfortable new jail, where the prisoners were all supplied with sets of clothes including two pairs of stockings and a wooden nightcap, and exercised individually in a commodious airing yard.

"It sounds delightful, sir," Juliana said politely.

"I have it, I have it!" cried Mr. Blake from his packing case. "The words 'shining' and 'lovely' should be transposed: 'The lovely blue and shining heavenly shell!' That does away with the awkwardness of the two *v* sounds coming close together."

"William, William," said the earl affectionately, "why will you not leave working for a while and go to sit with my Liz and read to her? She complains that she has hardly seen you this visit."

"I intend painting a picture for her, very soon," said William, obediently rising to his feet. "It shall be a Last Judgment; and it shall have an inscription to her; let me think now, something along the lines of 'Egremont's Countess may assuage, The flames of Hell that fiercely rage…'"

Pocketing his notebook, he wandered out of the gallery, and Juliana, having thanked Lord Egremont once again for his kindness, was about to follow his example, when, to her extreme horror, who should enter the place but Sir Groby Feverel! With great presence of mind, Juliana slipped behind a large statue as Lord Egremont turned to greet Sir Groby, and kept out of view, though her heart was beating so loud with fright and surprise that she wondered it did not betray her presence.

To her dismay the two men, though they left the gallery, now walked in the direction of the tennis court. Juliana did not, therefore, dare return by the underground way, as she had been intending, but no more did she dare linger in Petworth House, for fear of encountering Sir Groby again. She ran upstairs to seek the help of William and Maria, who were sitting in the schoolroom, arguing about whether carrots floated or sank, instead of getting on with their Latin, and in spite of the remonstrance of Mademoiselle Lord. Fortunately at that moment a messenger arrived from Mr. Leidenberg in the kitchen, asking if Mam'selle would be so obliging as to come down and advise on the wording of the menu for the Prince of Wales's dinner.

As soon as she was gone: "William, could you possibly be so obliging as to lend me a suit of your clothes?" said Juliana. "Just for a couple of hours? We are much of a size—I promise I would not hurt them!"

"Of course, Miss Jeannie—anything you wish," said William, who had inherited his father's tranquil disposition. "But what's the row? Why do you look so pale and frightened?"

"It is just that there is somebody in the house by whom I very much wish not to be recognized."

"We'll dress you up so that your own mother wouldn't know you," said William cheerfully. "It'll be a prime lark, won't it, Polly?"

"*I'll* help Miss Jeannie dress," said his sister firmly. "It wouldn't be proper for *you* to do that."

So, ten minutes later, disguised in jacket, breeches, and hat, Juliana stole cautiously down a side staircase.

She still did not dare pass through the tennis court, for that would be to attract notice; so, thrusting her hands into her pockets and endeavoring to stride freely and casually, like a boy, she passed through the main entrance and so through the gates into the town.

In order to reach the street leading to the Hermitage, she was obliged to cross the main square, in which stood the Town Hall. This she did apprehensively enough, pulling her hat well down over her ears and hardly daring to glance about her, for fear of encountering her mother or Captain Davenport. A loud clamor of voices as she reached the middle of the square did, however, induce her to take a quick look sideways, and to her unbounded relief she saw that Lord Egremont's order had already been put into effect, for the gypsies were just emerging from the Town Hall, a most motley and gaudily garbed crew, chattering among themselves, with expressions that varied from indignation at their wrongful detention to joy at its sudden ending.

Juliana was hurrying on her way, amused at the thought that none of them realized *she* was the cause of their apprehension and also of their release, when she almost ran up against a sunburned man who was following in the rear of the tatterdemalion procession. She heard him give a sudden gasp—their eyes met—and then she was running up the street, almost blind with shock, her heart beating even faster than after her sight of Sir Groby. It could not have been! she told herself incredulously. It is impossible that it should have been. And yet it was! She was certain that it had been. Brown-skinned, his hair bleached by the sun, much thinner than when she had seen him last, disguised in a long smock, a round hat, spotted neck-erchief, and leather leggings, she had surely recognized Herr Welcker!

I *must* have imagined it! she decided, when, pant-ing and flustered, she found herself safely back in the Hermitage garden. No doubt having just seen Sir Groby—of which, alas, there can be no doubt whatsoever—deranged and flustered my mind, predis-posed me to imagine things that are not so. For what in the world could Herr Welcker be doing with a band of gypsies?

There seemed absolutely no adequate answer to that question.

She asked Berthe, whom she discovered hanging out washing in the garden, where the gypsies came from, and who they were. Berthe shrugged.

"They are not English—they are not French. They come and go as they please. They have ships, and cross the sea; sometimes, *comme les gentilshommes*, they bring goods or escaped persons from France; sometimes they steal and poach. They are wild. They are their own masters."

Which did not advance Juliana's inquiry.

Madame Reynard was, not unnaturally, somewhat startled to see her protégée come home with an agitated aspect and clad in a suit of boy's clothes. She demanded to be told what was the matter, and Juliana was obliged to explain that a gentleman staying at Petworth House, Sir Groby Feverel, was a particular enemy of hers, and that she very much dreaded being recognized by him.

"Heavens, my dear," said Madame Reynard, "you seem to have enemies under every bush! No sooner does one go than another one arrives. It is a pity—I was about to inform you that your mother and Captain Davenport have quitted the town, leaving their bill unpaid at the Bull. And now, here is another peril! I am not at all surprised to hear that you detest Sir Groby, for he is a most evil man, and I have heard many scandalous tales concerning him. Indeed, Georges was very annoyed that he has invited himself, for they are not friends, *pas du tout*, and the reason Sir Groby gave, that he was writing a treatise on wood carving and wished to study the work of Mr. Grinling Gibbons, seemed exceedingly hard to credit. I fear, my child, that he has somehow got wind of your presence in Petworth, and invented this pretext to come here. Perhaps he followed Captain Davenport and the Bow Street Runners."

"Oh, what can it all mean?" lamented Juliana. "I believe that I had best leave your house, ma'am, and get clear away from here. I am nothing but a trouble to you."

"Nonsense, my child; you are giving me more amusement and diversion than I have had for years," Madame Reynard replied briskly. "Now—let us think what is best to be done. I must ask Georges to get rid of Sir Groby; that will not be easy, for Georges is so good-natured, he dislikes to turn away a guest. But perhaps we can say there is smallpox in the town, or some such thing." She laughed as she surveyed the anxious Juliana. "You look quite famous as a boy! Perhaps you had better remain one for the present—my nephew Jean! Fortunately the gentlemen must have come again last night—we could say you came with them—they have left an immense package in my *kiosque*; if it is tea, I fear it must have become wet on the crossing, for it weighs heavy as lead."

However the heavy parcel proved, when undone, to contain books.

"*Books!*" exclaimed Madame Reynard in disgusted astonishment. "Reading is an admirable occupation, I do not say to the contrary, but to make this perilous journey all the way from France, up the Arun River and then our brook, for nothing but a great bundle of dusty volumes, quite passes my comprehension, indeed it does!"

But Juliana was kneeling on the stone summerhouse floor, with tears running down her cheeks, opening first one volume and then another.

"*Ciel*, what a to-do! What is it that it is?" demanded Madame Reynard in astonishment.

"It is—how amazing!—it is, they are, all Papa's books that he left behind in France!" said Juliana.

Twelve

JULIANA RETIRED TO HER COUCH THAT NIGHT WITH her mind in a whirl. Three questions perplexed her, of which sometimes one came uppermost, sometimes another: What was Sir Groby doing in Petworth House, and had he caught sight of her that morning? If so, had he recognized her? What was Herr Welcker doing with the gypsies? She had no doubt at all as to whether *he* had recognized her; in spite of her altered hair color and boy's clothes, she was perfectly certain that he had known her instantly. And the third question was: By what agency had her father's books been brought to England? Or rather: Who had thought to bring them? It seemed plain enough that the smugglers were the agency that had ferried them over from France.

Somebody must be my friend, she thought—and who could it be but Herr Welcker? For he was the only one who knew about Papa's books. Yet how did he know that I was here? And how can I be sure that it is indeed an act of friendship, and not simply a shrewd means of winning my regard? For it *must* have been Herr Welcker who told my mother of my interest in Charles the First, and gave her the notion of employing Captain Davenport to beguile me—only, if that was the case, why did Herr Welcker propose to me himself? I fear his motives must be as base as everybody else's.

It was long, long before she fell asleep, and her slumbers were disturbed by miserable dreams.

Next day at noon, when the *Morning Chronicle* was delivered off the mail coach, Madame Reynard, scanning its columns, exclaimed, "Why, child! Here is an advertisement regarding you!"

"*Me*, ma'am? You cannot be serious?"

Nonetheless, Juliana's heart leapt. It is Grandfather, she thought; he has forgiven me and wishes me to come home.

"Never more serious," said Madame Reynard. "Regard for yourself."

With trembling hands, Juliana took the paper and read: "If Miss J— P—, surviving daughter of the late C— E— T— P— Esq., of Hampshire and Florence, will communicate with Box 10, Poste Restante, Chancery Lane, London, she will receive Information Greatly to her Advantage."

"That must be you, must it not?" demanded Madame Reynard. "Without doubt, my dear, this will be something relating to your unknown wealth of which we spoke the other day. You had best reply without delay."

"You do not think, ma'am, that it is some fiendish device of my mother to entice me into a trap?" Juliana said. The moment the words had left her mouth she

thought how timid and foolish they sounded, but
Madame Reynard took them with due gravity.

"To be sure we shall have to reflect on how it will
be best for you to answer," said she. "You should certainly not give *this* address for your direction—rather
give that of Milord Egg; Georges will be happy to
frank your letter for you, I am sure. Yes, that will be
best. Write as from Petworth House, giving particulars
as to yourself, and requesting more information; then
I will take your letter round to Georges, and he will
send it to you."

The note was written and rewritten several times,
until Madame Reynard was satisfied that no dangerous
information had been divulged; and she then bore it
off to receive Lord Egremont's frank.

Three days later a footman came round from Petworth House with a packet for Madame Reynard.
Inside was a note addressed to Miss J— P— at
Petworth House, requesting Juliana to present herself
at an office in Chancery Lane.

"Now what is to do, ma'am?"

"You must on no account go up to London," said
Madame Reynard. "Why, for all we know it is a plot,
and long before you had arrived in Chancery Lane you
would have been decoyed away to your doom. No,
no; I say, and Georges quite agrees, that whoever it is
must come down here to see you. You had best write
to that effect."

So Juliana wrote, "Miss J— P— presents her
Compliments & will be pleased to interview X— Esquire
in Petworth at a time suitable to his Convenience."

Back came a reply, some days later, naming a time

and day the following week and suggesting a meeting in Petworth House.

"Impossible!" said Juliana. "For who knows but Sir Groby may still be there."

Regrettably, Sir Groby had hitherto proved impervious to all Lord Egremont's not very strongly worded hints that his chamber might soon be required for other guests; since there were at all times some twenty or thirty chambers available, this argument was certainly not a very strong one.

Juliana wrote back suggesting a meeting in a private parlor in the White Hart Inn.

"I suppose that will have to do," said Madame Reynard, not wholly satisfied. "I shall, of course, accompany you, and I think it best that Georges does, also."

"Oh, ma'am, no! I cannot expect Lord Egremont to do that! Besides, I think I should be embarrassed to have him at this interview, which is probably very stupid; I daresay some old great-aunt has left me her teapot."

The following day Rosine came back from market with dramatic news: "*Un vieux monsieur*—a guest of Milord Egg—had been attacked and left for dead! What a horror! It is as bad as France—soon we shall all be garroted in our beds!"

"Which guest?" inquired Madame Reynard. "I do hope it is not that delightful Monsieur Blake. I find his poetry entirely sympathetic." And she recited dramatically, "*Tigre, tout en incendie, Dans les forêts de la nuit!*"

"No, madame, it was not Monsieur Blake, but an old nobleman, *le Sieur Groby Fièvre*. And it is thought that *les gentilshommes* must have attacked him, for he was found lying where he had no business to be, in the underground way leading to this house!"

"Heavens! What next! At all events, he is justly served," said Madame, "and whoever attacked him did us a good turn. Is he dead?"

"No, madame, but they say he is close to death. Monsieur Barrett told me."

"I daresay I had better take him some of my cucumber lotion," said Madame Reynard, "wicked though he is. Mrs. Garland probably knows no better than to clap a wasps' nest onto his wound, as I found her doing for poor Socket when the bull gored him."

Juliana was half relieved, half frightened, to hear of Sir Groby's fate. For who could have struck him down so brutally? She hardly liked to speculate. And what had Sir Groby been doing in the underground passage? Could he have observed her emerging from it before she was aware of his presence in Petworth House? Or had he merely been exploring at random?

On the day of Juliana's interview, Madame obliged her to dress very handsomely in a gown of cinnamon-brown Lyons silk (smuggled) adorned with cream-colored lace and ribbons, and she lent one of her own hats, a ravishing broad-brimmed Dunstable straw. "So! Now if you are an heiress, at least you look the part. Let us be off!"

They were, of course, too early in their eagerness, and stood for a moment or two outside the White Hart, in the town square, where, despite Lord Egremont's stated disapproval, a cock-throwing was taking place.

Three or four handsome cocks stood in a circle

crudely marked out with chalk, and, from outside the boundary of a larger circle, men in the crowd were throwing short staffs at them. The cocks had been carefully trained, and they succeeded in avoiding the staffs with considerable skill and agility by leaping into the air. One of them, however, had had its leg broken, but continued to jump, despite the objections of the man whose staff had done the mischief.

"Do 'is leg be broke, Bowyer's cocky be my fair winnings," he bawled angrily.

"Not so, Jarge Pullin. Don't 'ee be so tournate, now! Bowyer's cocky mun be stunned proper, 'fore 'e belongs to be anybody's winnings."

"So shut thy gob!" shouted a loud cheerful voice which had a familiar ring about it.

"What a cruel game," said Juliana in disgust. "Let us go into the inn."

As they turned to do so, she saw Lieutenant Cox's yellow head among the crowd, and swiftly tilted the brim of her hat so that he should not get a glimpse of her face.

In the entrance hall of the inn they met the lawyer whom Madame Reynard had consulted about her title deeds.

"What, are you back in Petvurrt again so soon, Monsieur Trockmorton?" she said. "We keep you busy, Milord Egg and I! Have you brought me news of the Glebe Path, *enfin*?"

"No, no, it is not on Lord Egremont's business that I am here, nor on yours, ma'am," he said fussily—he was a short, self-important little man, with pince-nez and an old-fashioned brown wig. "I am here on account of some young lady who, I fear, has more hair than wit. I only hope she arrives to the appointment and does not keep me waiting. But, forgive me, I am upon my hour, and must leave you."

Away he bustled and when, two minutes later, they entered the appointed private parlor, they found him there before them.

"*Eh bien, alors!*" cried Madame Reynard. "Here is a fine comedy! We are all on the same errand, it seems, Monsieur Trockmorton. Permit me to introduce to you Mademoiselle J— P—!"

"Why, what is this?" he said crossly. "Are you joking me, ma'am? I understand that you are frequently of a sportive nature."

"*Mais, au contraire*, altogether serious! This is the young lady for whom you have been searching, monsieur. She has been residing under my care because her friends forsook her; and Lord Egremont has taken a great fondness for her, and is prepared to vouch for her in every way possible, so quick, to your business, *monsieur le Notaire!*"

"Well, this is all highly irregular," said he, frowning.

"First of all, do you have with you any proofs, miss, that you are whom you claim to be?"

Juliana had anticipated this. Fortunately she had her certificate of birth, which her father had entrusted to her at the commencement of their journey. She had taken it in her reticule on the elopement with Captain Davenport, believing that it might be needed for a marriage ceremony, even one at Gretna Green.

Mr. Throgmorton scanned this document, pursing his lips together disapprovingly. "This seems to be in order," he said in a grudging manner. "But this is not to say that you are the person named in it. You might have acquired it anywhere."

"Well, I daresay Lady Lambourn would speak for me—if she had not turned me out of her house," said Juliana in a dispirited voice. "Or my grandfather, General Paget, if I had not angered him by running away from Flintwood to be married."

"You are not married, however?" said Mr. Throgmorton sharply. "You wrote to me as Miss Paget?"

"Yes, sir, I am still Miss Paget."

"Your father is not living, miss?"

Juliana shook her head. "He died upon his arrival in England."

Mr. Throgmorton nodded; he was obviously already informed of this fact.

"You were his only child?"

"Yes, sir."

He nodded again, and then asked, "Is there any person of standing and repute who was acquainted with you when you were residing with your father, who would be prepared to swear to your identity?"

Juliana reflected for a few moments. Then she said, "I daresay Mr. William Wyndham the British Representative in Tuscany, would verify that I am Miss Paget. He knew both me and Papa."

"Monsieur Guillaume Wyndham?" cried Madame Reynard. "But this is *formidable*! He is the younger brother of Milord Egg! Only imagine! You have been acquainted with him all this time, and we never knew it? Oh, Georges will be so delighted!"

"Well, well, there are various formalities that will

have to be gone through before the business is completed," said Mr. Throgmorton, obviously favorably impressed, however, by this connection. "It may be necessary to summon Mr. William Wyndham to England, failing other witnesses. But perhaps your grandfather may prove more accommodating than you expect, Miss Paget. There is, after all, a very considerable sum of money involved."

"*Eh bien*, monsieur, come to the point!" cried Madame Reynard impatiently. "This sum of money, how large is it? And from whom does it come? And when is Mademoiselle Paget entitled to it?"

Mr. Throgmorton did not like to be hurried. He set his fingertips together and looked over them in an admonishing manner at the impatient females before him.

"General Paget, as you may be aware, had a younger brother, Henry Paget, who also entered the Army, according to family habit, and pursued a successful military career."

"No, that I did not know," Juliana replied. "My grandfather never mentioned him to me." But then, she thought, Grandfather never mentioned *anything*, if he could avoid it.

"The brothers were estranged," Mr. Throgmorton said primly. "General Henry Paget—for he, too, rose to be a general—Henry Paget did not attempt to conceal his disapproval and indignation at the time of his brother's action in severing relations with his son, Mr. Charles Paget. His protest took the form of making a will in which he left his entire fortune to his nephew."

"In *my* opinion it would have been more to the purpose if he had helped his poor nephew during his lifetime, instead of leaving him to a life of penury in Florence," said Madame Reynard tartly. "However, continue, monsieur."

"General Henry Paget had very *little* money in his lifetime," said Mr. Throgmorton, directing a quelling look at Madame over his pince-nez. "However, shortly before his retirement last year he had the good fortune to be of service to an Indian potentate, whose life he was able to preserve during a period of civil war and insurrection. (I should perhaps have mentioned that General Henry passed most of his military career in India, serving under Lord Cornwallis.) This potentate, the Gaikwar of Baroda (I understand, a small but affluent state on the borders of Kashmir), was so obliged to your great-uncle, Miss Paget, that he made him a gift of money, jewels, and estates, the values of which, when realized, amounts to some five hundred thousand pounds."

"What?" exclaimed Madame Reynard, dropping her parasol. "He gave him half a million?"

"The sum would seem to approximate to that, certainly," said Mr. Throgmorton with ill-concealed disapproval. "Unfortunately General Henry did not long survive to benefit by the Gaikwar's handsome gift, news of which had followed him to England. He had returned here last autumn, but contracted a putrid sore throat, which he was unable to shake off, and which finally brought about his decease in May this year."

"Then," put in the irrepressible Madame Reynard—

Juliana sat stunned and silent—"*ce cher enfant-là* is liable to inherit—"

"One moment, madam, *if* you please," said Mr. Throgmorton irritably. "General Henry's will was simple enough. He left his entire fortune—as I say, a small one at the time when he made the will—to his nephew, should his nephew survive him. Should his nephew predecease him—or die while the nephew's daughter was still a child—the money was then left in trust for the said daughter, she to receive it on arriving at the age of eighteen years." He bent his gaze on Juliana's birth certificate. "Ah—I understand that your eighteenth birthday falls on June the twenty-fourth this year, that is to say, in eight days' time. However, the will also provided that, if Miss Paget should have married before reaching the age of eighteen—"

"Which she has not," said Madame Reynard.

"Then the legacy would pass into the hands of her husband, to be administered for her by him. General Henry Paget had no very high opinion as to the abilities of females to take care of themselves or their property," said Mr. Throgmorton, for the first time allowing a note of approval to creep into his voice. "Or, should Miss Paget have the misfortune to decease before her eighteenth birthday, then the money would pass to her next of kin."

"Her next of kin?"

"Probably her mother, if still living."

"*Mon dieu!*" breathed Madame. "So: who knew about this will, monsieur?"

"Before General Henry's death, very few persons,"

said Mr. Throgmorton, thin-lipped. "And of those, even fewer were aware of the Gaikwar's gift. Regrettably, in my opinion, General Henry had seen fit to write to his brother, informing him of the legacy. Consequently, I understand that Sir Horace Paget, realizing that once the news was out his niece was likely to become the prey of fortune hunters, instructed his daughter, Lady Lambourn, to find some respectable husband for the young lady before her expectations became public knowledge, so that by the time this occurred she would be in the care of some worthy and disinterested person. However, this plan proved unsuccessful."

"Did Lady Lambourn know about the will?" faintly inquired Juliana.

"No, she did not," shortly replied Mr. Throgmorton. "General Sir Horace, having no very high opinion of her intelligence, did not see fit to inform her. Of course, she learned about it at the time of General Henry's death, last month, when I understand she went into a fit of hysterics which lasted four days."

"Who did know about it?" asked Madame Reynard.

Mr. Throgmorton frowned. "*Most* regrettably," he answered, "I had an untrustworthy clerk whom I was obliged to dismiss last year for embezzlement. I have some reason to believe that this person, Francis Jenkins, in return for payment, may, at the time of the Gaikwar's gift, have passed information as to General Henry's will on to another of my clients." He set his lips, as if no persuasion would extract this person's name from him, but Juliana instantly thought of Sir Groby. She remembered her cousin saying, "Mr.

Throgmorton, his man-of-business, sent Pa a note about a marriage contract."

"What became of Jenkins?" inquired Madame Reynard.

"I have no idea," replied Mr. Throgmorton shortly. "As I say, he left my employ last summer and, I believe, went abroad. He was a most unsatisfactory clerk. He had left the acting profession to try his hand at the law, and I should not be surprised if he returned to the stage… Have *you* any questions to ask me, Miss Paget?"

But Juliana shook her head without speaking. The news had overwhelmed her. All she could think was, that if only her great-uncle Henry had written to her father before—if they had traveled to England last summer—if her father had known that such a sum awaited him—if he had not wished to finish his book before setting out for England—

"Oh, I cannot bear it!" she exclaimed, pressing her hands to her cheeks, down which tears were beginning to roll.

"Tush! That, miss, is hardly a normal way in which to receive news of a very handsome competence," said Mr. Throgmorton, disapproving to the last. He added more tolerantly, however, "Well, well, I daresay you would like some time to think over the information you have received. Perhaps we may appoint a date for another meeting to discuss arrangements for your formal identification. I would suggest tomorrow morning. (Tonight I dine at Petworth House.) And then I shall come down again on June the twenty-fourth (if all is in order) with papers for you to sign,

Miss Paget. For the moment I daresay I had best bid you good afternoon."

"Thank you, sir," said Juliana. Her eyes were too blurred by tears to perceive his extended hand; she stood up and moved uncertainly toward the door. All she longed for was fresh air and silence, in which to come to terms with this devastating news.

"One single moment, madam—" said Mr. Throgmorton, as Madame Reynard was on the point of following her young protégée. "With regard to your inquiry two weeks since, respecting the Glebe Path—as you are here, we may as well settle the matter—"

Juliana walked blindly along the passage and out into the street, disregarding Madame's cry of "*Attendez-moi, chérie!*"

The cock-throwing was still in progress; by now, with dusk falling and work hours over, a much larger crowd of people had assembled in the square. Anxious to get away from the press, Juliana edged her way along the wall and round the corner into the street that led up toward the Hermitage.

"Look out, missie, you've dropped summat!" cried a rough voice, and turning, Juliana saw something white on the cobbles. She stopped to pick it up—had a momentary glimpse of a gypsy urchin clad in ragged breeches and a red kerchief, who seemed to be staring at her in horror—then a powerful hand thrust her head dawn, while, at the same time, some object held under her nose and mouth gave out a choking fume of noxious vapor which she could not help inhaling. Her head swam, her legs gave way beneath her, and she sank down upon the pavement.

"Watch out for the lady, she've fainted!" the same rough voice shouted.

Dimly, Juliana apprehended that she was being lifted up; she felt herself laid on an upholstered seat, and heard the slam of a carriage door; then she felt a swaying, jolting motion which assisted her plunge into deep unconsciousness.

Thirteen

JULIANA NEXT OPENED HER EYES ON DARKNESS. AT first she felt dreadfully sick and confused, the effects of the drug still remaining to perplex her senses; she even wondered if she might possibly be dead, a horrible, close, dank, earthy odor all about her powerfully contributing to this impression. But after a long while she heard a cock crow, very faintly, in the distance, and then light began gradually stealing into the room where she lay.

It was a dismal little box of a place—the bedroom of some cottage, she surmised from the sloped ceiling, damp walls made of wattle and daub, the bare worm-eaten boards of the floor, and the lack of furniture. A small window hole was boarded over. It took Juliana some time to observe all these details, for she still felt exceedingly weak and unwell; when she attempted to raise herself up on one elbow, her head throbbed so badly that she was immediately obliged to lie down again. At last, however, she managed to push herself up, and found that she was laid upon a pallet on the floorboards. The door of the room was closed. She crawled over and feebly shook it, but it was secured on the other side.

"Help!" Juliana called, as loudly as she could, and she shook the flimsy door again. "Help, help!"

At first there was no reply, but as she continued to call, and to rattle the door, she heard sounds from below, as if her room lay at the top of a flight of stairs.

She heard a kind of grumbling groan, then a cough or scraping sound. After a while a man's voice said, "Our guest has woken up," and a woman's voice replied with a sound of irritable acquiescence, as if she resented being woken from sleep simply to be apprised of this fact.

"Do *you* wish to speak to her, or shall I?"

There was another irritable rejoinder, a negative, apparently. Then quick firm steps mounted a stair, and a voice, surprisingly close, spoke on the other side of the thin door.

"Miss Paget? Are you attending?"

Juliana recognized the voice immediately. She mustered what strength she had to reply in a calm, firm manner. "Yes, I am attending, Captain Davenport. And I wish you will let me out of this place!"

"Not so fast, my dear! First we need an undertaking from you."

"If you expect me to agree to marry you," Juliana said coldly, "you are a great way wide of the mark! I am not to be caught in that manner twice, I assure you!"

"In that case, ma'am," he replied, "I fear that you are liable to starve to death in there."

Juliana instantly began shouting "Help!" again, and rattling the door as hard as she could. Captain Davenport waited until she had tired herself out (which did not take long, as she was still very weak) and sunk down on the floor; then his voice, still just outside the door, said, in a pitying tone, "I am afraid there is not the least use in keeping up such a clamor, Miss Paget. We are in the middle of the forest; in the area known as Badlands, because it belongs to nobody, and is rarely visited. The keeper's cottage in which you find yourself incarcerated is ruinous and not entered from one year's end to another. Your skeleton may dry to dust here before it is discovered."

"If my body is not discovered," said Juliana quickly, "then I shall not be presumed dead and it will be many years before those who hope to inherit my fortune may do so!"

"Very true, my dear. So it is much more likely that your body *will* be discovered; doubtless your murder will be laid at the door of the brutal smugglers who attacked Sir Groby."

He let a pause elapse while Juliana wondered if the attack on Sir Groby had been public knowledge, or whether his awareness of the occurrence indicated that he had committed the assault himself; probably the latter, she thought.

Then he said, in a milder tone, "Come, my dear, do not be obstinate! We hold all the cards. You may as well be accommodating. After all, there is plenty of money to share among us. Your mother has a special license. We may be married by noon, and you back with your friends. Why do you not come downstairs and talk the matter over calmly?"

"I am perfectly calm, Captain Davenport," Juliana replied. "And quite prepared to come down."

She heard a key turned, and presently saw him. He looked different; shrunk down, somehow in stature, from the surly man with whom she had shared the elopement; and very, very different from the polished Captain Davenport of the Pantheon Rooms and St. James's Park. This man was pale, untidy, and haggard; his beard was untrimmed, his eyes were bloodshot. However, he seemed collected enough; he pulled Juliana to her feet (she found she was still too weak to stand unaided) and assisted her down a flight of stairs which were so narrow and so steep that they more nearly resembled a ladder.

The squalid little room down below was a degree warmer than Juliana's prison had been, because a small fire of sticks burned in the tiny hearth; and there was a narrow window, also, which assured Juliana that Captain Davenport had spoken nothing but the truth when he said they were in the middle of the forest, for it showed a close view of dense undergrowth. Juliana, however, had little attention to spare for anything but the woman who sat huddled on a stool by the handful of fire, fixing her eyes hungrily upon the disheveled figure of her captive.

"Well, miss," she said harshly. "How does it feel to be the underdog? Do you find that you like it?"

Juliana looked thoughtfully at the speaker, in whom she recognized the lady of the Ponte Vecchio, and of Lord Lambourn's house.

"How do you do, ma'am? I collect that you are my mother. How should I address you? As Mother? Or as Mrs. Paget?"

"Ay—ay—you are full of fine airs and impertinence

now—but after a few days without any food you'll sing another tune," the woman said loudly and angrily, her hands working one inside the other, as if she wished to take hold of Juliana and shake her. Indeed, she half rose up, but Captain Davenport, behind Juliana, said sharply, "Be easy now, Laura! Do not rush at things all in a pelted... I am afraid you will have to sit on the floor, my dear," he added, to Juliana, "since there is but one seat." He himself sat on the bottom step— for the stairs led straight into the little room—and Juliana, after glancing round her, sank weakly onto the ground, which was simply hard-packed earth, covered over with a layer of dirty-looking rubbish. The room was almost as bare as the one upstairs, save for a couple of sacks spread out in one corner, and a small basket, containing a loaf and a bottle of Geneva. A black pot stood near the fire. Captain Davenport, interpreting Juliana's glance, nodded ironically. "See the privations we undergo for your sake," he said. "But *we*, at least, are supplied with food, which I fear will not be *your* lot."

Laura Paget, still with ravenous eyes fixed on Juliana, began to mutter, rather to herself than aloud. "Oh, how I have *longed* for this moment! The petted, cosseted little darling—her father loved her so *much*! He took such care of her! Never let her out of his sight! Times out of mind I have lurked, and watched, and planned, and hoped—but he—weak, whining fool as he was—nevertheless always seemed to divine just as I was ready to pounce, and off he would go; and then there was the long pursuit to begin all over, discovering where they had flitted to. In Geneva—in

Milan—in Florence—each time I thought I had her. I had found out so much—talked to neighbors, learned the degree of his illness—all her follies and weaknesses—*il re Carlo!* Bah! And then—just when I had my decoy duck ready, my sweet Charles figure fitted to match her sickly tastes—off she went again. But now I have her, and can do as I choose with her."

"Easy, ma'am," said Captain Davenport warningly. "Take care now! Do not be overexciting yourself and mar all!"

"Why should I have lived a life of wretched anxiety and disgrace, all these years, while *she* is feted and pampered—vouchers to Almack's, introduced to Prinney's brothers—what has she done to deserve such respect?"

Juliana could not withhold a shudder as she studied her mother. It seemed only too plain that Laura Paget had become slightly unhinged by the uncertainties of her life, or by its hatreds, or by the exertions of her recent scheming. Juliana was not certain that reason would reach her at all, but trying it seemed the only course open to her.

"What do you want, Mother?" she said, in as calm a voice as she could manage. "If it is money, I shall have plenty for us both. I am very happy to sign a paper making over half my fortune to you. Will that not satisfy you?"

"No—no—that would not do—" muttered Laura Paget, turning from her survey of her child to stir the fire restlessly with a hazel twig. "No, she must give it all—all—"

"Signing such a paper would be impracticable,

I fear, Miss Paget," interposed Captain Davenport. "There would be all too much reason to suppose that you had signed under duress."

"I would say that I had not!"

"No, I fear you must resign yourself to marry me. The marriage need be of short duration only, I assure you!"

"Ay—he wishes to return to his slut in Southampton," muttered Mrs. Paget spitefully. Suddenly she rounded on Davenport, her eyes blazing. "If you had not spent half the money I gave you on that trollop, we should not be in this case now—forced to subsist on the charity of your friend—your havey-cavey Cox! Suppose he does not come back?"

"He will come back, ma'am, don't trouble your head," Davenport said easily. "He wants his cut! Young Cox has all his buttons, I promise you."

"But how can you hope to marry me?" said Juliana. "What clergyman would do it?"

"Why, my dear, there is not the least difficulty in the world. We have your mother—who approves of the match—we have her consent. And we have a clergyman—Mr. Wakeford, the rector of Barlavington, who stands under an obligation to my friend Cox—a little matter of a false entry in the baptismal register, which he would not wish brought into the public eye!"

"Cox and Jenkins," mumbled Mrs. Paget to herself. "Don't care for 'em. Never wanted 'em in. But couldn't carry off the gal on my own. Don't want 'em now, though. Who's to say—once Jenkins marries her—that I shall have *my* rights?"

"Jenkins?" said Juliana, turning to look at Captain Davenport, who appeared somewhat embarrassed. "Is that who you really are? Mr. Throgmorton's dismissed clerk? The ex-actor? No wonder you contrived such a sympathetic presentation of King Charles the First! I collect that, having milked Sir Groby, you then approached my mother with your valuable information and she was persuaded to hire you? Let me congratulate you. Captain Davenport is vastly more romantic than Jenkins! I see you had gauged my tastes to a nicety."

"Pray feel free to continue calling me Captain Davenport if you prefer," said he as jauntily as he could.

"I do not wish to call you anything at all," said Juliana. "You fill me with disgust. I find you wholly contemptible. I would sooner starve to death than marry you."

"Strong words!" He shrugged. "But it may not be a case of starving to death, my love. That sounds easy and peaceful, I daresay you think! But what would you say to being upended in a barrel of rainwater (there is one just outside, if it be not full of mud) and held there till you drown? Or having your throat cut with that"—and he nodded toward a rusty but sharp-looking butcher knife that lay by the basket.

Juliana shuddered in spite of herself.

"But if my murdered body is found," she said quickly, to banish the idea of that rusty blade sawing at her throat, "*you* will not stand to gain a penny, Cap— Mr. Francis Jenkins. All the money will then go to my mother—if she does not go to the gallows."

"Sharp, aren't you?" he said, half angry, half admiring. "But I can easily supply myself with a wedding certificate, you know. Mr. Wakeford would oblige with one, I feel certain."

"In that case," said Juliana, rising shakily to her feet, "I do not see that you have any need for my cooperation at all. You may as well ask Mr. Wakeford to forge the certificate directly—if you can get my mother to agree! And now, if you will excuse me, I shall lie down again, for I feel very ill."

"Suit yourself," replied Davenport laconically, but Mrs. Paget cried, "No, no Francis, how do you know she will not escape out of the window? You must cut her stays—cut her stays! Leave her only her shift, so that she cannot run out into the wood!"

"How can she possibly escape, Laura, while we are here?" he replied irritably, but as she continued to insist, in a high, piercing voice, that Juliana's stays must be cut—

"Oh, very well," he grumbled at last, and, taking up the knife, he walked round behind Juliana, ripped the brown silk dress apart with one dexterous tug, and slit her stay laces at the back so that they and her petticoat fell off and she stood shivering in her shift.

"Oh!" she gasped furiously. "How dare you? How *dare* you?"

"Just a precaution, my love," he replied calmly, wagging the knife at her before returning it to the basket. "Here—you may have one of these if you wish to cover yourself," he added, averting his eyes as if in distaste from her bare limbs, and he tossed her one of the sacks. Furious, cold, shaking, shamed, and terrified, Juliana glanced toward the door, wondering whether to make a dash for it, but Davenport, catching her eye, slightly shook his head in what was almost a pitying manner, and she knew that it would be hopeless; still too sick and weak from the effects of the drug, she would be unable to run more than a few yards. Climbing the stairs, she huddled back on her pallet, pulling the sack round her as best she could.

Soon, to her unspeakable horror, she heard her mother's voice, angrily urging Davenport.

"Don't be a whining milksop, man, you were not used to be so nice! Why, I can remember times when you were as hot and hard to hold back as any stallion. What ails you, fool? Hurry on up and take her—then she is ours for sure, she will be glad enough to put out her little finger for your ring."

A low mutter followed, evidently Davenport objecting to her command, then her voice rose to an angry shriek.

"Coward! Gaby! Do you call yourself a man? You are no better than a eunuch. If you do not go up there, I declare I shall take the knife and so spoil her looks that no other man will even wish to touch her."

"No, ma'am—Laura, do not—pray, pray be calm, I beg of you! Think what you are about—think what you are doing—your own daughter! Oh, very well, I will go up—"

Juliana heard him step on the stair. Looking about her desperately, she noticed the glitter of rusty metal in a corner, and snatched up an old meat skewer which must have been lying there for years past. Preparing to sell her honor dear, she faced Captain Davenport as he came through the door.

"I warn you, sir, I shall defend myself as long as my

strength holds out," she said breathlessly, retreating to the corner of the room, and she held the skewer in front of her.

"Oh, it is of no use, I can't do it," said he, with a kind of savage irritation. Laura Paget was shouting obscenities from below.

"Coward! Coward! Do it, or I shall call you the most arrant coward I have ever come across."

He swung furiously round and ran down the stairs again. Juliana was terrified at the sound of the quarrel that followed. Discovering two staples, on the door and the jamb, she contrived a bolt with the skewer, so that when, presently, her mother ran upstairs and shook the door, shrieking insults, she was unable to get in. After a time she went down again, and a long, muttered colloquy took place. Juliana crawled weakly back to her pallet, and sometime later she must have fallen asleep again.

When she woke she realized with dismay that entry had been effected into the room. The skewer had been dislodged from its shaky position and removed. Worse, the drugged material must have been held to her nostrils again while she slept, for she had the same nauseated, dizzy sensation, in even greater degree, that she had experienced before.

Downstairs, as before, she could hear voices arguing; but now there seemed to be three of them. She could distinguish two men's voices, besides the shrill, bird-like tones of her mother.

No wonder, she thought vaguely, that Papa could not endure being married to her. No wonder he fled from her...

"Damn your impudent selfishness," Laura Paget was crying. "Why do we have to remain here like beggars while you lounge at your ease in Petworth?"

"Because, ma'am, I happen to have a house in Petworth, whereas you have run out of money," came Lieutenant Cox's voice, loud, cheerful, and self-satisfied. "And because it's best we ain't associated in people's minds, and because someone has to keep guard over the young lady. But don't fret—I have brought you enough Geneva to warm you nicely—a whole tub—nineteen bottles' worth—I hope you are duly grateful! It cost me a pound and sixteen shillings, and I do not begrudge it in the slightest."

"Have you brought some bread and meat?" asked Davenport's voice sharply.

"Ay, ay, plenty; a lovely handful of mutton chops for Madame here to sizzle over the embers. That should tickle up the nostrils of our little captive up yonder; I daresay she will very soon be ready to cry 'I will!'"

"Well, I can tell you, she ain't at the moment," growled Davenport.

"No? Give her two or three days of fasting, and she'll come around. Or do you reckon she would sooner have me for a bridegroom? I'd be ready—you know that!"

"I also happen to know that you've a wife already at Clapham!"

"What has that to say to anything? You are as good as wed to your Tillie. By the by, what became of the brat?"

"I neither know nor care!"

Juliana heard a clink, and then Laura Paget's voice. "Fuller than that, idiot! I need more than a niggardly couple of teaspoonsful to keep out the cold in this hideous damp hovel!"

"I am sorry that you don't like it, ma'am; it was the best accommodation I could think of on the spur of the moment. And you must agree it makes a handy prison—not quite so choice as old Egremont's, with his nightcaps and his two pounds of bread a day, but even more secure." Cox laughed heartily, and there were further sounds of clinking. Although she intended to keep listening, Juliana presently fell into a drugged sleep once more. Vaguely, through its mists, she heard the voices downstairs become loud, rise to a pitch of quarrelsomeness, then die down. Later on there came soft steps on the stair, and the door opened. The light of a candle illuminated her wretched little room.

"Miss Paget? Are you there?" inquired a soft voice from behind the candle flame. "It is quite all right to come out now! Both your mama and Captain Davenport are enjoying the sleep of intoxication. I took the liberty of lacing their Geneva with laudanum! Dear, dear, they have left you in a pickle, have they not?"—as she staggeringly rose to her feet. "I wish I could carry you down the stairs, but I fear they are too steep; but you may take my hand; so—that's the dandy. Down you go—very good!"

Arrived in the downstairs room, Juliana peered about—it was dark now, and the place was lit only by the candle and the dying fire. She could see both her mother and Davenport sprawled out on the floor, evidently dead drunk.

"My—my dress—" she managed to articulate. Lieutenant Cox—for it was he—looked about briefly, then stooped to pick up a shred of material.

"Alas—I fear your mother must have burnt it—" He tossed the piece into the fire, which blazed up briefly. "Here, you had best take her shawl instead. Do not trouble yourself—it is all thick woodland, there is no one to see you."

Shivering, Juliana wrapped herself in the shawl he gave her, then followed weakly as he led the way outside.

The night was cool and damp, very dark, with no stars. Juliana sniffed hungrily at the smell of wet undergrowth and forest earth, so much preferable to the fetid smell of the hut.

"I am afraid I am too weak to walk," she said simply. "Have you a carriage?"

"A carriage? No, my dear. But old Brown Peg brought me and the tub of Geneva, and I daresay she can make shift to carry us both back. A moment, though, till I make up a fire to warm the bones of that previous pair—no need to leave them to freeze to death—" She heard him laugh, briefly, his step as he turned back into the house with something in his hands; then she saw the reflected light as a flame leapt. A moment later he was back, beside the dark, warm bulk of a horse.

"Hup you go now, my dear, and hang on to the crupper! That's it—so—now I mount in front of you, and all you have to do is keep a firm hold of my belt. Capital! Off we go; old Peg knows her way through these woods better than any exciseman."

Indeed, the mare, invisible in the darkness, picked

her way sure-footedly among the trees, while Juliana dazedly clung on to Lieutenant Cox's belt. Presently he began to laugh.

"Butter my wig, what a pair of muttonheads! I am sorry, my dear, to laugh when you are in such a case, but I cannot help it when I think how capitally I have fooled them! Eh, me and old Sir Groby too! He was watching out for them like a hawk, had them followed to Petworth as soon as Dav made the mistake of going up to town for the Runners. (And much use *they* were—putting the cry on a set of gypsies who were in France at the time you vanished.) Down comes old Sir Groby, sniffing about, and I very soon have *him* dispatched. And now, if that pair choose to drink themselves into Valhalla, I daresay neither you nor I will weep, my love, hey? I'll soon have *you* in safety—in a close, quiet little room, where you can lie as snug as a dormouse all winter long—come up, mare!"—as she stumbled, crossing a brook. "Watch how you go, old Peg, it's not often that I ride you with five hundred thousand gold shekels clinging on to my belt."

"Where are you taking me, sir?" asked Juliana, stirred to vague alarm by his words.

"Why, to my father's house at Newgrove, where else? I wouldn't invite that havey-cavey pair there— but there's a little private room that will just suit you— with your interest in the Stuarts!" He chuckled. "Ay, you can sit in there and think about Charles the First, and Charles the Second, and Charles the Third, too, if you've a mind to. And where you and I can talk and kiss without fear of interruption."

"Sir—Lieutenant Cox—pray, pray take me back to Madame Reynard's house—to the Hermitage—I am sure Mr. Throgmorton will pay you a great reward if you do so," Juliana said.

"My dear girl, you must be funning! A reward? Why accept a slice, when you can have the whole cake? You are so delightful and charming, Miss Paget, that I cannot rest until I have made you mine, all mine. Hey up, mare!"

They had now come out of the wood into fields, and he kicked the mare into a canter.

"B-b-but you have a wife in Clapham!" Juliana managed to articulate.

"Never mind her, my dear! A wife in Clapham is easy got rid of—one way or t'other. If she won't go easy, I'll prune her off as I did Rosie the baker's daughter…"

By now they were galloping at a rapid pace. Juliana looked down at the shadowy ground. If she threw herself off the mare, she would probably break her leg. Then she would not be able to run, and he would easily be able to recapture her. Perhaps they might come to a gate or stile, where he would be obliged to slow down; that would be the time to throw herself off, just as he had passed through the gate.

She had reached this point in her incoherent planning when a voice cried, "Halt!" The mare snorted, and Juliana was suddenly aware of black figures moving out from the darkness of a hedgerow ahead of them. Peg threw up her head, and Lieutenant Cox cursed at her; next moment Juliana, leaving go of Cox's belt, pushed herself violently away from the mare and fell sprawling onto hard grassy ground. As she hit the ground she heard a pistol shot and saw a red spark of flame; the mare screamed and wheeled about. Juliana heard a confusion of voices shouting, and then nothing more.

Fourteen

SHE WOKE TO BROAD DAYLIGHT, AND A SENSE OF complete incredulity. For she found herself back in her own room, in her own bed at the Hermitage—sunlight on the apple trees outside the window, Berthe just coming through the door with a steaming cup on a tray. Could it all have been an appalling dream? But no—as Juliana tried to sit up, she realized that she ached in every limb, and that her head still swam horribly; also her left arm was bandaged and felt very sore when she tried to move it.

"Ah, you poor little cabbage, you are awake then—wait one small moment while I call Madame," exclaimed Berthe rhetorically, putting down the cup, which smelled as if it contained hot wine and cinnamon. Madame Reynard was, in fact, close behind her, and came swiftly to the bedside to embrace Juliana.

"Oh, *chérie*, what a fright you gave us. We have been in despair!—we feared we had lost you forever—that your terrible maman had abducted you in order to acquire the treasure of that Rajah or Nawab, or whatever he was—oh, how happy we were to see you safe back!"

"But, Tante 'Lise—how did I get back? Who brought me? I remember nothing!"

"Who brought you? Why, the gypsies did—two great black-haired fellows like Beelzebub and Asmodeus, an old witch in a shawl, a young girl, and a little imp with a red kerchief, who told me his name was Pharaoh, though I daresay Child of Satan would do equally well. They said that they had found you insensible in a field, up near Brinksoles, with Lieutenant Cox dead as a herring nearby, and his mare lamed by stumbling about with her foreleg through her rein."

"Lieutenant Cox *dead*! What killed him?"

"A bullet through his head," replied Madame Reynard calmly. "The gypsies all declare that is how they found him—and as he was known to be involved with *les gentilshommes*, it is thought he must have been killed in some smuggling affray. His parents have been summoned back to Newgrove from Bath; other than them, I do not think anybody will grieve at his loss."

Juliana recalled his saying. "There's a little private room that will just suit you..." She shivered, and lay silent. She wondered what had become of her mother and Captain Davenport—Jenkins. How long had it been before they had woken and discovered that their accomplice had betrayed them?

"My child, I must ask you one question," Madame Reynard said, looking at her carefully. "I do not think you are quite ready to tell your tale yet, but this I *must* know, in case there is need to send for a physician. Were you violated? I dislike to distress you, but did either of those men force you to go to bed with him?"

"No, madame—thank God," Juliana said weakly. "I must confess I feared very much that Captain Davenport would do so—because, on our elopement, before, he had been so—so very urgent—but I think the presence of my mother constrained him—"

"He was her lover?"

"I do not know... I think it possible. And their accomplice—Lieutenant Cox—I think his intentions were very bad, but he was shot before—"

"It is enough." Madame Reynard's voice was full of relief. "And you have no pain, no wound, no bleeding? *Bien*. We will talk fully when you are more rested. Now drink Berthe's posset and sleep again. You are among friends once more, and we shall see that no harm comes to you."

Twice more Juliana slept and woke, drank Berthe's potions, and slept again. Then she awoke clear-headed and calm, and ready to tell her tale. At that point Madame Reynard insisted on summoning Lord Egremont. "He is a justice of the peace, if wrongdoers need to be brought to judgment, it is best that he hear it all from the start."

So Juliana told her tale from the beginning. When she described the little house in the forest, Madame Reynard and Lord Egremont looked at one another significantly, but neither spoke. When Juliana came to the end, Madame Reynard said, "Are you feeling strong, *chérie*? Strong enough to hear a somewhat shocking piece of news?"

"I—I think so," faltered Juliana. "What is it?"

"Two days ago some charcoal burners over at Brinksoles noticed a great column of smoke going up into the sky from the part of the forest known as Badlands. They went to see what was causing it, and found the old keeper's cottage burning; it had already burned almost away, and they could not put out the fire. But when it all died down, a body was found in the ashes."

"One body?"

"Yes. It was so burned, they do not know if it were man or woman."

I wonder which of them it was, thought Juliana, shivering. Was that Cox's work—just before we left? Somehow the horror of that death, in the dreadful little house, combined with the doubt as to who had died to make the thought of *the other*, still alive, particularly terrifying... She repeated aloud, in a trembling voice, "I wonder which of them it was."

Lord Egremont said firmly, "My dear Miss Juliana, you have been subjected to a shocking experience, but you must now endeavor to put it quite out of your mind. Your friends are all around you, and we are going to keep a most careful watch over you, never fear! We shall also institute a search for the survivor of that fire. Meanwhile, as it is only three days now till your birthday—"

"Three days?" cried Juliana. "Why, what is today? I had thought it was Tuesday?"

"No, my child. It is Thursday. You have lain sick for two days. And now," continued Lord Egremont, "I have a surprise for you; a pleasant one, I hope."

"What can it be, sir?" Juliana felt she was hardly equal to any more surprises.

"Your Grandfather, Sir Horace, is here, and wishful to see you."

"*Grandfather?* Oh, I would like to see him above all things!"

At her heartfelt cry of joy, some muttering, which had been going on outside the door, resolved itself into Berthe, standing aside, and Sir Horace, stumping forward with a very red face.

"Grandfather—" cried Juliana, opening her arms. "Oh, I am so *very* sorry for what I did! I wish now that I had never left Flintwood!—No, I do not, for then I would not have met dear Madame Reynard, and Lord Egremont. Please, Grandfather, say that you forgive me!"

Sir Horace made an inarticulate sound—took one of the hands stretched out to him—then as Juliana looked at him pleadingly he fairly took her in his arms and hugged her.

"Good God, child," he then said, surveying her, "what *have* you done to your hair? You look like I do not know what!"

"Aha! Now he has truly accepted her," muttered Madame Reynard to Lord Egremont, and they tactfully left the room (which indeed was hardly large enough to contain them all), leaving Sir Horace with his granddaughter.

They were both trying to say different things to one another.

"If only you had been at home! You would have seen through Captain Davenport's pretensions in one moment. How could I have been such a *fool*?"

"Why did you not *tell* me that your father

had written books under the name of Charles Elphinstone? The silly fellow—why could he not use his own name?"

"I have felt so bad about you, Grandfather—I longed to tell you all about everything. Oh, if only you had *told* me that I was to be an heiress, I would have been on my guard. Can I get rid of the money? Give it away?"

"I have all your father's books in my bedroom; have read them over, I cannot *tell* you how many times— never realizing they were his! I have always, as you know, been fond of history—"

"No, I did not know that—"

"A letter came to you from Mr. Murray, which I opened, not knowing what other course to take—then all became plain—"

"And then, when I was living with Madame Reynard, I longed to write to you but did not dare—I thought you could not approve of her—"

"Madame Reynard is an excellent sort of woman," said Sir Horace. "In her way! Ahem! Knew her many years ago in Paris—took her to the Comédie a few times—she cured me of a phlegm—of course, in my young days, gels of your age would not have been allowed anywhere near women of the world such as Madame, but—but—times have changed, I understand. Nothing, I daresay, compared to what goes on in London. And I find that she has taken very kind care of you—can see *that*. As for Egremont—singular sort of fellow—a bit queer in his attic, if you ask me. Still, he has some excellent notions about cultivation—"

"Oh, Grandpapa, I am so happy to see you!"

"Well, m'dear, we'll agree to say no more about what's past, eh? Mind you," he added unfairly, "if you had agreed to marry Mr. Arpel, none of this need have happened."

"But how could I agree to marry him? I had never even met him!"

"Never met him? Gel's got moonshine in her brain-box," grumbled Sir Horace. "Far's I can make out, you have been practically living in one another's pockets. Arpel contrived to find you for me—"

Juliana would have demanded further explanation, but at this point Madame returned with a large basin of pottage, and orders that the General must quit her patient before she became overtired.

"How does Sir Groby go on?" inquired Juliana, as Madame remained while the pottage was eaten.

"He is recovering. I have been to see him several times. But I fancy his days of abduction and plotting are over; he is become, all of a sudden, an old, old man. He is to return to town tomorrow, so he will not be here for the Fete."

"I need not attend it, need I?" said Juliana.

"Not the grand dinner if you do not wish it, chérie. But I think Milord Egg would be disappointed if you did not attend some of his festivities. Besides, the Prince of Wales is coming, as you know, and he has expressed a most particular wish to meet you."

"But how does he know about me?" said Juliana. "Oh—I suppose from his brother. How—how tiresome. I would very much rather not."

❦

However, next day a message arrived from little Prue, who had been laid up with a megrim of the bowel, to ask if dear Miss Jeannie would go to Petworth House with Mistigris, and accompany Prue to see the festivities.

"May I do that, Tante 'Lise?" said Juliana. "I can hardly deny her. What is going to happen to that poor child, do you suppose?"

"Oh, Milord Egg will find some means of discovering her mother," Madame Reynard said comfortably. "Or, if he cannot, she can stay at Petvurrt House and when she grows up we can establish her in some respectable trade. Maybe I open a shop, a modiste's establishment—Madame Reynard, modiste; or Madame Fox, maybe... Yes, you may certainly accompany Prue about the park, my child, and do not fear that another attempt will be made to abduct you, for Georges has instructed Darner and Goble, his two stoutest footmen, to attend on you wherever you go!"

"Oh, heavens," said Juliana, laughing, "I shall feel like the Queen of Sheba."

The day of the fete dawned cloudy and damp. But the people of Petworth, quite undismayed by the weather, had been in the park since dawn. The day's program was to include sports during the day, with long-bowling, quoits, hunting the pig (Lord Egremont was providing a pig as prize), sack races, wheelbarrow races, ordinary running races, besides a pugilistic exhibition, archery and shooting at the butts, rope dancers, jugglers, and fire eaters. A dinner would be served to the townspeople in the park, at three, consisting of roast goose, roast mutton, batter puddings, beer, tea, boiled shin of beef, tripe, and apricot tarts, made with fruit from Lord Egremont's own succession houses. The gentry indoors would not eat until six, as the Prince of Wales kept town hours, and was not expected to arrive from Bognor, where he was staying with Lady Jersey (the Princess of Wales being in an Interesting Condition, consequently unable to travel) until midafternoon.

Juliana spent the morning signing papers in the presence of Madame Reynard, her grandfather, and Mr. Throgmorton. When the papers were all signed— and there seemed an infinite number of them—Mr. Throgmorton formally congratulated her, and her grandfather gave her a kiss. He also gave her a gold locket which contained a portrait of her grandmother, and Madame Reynard gave her a charming little peridot brooch.

"I do not give you diamonds," she said, kissing Juliana, "because they are very boring, and now you will be able to buy any number of them for yourself. Besides, I have a better gift in mind for you."

Juliana could not feel the slightest pleasure in the acquisition of her great wealth. Her only wish was to get rid of it; perhaps, she thought, she might endow a home for poor children, or almshouses for the elderly; or give some to Lord Egremont to start a school. No one will ever like me for myself alone, from now on, she thought dismally; I may as well resign myself to a life on the shelf.

When the papers were all signed, Sir Horace,

declining Madame Reynard's offer of a nuncheon, announced his intention of setting off immediately for Flintwood.

"Grandpapa! Will you not stay for Lord Egremont's dinner and to meet the Prince? Or see the fireworks?"

"Not I, miss! I have not the slightest wish to see the Prince of Wales—he is a pestilent fellow, a shallow-pated trifler—and as for fireworks, I do not regard them. I have seen too much of the real thing. No, no, I shall be more comfortable when I have my feet under my own table again, and I strongly recommend that you follow me without delay, child. Besides, the house seems quiet without your chatter."

Juliana promised that she would soon set out for Hampshire. She longed for the silence and spaciousness of Flintwood—and yet she would be very sorry to part from Madame Reynard, whom she had come to love dearly. Life is very difficult, she thought, and then laughed at herself for finding it difficult with half a million in her pocket. Yet she felt strangely lonely; surrounded by friends and kindness, she knew that something important was lacking.

When Sir Horace had departed, she helped Madame Reynard with her toilette for the grand dinner; it would be excessively boring, Madame said, but she had promised to help her friend Lizzie, who, though far from well, was obliged to rise from her couch and act as hostess. By the time Juliana and Rosine had decked Madame with all her diamonds and put her into a gown of silver tissue embroidered with flowers, she looked very splendid. Juliana herself had a new dress of blue muslin, embroidered with black butterflies, over a black silk underdress, and hat with blue ribbons; when she went to collect little Prue, the latter exclaimed that she looked exactly like a Pharisee, which, it seemed, meant a fairy. Although recovered from her megrim, Prue still looked a trifle pale, and Juliana suggested that before proceeding into the park, they should watch from a window and see the Prince of Wales arrive. Accordingly, they sat in an upstairs window seat, Prue clasping Mistigris, and so were able to see the long procession of coaches come bowling through the park, headed by a bright yellow one with maroon blinds. Tremendous cheers went up from the townsfolk assembled on the grass, as the carriages came to a halt, and elegantly dressed personages began getting out.

"Look, Prue, *that* must be the Prince of Wales—the very fat gentleman all dressed in purple and blue stripes with a silver waistcoat."

"*He* the Prince?" cried Prue. "Why, he be fat as a pig! He bain't my notion of a prince!"

Juliana was eagerly looking among the Prince's retinue, trying to keep down the half-formed hope that she might see Herr Welcker; but there were so many people that it was hard to distinguish one in particular; and why, in any case, she asked herself, should she expect him to be there? But she kept turning over in her mind that brief, extraordinary glimpse of him among the gypsies, which she had never mentioned to anybody.

The Prince and his train proceeded into the house, to be welcomed with a light refreshment. Juliana now proposed that she and Prue should walk through the park to see the sports. She was greatly embarrassed by the two burly footmen, Darner and Goble, who instantly fell in behind her; she could not help feeling very absurd. However, there was plenty to look at; they were able to watch a sack race and a wheelbarrow race and some wrestling and long jumping, which appeared to afford equal pleasure to little Prue and the footmen.

Presently a light rain commenced falling, which made Juliana glad she had brought her parasol.

"Let us go and see what is happening under those trees," she proposed, shivering as the damp crept through her shawl. "We shall be sheltered there from the rain." Privately she resolved that Prue must soon return indoors again.

From the slope leading up to the trees they had a view of the three immense rings of white-covered tables set up for the townspeople's dinner—they resembled nothing so much, Juliana thought, as some mysterious primitive monument.

A group of massive trees—oaks and chestnuts—grew on top of the knoll they were ascending, and in their shelter an archery contest was taking place. A target had been set up at which competitors were shooting. But the sport was somewhat slow and argumentative; little Prue soon became bored, and began tugging at Juliana's hand to go in search of livelier spectacles. Suddenly, however, the dignity of the proceedings were interrupted by laughter and shouts.

"Catch 'un! Grab aholt of Lordy's gilt, afore she gits into the woodses!"

A large excited pig came dashing into the midst of the archers, overthrowing the target and causing wild havoc. Little Prue shrieked, and let go of the monkey's leash; Mistigris, snatching this unlooked-for opportunity, scampered up the nearest tree, a huge chestnut with a trunk so creased and seamed that the monkey could run up it like a flight of stairs. Meanwhile the pig fled away with all the archers and their audience in pursuit.

One of Juliana's attendant footmen rather reluctantly offered to go up after Mistigris, but Juliana, thanking, shook her head.

"He does not know you, and he is very timid; besides, all the noise has scared him. He minds me fairly well and I think it will be best if I go after him; the tree looks easy enough to climb. Prue, love, hold my parasol."

Accordingly Juliana began carefully drawing herself up the serrated surface of the tree; the light slippers she wore proved admirable for the purpose, as she could dig her toes into the deep cracks in the bark.

Mistigris, huddled in the first fork, hailed her approach with chattering enthusiasm, and obviously expected her to pass the afternoon with him in the tree.

"Yes, it is all very well for you, you wretch," said Juliana, making a successful grab for the dangling leash, "but what Grandfather would say if he could see me—oh!"

This cry of astonishment was caused by the sight of a long arrow which had struck the tree trunk just beside her arm with a loud, resonant thud, burying its steel point deep in the wood; it stuck there quivering, and Juliana, looking below, called urgently, "Take care! Oh, pray take care!"

Her voice was drowned by Prue's joyful shriek of "*Davvy!* It's Davvy!" Then the child's tone changed to one of horror and she screamed, "Davvy, what be you *doing*? You must not shoot at Miss Jeannie!" Juliana saw a man pulling back a bow, prepared to shoot again. She scrambled down the tree with desperate haste, clasping Mistigris against her; another arrow whistled over her head, missing her by inches.

As she dropped to the, ground, she heard angry shouts, and turned to see two men locked together in a furious conflict; next moment, one of them, pulling free from the other one's clutch, succeeded in felling his opponent with a savage blow from the shoulder. Muttering vindictively, the second man struggled to his feet. It was Captain Davenport—Juliana still could not think of him as Jenkins. Darner and Goble sprang forward to seize him, but the man who had knocked him down said, "Stand back! This is my affair."

Juliana stifled a gasp. For in the other man she recognized Herr Welcker: a Herr Welcker very different from when she had seen him last, ragged and grimy. Now, though still much sunburned, he was precise to a pin, clad in elegant morning dress—except that his neckcloth had come untied, his hair was disarranged, he was bleeding from a cut on his cheekbone, and he looked very angry indeed.

Steeping forward, he seized Davenport by the arm. "Why were you shooting at Miss Paget?"

"She's a cursed jilt," muttered Davenport, who

looked, Juliana thought, far more frightening than
when she had seen him last. His eyes were bloodshot
and wild, he had a perceptible streak of white on his
dark disheveled locks, and there was a great blackened
burn on the back of his jacket. He said, "I'll lay my
hands on her sooner or later—see if I don't! And if
I can't have her—nobody shall!"—endeavoring to
break away from Herr Welcker's hold. It seemed plain
that the experiences of the last few days had deranged
his mind. Little Prue cried out, "Davvy!" fearfully,
but he growled, "Shut your mouth!" Then, evidently
realizing that he was outnumbered, he twisted suddenly, thrusting Herr Welcker to one side, and darted
off, bounding over the grass with astonishing speed.
Welcker was up in a moment and after him—so
were the footmen. Juliana and little Prue also ran in
pursuit, the former filled with dreadful apprehension.
Davenport had seemed so strange! What might he not
do if he entered the house?

He had directed his course toward the pleasure
gardens, from where a door led into the tennis court.
Possibly he had intended to make his escape by the
underground passage; he had reached the court and
was heading for the door when Herr Welcker over-
took him and seized him again.

The two footmen arrived shortly after.

"Best turn him over to Lordy," one of them was
saying as Juliana reached them—little Prue, wailing,
had been left far behind.

"I'll fight you, I'll fight you all!" screamed
Davenport. "I'm not afraid of you! I'll fight you for
her!" Then he perceived a case of dueling pistols

which had been left in the court; evidently someone had been using the room as a shooting gallery, for a target hung against the end wall.

"Will you fight?" he said again to Welcker. "Will you fight me? Or are you a miserable sniveling coward?"

Herr Welcker glanced around, and saw Juliana. "I'll fight you," he said to Davenport. He was very pale. "I'll fight you if you will then guarantee never to pursue that lady again."

"If I lose, you mean!" shouted Davenport, with a loud, crazy laugh. "But I shall not lose. You!" he said to one of the footmen. "Load the pistols and see fair play!"

"Oh, pray do not—!" Juliana cried out, but nobody was paying any attention to her, and she crept into the netted gallery while the two men took off their jackets and the pistols were loaded. Then the duelists retired to the ends of the gallery, and Darner, the elder footman (looking very nervous), stood where the net met the wall, holding a white cloth (Herr Welcker's neckerchief).

"When-as I drops this-yurr wipe, an' says 'Fire,' then I wants ye to fire," he said. "But 'tis all wrong, an' I 'opes Lordy don't give me a blasting an' my marching orders for it. Are ye ready? Fire!"

Both pistols cracked, and Davenport, who had been standing close against the back wall, slowly subsided, leaning against it, until he was sitting on the ground. Juliana, who had been turning her eyes fearfully from one man to the other, observed a spot of red appear on Herr Welcker's white-sleeved arm. It rapidly increased to a scarlet patch.

At this juncture, the door leading to the house burst

open, and Lord Egremont appeared. He exclaimed, "For heaven's sake, what is going on here? Are you all run mad? Darner—Gable—what is the meaning of this?" Then his gaze took in the two wounded men, Davenport rolled over in a faint, Herr Welcker with a rather rueful smile upon his countenance.

"I must apologize, my lord," he said. "Pray do not be blaming your servants! It was entirely my fault—it seemed the simplest solution to the business. No, that is not quite true," he added reflectively. "I am afraid that I lost my temper. That fellow there was the man who had abducted Miss Paget."

Darner, who had been examining the injured Davenport, now reported, "'E bain't 'urt bad. Ball be lodged in 'is shoulder, likely."

"Carry him off to one of the servants' rooms and keep him under close observation," directed Lord Egremont. "I will deal with him later. And I daresay Madame 'Lise will doctor his wound. As for you, Herr Welcker—I am greatly shocked that such a thing should happen in my house while the Prince is visiting it—but I realize that you were provoked. We will say no more about it. Is your injury of a serious nature?"

"Merely a flesh wound, my lord," replied Herr Welcker, binding his handkerchief round it. He then looked up and saw Juliana, who, white with anxiety, had run out of the gallery and now stood close by. A sudden smile irradiated his face.

"My dear Miss Juliana! I must apologize to you, too, for this disgraceful fracas! But I trust that wretched man will annoy you no more from now on."

Lord Egremont, hearing Juliana's name, turned and said, "Ah, my dear child, I was just searching for you when my attention was attracted by the sound of pistol shots. His Highness wishes you to be presented to him. Will you come with me, if you please?"

"Oh, no!" cried Juliana, horrified. "Just *now*—when I am in *such* a pickle—with my dress all green and torn from climbing trees—and Madame's monkey—"

"I will accompany you," offered Herr Welcker obligingly. He put on his jacket and retied his neck-cloth in two expert movements. "But perhaps it *would* be best to get rid of the monkey—"

Luckily at this moment little Prue arrived, panting and indignant, and was instructed by Lord Egremont to "take the monkey and go to Mam'selle Lord." Being much in awe of him, she did so without argument.

Juliana, setting her dress to rights as best she could while walking along, was escorted down a corridor and across a court to the great carved and paneled Grinling Gibbons Hall, where the Prince of Wales was seated in state, conversing with the various guests invited to meet him by Lord Egremont.

Juliana studied the Prince with interest as she approached. He was like his brother, but better-looking, she decided. He certainly was remarkably fat—she judged that the estimate of seventeen stone could not be far off the mark—his complexion was rather flushed, his curly hair somewhat thin, but his blue-gray eyes were large and bright, and his smile as he stood up to greet her was so full of charm that Juliana saw at once what people meant when they spoke of the Prince's irresistible fascination. She made him a profound curtsy, to which he responded with an astonishingly graceful bow.

"My dear Miss Paget! I am so delighted to meet you at last. I have been hearing about you forever—from my brother Clarence, who spoke most highly of your charm—but chiefly from my friend Augustus, yonder"— and he nodded toward Herr Welcker, who bowed.

"And so *you* are the dauntless young lady who rescued Augustus from a French mob and sailed with him over the Isle of Wight," the Prince continued, surveying Juliana with a look in which friendliness, admiration, and a gleam of fun were mixed with something else very unnerving; it makes me feel as if he can see right through my blue dress to my shift, she thought. "And not only are you a beauty and a heroine, but I hear you have just inherited half a million from old Brandywine Paget as well. That seems almost too much. Unfair to other mortals!"

"No, Your Highness, excuse me," interposed Lord Egremont, "it was not from General Brandywine Paget that Miss Paget received her legacy; he is still alive, I am glad to say, and is the young lady's grandfather; it was from his brother, Seringapatam Paget, her great-uncle, that she inherited."

The Prince nodded irritably, as if he hated being corrected.

He went on, "And your father, I understand, was that excellent historian whose books on Villiers and Wentworth I have read with so much enjoyment. And I hear with delight that one on my great-great-grandfather, Charles the First, is in course of publication. I shall look forward to that with the keenest pleasure. Alas, he was a sad loss, your father; we could have done with many more works from his pen."

Good heavens, thought Juliana, while she was making civil replies to these remarks, *could* King Charles the First really have been the great-great-grandfather of this man? How very extraordinary!

"I hear from my friend Augustus that Charles the First is quite your ideal of a man and a prince," His Highness continued, in a somewhat languishing manner. "But I hope that having *his* image in your mind will not render you too hard-hearted toward *other* princes, ma'am?" He took her hand in his rather limp and moist one, and gave it a gentle squeeze. Good God! thought Juliana, very much disconcerted; he is flirting with me; what must I do now? Anxiously looking past the Prince of Wales, she caught Herr Welcker's eye fixed on her with a look of such amused sympathy that she instantly felt more at ease.

"Meeting Your Highness must necessarily demote your great-great-grandfather to second place in my esteem, sir," she said, smiling up at the large florid good-natured face above hers. He beamed back, delighted, and Juliana, anxious to quit a vein which she knew she could not continue, said, "Sir, pray enlighten my ignorance on a point that puzzles me?"

"Anything, my dear Miss Paget!"

"You have alluded to your friend Augustus. You refer to Count van Welcker?"

"Yes, my dear."

"But I thought his name was Frederick?"

"His full name is Frederick Augustus Arpel, Count van Welcker, my child"—Juliana gave a gasp—"and I am infinitely obliged to you for saving his life, since, besides bringing me all kinds of treasures from Europe"—Juliana thought of the Sèvres and could not forbear a smile—"the political and military intelligence that he has brought along with the pots and pans has been of inestimable value to our government."

"Good God! You mean, sir, that Count van Welcker is a sp—"

"Hush, my dear. Walls have ears," said the Prince, glancing at the remarkable Grinling Gibbons carvings, which did seem particularly generously endowed in this respect.

Lord Egremont now came up with a member of the local gentry who was to be presented to the Prince, and Juliana, much relieved, was able to make another deep curtsy and retire to the side of the room, where Herr Welcker immediately joined her.

She burst out at once. "*You* are Augustus Arpel—but why did my grandfather not know that you are Count van Welcker?"

"Ah, well, when I was engaged as his aide in the American war, I had not inherited the title, which came from an uncle. And since then we had quite lost touch; I have been out of England a great deal, as you know. Indeed, I was not aware that you were the granddaughter of my old chief; I thought your grandfather was the other General Paget. However, of course, when I received your grandfather's letter—"

Juliana blushed, wondering what Sir Horace had said.

"When I received a letter informing me that you had vanished, and asking for my help in tracing you—"

She interrupted him. "Grandfather asked for your help? I do not understand."

"Why," he said, "in my various missions I am frequently in communication with all kinds of odd folk. Sir Horace thought I might have means of acquiring information—"

"The gypsies!"

He laughed, and said, "The gypsy tribe know no frontiers. What is a war between England and France to them? But it certainly was awkward when, returning from a mission to France to commence the search for you, we were all clapped under hatches for your murder, my dear! I cannot express my relief, Miss Juliana, both at your most obliging intervention and at the discovery that you were not murdered but alive and more delightful than ever."

He took her hand gently in his own—his clasp, unlike that of the Prince, was warm and firm—and continued, "I am indeed sorry, my poor child, that your suitor turned out so badly. If I had known in London what I learned later, I would never have carried your message to him."

His kindly face was grave now, and rather somber.

"Oh, Herr Welcker, I was so mistaken in him! I will never, never believe anybody ever again. He was so different when we eloped! And when he kissed me, it was quite horrid! All he wanted was my money, and how I wish I had not got it. It has done nothing but harm. I would like to give it all away."

Count van Welcker looked much more cheerful at once. "Well," he said, "you *can* give it away, you know! Nothing obliges you to keep it. If only—"

At that moment a movement in the crowd began. "Oh, dear," he said. "Prinney is going in to dinner. Do you dine here, Miss Juliana?"

"No, sir, I cried off. I do not feel strong enough for a great dinner. I am going back to the Hermitage."

"My dear Miss Juliana—might I be permitted to come round and call on you after dinner?"

"Will not His Highness have need of you, sir?"

"His Highness can manage without me very well."

There was such an anxious, intent look suddenly in his eyes that she found her heart beating faster as she slipped away. It was odd, she thought, to be able to run through the town without fear of being seen or pursued; she could still hardly believe in her freedom. She felt all of a sudden very lighthearted. The streets were empty; the inhabitants of the town were still in the park, making merry.

Berthe and Rosine, however, had remained at the Hermitage; like General Paget, they were not interested in fetes; and they preferred their own cooking to Lord Egremont's feast.

"Mademoiselle looks tired," said Berthe. "She will be the better for a bowl of good soup. Eh, poor Madame! Doubtless she wishes she were at home too. Did you see the Prince, mademoiselle?"

"Yes, I saw him," said Juliana. "He was very fat." Not a bit like Charles the First, she thought. But still, I liked him.

"Mademoiselle laughs," said Rosine sympathetically. "She has been well amused."

"Yes, I have!" said Juliana, thinking how difficult it would be to explain that she was laughing because she had suddenly realized what a very dull man Charles the First must have been. Good; but dull.

Some two hours later, Madame Reynard returned, accompanied by Count van Welcker.

"The Count kindly escorted me home," she said, "lest I should be kidnapped by highwaymen or brigands! And now I am going to my couch, for I am fatigued with a thousand and one civilities. Amuse each other, my children; but do not let this rake of a Count keep you up too long, *chérie*. Rest well, my very dear child; I shall see you in the morning. *Bonsoir!*" She kissed Juliana good night, but turned at the foot of the stairs to say, "I have given you another birthday present, and I have instructed the Count to tell you about it."

"Is she not a delight? I sat next to her at dinner," he said, taking Juliana's arm and strolling with her into the garden. "May we walk up and down this grassy alley? Shall you take a chill?"

"Certainly not," said Juliana. "My feet will get wet, that is all."

The rain clouds had disappeared at sunset, and a wonderful pink afterglow filled the sky. Juliana picked a sprig of honeysuckle blossom and sniffed at it. She said, "Count van Welcker, I am sure I have you to thank for bringing me my father's books? I was so touched, so deeply grateful—"

"Ah, it was nothing," he quickly replied. "I had to go to France on government affairs—I found a messenger to negotiate—it was a simple matter! Now let me tell you about Madame Reynard's birthday present. 'What can one give a girl who has just inherited a fortune?' she said, and then she began to laugh and exclaimed, 'I have it! I will give her the memory of how she had to play cache-cache and run through the underground way! I will give her my house when I return to France!'"

"Her *house*? *This* house? But oh, how can she ever bear to leave it?"

They turned to look at it, standing among its young apple trees, against the pink sky. The valley down below lay hushed, except for the distant bleating of sheep and lambs. But over in Petworth Park the revels were still at their height; voices could be heard singing and shouting; and the occasional crackle of a firework.

"Prinney was just about to give one of his violin recitals," Count van Welcker said. "I daresay he will be very annoyed when he finds that I slipped away. *How* glad I am to miss it!"

Then he turned toward Juliana, and said, "Miss Paget—I addressed you on this subject once before at your aunt's house. Believe me, I was not then aware of the gold collar round your neck. However, at that time—as in our dear balloon—your thoughts were all directed toward Charles the First. That has not prevented mine toward you from growing stronger and more tender with every passing week. Dare I inquire whether Charles the First has now suffered an eclipse—whether there can be any possibility of your sentiments having undergone a change? I am quite wealthy (as you may not know), I can support you in modest comfort, and, if you wish, we can consign all your fortune to the devil… Do you find yourself able to give me an answer, dear Miss Juliana?"

He took both her hands, looking steadily into her face, and moved toward her as she looked up at him, smiling.

"Oh, but please don't go down upon one knee again," cried Juliana. "The grass is so wet!"

"I was not going to go down upon one knee," replied Count van Welcker. "It is odds but you've left a needle sticking somewhere in that grass! I was going to take you in my arms."

"How very odd," remarked Juliana, some time later. "When Captain Davenport kissed me I did not like it at all."

"But this is different, hmm?"

"No, that is what is strange. It is *not* so different— and yet, now, after all, I find that I do quite like it!"

Historical Note

I have anticipated in one respect. The Prince Regent did not, in fact, come to Petworth until 1814, when Lord Egremont received him, Alexander, Emperor of Russia, the King of Prussia, the Prince of Wurtemberg, and the Grand Duchess of Oldenberg, with their respective suites. "The Russian attendants in the train of the Czar are yet spoken of by townsmen, who recollect their grotesque appearance and the circumstance of their evincing a partiality for oil by drinking it from any lamps…as well as devouring the soap placed in their bedrooms." (From *Petworth: A Sketch of Its History and Antiquities*, by Rev. F. H. Arnold, 1864.)

J. A.

The WEEPING ASH

WHEN SIXTEEN-YEAR-OLD FANNY HERRIARD BECAME, through the instrumentality of her father the Rev. Theophilus and with his full consent and approval, betrothed to forty-eight-year-old Thomas Paget, the regulating officer of Gosport, she was under no illusion as to the romance of the match. She did not make any attempt to convince herself that Mr. Paget was a heroic or dashing character—despite the fact that he preferred to be called *Captain* Paget: in point of fact, as she knew, a regulating officer was hardly to be distinguished from a civilian—and besides, Papa said that Mr. Paget only carried the rank of lieutenant. Moreover the prospective bridegroom was a widower, with two daughters already older than Fanny herself, and one younger, and until this year he had possessed little more than his pay of one pound a day and additional ten shillings subsistence money. (His previous wife, it was to be inferred, had been able to bring him some money of her own).

Recently, however, Captain Paget had benefited by a stroke of good fortune which, quite unexpectedly, enabled him to contemplate a second marriage, one this time for pleasure rather than for convenience. A distant cousin of his, whom he had never even met, having herself succeeded to an immense—and quite unanticipated—legacy, just as she had contracted an alliance with a wealthy man of rank, had the happy and liberal notion of seeking out the more impoverished members of her family and sharing her good fortune with them. The astonished Thomas, therefore, found himself not only endowed, out of the blue, with a handsome competence, enough to enable him to buy a thriving business, but also possessed for an indefinite period of a larger and much more comfortable house than his own, at a very reasonable rental.

The reason for this additional piece of luck was the devoted attachment of his generous cousin Juliana to her new-wedded husband, a Dutch nobleman who, up to the time of his marriage, had served as an equerry and intelligence agent in the entourage of the Prince of Wales. However, during the previous year, 1796, Count van Welcker had been delighted to find himself repossessed of some family estates in Demerara, upon the recapture of that region for the British by Laforey and Whyte. In consequence of this, the count was obliged to take leave of absence from the prince's service and make a journey which might be of some years' duration. His bride, unable to contemplate the prospect of such a long separation, had elected to accompany him, and she therefore obligingly offered Thomas Paget her own house in Petworth until the (doubtless far distant) date of her return.

With all these advantages, it could not be said that Captain Paget was particularly handsome or interesting in his person: he was a plain, square, dry-looking man, with sandy hair, rather thin lips, pale blue eyes, two fingers missing on one hand, discolored teeth, and a curt, short manner of speaking; but still it was to be hoped that having been the recipient of such generosity would release in him hitherto suppressed qualities of kindness and liberality; and in any case several of Fanny's unmarried sisters (she was the youngest of eight) thought, and said, that Fanny had done very well for herself, very well *indeed*, considering that Papa could afford to give his daughters only £200 apiece as dowry. The Rev. Theophilus Herriard was a hard-working Church of England rector, long since widowed, and his daughters might think themselves lucky to catch husbands at all.

Only Fanny, a shy, sensitive girl with a considerable reserve of delicate pride, knew the full measure of her own luck: that she was enabled, by this marriage, to get away from home before her sharp-eyed siblings could discover the intensity of the anguish that she was going through on account of her rejection by Barnaby Ferrars, the squire's happy-go-lucky son.

"*Marriage?*" he had said, laughing heartily. "You thought we might be *married*? Why, goosey, my father would never allow it! No, no, my dear little sweetheart, we must be like two butterflies, that flutter and dance and kiss in mid-air—so!—and then flit on to other meetings; you will find some good, kind, wormy fellow who will cosset and spoil you all the days of your life; and I—I shall never forget you, dear little wild rose, and the happy haymaking we passed together, when I am married to some dull lady of fortune who will help repair the inroads that my father's gambling has made on his estates. Gold—gold I must be sold for gold, my angel—" and he had tickled her chin with a buttercup. For their flirtation—innocent enough, heaven knew—had taken place during a warm and beautiful June, when the whole village— schoolchildren, grandparents, squire's sons, and rector's girls—had all helped in the meadows to get in the splendid crop of hay. But then Barnaby's father, Squire Ferrars, had fulfilled his promise to buy his son a commission in the Hussars. Fortunately by the day, some weeks later, when Barnaby came whistling along to inform the Herriard family, assembled for evening tea drinking, of his imminent departure to join his regiment, Fanny, too, had been able to gather the shreds of her pride and dignity around her— it was that little air of self-possession and reserve which, did she but know it, had attracted his notice to her in the first place—and could tell him, with cool decorum masking a breaking heart, that her own betrothal had been arranged; that she would be marrying Captain Paget, a school acquaintance of her father's, in September.

"Why, that's famous! Dear little wild rose, I'm delighted to hear it. Good luck to you both," said. Barnaby, not very interested; and after he had informed the Herriards that his regiment was ordered out to India to keep a sharp eye on Tippoo Sahib, he bade them all a care-free good-bye and swung happily off into the dusk.

"Barnaby's very pleased with himself," said Harriet. "You'd think the squire would wish him to marry and get an heir before he goes off abroad," said Maria.

"Maria, such thoughts are unbecoming to you and, in any case, no concern of ours," reproved her father.

"At *one* time I quite thought that Barnaby had an eye to our Fanny," said Kitty with a spiteful sidelong glance at her youngest sister. But Fanny said nothing, merely bent her head lower over her stitching—they were all hemming sheets for her bride linen—and was immensely relieved when the rector said, "Enough chatter, children; it is time for evening prayers."

By September the hot, haymaking weeks were a thing of the past, long forgotten, and it was in weeping gray autumn weather that Captain Paget assisted his youthful bride into the carriage which, after the simple wedding ceremony had been performed by her father, was to take them from Sway, in the New Forest, where Fanny had spent the whole of her life up till now, off to the new home in Sussex.

It was a cold and dismal journey. Rain penetrated the cracks of the ancient hired conveyance, turned the roads to quagmire, and reduced the stubble fields on either side of the turnpike to an uninviting dun color, but nevertheless Fanny, who had never traveled in her life, was prepared to find interest in all that she saw. Although she did not feel it likely that she would ever come to *love* her taciturn bridegroom, she was exceedingly grateful to him for taking her away from her sharp-eyed sisters and a home which had come to be associated with excruciating unhappiness; she fully intended to be friendly, affectionate, and biddable, to do as much as lay in her power to make her marriage a success.

However she soon found that her polite questions and comments about the villages they passed through met with but a brusque reception; the necessities or Captain Pagers rather dismal profession took him traveling about the country for large parts of every week, on horseback or by coach; landscape was of no interest to him, and his only present wish was to reach home and inaugurate the new period of connubial comfort with as little delay as possible; sharply, ignoring Fanny's polite remarks, he ordered the coachman to flog up his brutes of horses and get them to Petworth before the rain turned to a deluge.

Fanny prudently resolved to keep silent; but after a few moments a wish to learn something about the house toward which they were bound made her forget her resolution, and she inquired wistfully:

"Will your cousin Julianna be there to greet us, sir, when we arrive?"

A cousin, such a kindly, well-disposed cousin, would, she thought, be more inclined to be friendly than those three rather daunting unknown figures, her stepdaughters, whose presence their father had not considered necessary at his wedding.

"Juliana? No, no, she is halfway across the Atlantic already, she and that fancy Dutch husband of hers."

Considering the benefactions that Countess van Welcker had heaped upon him, Mr. Paget's tone did not sound particularly cordial, Fanny thought; it is much harder to receive gracefully than to give, and perhaps he was already discovering that to be the recipient of such generosity posed its own problems.

"What is the name of your cousin's house, sir?"

"It is called the Hermitage," he replied shortly, his tone suggesting that he considered this name far too fanciful and would, if it lay within his power, change it to something plainer. He added, "I believe there was once some monastic foundation upon the site; no doubt the name derives from that."

"The Hermitage!" Fanny shivered; to her the name had a chill and dreary sound. She pulled the carriage rug more closely around her shoulders. "And what is the house like, sir?"

"Like? *Like?* Why, it is just a house."

"No, but I mean, is it old or new? Does it lie within the town of Petworth or in the country outside?"

Captain Paget replied briefly that the house was a new one built within the last twenty years, he understood, and that it lay on the edge of the town, which numbered about three thousand inhabitants.

"It will be very strange to live in a town," murmured Fanny, and added in what she hoped was a cheerful and lively manner, "I greatly look forward to seeing the shops and warehouses and the stalls in the marketplace."

"I trust your recourse to them will be infrequent. A good housewife contrives all that she may without quitting her own home," was her husband's somewhat discouraging rejoinder.

Fanny had learned already that there were to be four servants in her new home: a cook, a housemaid, a knife- and bootboy, and an outside man who would sleep over the stable and attend to the garden and the horses; she found the prospect of responsibility for ordering such a large establishment an alarming one and said timidly:

"And shall you continue in your profession, sir, now that you have bought the mill?" For she had been told that, with part of his cousin's gift, Captain Paget had been able to acquire a small flour mill at Haslingbourne, a mile outside the town of Petworth, the revenues from which would make a comfortable addition to his income.

"Continue in my profession? Certainly I shall!" he said sharply. "What can have given you the notion that I should not?"

"I did not—I had not meant—" Fanny knew that she must never, at any cost, betray how odious she thought her husband's calling; she faltered out something about regretting that it required him to be so much from home.

Thomas Paget glanced impatiently out of the carriage window—they were slowly descending a steep hill and the driver had been obliged to put on the drag, or the vehicle would have rattled away faster and faster, out of control. Fanny, looking out in the other direction, over a wide prospect of blue-gray, misty weald without a house in sight, battled desperately with the onset of tears. Her throat felt tight and choking; she swallowed and clenched her hands together. For the thousandth time she remembered an afternoon during haymaking—the peak and pinnacle of her flirtation with Barnaby, as it turned out, though at the time she had thought it but a prelude to greater and greater happiness. He had encountered her behind a new-made rick and rained a shower of light, laughing, impudent kisses on her face and neck, until the voices of two other approaching haymakers made them fly guiltily apart. Dizzy with joy, her blood sparkling in her veins like home-brewed cider, she had believed during that moment that a life containing unimaginable radiance and bliss lay stretched ahead of her.

And it had all ended so soon!

READ ON FOR A LOOK AT THE NEXT GENERATION
IN JOAN AIKEN'S PAGET FAMILY SAGA.

The GIRL *from* PARIS

May 1859

"YOU WOULD CONSIDER PARTING WITH *MISS PAGET*?"

Lady Morningquest was a tall, impressive personage, with a commanding air, an aristocratically curved nose, and a high, incisive voice; her tone indicated disapproval, such as might be displayed by the donor of a handsome and valuable gift, on discovering that the recipient intended to pass it on to a charity bazaar.

Her companion, however, wholly undisturbed by the note of censure, replied equably, "Well, you see, *ma chère amie*, this is how it is: certainly I am devoted to *la petite* Elène Paget, I regard her as I might my own daughter (if I had one)—and *that*, my friend, is the very reason why I would not wish to stand in the way of her advancement. In the city of Paris, how much wider a vista would open before her. Without doubt, as your protégée, dear madame, she would have the opportunity to hear the words of savants, of philosophers—there is the Comédie, the Opera—whereas, here in Brussels—pfah! What a narrow, provincial scene!"

Nevertheless, Madame Bosschère glanced with some complacency about the room in which the two ladies were standing. It was the salle, or largest classroom, of her school for young ladies, a handsome spacious chamber with double glass doors opening on one side into a hallway tiled with black and white marble, on the other into a garden half screened by a large grape arbor. Everything in sight glittered with cleanliness and prosperity.

Lady Morningquest also turned to survey the room benignly through her lorgnon, before repeating in a tone of perplexity, "You are really offering me Ellen Paget? But, *ma chère*, I thought she was your right hand in the school, your *première maîtresse*? I fear she might be wasted in the post I am seeking to fill; though, of course, I should be happy to have my dear little goddaughter in Paris! But I had hoped merely for some worthy person—steady, sober, not prone to agitations or high flights—perhaps a young teacher who found large classes too formidable; or an older one, approaching retirement, wishful to secure a less exacting position in a quiet household—"

Here Lady Morningquest paused, possibly arrested by the recollection that no stretch of truth could designate the Hôtel Caudebec a quiet household.

But Madame Bosschère had not noticed her hesitation.

"My dear friend, Mademoiselle Paget is as steady, as sober, as could possibly be desired, I assure you: imbued with sense and integrity, she has the head on her shoulders of a person three times her age! *Elle est pleine de caractère*—formidable, indeed—honest as the day, wise as an advocate, upright as a judge!"

Madame spoke in rapid French, which had the effect of making these qualities seem, somehow, less reliable. But she added with vehement sincerity, "I say all this to you in full confidence, I who know her thoroughly, and have done since she was a *petite fille*. She is ruled by conscience—your English Calvinist conscience! She would not knowingly commit the slightest fault, she would bitterly repent the most trifling error."

In that case, and if she has all these virtues, I wonder why you wish to be rid of her? reflected Lady Morningquest, intently regarding her *chère amie*, who bore the scrutiny with aplomb. Usually, at this time of day, late morning, Madame Bosschère would not yet have assumed her full toilette; she would be comfortable, though perfectly businesslike, in wrapper, muslin nightcap, shawl, and felt slippers, bustling about the administrative duties of her school. But in honor of her august friend and patron she had today dressed early and appeared convenable, if not downright elegant, in dark-brown silk, admirably fitted to her plump figure, and a Brussels lace fichu. Madame was not tall, but she possessed immense dignity; she neither flushed nor paled under the thoughtful gaze of the ambassador's wife. Indeed a skeptical observer might have wondered how her face could remain so unmarked by the traces of care and authority; was this due to an untroubled conscience, or a lack of scruple and sensibility?

"Let me see," said Lady Morningquest, "how long has the child been with you?"

"She is hardly a child any longer, *chère amie*! She came to us when she was fifteen; her elder sister Eugénie was still with us at that time; *non*—I mistake—it was Catherine, the middle one. Eugénie had already left to wed her baronet. Two years *la petite* studied here as a pupil; one, by her own request, as pupil-teacher; and now three as full teacher. During which time, as you say, she has become my right hand."

"Has she never been home during that time?"

"Oh, *mais oui, bien sûr, plusieurs fois*. The father, who is a very correct English gentleman, as you know, madame, requested permission for her to attend her sisters' weddings, and the christening of a niece; and his own wedding…but each time she returned, and I believe was happy to do so. I understand that *la petite* is *not* loved by the father's second wife."

"Six years in all." Lady Morningquest counted thoughtfully on her thin, beringed fingers. "So she is now twenty-one."

"And how deeply indebted I am to you, dear friend, for introducing me to the Paget family; for giving me the chance to acquire such a treasure! Indeed all three Paget girls were amiable, well-disposed, serious young ladies—"

"You would hardly call Kitty Paget serious?"

Madame gave an indescribable grimace, half moue, half shrug.

"Serious when it came to her own interests! A light heart, but a hard head. I understand she married an exceedingly wealthy bourgeois—how do you call him?—an ironmaster."

Madame pronounced it *irrenmastaire*. There was

considerable irony in her tone; bourgeoise herself to her blunt fingertips, she nevertheless had the same dispassionate regard for her friend's aristocratic connections that she would have for a piece of fine Meissen or Dresden; it was plain that she deplored the social aspect of Catherine Paget's marriage while admitting its utility.

"You think Ellen would be less hardheaded? Less regardful of her own interests?"

"*Douce comme une ange!*"

The benevolent Directrice seemed to be assigning some rather contradictory characteristics to her young assistant, reflected Lady Morningquest. But she merely remarked, "Ellen will need more than gentleness, I fear, if she is to hold her own at the Hôtel Caudebec. She had need, rather, to be a female Metternich."

"And she can be that too," responded Madame Bosschère without a blink. "But are matters, then, come to such a pass in your niece's establishment?"

"They could hardly be worse! That young man is behaving like a monster to my poor Louise. He neglects her atrociously—gambles all day and most of the night; his companions are drawn from the worst sections of society. And the wretched Louise, instead of trying to grapple with the situation, merely reclines in her boudoir and reads philosophy! As for the child—I am in despair. A village brat would get more care. I tell you, madame, the ménage is a disaster—I have a migraine for two days after each visit."

The widow looked suitably horrified by these revelations. "*Tiens!* It will be difficult, I concede. But I do believe you have found the right person for the task, my friend. I am certain that such a situation would not daunt *la petite* Elène. See, here she comes now."

The two ladies were standing on the estrade, or teacher's dais. Leaning on its balustrade, they surveyed the bustle of activity now commencing in the long classroom, as the young-lady pupils prepared the establishment for an evening's festivity. Today, May 5th, was the feast of St. Annodoc, the school's patron saint, and was traditionally celebrated by a collation in the school garden, a dramatic performance, and a dance, to which parents and selected friends were invited. Hence the arrival of Lady Morningquest from Paris. Her daughter Charlotte was to play Ophelia in a heavily edited version of *Hamlet*, and though Lady Morningquest, a realist, expected small pleasure from the performance, she had traveled to Brussels since she had her own reasons for consulting Madame Bosschère.

Now she turned with interest to follow the direction of the headmistress's glance.

Although drawn from the cream of Brussels society, the young-lady pupils at the Pensionnat, many of whom continued their education till the age of twenty or beyond, were, in general, tall, big-boned, and brawny. Exuberant today, and unrestrained, since it was a holiday, they laughed and screamed like herring gulls, energetically lugging the furniture so as to clear the floor. Some brought in vases of flowers, others directed the aged gardener where to place blossoming orange trees in pots, and palms in tubs—all this without the least embarrassment, despite the fact that most were *en deshabille*, clad in calico print wrappers, their long flaxen hair in curlpapers, their large feet in list slippers. Every now and then a shout would come from the *salle à manger*, where the hairdresser was established with his curling tongs: "Mademoiselle Eeklop au coiffeur!" The few English or French girls in the group were instantly recognizable because of their smaller stature, darker coloring, and greater modesty of demeanor.

A young lady differing from the rest in that she was already dressed, in a dark-gray gown whose Quakerish plainness of cut was mitigated by a decided elegance of line, appeared to be in charge of the proceedings, and was giving orders to pupils, gardener, and servants, in a low, clear, decisive voice which was immediately and unhesitatingly obeyed by everybody, despite the fact that she was several inches shorter than most of her charges.

"Yes—that will do very well, Emilie—the pots in rows across below the estrade, and the ferns in those baskets along the side; *non*, Marie, together, not separately. We shall need a great many more. Clara, run and tell the little girls in the *première classe* to come, as many as can be spared, and they can act as porters running to and fro. That will keep them out of mischief, too."

At this point, looking up, Miss Paget perceived the headmistress and her guest. She smiled quickly at them, revealing an unsuspected dimple in her thin cheek, and curtseyed, saying in a friendly way, "Excuse me, madame, that I did not observe you before! There is so much to do that one need have eyes in the back of one's head. Lady Morningquest, how do you do!

Charlotte has been counting the hours to your arrival.
She is going over her lines in the Green Room—shall
I send her to you?"

"No, no—leave her to con her part," said the fond
parent. "I had rather be sure she knows it by rote and
will not disgrace the family. There will be plenty of
time to talk to her after—and you, too, my dear, I
hope, when you can be spared! I have messages from
your father and your sister Eugenia, for I have been
in Sussex recently. But I will not distract you now."

With another quick, smiling curtsey, Miss Paget
availed herself of this dismissal to dart across the room,
exclaiming, "Maude, Toinette, take care with that bench,
or you will mark the plaster. Set it down *away* from the
wall—so—then you can drape the baize over it."

"What a pure Parisian accent she has," remarked
Lady Morningquest approvingly. "Her speech has not
been contaminated by your hoydens of Flemings."

"She takes pains to converse every day with our
dear old Mademoiselle Roussel, who has the diction
of a truly cultivated person."

"She need do no more than listen to yourself and
your cousin, my friend. Both your accents are exquisite. How is the Professor?"

"He is well, I thank you, madame," responded
the Directrice; but a slight cloud became evident on
her brow, and this was not missed by the alert eye
of her guest.

"I had no idea," idly remarked Lady Morningquest,
watching the activities of Miss Paget through her lev-
eled lorgnon, "that Ellen Paget would turn out such
a pretty girl. Her sisters were handsome creatures

enough, but she was an ugly, skinny little shrimp of a thing when I saw her last, all hair and eyes and hollow cheeks. She is a credit to you now, my friend."

"Pretty? I would not go so far as to call her that," replied the headmistress rather sharply. "One does not require prettiness in a teacher; in fact, it is a disadvantage, leading to unhealthy devotions among the pupils, and unsuitable regard from visiting teachers."

Aha, my friend, thought Lady Morningquest; so that's where the wind sits? She remarked mildly, "Still, it is an engaging little face."

More fitted to the stage than the classroom, she reflected, surveying the expressive countenance of Miss Paget. If she had any theatrical gifts—and had not been a gentleman's daughter—she could have made her way on the boards as a soubrette. Her face was piquante and pointed, with wide-set dark eyes and a neat, straight little nose. Dark, strongly marked brows kept her from insipidity, and so did a charmingly shaped mouth, always curved in what seemed the beginning of a smile even when she was serious. Dark hair, confined in a knot on the nape of her neck, was so fine and soft that tendrils escaped at the back and also curved down over her brow, giving her an air of childlike appeal. Viewed beside her massive pupils, she seemed more of a child than they—until her firm, confident voice made itself heard.

"Softly, Léonore—ease it through the door. See—there comes Monsieur Patrice—you do not wish to knock him down!"

"*Quoi donc—mon cousin*—what is he doing here at this hour?"

The cloud deepened on Madame's brow, as the pupils parted respectfully to allow a slight active man of her age, or a little younger, to make his way to the dais.

"Ah—Miladi Morningquest—*bonjour*—" He made a hasty, nervous bow in the direction of the distinguished visitor, but Lady Morningquest could see that he wished her at the devil. He continued rapidly to his cousin, "Marthe, here is catastrophe! I told you how it would be if the wretched girl was permitted to go home for her *jour de fête*—"

"What?" exclaimed Madame Bosschère, grasping his meaning with positively telepathic speed. "Not Ottilie de la Tour? You do not mean to tell me that some misfortune has befallen her—?"

"What did you expect? Not five minutes ago a servant delivered *this*!" Furiously, almost grinding his teeth, he flourished a crumpled piece of paper embossed with a coronet. "Broke her miserable nose riding one of her father's horses in the park—without permission, I need hardly say! I wish it had been her neck! Now her idiot mother writes that she is under a doctor's care and cannot return to school. *Du reste*, what use to me would be a Hamlet with nose bound up in court plaster? I should be the laughingstock of my colleagues at the Seminary. Oh, these cretinous giggling lumps of girls, with their fetes, and parties, and their minds on nothing but pleasure—how can one do anything with them? I would tie all their necks together and drown them in the Senne! Why in the name of reason did you allow her to go home before the performance?"

"My dear cousin—her father is the Count of—"

"Count of—*chose!*" growled Monsieur Patrice. It was plain that he was in a highly overwrought condition, almost beside himself with exasperation. He was a dark, sallow man, clean-shaven and quick in his movements. He wore his hair *en brosse*, unfashionably short, and was dressed very plainly in black garments of clerical cut, with a scholar's gown flung over his shoulder. Not an impressive man at first sight, thought Lady Morningquest; but what did make him remarkable was the look of lambent intelligence in his eyes, which were the dark purple-gray of a thundercloud. His mouth was thin and mobile, his brow scarred with thought.

Madame said soothingly, "Is there not an understudy, *mon cousin*? It is a pity about Ottilie, I agree, she is thinner than most of those *paysannes*, she has more the appearance of Hamlet, but still—"

"Fifine Tournon!"

Madame looked at him blankly, then remembered. "Oh, *mon dieu!* Called away to her father's deathbed!"

"Now, do you see? It is crisis—catastrophe—chaos!"

In this extremity, Madame became Napoleonic. With knitted brow she reflected for a moment or two, then pronounced, "There is only one thing to do. In such a case as this, *les convenances* must be put aside—as I am sure our dear friend and guest here will readily agree—"

"Indeed yes!" hastily said Lady Morningquest. "But, madame—Professor Bosschère—my dear friends, forgive me—I am shockingly de trop, and you must wish me a thousand miles off. I shall take myself away, for I have a dozen errands to perform in

Brussels. I grieve to leave you in such a predicament, but I am sure that all will arrange itself in such capable hands—by the time I return this evening you will have trained a substitute—"

She might as well have spoken to the potted palm beside her. Neither of her companions paid the slightest attention.

"Marthe, I am relieved that you agree with me!" exclaimed Professor Patrice. "I knew you would see it as I do; there is only one person who knows the part, and, furthermore, can take the role and play it with intelligence at such short notice—"

"Yes, my cousin, you are right, but, *mon dieu*, there will be so much delegation of duties to arrange; let me see now—how can we manage it all—"

"Francine!" Patrice grabbed the arm of a passing child. "Run, find Mademoiselle Paget, and bring her here."

"I will leave you for the present," repeated Lady Morningquest.

Madame was still thinking over the day's program.

"There is the collation to supervise—but old Roussel can do that; yes, and Elène can greet the parents, and preside at the prize-giving after the first few minutes—for I shall be too much preoccupied, so soon before the performance. Elène can do it—not with my polish, it is true, but ably enough. It will be valuable experience for her, furthermore, since she must learn to comport herself in polite society."

Patrice looked puzzled.

"She—Mademoiselle Paget?—greet the parents? Give out the prizes? What can you mean?"

"Why, you would not have Roussel greet them?

The poor woman would die of terror and twist herself in knots. And Maury is too unpolished. No, if I am to take the part of Hamlet—and I do not see who else could do it—little Paget must manage as best she can for the first part of the afternoon."

"*You—you*—take the part of Hamlet?"

Now it was the Professor's turn to stare; indeed he received this announcement as if it had been a cannonball.

"But of *course*! What else?" Madame seemed equally taken aback. "Whom—then—did you have in mind?"

"Why, *she*—Mademoiselle Elène!"

For the first time, watching the two faces as they confronted one another, pale-cheeked, red-cheeked, Lady Morningquest thought she detected a cousinly resemblance in the square jaws, the flat cheek structure, the thin, firm-lipped mouths. But the eyes were different, hers opaque with shock, his fiery with purpose.

"*Mais—c'est une bétíse—inouï—!*"

"I will leave you to your discussion," the visitor reiterated, and at last received a hurried, harried nod from her hostess, and a curt bow from the Professor. Hardly a discussion, Lady Morningquest thought with a private chuckle, as she descended the three steps from the dais, carefully lifting her gray lace skirts clear of the chalk dust and the palm spores. For Madame was saying, in a low, vibrant tone, "There can be *no possible question* of Elène Paget playing the role of Hamlet."

"But she *knows* it—she has been present as chaperon at all the repetitions—"

"Firstly, she has far too many other duties to perform during the day, from which she cannot possibly be spared. Secondly, how could I ever explain such a thing to her father in England? It would be *épouvantable*—wholly unsuitable. A young girl, in my care! All the world would consider it a gross dereliction of duty on my part. Whereas I, the Directrice, a widow and woman of the world—for me it is unusual, to be sure, but I am above scandal, and it will be an encouragement to the parents to see how I take part in the children's activities—"

"But—!"

"Say no more, Patrice! Any dispute on this matter is wholly out of the question."

As Lady Morningquest crossed the black-and-white-tiled hall, she saw Miss Paget run in from the garden, breathless and pink-cheeked. "You sent for me, madame?" the visitor heard her ask.

"Ah, yes, my child, here we have a little crisis—"

Lady Morningquest allowed herself a small ironic smile at the thought of the ensuing tripartite conversation. Patrice is no match for his cousin, she thought; Madame Bosschère will certainly have her way. Heaven only knows what she will make of the part of Hamlet—a forty-year-old Directrice! I am sorry, now, I did not manage to drag Giles to Brussels. But it's as well she won't allow Ellen to take the part—a taste for amateur theatricals is a complication we don't need at the Hôtel Caudebec.

At this point the ambassador's wife became aware of the arrival of her daughter, tiny blonde Charlotte, clad, like the rest of her schoolmates, in a calico wrapper and curlpapers.

"Mamma! You are here! *Grace à dieu!* Léonore said she had seen you. Are you come to wish me luck?"

"My dearest child! Gently, I beg you—you will ruin my coiffure! And—merciful heaven—*look* at you! You are an absolute fright! If your father could see you now—and in the lobby, too—"

"Oh, nobody cares today," said Charlotte blithely. "And there is none to see, except old Philipon, and he is half blind. Still, come into the little salon."

Charlotte dragged her mother into a small reception room, stiffly furnished with gray-brocade-upholstered chairs and sofa, a green porcelain stove, glittering lustres, and a console.

"Listen, Mamma!" she said. "It's so exciting. Ottilie de la Tour, who was to have played Hamlet, has broken her nose, and so Miss Paget is to have the part instead. We are all so delighted!"

"Who told you that?" demanded her mother, reflecting on the rapidity with which rumor spreads in a school.

"Oh, everybody knows. *Du reste*, who else could possibly take it on? Oh, I am so happy! I adore Miss Paget—she is my *beau ideal*! And to think of playing Ophelia to her Hamlet—Véronique and the others are all dying of envy. All of our class worship the ground she treads on—"

"Then you are a lot of very silly girls," repressively answered her mother, with the private conclusion that it was just as well Ellen Paget was to quit Madame's establishment. "And, in any case, you are quite out. Madame Bosschère is to take the part herself."

"*What?*" Charlotte's jaw dropped comically. She looked horror-stricken. "No, Mamma, you can't be serious? Why, Monsieur Patrice would never,

never allow it. He thinks the world of Miss Paget. He would have had her play Hamlet from the start if Madame permitted. Now she will be *obliged* to give in."

"Indeed she will not! And she is quite right. *Les convenances* would be outraged."

"But why? If it is proper for me to play Ophelia—"

"That is quite another matter. You are only fifteen. But Miss Paget is a young lady, earning her living."

"I don't see what that has to do with it. And anyway, she won't for long. Everybody says Monsieur Patrice is sure to marry her. We are all going to put our money together, as soon as he pops the question, and buy a beautiful silver epergne, with all our names engraved. Not that he is anything like good enough for her, cross old thing! But you can see he dotes on her—his eyes follow her all the time."

"Charlotte!" exclaimed Lady Morningquest sharply. "I wish you will stop talking such ridiculous rubbish. It is harmful to both parties and, I am sure, entirely without foundation."

"No, Mamma, it is not. Véronique heard him, in the music room, calling Miss Paget his *chère petite amie*!"

"Charlotte, I do not wish to hear any more of such ill-judged and disgusting gossip. In any case, Monsieur Patrice would not be able to marry Miss Paget; did you not know that it is a condition of the Seminary where he is a Fellow that he remain a bachelor? It is only by special dispensation that he may come here to teach in his cousin's school."

"Well, if he married Miss Paget he could leave the Seminary—could he not?—and they could start a school together somewhere," argued Charlotte, but she looked a little dismayed by this news.

"Charlotte, I do not wish to hear another word on the subject. It is vulgar, mischievous, and, I am sure, a complete fabrication. Now I am going into town to buy lace, and I suggest that instead of indulging in addlepated speculation, you apply yourself to studying your part."

"Oh, I know it well enough," cheerfully responded Charlotte. "The part of Ophelia isn't very long, you know. And Miss Paget has been coaching me. *Au revoir, Maman, chérie, à ce soir!*" and she danced away down the hall.

Very thoughtfully, Lady Morningquest went out to her carriage and had herself driven through the leafy faubourg and along the rue Royale. She did not observe the stately houses, rosy brick or colorwashed, on either side of the wide streets. She ignored the blossoming trees, hawthorn and chestnut in their spring foliage, poplars and laurels in the park where crinolined little girls bowled hoops. She was deaf to the cheerful carillons celebrating the birthday of St. Annodoc.

Am I doing the right thing in transplanting that girl to Paris? she was asking herself.

About the Author

The daughter of Pulizter Prize–winning poet Conrad Aiken, the late Joan Aiken started writing at the age of five. During her lifetime, she published more than one hundred books for children and adults. She received an MBE from the Queen for her services to children's literature, and is well known for her Jane Austen continuations.